Fa[illegible]aw

LAURENCE BRADBURY

Laurence Bradbury

Novel Ideas Publishing

Fatal Flaw

Copyright

First published in Great Britain by Novel Ideas Publishing
2011

www.laurencebradbury.com

ISBN-13: 978-1466497351

For

The Hero of

Arundel

Introduction

I have my father to thank for arousing this writing passion of mine. You see I used to travel a great deal with my car and plastics design work and would send him monologues from the places I visited. A playful soul, he once asked me to send him a letter in the style of Sherlock Holmes. This was the first of many characters and their adventures in far flung corners of the world. If it wasn't for the detail in the letters from Japan, Thailand and Hong Kong this novel could not have been written. I spent quite some time in these countries, so if you enjoy travel, well researched facts and a flavour of a destination you'll find it in this and subsequent novels.

I also owe a debt of thanks to an Interpol agent (who wishes to remain nameless). He sat next to me on a long-hall flight from Brussels to Tokyo. The conversation introduced me to the underworld of art theft, the global infrastructure of criminal organisations, and the resources targeted at retrieval. It is thanks to this stimulating chance encounter that Fatal Flaw is a reality.

I sincerely hope you enjoy it!

CHAPTER 1

The sun rose spectacularly through the broken cloud, casting beams of sunlight onto Kawaguchiko Lake. A near perfect reflection of Fuji illuminated and transformed the still water into a work of ephemeral art. Few sights throughout the world could compare.

Hideo Matsumoto had viewed sunrise from this same place on the lakeshore for as long as he could remember and remained in awe of its beauty. He'd loved the valley all of his life and would never forget the day he had taken possession. It had used the full resources of his organisation and the sale of his first legitimate business to achieve it, but it had been well worth the sacrifice.

He briefly closed his eyes and breathed deeply for a moment of meditation. No other month smelled the same. Of all the months of the year, May unquestioningly wore the crown. With the cherry blossom in full bloom and the birds in full song, none other could equal it.

'If only life was as simple and as beautiful as this.' He thought, working quickly to capture the moment on canvas before the magic passed.

Concentration did not come easily. He knew he had little time left to fulfil his commitments before the gathering at the end of the month and his logistical burdens of security and organisation played heavily on his mind.

'Rash promises will be the death of me.' he mused, as he considered his commitment to Robotti, the infuriating American he'd met during the New Year celebrations. Now

he had to 'come up with the goods,' as he had put it, and complete his side of the bargain.

In principle the remaining task was easy; after all, the American team had already executed the most demanding component of the plan. He had to be patient. A week, perhaps two and the prize would be his. A prize, worthy enough to satisfy his honour at this year's event, and spectacular enough to ensure his position amongst the Oyabun elite forever.

Stepping back from the easel he compared his efforts against those of the Creator and smiled. "Not bad." He said and set to cleaning his brushes.

An archway of cherry trees lined the blossom-covered pathway leading from the lake up to the terrace. He paused momentarily at the edge of the stream separating the extensive lawns from the orchard and admired the view.

Even at a distance the house was impressive. Styled on the castles of the great shoguns, the white, three tiered pagoda structure epitomised the empire he had created over the past twenty years. With accommodation exceeding that of most hotels it served his needs perfectly as a base for operations and would perform the task of housing the gathering with ease.

Meena, his Filipino maid bowed low as he entered the breakfast terrace. "Matsumoto-san, ohayou gozaimasu." She greeted.

'Kumagai-san, is he here yet?' He inquired, barcly acknowledging her presence.

'Arrived late last night sir.'

'Good. Have him join me for breakfast at seven, tell him to be punctual.' He said, and almost as an afterthought, 'Collect my painting equipment from by the lake, would you?'

Meena again bowed low.

Shedding his pure silk Yukata robe, Matsumoto changed into his western attire. Gucci shoes, a crisply starched Dior shirt and a dark blue Boss suit, collected during a recent visit to Berlin and a style best suited to his stocky yet powerfully built figure.

He admired the result in the full-length mirror. Good living and constant light exercise had kept him in shape. For a man of sixty years he had worn well and knew his physique would not have been out of place on a man twenty years his junior.

Meena appeared at the entrance to the dressing room and remained silent until she had been noticed.

'Yes?'

'Breakfast is served on the terrace and Kumagai-san is waiting for you in the library.'

'Have him wait for ten minutes then bring him to my table for coffee.'

'As you wish sir.'

Moving to his study, a windowless room, illuminated solely by brass picture lights, he stood before the centrepiece of his collection. A disturbing explosion of colour, swirling skies over wind swept golden fields. "At one million dollars, this was truly a bargain," he thought, as he focused on the signature of Vincent in the lower right hand corner.

He released the concealed catch, a detail in the swept frame, and the painting slid silently to the side, revealing the dull, grey textured surface of the safe. With six light touches on the keypad the door eased open. He reached inside and removed the package containing

Kumagai's briefing and three million yen in cash, an ample sum for the task.

Matsumoto knew breakfast was a good time for business, as an early riser, it gave him the edge over his peers, who, almost without exception, performed with clouded judgement at this time of day.

Kumagai arrived as he settled down to the routine of rice, fish, miso soup and o-cha, the green tea he had loved since childhood and which grew in abundance on his estate. The Gyokuro tea had been an excellent investment, both financially and aesthetically. Mile after mile of hilltop topiary lining the valley walls, resembling perfectly shaped green waves on the hillsides.

Always keeping eye contact, Kumagai bowed respectfully at the waist and waited for permission to sit. He had the self-assured air of a man confident in his own abilities and a solid stance reminiscent of disciplined military training.

With a brief nod, Matsumoto motioned for him to take a seat. 'I am pleased that you could join me at so short a notice,' he said, indicating that Kumagai should help himself to coffee, 'I trust my staff have made you comfortable?'

'Perfectly, thank you.'

'Good. For a man with your special talents and contacts, you should make light work of this.' Said Matsumoto, sliding the package across the table. 'I need something rather special this time. You have twenty-six days in which to complete it, the sooner of course the better. Your deadline is the end of May. You must not fail. There's enough in here to complete your objective. Half of this amount is for your living expenses; the other half is for you. Your travel costs can be direct billed on the American Express card, sign it before you leave.'

'Can it be traced?'

'Back to you? No. Payment of the card will be covered by an offshore account; it's quite safe I assure you. I would like you to read the brief while you are here, and remember, please, no loose ends.'

Matsumoto stood and walked to the shallow wall at the edge of the terrace as Kumagai read in silence. "Who else knows it will be here?" He asked finally.

'No-one. The representative believes it to be a facsimile, a copy, to be used as an example of the real thing. This is also reflected in the import documents. As you have read, the item was substituted last month in Houston. Smuggling it in would have been far too risky. This way it is much better, don't you think? All you have to do is make the second switch. Can you do it?'

Kumagai smiled. 'Yes, I can.'

CHAPTER 2

Alexander had to admit it, there was nothing quite like a dog's nose in your eye, to give you that wide-awake feeling, first thing in the morning.

He had tried everything. Pushing him off the bed, buying him a basket, even locking the bedroom door didn't help, the whining kept him awake all night. What ever he did, the result was invariably the same, a spread-eagled Border collie on the pillow next to him every morning as the alarm went off.

Alexander Webb and Maverick were a team. They had been together for a full eight years, through puppy youth to brotherhood and were almost inseparable. Unerringly faithful and incomparably bright his tricolour Border collie was a Christmas gift from an old flame. The flame had long since dwindled, but the fire that burned in Maverick's eyes was a constant pleasure to him. His expressions always keen and his appetite for games limitless.

Dutifully Maverick sat by his side as he shaved. The face in the mirror looked tired. The LX4 project was nearing completion and though stimulating had caused many sleepless nights. Five further days of pressure, resulting in the decisive presentation to Tri-Star on Friday and it would be over.

It was raining again, the fourth day in a row. With April having been dry, May appeared to be exacting it's reprisal with a vengeance. The old Alfa Romeo spider burst into life at the first turn of the key, purred out of the driveway and headed westwards along the sweeping coast road to the office. It had taken considerable time and money to restore to its now near perfect condition and it sang musically with the feed in of more power.

Maverick sat alert in the passenger seat, full of expectation as Alexander deftly negotiated the challenging curves with perfect line. There was no doubt, with slick gear changes; the country roads of Sussex were an unequalled pleasure.

'One day we'll be making this journey in a Ferrari,' he said, for the benefit of Maverick. 'Though by then, we'll probably be too old to enjoy it.' A smile crossed his face as he imagined a bottle of Benylin rocking arthritically in the glove compartment and a Zimmer frame creaking in protest on the roof rack.

The design office was always deserted early on a Monday morning, an ideal time to review the status of the project.

With coffee in hand, Alexander powered up the design workstation and highlighted the LX4 icon. Gradually, piece-by-piece, a computer model of a revolutionary sports coupe filled the screen.

The all thermoplastic body had long been completed, it was now a matter of fine details, tuning the chassis and ironing out the bugs in the electronics controlling the four, delta generation electric motors. Checking the delivery and programme sheets he could see the Sodium Sulphur batteries had been delivered late on Friday evening, and would be built into the working prototype towards the end of the day.

It was finally coming good. The normally expected blind panic as a project neared completion would not be required, a feature all too common in the past. Fortunately, on this occasion, the programme and timing plan had run like a dream. The team still performed with the same enthusiasm they had shown on the first day and if the bench testing were to be believed, the results would far surpass the expectations of his Japanese clients.

He called Maverick to his side, fed him a biscuit and a saucer of coffee then turned his attention to the circuit diagram for the electronic transmission.

'Morning Alex, how's it going?' Asked Greg, appearing in the doorway.

'We're getting there, come in. I'll have the mod's ready by lunch today, OK?'

'Fine with me. I've arranged the track for eight o'clock in the morning, does that give you enough time?'

'No problem.'

'That's what I thought.' Said Greg, feeding Maverick another biscuit. 'You spoil that dog Alex.'

'So do you.'

'Yes, I suppose I do.' Said Greg closing the door behind him as he left.

'Big day tomorrow Mav,' said Alexander, stroking his hand through the soft fur, 'God help us if something goes wrong.'

Greg Matthews, the Director of Global Design had given Alexander a free reign on the LX4 project, and soon the result of two years of his life would be in his own hands for the final round of testing. The thought made him tingle with a feeling somewhere between pure excitement and fear.

By noon the design centre was a hive of activity. 'Stay here Maverick,' he said, 'I'll be back soon and we'll go and get a bite to eat.'

With the modified drawings under his arm, Alexander left for the prototype build department on the south side of the complex.

Global Design had a well-earned international reputation for mixing the best of traditional craftsmanship with the cutting edge of modern technology. Intricate hand draughting skills, reflecting years of experience were never better placed than in the advanced feasibility drawing office, where full size hand drawn layouts of the cars of tomorrow covered six metre long layout tables. By comparison, further along the corridor, the lights were dimmed and the blinds drawn, in an attempt to eliminate as many stray reflections as possible from the computer screens of the detail design, surfacing and stress analysis engineers.

Each project had its own electronic card key security system. A necessary selling point if a client wanted to develop a new car or product style in secret. Its value was clear; it was one of the reasons why Global Design's customers kept coming back. Nevertheless, the constant stop start journey never failed to irritate Alexander on his frequent visits through the plant.

Travelling down the stairs, he approached the most security sensitive area of the site, the clay modelling and prototype workshops. As before, the fifty metre wide and one hundred metre long building was sub-divided into separate secure areas. Most of which were off limits to all but the vehicle project managers and their design teams. The LX4 workshop was at the far end. Inserting the credit card passkey into the control box, he typed the four-figure code on the calculator style keypad. A buzzer sounded and the door unlatched.

In the centre of the room, the printed silver bodywork shone like a mirror. Fred Deans sat inside, putting the finishing touches to the leather trim, as his son, Peter, worked on the transmission.

'How's the family business coming along?' Alexander asked.

Fred looked up, with his usual beaming smile. 'Hi Al, got a new one for ya. What's the difference between a coyote and a flea?' He asked.

'I don't know Fred, what is it?'

'One howls on the prairie and the other prowls on the hairy.'

'Well there'll be no fleas on you then Fred.' Fred had been nearly bald for thirty years. They both laughed.

Walking to the back of the car Alexander handed the drawings to Peter. 'I think this should work Pete, I've kept the modifications down to a minimum.'

Rolling them out onto the table, Peter stood thoughtful as he evaluated the changes. 'Yep, this'll do it,' he said positively. 'Fancy a cuppa?'

'No thanks Pete, Maverick and I are off down the pub, join us if you like.'

Peter shook his head. 'Too much to do old chap, let's do it on Friday, after the show.'

'I'll set it up. It's a date.'

With that Alexander returned to his office. Maverick was curled up asleep under the desk. 'Come on boy, let's go for lunch.' Maverick sprang to his feet, and with tail wagging, followed Alexander out to the Alfa.

At last the rain had stopped and brief glimpses of the sun could be seen between the breaking clouds.

The King's Tavern, five minutes from Global Design, had been their watering hole practically every day for the past two years. It was a traditional, Old World pub, which had started life as a coaching inn a couple of centuries earlier. Inside, the oak beams in the ceiling and the recent rustic style refurbishment gave an atmosphere of quiet relaxation, perfectly in keeping with its peaceful countryside image.

Without asking, a pint and a half of Guinness was placed on the bar, as they entered. The pint in an ornate glass bottomed pewter tankard, a leaving gift for Alexander from his previous employer and the half in an earthenware bowl with the name Maverick printed in bold black letters on the side.

'Now, will you two gentlemen be requiring a bite to eat?' The landlord enquired.

'A couple of steak and kidney pies please George.' Answered Alexander taking his seat. Moments later they were brought, piping hot, to the table.

Alexander lifted the crust from one of the pies and left it to cool at the table's edge. 'You'll have to wait a bit Mav, it's a bit hot.' He said and lowered his bowl of Guinness to the tiled floor. 'Here, drink your beer.'

'Alex! I knew I'd find you here.'

A brief, almost sisterly kiss landed softly against his cheek as she settled into the remaining space between his folded jacket and the upright piano.

'Did you miss me?' She asked.

Looking into her pale green eyes, his expression said it all. 'I never knew a month could feel like a year.' He said with an honest smile, the sight of Amanda pleased him enormously.

She kissed him again, this time with a passion, exploding like a cork from shaken champagne. 'I missed you too.'

They sat in silence for a moment listening to each other's thoughts until finally Alexander asked, 'Will you meet me from work tonight? I'd like us to spend some time together.'

She nodded and smiled. 'My time is yours.'

'Just the way I like it. You must tell me everything about your trip, how did the interview go?' He asked.

She looked down at his half empty tankard, searching for the words. '*How do you say good-bye and I love you in the same sentence, and mean it!*' She thought. She turned to face him, exploring his eyes for strength.

Something was wrong, he could sense it. 'No luck?'

'New York is just like the movies,' she said, lowering her gaze, 'I never expected them to like me or my work.' She reached into her purse and handed him the cheque.

'$20,000!' Alexander exclaimed. 'That's bloody marvellous!'

'It's a retainer.' She said. 'They've asked me to choreograph the stage production of "Gone with the Wind". It's a once in a lifetime chance.' Tears started to form in her eyes 'It's scheduled to open on Broadway in October.'

'Then why the tears?' As soon as he'd asked, he knew. He placed his hand against her cheek and turned her face towards him. Their eyes met again. 'When do you leave?' He inquired softly, knowing something like this would happen sooner or later.

'I fly back at lunch time tomorrow.' She said.

'Well at least that gives us nearly twenty four hours together,' he smiled, hoping the pain didn't show. 'I'll call work, we'll spend the afternoon together, OK?'

CHAPTER 3

Putting the kettle on is a reflex practised by most of the western world, and with fervour by nearly all British households. It was no exception in the Webb residence. Within moments of entering the house Alexander had the appliance approaching the boil and the Assam tea bags ready in the Royal Albert 'Old Country Rose' mugs. The twin-bayed seaward-facing bungalow always seemed to come to life when Amanda stayed. Its character changed, moving magically from a house to a home with her presence, and he was sure that somehow it would miss her when she was gone.

She was sitting on the Chesterfield sofa, stroking Maverick as he entered the living room.

'Tea is served ma'am. Would madam care for some cake?' He asked in his best butler voice.

'No thank you Jeeves, that will be all. Be so kind as to inform the master his finely tuned body will soon be required in the boudoir.' She commanded, continuing the jest.

'Very good Mi-lady.'

They both chuckled as he sat down and Amanda nestled her head on to his shoulder. 'It won't be so bad,' she said, 'I'll be back for your birthday. It's only six months, the time will fly by. You'll see.'

'You're probably right. Fancy an early night?' Asked Alexander, as flippantly as he could.

Amanda smiled, *'I was hoping you would say that'* she thought.

'Or shall I put some music on instead?' He said, knowing she had already made up her mind.

Amanda took his hand and held it warmly against her breast. 'Don't change the subject. You can be so cruel Alexander Webb. I've been celibate for a month, if I wait one more minute, I swear I'll take holy vows.'

'You drive a hard bargain Miss Amanda James, how could I possibly refuse.' Alexander carried her to the master bedroom and laid her head onto the pillow, gently kissing her delicately decorated eyes.

'I do like that,' she said softly, 'reminds me of bedtime. My mother used to kiss me there when I was a child.'

Then, almost under his breath, he said, 'I'm almost certain she didn't kiss you here.'

'It's a little late to close the curtains now.' Thought Alexander, as the room filled with the golden glow of sunrise. Quietly he rose and tiptoed to the kitchen to make coffee. It had been a fitful night's sleep, troubled by a dream of Amanda leaving in a sleek silver sports coupe. She was right of course, six months would pass quickly, and however unlikely, there was always the chance she would come back. Unlikely was the key word. Once her talents had been seen by the powers of Broadway, it was more than likely she would become a feature for years. He knew her gifts better than anyone, probably better than Amanda herself.

He placed a CD into the old Denon player, turned the volume down low, picked up yesterday's mail, still unopened by the front door, collected his coffee and returned to the bedroom. He chuckled softly in the doorway and shook his head. As expected, Maverick was in his place on the bed, next to Amanda. "*C'est la vie.*"

The view over the sea was spectacular. A beautiful morning, the prospect of an exciting day, yet, within a couple of hours he would have to say good-bye to one of the few people he truly cared about. Trying to make light of it he reflected, *'Well, two out of three isn't bad.'*

Amanda watched him as he sat motionless at the desk, by the window. She was glad she'd come back, even though it was for a short time. The room was just as she'd left it four weeks ago. Nothing had changed. The display of subdued oil paintings they'd bought together last summer in the Isles of Scilly, were still on the walls. Alexander's collection of minerals and fossils still gathered dust and the photograph of Maverick still took pride of place on his desk. Nothing ever changed.

Concentrating she could hear the faint strains of music filtering through from the study. She loved the music of Chicago, it was the same track, "Remember the feeling" that had played the first time they had made love, almost a year ago. It was so much less complicated then. Alexander turned to face her and smiled. *'If only you could come with me.'* She thought.

He moved to her side and sat perched on the edge of the bed. Softly he kissed her, and then whispered in her ear, 'Get dressed.'

During breakfast she talked about New York, and how the American TV showed it as a dangerous place, full of gangsters and bank robbers, when in truth it was mostly full of honest hard working people trying to make ends meet.

'Trying to make ends meet, is what I've done all of my life.' She said. 'If I was honest with you, I always thought it would be this way. Now it looks like there could be a future where money worries are a thing of the past. Alexander, this could be the start of a whole new career for me. You never know, if I'm lucky, they'll offer me a permanent choreography position. We'll be set for life! How would you feel about joining me and living in the states for a while?'

At the back of his mind, Alexander had known this question would come; it had even crossed his mind that morning. 'Last night, I lay awake for a while, wondering how it would be. This musical of yours is sure to be a smash hit. Knowing you, it couldn't be anything else. They'd be crazy not to ask you to stay on a little longer. Let's face it; you're the most talented woman I know. And not just on the stage!" He said with a knowing smile. "If I was in your shoes, I couldn't give it up, I know that for sure. Looking at it from my point of view, you know as well as I do, there's not much scope for a car designer in New York, the best jobs are further up north in Detroit.'

Apprehensive, Amanda stared deeply into her untouched bowl of cornflakes. She knew the time had come to ask her most dreaded question. A question she'd had in her mind since the end of her American visit. 'Are you saying that we should give ourselves a chance to start afresh?'

'Maybe it's the most selfless gift we could ever give each other.' Said Alexander sincerely. 'You know I'll miss you, that's why it makes sense. If we're apart for so long, you're sure to meet someone else, and it would hurt me to think that you'd be feeling guilty.'

'Like now? You really are impossible Alexander. You don't make it easy do you.' She reached across the narrow table and kissed him tenderly.

They left for the station a little after seven. It was good to be able to drive the Alfa with the top down for a change. Amanda's long blond hair blew freely in the wind; she looked radiant. 'This is exactly how I will remember you, until we meet again.' He said.

Maverick stayed in the car as Alexander and Amanda walked to the platform. At the door of the Intercity First Class carriage they fell into each other's arms, 'You will be careful won't you?' He said, his concealed emotions rising hard against his fragile facial mask.

Closing the door behind her, she leaned out of the window. 'Of course I will and I'll write to you as soon as I settle in.' A single tear traced a thin line down the contour of her left cheek and fell wasted to the pavement. 'Remember,' she said, brushing her hair from her face, 'I do love you. Twice as much as I did yesterday, but only half as much as I will tomorrow.'

The train disappeared into the distance bound for London Victoria station. Alexander watched emptily as her face and waving hand diminished into an almost indiscernible speck. He turned and walked back to the Alfa. *'I wonder if Maverick will miss her.'* He thought, opening the door and placing the key into the ignition. 'It's just you and me again kid.' He said.

CHAPTER 4

The test track was almost deserted; he'd never known the security so tight. He switched on the radio mic linked to his tight fitting Arai racing helmet and spoke. 'Is there anybody there?' His voice echoed ghostly over the pits address system.

'You're coming in loud and clear, Alex,' said Greg from the observation tower, 'Let's see if the telemetry works, start her up.' The screen in front of him resembled a flight simulator video game. The four oil-cooled twenty-four pole DC motors showed idle, power reserve one hundred percent and speed zero. All motor, transmission, brake and battery sensors showed green. 'Everything's OK Alex, she's all yours.'

Selecting drive, Alexander gingerly pressed the accelerator; silently the car rolled forward, progressively picking up speed. 'The speedo now reads thirty miles per hour, power drain five kilo watts, are you getting the same data Greg?'

'Yes Alex, the system's working perfectly.'

Before any further testing, experience had taught him that early brake testing was an essential safety precaution. With sixty percent of the vehicle weight at the front and forty percent at the rear, there was almost no hint of dive even under quite violent braking. 'The brakes are fine,' he said, 'I'm approaching the chicane, let's see how she handles.' Entering the first corner at forty miles per hour, and gradually feeding in more power, the car negotiated the esses as though on rails. With the centre of gravity lower than six inches above the floor, this was to be expected. The mile long straight was now in his sights. "The speed is now sixty Mph, I'm going to find out how fast she can go." He said and floored the throttle. The push in his back was quite unexpected as the needle on the speedo raced urgently through one hundred. Trees bordering the circuit Armco flurried past with increasing swiftness and detail began to meld into flashes of colour as the LX4 consumed tarmac. The sensation felt unusually strange. Chaotic uncontrollable action outside yet inside the cabin a pervading sense of calm and order. Theoretically there were ten miles per hour to go. He glanced at the rising needle. It was slowing. Then, as though on cue at the terminal speed of one hundred and fifty five the corner of the bonnet nearest to him started to vibrate. A satisfied smile grew irresistibly on his face behind the visor. There always had to be something.

Easing the speed back to one hundred and twenty he settled down for what he hoped would be the longest part of the test. 'Everything seems to be working perfectly Greg, according to the sound measuring equipment, the noise in the cabin is roughly equivalent to a Jag travelling at thirty and most of that is road noise. Right, as the actress said to the bishop, let's see how far we can go.'

At noon, Greg knew the presentation on Friday would be a major success. The LX4 had already covered four hundred and fifty miles, and according to the telemetry readout there was still a power reserve of thirty percent. 'Alex' he called, 'Before we break for lunch, I think we should record a few sprint times.'

The Test Track canteen was just like a nineteen fifty's truck stop, and just as uninviting. Gathered around a large white Formica topped table, the test team sat, discussing the morning's test results. Computer printouts and hand written notes covered the table's surface.

Greg was the last to arrive. He had been out to his car and was carrying a bottle of Champagne and a nest of paper cups. 'For the best engineers in England!' He acclaimed, popping the cork and poring generously. 'Ladies and Gentlemen, I give you a toast, the Tri-Star LX4. The world's first; production feasible, Usable and Saleable electric vehicle. Well done, all of you!'

Raising their cups, all present saluted the toast.

'Alexander,' continued Greg, 'tell me, what should be done to the vehicle before we present it?'

'At high speed we get some bonnet vibration, it may only need an adjustment to the lock cables and bump stops, we don't know yet, Peter will look into it this afternoon. The motor's oil coolant system seems to work well; the highest temperature recorded during regenerative braking was thirty five degrees. A good ten degrees inside the safety zone before the magnets demagnetise. In general you could say I'm pretty happy with the result.' Alexander grinned widely; it was a masterpiece of understatement.

After lunch, they loaded the car back onto the transporter and headed for the Design Centre.

The office was buzzing with excitement when Alexander and Maverick arrived. They had heard everything. Mark Goodyear, his electronics engineer had patched into the car to pits radio on his FM receiver and had relayed the progress to the design group, blow by blow, as it happened. Alexander had never known the morale so high. He called Greg on the telephone and told him of the atmosphere, and invited him down for a drink with the group. There was nothing else he could do; he knew the productivity for the rest of the day would be zero.

The preparation for the presentation was complete, and like most of his colleagues Alexander arrived early for work that Friday morning. A car had been dispatched to gather Higaki-san; the President of Tri-Star from his Brighton hotel and the LX4 had been placed resplendent on the turntable at the end of the boardroom, lit to perfection. They were as ready as they could ever be.

Collecting his laptop with footage of the test and PowerPoint presentation he headed for the conference centre to confirm the presence and function of the equipment. All was in perfect working order. *'Great minds think alike.'* He mused. The tell tale witness of a gabardine rain coat resting on the back of one of the leather-backed chairs showed that moments earlier Greg had presumably conducted his own similarly prudent inspection.

Higaki-san accompanied by his entourage arrived soon after Alexander had completed his final run through. He greeted him with the warm handshake of a friend and offered the same to Higaki-San's senior ranking colleagues, Marketing Director, Saitoh-San and Production Director, Sagawa-San. Both of them had renowned reputations for shrewdness and he was well aware both of them would have a major influence on the future of the project.

Assuming his position behind the lectern, Greg Matthews sporting his favourite dark blue pin stripe suit and champagne tie began his introduction of the company for the benefit of the first time visitors. A ten-minute video presentation followed extolling the virtue of Higaki's decision in placing the order for development with them and culminated with the soft hushing sound of drawing curtains to reveal the gracefully rotating form of the LX4, the fruit of their labours.

Taking his place Alexander talked in detail of how the development had progressed from the early design concepts, through the engineering stage and tooling to the present working prototype. Amanda would have been proud of him, he thought. Just as an actor draws his audience to a climax he had lead them from indifference, through the months of testing, the video of the car on the track and on to restrained enthusiasm.

Sagawa-San, stimulated by the potential of the project betrayed his excitement through impatience. 'In your opinion, how long would it take to transfer this technology to Tri-Star?' He asked.

'Somewhere in the region of six to eight months.' Replied Alexander confidently. 'From the beginning we have operated the Tri-Star engineering procedures. All component CAD files are complete and where possible, approvals have been sought from the respective legislative bodies. Full vehicle type approval I would estimate at one year after the transfer. Conceivably it could take less. Electric vehicles are some what easier to homologate than those conventionally driven.'

Saitoh-San considered his notes thoughtfully. 'I understand the logic behind using plastic body panels for their weight advantages Webb-San, taking that as a given, can you conceive of any additional benefits we may exploit as a consequence of using them in the near or perhaps the longer term?' He asked.

'Yes indeed, Saitoh-San.' Replied Alexander, walking to the LX4. 'In addition to the fifty percent weight saving per body panel over steel, plastics were chosen for three principal reasons at the project outset. Cost, styling freedom and low speed impact protection. Of these, cost and styling have proven to be very closely linked. Niche marketing would seem to us to be the key to success. We have designed the galvanised chassis of the LX4 to accept three basic body styles. Through a relatively small investment in injection mould tooling, the body shape can be altered from the sports coupe we have here, to either a saloon or commercial derivative.

'You will also notice that the super structure has been developed with corrosion resistant materials, eliminating any requirement for painting on the vehicle. In our concept, a single galvanising bath adequately affords the same level of protection to the car as the fifteen million pounds capital investment required for a new painting plant.

'So, having decided not to paint the exterior on-line, we had to come up with something else. We could of course have painted the panels off-line, but this only served to double the cost of the components and didn't offer us the styling freedom we were looking for, no, we had to find a viable alternative. Taking our inspiration from the packaging industry we investigated the possibilities of printing directly onto the moulded parts. In-mould coating and in-mould printing were both evaluated and found wanting. Sublimation printing, on the other hand, answered our requirements perfectly. A well-established technique in packaging and about half the price of painting, we felt it was a natural progression to apply it to decorating body panels. The freedom offered by the process frankly stunned our stylists. The process itself is quite simple. A film, printed with a computer generated styling theme; for example, a silver background with the

Tri-Star logo as seen here on the bonnet of our car, is held onto the body panel by vacuum. Heat is applied and the ink on the film is transferred to the plastic, impregnating the surface. The film is flexible enough to accommodate most body form variations.

'I can envisage a day gentlemen, when a potential customer visits the Tri-Star show room and not only chooses a colour for his new car, in one of three interchangeable body styles, but assisted by a skilled sales executive, he can chose a colour scheme unique to himself, there and then at a computer terminal. Then, just as you would send a message to a printer from your PC at work, his message is sent to the plant to print his body panel films, at no additional cost to you the manufacturer.'

'An exciting concept Webb-San. I can see I have touched on your pet subject.' Observed Saitoh-San.

Alexander smiled. 'One of many, Sir.' He said coyly.

'Who will be responsible for recycling all of this plastic?' Asked Sagawa-San thoughtfully.

'I believe Tri-Star should be.' Answered Alexander opening the car's passenger door to retrieve a bag of granulated plastic. 'It makes good economic sense. This used to be a car bumper. Another bumper has been recycled and now serves as the roof of this vehicle.' He said patting it lightly with his hand. 'The properties of the material do not degenerate much in life so with minor additives I can see no reason why your vehicles of the future should not take advantage of those produced in the past.'

'You and your team would seem to have thought of everything Matthews-San.' Said Sagawa, placing his pen at the foot of his notes and easing back into his chair.

'Thank you Sagawa-San,' responded Greg, pleased by the comment, 'we have tried to.'

Higaki-san had been sitting quietly, without comment since his arrival. He stood and walked to Alexander's side at the car. "Gentlemen, from what we have witnessed this morning, I believe we have in the LX4, a product, which if put into production could revolutionise the Automotive Industry. As a consequence our company will be viewed world-wide as a leader in its field. There is much kudos to be gained from this.

'The risks, we all know, are high. Yet, so are the longer-term rewards. In a year or two the market will be ripe for picking. Even as we speak, Germany and America are paving the way forward to greener cars and in no place more so than in the state of California. Who, with their changing legislation towards zero emission vehicles, guarantees an initial potential market of three million sales. I am confident we can capture a sizeable share of this market and cover our investment. My proposal is that we proceed without delay. If any of you disagree, raise your objections now. On this one, we must all be in accord.'

The room was silent.

'Very well, the decision is made. Matthews-San, I will require the services of some of your staff for the technology exchange which Saitoh-San mentioned and also I will need your company's assistance and experience during the production planning stage, will this be acceptable?'

Greg nodded in agreement. 'Perfectly. My company is at your disposal, sir.' He said.

'Webb-San.' Higaki continued, 'Would you be prepared to lead our Tokyo development team? You have my word you will be well looked after.'

Alexander, surprised by the sudden turn of events, for once was lost for words. It occurred to him that the only thing to keep him here now that Amanda had gone, was Maverick. He turned to Greg, and for fear of demonstrating a weakness in his loyalty to the project, lowered his voice. 'Maverick will need a home for six months. He trusts you, look after him for me?' He asked.

'No problem. We'd love to have him, we'll treat him like one of the family.'

His concern appeased, Alexander returned his gaze to the Tri-Star President. 'Higaki-san, I would be honoured. On condition, that I get to chose my own team, and have full decision making responsibilities.'

'You have my word, it shall be so. I will appoint you a secretary to make the appropriate arrangements. Thank you Gentlemen, it would seem that you have sealed our future. Your company has served us well. I think I speak for all of my colleagues, when I say, we are delighted!'

CHAPTER 5

'Kangei! Welcome aboard,' Greeted the pretty Kimono clad stewardess, 'May I see your Boarding pass please? Ah yes, Mr Webb, please permit me to show you to your seat.'

It was Alexander's first visit to the Pacific. He had often flown on 747's to Detroit in the past, but they were nothing like this. The wide-bodied Boeing 787 Dreamliner would be a new experience. He settled into the comfortable window seat of All Nippon Airways flight NH202 and breathed a sigh of relief. Frank Sinatra's portrait on the cover of the in-flight magazine looked to be doing the same and was complemented by the mellow tones of 'Come fly with me' over the tannoy system.

It had taken every minute of the past five days to prepare for this moment, now it was time to relax. Heathrow Airport proved tolerable this time, unlike the irritating security queues at Heathrow terminal four just a few weeks ago, check-in and customs formalities had been quick and courteous. As expected, the Wednesday traffic was light. He'd arrived well before the early evening flight and had ample time to buy the obligatory Glenmorange malt whisky for Higaki-san. A drink he had introduced to him over dinner the previous Friday evening with great success.

The stewardess bowed and handed him a small hot towel and a sumptuous menu, a choice between traditional western cuisine and the culinary delights of the East. 'Would you care for a glass of champagne before we take off, Mr Webb?' She inquired.

Alexander nodded politely. 'You ask so beautifully, how could I possibly refuse?'

'Are you always so eloquent Mister Webb?' She said teasingly.

Taking the glass, he smiled. 'Hardly ever, I save it all for when I'm travelling.'

The acceleration force in his back was reminiscent of the LX4 test drive, as the Rolls Royce Trent 1000 engines, each producing 74,000 pounds of thrust, powered them skyward. All thoughts of the car soon faded away and he stretched happily in the reclining seat. He peeled open a bag of salted peanuts and settled down to review the video selection available for his personal LCD television.

By the time he stood admiring himself in a Russian fur hat at Moscow Airport's duty free, he positively glowed, and was sure that the constant stream of Gordons gin and tonics were only partly to blame for his apparently successful proposal of marriage, to Kiki the stewardess.

The second leg of the flight, over mainland Russia was spent wrapped in a land of dreams. An attempt to condition his body to the nine hour time difference between England and the land of the rising yen.

Seven hours into the second flight he stirred to Kiki's gentle touch on his shoulder. He could faintly hear his name being called as her soft lyrical voice coaxed him back to consciousness. 'Webb-San,' she said, 'We will be arriving in Narita in a little over an hour, I thought I should wake you, I hope you don't mind. Did you sleep well?'

Her face was a vision. 'Very well, thank you. I was dreaming of a Japanese beauty guiding me around the romantic and colourful spectacles of Tokyo. Are you free tomorrow?' He asked playfully.

'If only I was.' She smiled and passed on to the passenger behind him.

He spent the next few minutes filling out the immigration and customs forms, then, with the complementary ANA tooth brush and shaving kit in hand, headed for the washroom.

Refreshed, he sat gazing out of the window as the plane gradually descended beneath the clouds. He could see the Japanese coastline sharply defined against the deep blue of an apparently calm sea. From this viewpoint the similarity to an English landscape was uncanny. The patchwork of fields bordering small villages and woodland so closely resembled the rolling hills of the South Downs that he could scarcely believe he was on the far side of the world. Lower still and the detail in the villages became clearly visible. The sight of so many houses with blue tiled roofs made him reconsider. *'You'd never see that in Littlehampton.'* He thought.

For such a large plane the landing was surgical precision. Kiki came back to him. 'The Captain informs me, we are the first of five aircraft landing almost at the same time. When you leave the gate go as quickly as you can to immigration, if you take your time you'll be queuing for hours.' She smiled warmly and handed him his jacket. A folded piece of paper containing her address and telephone number stood proud in the breast pocket. 'If you have time, call me, there is much to see in Tokyo!'

The grey chauffeur's uniform appeared out of place amongst the hoards of holidaymakers milling around the arrivals hall and the middle aged Japanese wearing it looked just as uncomfortable. In his hands he held a board with the legend "Global Design" in perfectly printed black letters high up against his chest and having a clear description in his mind, he scoured the arriving passengers with a practised eye.

With trepidation he stepped forward and lightly touched Alexander on the arm. 'Mister Webb?' He enquired.

'Yes?'

'Welcome to Japan. My name is Kuro. I am pleased to meet you!'

They shook hands.

'I hope you had a pleasant trip. You have luggage?' Asked Kuro politely.

'Just these two.'

'I take for you OK?' He said, offering his hands to receive the two matching cases. 'You stay long time, yes?'

'Six months.'

'I could have guessed.' Kuro grinned, struggling arch-backed with the full thirty-kilogram allowance, out to the waiting Limousine.

Alexander sank back luxuriously as the large black car surged forward, slipping quickly into the freely flowing traffic. Despite the strength sapping flight he tingled with excitement. From the second after Higaki's request for his presence, the thrill of expectation had steadily grown, and now, with the realisation that he'd finally made it, the sensation had a new intensity. He'd read much about the land that was to be his host over the past week and marvelled as the images described exotically in the tourist travel guides developed before his eyes.

With the traffic slowing to a crawl Kuro turned from the highway in search of an expeditious route through the city.

Tokyo's size, its maze of streets without names, the masses of people, the signs in Japanese and the constant movement all added to Alexander's bewilderment. 'How am I ever going to find my way around?' He mused, airing his thoughts aloud.

'Simple!' Said Kuro. 'You take a cab!'

One and a half hours after leaving the airport they arrived at the hotel, all of the stories he had heard about Tokyo's traffic congestion having proved to be true. A claret liveried footman approached the car, opened the door and stepped aside. 'Good afternoon Sir.' He said sombrely. 'Welcome to the Hotel Okura.'

One of the leading hotels of the world, the Okura was to be his home, all be it for one night. His faxed itinerary showed a move in the morning to a company guest apartment, some two miles distant, west of the hotel, in an area called Sendagaya.

The suite was a sensitive mixture of western and oriental design, with shoji screens separating the entrance room with its desk and bar from the sitting room, overlooking the swimming pool and Tokyo tower. Through further screens to the right he found the bedroom, equipped with two twin beds and an adjacent marble bathroom. All was pleasing on the eye and elegantly decorated in sympathetic pastel pinks. He liked it, and said as much to the porter arriving with his cases.

The telephone rang. He took it in the sitting room gazing out at the skyline.

'Ah, Mister Webb, welcome to Tokyo.' Greeted the voice. 'My name is Akiko Takino, Higaki-san has assigned me to look after your personal and secretarial needs during your stay with us. I am calling from your hotel's reception, will you come down to meet me, or shall I come up?'

'Do, please, come up.' He stammered, expecting at least an hour's respite before the news of his arrival reached the Tri-Star offices. 'I'm just about to unpack a few overnight things, I'll be through by the time you arrive. Room one thirteen.'

Takino entered and after the brief formalities of introduction, took a seat by the window. She had an air of efficiency Alexander would normally have associated with a businesswoman well beyond her years and a comforting manner he knew instantly he could work with. Not what he would term attractive, her nose was a mite too large for her otherwise delicate facial features. She was slim, well poised and wore her knee length skirted pinstriped suit with elegance. She crossed her legs femininely, opened a manila file on her lap and looked engagingly through her patterned frame glasses for his attention.

'It has been some time since I last made international arrangements Mister Webb, I hope you found everything satisfactory.' She said.

'Your preparation has been impeccable. The flight ticket was waiting for me at the airport, the chauffeur driven car and now this superb hotel, in a word; perfect. You will have to be careful, I could easily become accustomed to this style of living.'

'If it pleases you, I shall see to it that it continues. Higaki-san wishes for you to enjoy your stay with us. My intention is to carry out his wishes to the letter. For the remainder of the week, he recommends that you explore Tokyo. I'm sure you will agree it is an ideal opportunity for you to acquaint yourself with your new surroundings and adjust to the unsettling effects of the time difference. If you need a guide, most of the time the car and I will be at your disposal.'

'Thank you, that's very thoughtful.'

Takino laid a pile of maps on to the table. 'You have a camera?' She asked.

Alexander pointed to a case at the foot of the bed. 'I thought I might need it!'

'I'm sure you will. I'll highlight a few areas worthy of interest and within easy reach of your apartment. Few are close by, so I suggest the best way to see the city is via the subway or JR line surface trains, they are cheap, quicker than a car or taxi and as regular as clockwork. I should warn you though, they can be a bit crowded. This English subway map should help you find your way around.'

Alexander unfolded it and studied the maze of tracks uncertainly. 'Excellent.' He said, hoping she would be with him on the occasion he would have to use it.

'Tomorrow, Friday, is a busy day for me, I will have to return to the office after seeing you to your new home. If you need me, you can always reach me on one of these numbers.' Takino wrote her business and private telephone numbers beneath the key of the map and turned it to face Alexander. 'Any time, day or night.'

She continued for the next hour and a half, recommending restaurants and advising on local customs then slipped an envelope across the table in front of him. 'I have opened an account for your use at the Sumitomo bank. A deposit has been made to ensure your comfort and I have brought some yen with me for your immediate expenses. I hope it is enough, if not, we can arrange for further withdrawals on Monday at the office, if you think it is necessary.'

He thanked her and slid the envelope and the map securely into his wallet. 'I am unsure how much Mister

Higaki has told you about my assignment, so if you will bear with me, I'll fill you in on a little of the history.'

He talked in detail about his expectations of the job and the crucial role she would have to play. Takino visibly warmed to the prospect of pushing back the restrictions of her secretarial position and embraced her new task as his personal assistant enthusiastically. Alexander sketched the outline of his objectives for the next six months on the hotel's note paper and in line with her suggestion, agreed to draw up a plan for each item's implementation on his first day of work.

Outside the sun had set and the illuminated Tokyo tower, partly hidden behind the Shuwa building, looked spectacular.

'Are you hungry? I'm starving.' Admitted Alexander. 'What's the food like in the Okura?'

'The Okura prepares some of the finest food in Tokyo. What would you like, French, Japanese or Chinese? We have eight restaurants to choose from.'

'I think I should ease my way in gently.' He said.

The Chateaubriand was cooked to perfection, and perfectly complemented by the silky texture of the '88 Chateau de Chambert, Cahors.

Akiko Takino talked with interest about her family and professional life, placing emphasis on the fact that it was only her status as a woman that was holding her back in the male dominated society. Alexander could sense her resentment and couldn't help but draw a comparison to the way it would be back home. Hopefully, an equally talented woman would be identified and nurtured into a position in keeping with her abilities. He wondered if the responsibilities he had placed on her shoulders would be seen as an affront to the Japanese system and decided to seek Higaki's advice on the subject, at the earliest opportunity.

By eleven the jet lag was taking its toll and they parted as friends, agreeing to meet at nine the following morning.

Alexander had checked out and was waiting in the reception area by the entrance as Akiko and Kuro entered on the dot of nine.

'Good morning, Webb-San.' She said.

'Ohayou gozaimasu, Takino-San.' He responded, with a pronounced English accent.

'You are a quick learner, Webb-San, this is good. Twenty more years and we will think of you as a Japanese, ...Over the telephone of course.'

'Of course.'

Laughing, they collected his bags and walked to the car.

CHAPTER 6

The three-bedroom apartment was perfect; it even had a balcony overlooking the park. His every request had been taken care of in advance, even down to the satellite television that would ensure his sanity on the nights when homesickness gnawed away at his soul.

'I'm sure I will be happy here, it's much better than I could ever have expected. Can I get you something to drink?'

'Thank you, but no, I really must be getting back. There's food and drink in the refrigerator and a selection of English books on the table in the hall. You have my number if you need me. Good luck Webb-San, I trust you will have a pleasant weekend.' She smiled, placed the key onto the tray beside the door and left.

Alexander sat with his coffee looking through Takino's list of recommended sights and consulted the map for directions. The nearest, he judged, was barely a five minute walk away. *'Decision made.'* He would spend the morning visiting the Meiji Jingu shrine.

According to the brochure, the Emperor Meiji and his wife the Empress Shoken were enshrined here after the Emperors death in 1912. Ever since the Japanese people had worshipped them as deities.

'Clearly the place to show off your best Kimono.' He thought, as at least half of the women there were doing just that. A mixture of sounds, chanting and clapping, flowed from a large elaborately decorated building at the far end of the courtyard.

Full of curiosity, Alexander stood watching the service for a while. The pattern of the proceedings was impossible to follow. His concentration drifted to a large six-foot diameter drum to his right and to beautiful, almost Indian style ornaments either side of the centrepiece of the shrine, an ornate altar. Two priests in bizarre red kimonos, black helmets and black lacquered wooden shoes chanted, as the congregation stood silent. A woman to his left bowed towards the shrine, tossed a coin into the wooden slatted offerings box, clapped her hands loudly and bent her head in an attitude of prayer. A minute passed, she raised her head, clapped her hands again, bowed and walked out. Intrigued by the ritual, Alexander copied her, assuming the wooden grid to be some form of oriental wishing well and wished for someone to cook his breakfast in the morning, after of course keeping him warm all night.

He decided to move on. Walking through the woods he followed the signs to the Treasure Museum, housing a collection of personnel effects of the Emperor. He stood in front of the royal carriage admiring the craftsmanship when a soft American voice drew his attention. 'They sure knew how to live in those days.' She said.

He turned to face her and tried in vain to hide his expression of surprise. 'Indeed. There's a lot to be said for travelling in a state coach, you see a great deal more at a slower pace.' He said, exploring her features for a flaw, there was none. Her shoulder length blond hair framed a face of classical beauty, her lips were full and welcoming and her eyes alive with the joy of life. *'A man could easily lose his soul to those eyes.'* He imagined.

'We seem to be the only Westerners here.' She smiled.

'Yes, it's peaceful isn't it? The Japanese are so well behaved.' He said, copying her smile. 'You live in Tokyo?'

'No, only visiting, although given the chance I don't think I'd refuse. It's so different that it would take me a year to decide whether I liked it or not. The first time I came to Tokyo was in the middle of last year, it was so hectic what with the work and all that I didn't have a chance to see anything, so you could say, this time I'm making up for it. I have it all mapped out.' She said, presenting an open page in her diary. 'Have you seen the Senso-Ji temple in Asakusa yet? I'm told it's quite superb.'

'I'm afraid I haven't. This is only my second day here, and my first seeing the sights, so far I can't complain. I see you've have been taking notes, you have a special interest in Japanese history?' He asked.

'Not really, more of a hobby actually. Some ten years ago I worked as a researcher for the Smithsonian Institute and now I suppose it's just a habit, you never know when it will come in useful.'

'As you say, you never can tell.'

They walked out into the surrounding woods, retracing the pathway he'd taken from the shrine. 'Allow me to introduce myself,' he said, 'Alexander Webb at your service.' He bowed low in good Japanese fashion.

'Sonya, Sonya Martin. Pleased to meet you.' She smiled, and copied the bow.

'What are your plans for the day?' He asked.

'I think I would like to see that temple in Asakusa, You will join me, won't you?'

Alexander could hear a strain of desperation in her voice, and wondered why. Before he had the chance to ask her, she supplied the answer. 'This is no place for a woman

Alex,' she said, slowly walking forward, 'my company made a mistake sending me here, you know.'

'Why?' He asked.

'Well, you see, a man doing business here is looked on with respect, a woman on the other hand is never taken seriously. It's almost impossible to get them to agree to anything I say. They are so bloody arrogant.'

He could clearly see the frustrated anger in her deep blue eyes. 'You are the second person in twenty four hours to tell me that, and the last one was Japanese. I guess there's not much that either of us can do about it. Remember, they've only been doing business with the west for a hundred years, maybe some things take a little longer. What you need is a diversion, something to take your mind off it. That, I propose, is where I come in. From now on, I see it as my sworn duty as an English gentleman, to ensure, that for rest of today, you are either laughing, smiling or eating.'

She grinned happily at the prospect. 'Lead on Sir Knight!'

Alexander consulted the rail map and plotted the course to Asakusa. 'Have you ever travelled on the trains here?' He asked.

'Several times, it's quite easy. You buy the cheapest ticket in the machine, make your journey and at the end the guard tells you how much you owe, it's that simple.'

'Then let's do it.'

They boarded the overland JR train at Harajuku. Sonya told him that it was called the Yamanote line. 'Basically the Yamanote is like a railway ring road around central Tokyo, If you live inside the ring you are either a Gaijin, a foreigner, visiting Tokyo or you are seriously rich.'

They changed trains in Ueno, an area renowned for its museums and arrived in Asakusa in blazing sunshine. Sonya consulted the map. 'It's this way.' She said.

They walked past restaurant after restaurant, each having it's own unique display of plastic food in the window. 'I have a feeling that we could easily get by here without knowing a single word of Japanese,' said Alexander, 'All we'd need to do is point and pay.'

'I can handle that.'

'What, the pointing or the paying?'

'You choose.' She said gaily.

'If you insist. Later.'

The Hozo-mon entrance gate to the Senso-Ji temple was impressive, it's thick red columns supporting an elaborate oriental style tiled roof. In the centre hung the largest paper lantern he had ever seen and beneath it, a blue robed monk in a wide domed straw hat, stood silently in the shade. Past the gate and a narrow road lined with tourist shops, decorated with smaller lanterns lay before them. It was crowded.

Thousands of pigeons flocked around a kiosk at its end, enhancing the skies of the main temple. Alexander bought a packet of seed and handed it to Sonya. 'Feed the birds two hundred yen a bag.' He sang, mimicking the song from Mary Poppins.

Within seconds the pigeons had flocked to her, perching on her head, her arms and her shoulders. 'One for the album.' He thought and raised his Canon EOS camera for the picture.

'Watch the birdie!' He said.

She laughed. 'Which one?'

Twelve hanging gold lanterns illuminated the inside of the temple filling it with a surreal glow. The air was filled with incense and in the centre stood a huge, highly detailed, gold plated shrine, flanked by rows of brightly coloured flowers. 'It's beautiful,' she said, 'I'm glad we came.'

'So am I.' Said Alexander taking her hand.

They walked out to the five-tiered pagoda, topped with what looked to be a two hundred year old radio aerial, gleaming in the sunshine. 'Do you think they can get Radio Tokyo?' He asked.

Sonya chuckled.

It was mid afternoon and the crowds were getting thicker by the hour. 'What kind of food do you like?' Alexander could feel his stomach rumbling for nourishment. 'Is there any thing you would recommend?'

'I think you should try Tempura. It is a traditional Japanese dish, although it was first introduced here by the Portuguese, a couple of hundred years ago. Everyone who try's it seems to like it, I suppose you would call it a soft touch for the western palate.'

They found a Tempura restaurant with ease, clearly recognisable from the display plates in the window. Alexander called the waiter and Sonya pointed to what she considered to be the best choice.

Fish, prawns and sliced vegetables were lightly coated in batter and deep-fried as they watched. They were each given bowls of Soya and horseradish sauce into which they were told to baste the battered food, a way of adding spice to the delicate tastes.

A bottle of Asahi super dry and a couple of glasses were placed on the table. Alexander poured. 'I hope you like beer Sonya, I think that's all they have. Tell me, what brings you to Tokyo?'

'Oh, lots of glamour,' she said, 'I'm here as a representative for Gem International, we buy and sell precious stones. Our speciality is the top one percent of the business.' She handed him her card. The stiff white card had Sonya Martin, International Sales Executive embossed in fine gold letters. 'My company has been given the task of compiling a Japanese national gem collection, so I'm here getting approval for the samples.'

'Surely that is very dangerous work, shouldn't you have a body guard or something?'

She laughed, 'You don't think they would trust me with millions of dollars in gems do you, even I would think twice if I was carrying something like that in my hand bag. No, the gems are normally flown in under heavy security.'

'Then how do you convince the powers that be, to buy what you have on offer?'

'That is really very simple. Firstly we show them photographs of the gems under our control, then on the next time we visit, we show them glass samples of the stones they have chosen. Something they can hold and touch. The cut and shape are direct copies of the originals. I have a box of samples in my hotel room, would you like to see them?'

'Very much.' He said, placing his napkin onto the table. 'You chose the meal, so I'll get the bill. That was the deal, right?'

'You cheated! You asked for my recommendation.'

'Precisely.'

Sonya was staying at the ANA hotel near the Roppongi nightlife district, in the heart of Tokyo. They decided to take a cab. An orange coloured taxi pulled to the side of the road at the sight of Alexander's raised arm and the near side rear door opened automatically. Despite obvious heavy use the interior trimmed with crystal white seat covers appeared spotlessly clean. An item Sonya observed she would never have found back home.

'Konnichiwa - good afternoon,' she said, 'ANA hoteru o kudesai.' At the request the white-gloved taxi driver sped off.

'Do you speak much Japanese?' Alexander asked.

'Not as much as I would like to and it's probably not enough to hold a business conversation. But I get by. It's amazing what you can pick up from those mail order courses. I listen to them while I'm in the car and always when I fly.'

'You must teach me some.' He said.

'It will be a pleasure, maybe later over a night cap.'

The Taxi pulled up in front of the hotel with the princely sum of eighteen hundred yen on the meter. Alexander paid him and they walked together in to the reception. She collected her key from the desk and escorted him up to her room.

On the bed lay a dark brown Cartier travelling case. He sat next to it as Sonya took a bottle of champagne from the mini bar. Moving to his side she raised her glass and chinked it against his smiling. 'To you Alexander, and a wonderful day.'

'And to you. A very special lady. I'm glad we met.'

She opened the case and folded it flat on to the bed.

In one side she had her passport, diary and business files. Beneath the divider lay her washing kit and a few over-night items. She withdrew and a file containing Gem International stationary with detailed descriptions of the stones. Using the first sheet as an example, she explained that each stone was graded with a system falling under the four C's. Cut, clarity, colour and weight, expressed in carats. On the other side, in a smaller case with a velvet-lined lid, lay a tray divided into sixteen sub-compartments, in each of these lay the gems. It was enough to take his breath away. 'They look real!' He said.

'They do don't they. They all have names you know?' She picked up one of the diamonds and held it to the light. 'This is called the Star of Tibet. It weighs ninety four carats, brilliant cut and is one of the biggest diamonds in circulation. It's almost as big as the Kohinoor, that's one hundred and eight carats and is part of your crown jewels.' She replaced it and picked up another, the largest stone in the box. 'This is an emerald cut, pigeon's blood, ruby. It's called the Chandra Ruby. At a hundred and fifty seven carats, I've never seen one larger.' The third stone she selected was a dark green emerald. 'This one is special, it's the Cougar's Eye. The original is almost flawless, very rare amongst emeralds and by far my favourite.'

'My favourite would be the ruby. Big is best has always been my motto.' Then almost childishly he asked, 'Would you mind if I photograph them?'

'Not at all, be my guest.' She said excitedly, having difficulty concealing her delight at finding someone as enthusiastic as she was in the gems.

'We'll have to go to my apartment, I need to use a close-up lens, do you mind?'

'No problem, I'd love to see your apartment, I'll bring the case.'

The time had flown by, it was now dark, or as dark as it can get under the illumination of more than a million fluorescent lights. The traffic was as chaotic as ever. It didn't seem to matter. Sonya moved closer to him as he placed his arm around her.

'You're a breath of fresh air.' He said, as the taxi negotiated its way towards Sendagaya.

At the apartment Alexander scoured the cupboards for a cork screw. 'I only moved in this morning, I haven't a clue where any thing is.' Takino-San had stocked the shelves with a myriad assortment of convenience foods, most with Japanese cooking instructions. *'Looks like I'll be eating out a lot.'* He thought.

Taking the chilled bottle of Pouilly Fume from the fridge he returned to the living room. Sonya had placed a CD of Bread into the HI-FI and the lights were dimmed. He looked into her eyes and watched her pupils grow larger. 'Will you stay tonight?' He asked.

'If you would like me to.' She said.

He drew her into his embrace and kissed her lovingly. Seldom before had he felt so comfortable with someone, especially after such a brief period of time.

She stroked the side of his face. 'You look good in my lipstick Alex.' She said, wiping it away, 'You had better take your photographs, before we are distracted further.' Her smile was both promising and tantalising.

Sonya opened the case as Alexander set up his camera equipment and placed each stone in turn onto the glass-topped table. A lamp shining from beneath highlighted every detail in the gems.

'Here! Take a look at this!' He said.

Looking through the eyepiece she could see the flaw. She knew it would be there. She had seen it herself a few days previously on the flight to Thailand on route to Japan. An almost perfectly shaped sword, a scimitar, in the centre of the stone.

'How unusual,' she said, 'it must have been a fault in the casting. I'm no gemmologist, but it looks like something you would find in the real thing. If there's a replacement when I return to the states, I'll send it to you as a souvenir.'

'I'd like that.' He said, 'A keepsake.' He placed the blood red stone back into the box and moved on to another.

With the camera equipment packed away, again they sat together. 'Are you working tomorrow?' She asked.

'On a Saturday? We Brits never work on a Saturday. And you?'

'My next appointment is at lunch on Sunday. What do you think we should do from now, until then?'

With that he took her hand and led her into the bedroom.

Facing each other he eased the neckline of her summer shift over her shoulder, and let it fall. She stepped from the dress and placed her hands against his chest, raising them slowly to caress his face, drawing it closer. His arms were around her again, warm and tender. They kissed long and hard, the passion rising in both of them. Still slowly and controlled she unbuttoned his shirt, eased it softly over his shoulders and allowed it to slip untidily to the floor. With all clothes cast aside they stood face to face, searching each other's eyes, without shame.

Making no attempt to cover herself, she reached out in need and opened her lips to meet his as Alexander came toward her. His body was hard and reassuring against her skin. His hands gentle and knowing. They eased themselves to the bed and kissed again. At his touch she was wet, an uninhibited release, tingling every nerve in her body. She traced his back with her nails and sighed with release as he entered her. He could feel her shake with pleasure beneath him as each gentle rhythmic movement drew them closer together.

They lay gazing into each others eyes, 'I think I'm falling for you.' She said, running her hand lazily through his hair.

'It's funny, I was just thinking the same thing.' He whispered, closing his eyes. The mixture of love and guilt was there. He knew it would be. His life with Amanda had been full of promise until it had been dashed by their careers. He hoped she would find someone soon, hopefully someone who could make her feel the same emotions he was feeling now for Sonya. The excitement of new love, the sense of commitment and the most human need of all, the need to share in another's life. He opened his eyes again and stared deeply into hers.

'I know so little about you Alexander, tell me, why are you here?'

'I live here.' He joked

'Fool,' she chuckled, 'No, why are you in Tokyo.'

Alexander eased himself up on to the pillow, as Sonya rested her head against his chest, under his arm. 'Are you laying comfortably, then I shall begin. Our story begins in a land far, far away. A land of poets, romantic rolling hills, puppy dogs called Maverick and yours truly, a frustrated car designer looking for a way to clean up the world…' He talked in detail of how the project had begun and passionately of where he could see the future.

'This is really exciting,' she said, 'so when do you start to make these cars?'

'Well my team arrive at the end of the month, up until then I'm pretty much left to my own devices. We will probably be making cars for real in about two years.'

She could see Alexander had other things on his mind for the immediate future. 'Would you like a massage?' She asked.

It was noon before they finally rose. Sonya walked to the kitchen wearing his shirt, 'How do you like your egg's.' She asked.

'Oh, as they come, the same as you probably.' His smile almost grew to a laugh as he recalled the wish he had made at the Meiji shrine, the day before. I'll have to tell her about that, he thought and walked happily naked to the bathroom.

Dressed and clean-shaven he joined her in the Kitchen. 'I was just thinking, I've heard of a place here in Tokyo, called Akihabara, they call it Electric City. It's supposed to be full of gadgets and electronic wizardry, a veritable feast for an engineer and I'm a sucker for gadgets, what do you say?'

'Sounds like fun!'

CHAPTER 7

Within the hour they were walking through street after street of hi-fi's, Computers and Video's.

'Do you have anything special in mind you want to look for?' Enquired Sonya.

'I've always fancied one of those personal hi-fi's. You know the type? The kind you slip into your top pocket.'

Crossing the road they stood before a store with a giant illuminated satellite dish above the "Tax Free for Tourists" sign over the entrance. 'Laox, funny name for an electronics shop?' Puzzled Alexander. 'A name better suited to a drug store or a chemist I'd have thought. Sounds like a laxative.'

'Electronic laxatives, now there's a thought.' Quipped Sonya, taking his arm, 'Let's see what they've got.'

'Can I help you sir.' Asked the shop assistant, a young man in thick-lensed glasses.

'He must have good eyesight to see through those?' Whispered Sonya.

'Yes please.' Requested Alexander, coughing lightly into his clenched fist to conceal his rising chuckle. 'I would like to see a selection of compact digital recorders, something with fine music quality.'

'The latest Sony model has many features, sir.' Taking it from the shelf, he placed the music recorder, little bigger than the memory card it would contain, onto the table. 'This model is very popular with western journalists.'

He said. 'Its main feature is the automatic on-off recording facility. After you switch it on, the machine is paused, recording starts the moment you start to speak, and stops after ten seconds of silence. It will of course allow you to download music from your PC or the web with a very acceptable level of quality, and, there is also a built in radio. Is this the kind of thing you were looking for, sir?'

Alexander weighed it in the palm of his hand and turned to Sonya. 'Definitely one of those things that you really don't need, yet, when you leave without buying, tend to regret it. Ideal for eaves dropping on the boss eh?' He said.

'Forgive me for listening to your conversation Sir, but if you are looking for something unusual, I think perhaps I have just the thing.' The assistant placed a super-compact video camera on to the counter. 'This is very special!' He announced proudly. 'Released for general sale last week. It's the smallest model on the market and works the same as any other video camera with a hard disc drive, except for one new and innovative feature. The dome in the front casing houses a special sensor, a sound and motion detector. At the first sign of sound or movement within a ninety-degree field of view, the camera will begin recording automatically. It was originally developed as part of a security system, although we find most of our recent sales have been to nature photographers.'

'Intriguing!' Alexander switched on the camera, standing still in front of it. He took a step backwards, and sure enough, the recording started. 'How does it stop?' He asked.

'It is the same system as is in the tape recorder, after ten seconds of silence or no movement, it will automatically pause the recording.'

'Is that so?' He took the machine in his hands and scanned the room through the viewfinder. 'What do you think Sonya?'

'Ideal for sight seeing.'

Alexander agreed and turned back to the counter. 'Thank you for the demonstration, enterprising of you, we will take them both.'

'You are welcome Sir. If you have a moment I will fill out the necessary forms. Tax free?'

Alexander nodded and offered his passport.

'Thank you. As a business purchase I can also offer you a further five percent discount if you have a business card.'

'Even better!'

Sonya placed an arm around his waist and whispered in his ear, 'That's proof of the difference between men and boys, Alex.'

'What is?' He asked.

'The cost of their toys!' She said and kissed him lightly on the cheek.

Leaving Akihabara they headed for Ginza. A shoppers paradise famous for having the most expensive real estate in the world. Sonya was now in a spending mood. Drifting from one department store to another, buying clothes for herself and gifts for her friends back in the states.

They were both shattered when they returned to the apartment.

'I'll run the bath,' said Alexander, 'I think we both could do with it.'

'You're a mind reader Alex, my feet are killing me. If you'd like, I'll treat you to a Japanese speciality, a soap massage. It's a fact, there are parlours here in Tokyo called Soapland, for just that purpose.'

'Now how would a nice girl like you, know a thing like that?' he asked.

'I read it in a book.' She replied coyly.

Alexander lay with his head on the pillow thinking of how happy he felt with Sonya at his side. 'Will you be in Tokyo for long?' He asked.

'Until next Friday, I wish it was longer. I'll miss you terribly when I'm gone.'

'Would you stay longer if I asked you too?' He said.

'Are you asking me?'

'I know we've only known each other for a couple of days, and I realise you have commitments back in the States, but I feel if we part on Friday we could both loose something special, who knows, maybe something very special.'

'Are you asking me to marry you?' She said tenderly.

'I would love to have the time to find out.' Gently he ran his fingers through her hair and kissed her lightly on her forehead. 'Most of the time I make quick decisions and hope for the best, in fact I feel like making one now. I just think a couple of weeks would give us both enough time to sort out our feelings, it would give us the chance to see if we would be good for each other. I wouldn't ask if I didn't think we'd have a future together. You will stay for a while, won't you?'

She snuggled up to him, placing her head on his shoulder, 'Yes please.' She said.

Sonya dressed quietly, as Alexander slept. It was nine am, plenty of time to get to the hotel, change and check out before her noon appointment she thought. Taking the tray of gem samples from the case, the only thing she would need for the meeting, she was nearly ready. She placed a brief note saying she would return later on the pillow beside him and kissed him gently before she left.

Within a minute, a taxi with its red "For Hire" light glowing, pulled up in front of the apartment, and she was on her way.

The ANA hotel was always busy, even on a Sunday morning. Every one she saw seemed to share in her happiness. She had never felt so complete, even the concierge commented on how radiant she looked. She would normally blush at such a remark, but not today. Who would have thought, She could soon be a married woman. Married to someone she could truly love. It had happened so fast, she had trouble believing it was true.

Throwing the gem case onto the bed, she slipped out of her dress and skipped whistling to the bathroom.

Reaching behind the bath curtain she searched for the shower tap. In that second the world stopped.

A breath, She'd heard a breath.

Adrenalin coursed through her veins in the same instant as a hand closed over hers. She froze. She was not alone.

Slowly the curtain slid to the side.

A Japanese face. Cold black eyes. What did he want?

A white-gloved hand moved swiftly, covering her mouth, muffling her screams. Tears of fear formed in her eyes and her muscles grew taught. She raised her hands to protect herself. It was in vain.

A blinding flash of pain exploded in her senses as the crushing blow found its mark. The room grew dark, and with it the image of a man in uniform.

CHAPTER 8

No pulse, Pupils dilated. 'Shit!' He said, cursing his own incompetence. He'd hit her too hard. The single blow to the bridge of her nose was only intended to knock her out. He would have to work harder at his technique.

Not to worry, occupational hazard, these things happened in this line of business and it wouldn't help to dwell on it. Her own fault anyway, stupid bitch, she shouldn't have taken it with her in the first place. Impassively, he shrugged his shoulders, reached his hands beneath her arms and laid her out flat on to the tiles.

Making it look like an accident would take meticulous attention to detail and the right setting, he knew that, and began the task of removing the remains of her clothing.

'Not a bad looking woman!' He thought, standing her in the bath, poised as though stepping out. 'Careful dear, hotel bathrooms are notoriously dangerous places.' He said, imagined the slip and gently guided her head to the side of the sink. The fatal moment. He pictured the fall as though in slow motion, lowering her inch by inch to the marbled floor. The position looked perfect, somehow natural, a work of art.

With the showerhead in his hand he turned on the flow. A gentle trickle at first to wet her hair and body, then with increasing force, aimed it at the bath, screen and walls. He took the Romanstar soap from its plastic container and rubbed a little in her eyes before placing it in the soap dish to give it a liberal soaking.

The box itself would be his "piece de resistance." He closed her hands over it, pressed hard and discarded it into the wastebasket. A simple clue yet sufficient. With the only prints on it, hers and the hotel maid's, the scene of crime staff would undoubtedly arrive at the only possible conclusion, an unfortunate accident.

Picking up her clothes he moved to the bedroom and arranged each piece naturally beside her dress on the bed. That was about it, he'd covered everything.

Now to the case. Lifting the catch, he opened the lid. Removing one of the stones he examined it carefully against the daylight and compared it with the copy from his pocket, it was a good match, the counterfeit was truly an excellent piece of work. He placed it into the same numbered compartment and re-closed the cover.

A thorough check of his uniform in the full-length mirror confirmed the absence of visible splash marks, and a final glance around the room showed no signs of his presence, time to leave.

The hallway was clear. He took the stairway down to the lower ground floor and the hotel's shopping arcades. No one would remember him there. *'Let's face it,'* he thought, *'who looks for direct eye contact with a policeman or security guard unless they really have to.'*

His car was parked a few minutes walk away, he took his time. To attract attention now would be foolish.

CHAPTER 9

The barking of a lone dog in the park had roused him. It was approaching noon. Alexander lay motionless for a while listening. Thoughts of walks on the downs sprang to mind and weekend romps on the beach, happy times, times he looked forward to sharing with Sonya. 'Can you hear him?' He asked to the darkened room, 'Sounds just like Maverick.'

There was no answer.

Reading the note, he remembered her lunchtime appointment. If all went well in the meeting, she would probably be wined and dined and presumably wouldn't return until late in the evening. He wondered if she was on commission and imagined with ease the face of her bank manager as she deposited a percentage of a national gem collection.

He would start the day with a coffee, he decided, slipped on a tracksuit and walked barefoot to the kitchen.

Settling down at the table he unpacked his Toshiba Laptop computer plugged it into the mains and called up the LX4 implementation plan. There was still much to do and little time in which to accomplish it. With his Design and Engineering staff arriving at the beginning of June, accommodation, a suitable work place and the necessary equipment would all have to be found and approved in advance. His first task would have to be the identification of their immediate needs.

Alexander was a pacer, thinking best on the move. He placed his new 'tape' recorder on to the table, switched it to record, stood and walked to the window. He described in detail the working environment he wished to create. The type of people he required from the Tri-Star staff to complement his own team and in his own estimates, the levels of expenditure he expected for the first six months of what Higaki-san had termed the Technology exchange period.

Mid afternoon he called Akiko's number, frustrated with the progress he was making alone. 'Hi, it's Alex. I hope you don't mind me calling you on a Sunday.' He said.

'Not at all,' she replied. 'Anything wrong?'

'No, not really, I need a little advice that's all.' He said. 'I'm working on the start-up proposal for Higaki-san, a few thoughts on how best to begin with the new programme. Presentation's my problem. How is it done in Japan? Typed report, overheads or a full blown, U.S. style, computer slide pitch?'

'You're supposed to be sight seeing!'

'I was. Something came up.'

Takino detected a note of cheekiness in his voice but thought it prudent not to enquire. 'Higaki-san likes to see the people presenting to him, likes to see their faces. I would suggest a written report and a presentation on your laptop. Can I help?'

'I really don't like to impose. However, if you know of a shop near here where I could buy a computer printer, I'd be grateful.'

'Your office equipment was delivered on Friday. If you wish, I can pick it up from the Tri-Star building and be at your apartment within the hour.'

'Are you sure it will be no trouble?'

'Quite the reverse.' She said. 'My parents have visitors today, it will give me the perfect excuse to leave for a few hours.'

True to her word, she arrived fifty minutes later, struggling with a large box. 'Hey, let me help you with that.' Said Alexander, taking it from her and placing it on the table by the computer. 'What would you prefer, tea or coffee?' He asked.

'I'll fix it, I know where everything is.' She said.

'That's more than I do.' Mumbled Alexander.

'How about a nice cup of tea.'

Alexander unpacked the printer, plugged it in, and set to modifying his software to accept the Hewlett Packard colour LaserJet.

'You type very slowly Webb-San,' said Akiko, appearing with matching mugs, 'would you like me to help?'

Alexander raised both of his index fingers and shrugged, 'If you don't mind. These are the only two I could teach and they're as thick as I am.'

They worked together until late in the evening. Alexander had lost total track of time. He had told her over dinner of the events that had happened since their last meeting on Friday morning and had promised that she would meet Sonya later in the day.

The clock had just past eleven and he was becoming concerned. 'I'd have thought Sonya would have been here by now,' he said, 'I'll call the hotel, see if she's returned from her meeting yet.'

The call was answered promptly. 'Good evening, ANA hotel reception, may I help you?'

'My name is Webb, will you connect me with Miss Sonya Martin's room please?'

'Certainly. One moment Sir.'

There was a pause, longer than he'd expected and a male voice came on the line. 'Good evening Mr Webb, My name is Shizuo Sonoda, I am the hotel manager. I believe you wish to talk to Miss Martin.'

'Yes, that's right, is there a problem?' Questioned Alexander.

'May I ask sir, are you a friend or relative of Miss Martin?'

'I'm her...' What should he say? 'I'm her boyfriend' He decided. 'What's this about?'

'Are you calling from inside Tokyo Sir?'

'Yes, why all the questions?' Asked Alexander, becoming irritated.

'If you have some time sir, I would like you to come to the hotel. It is better if we talk in person.' Sonoda said.

The words brought instant concern to his voice. 'I can be there in fifteen minutes. Please, tell me what is wrong.'

'If you don't mind Sir, I'd prefer to discus the matter when you arrive.'

Alexander hung up the phone. 'Akiko, there seems to be some kind of problem at the hotel, they want me to go down there.'

'I will come with you, you may need me to translate.' She said.

'She's probably drunk, and wrecked the place, or run off without paying.' He said, attempting to hide his anxiety. He was sure neither of these was a possibility.

Sonoda and another man, who introduced himself as a Detective Inspector from Tokyo's Azabu Police station, met them at the entrance.

Alexander grew increasingly anxious as they were escorted to the manager's private apartments. Sonoda beckoned them to take a seat in the low backed leather sofa and took his place opposite on similarly styled chair. He leaned forward, resting his elbows on his knees with his hands lightly clasped together.

'Thank you Mister Webb for coming to see me so quickly,' he began, in sympathetic tones, 'I only wish it was under happier circumstances.' He paused, as if searching for an easy way to say it. 'I regret to have to tell you that we have had an accident in the hotel, involving Miss Martin. It happened sometime earlier today in her room. Apparently, she had fallen, stepping from her bath after a shower. It was a bad fall I'm afraid, she'd hit her head hard, a blow from which she never recovered. I'm truly sorry.'

Alexander sat silent in disbelief. Impossible. They were mistaken. It must be someone else. 'Are you sure it was Sonya Martin,' he said, his hands beginning to tremble, 'don't you have any other Martin's staying in the hotel?'

'I'm afraid not. A maid turning down the sheets discovered her at around six this evening. There's no mistake.'

No mistake. Fateful words. He felt he was underwater, moving slowly, hearing voices from a distance, filtered through cotton wool. Accidents happened to other people, never anyone you knew, it was a law.

'Is she still here?' He asked, finally focusing on Sonoda's discomfort.

Sonoda relayed the question to the Inspector in Japanese, he nodded, stood and indicated that they should follow him. He led them silently across the lobby, into the lift and up to the tenth floor. The room had evidently been checked thoroughly by the police, silver finger print dust covered most surfaces, and was now empty of all of her personal belongings. On the bed, Impersonal, lay a long black plastic bag. As they entered a policewoman unzipped the top portion, permitting a clear view of her face.

Alexander's reaction was natural. Although keeping his composure, a tear of loss began to trace a path down his left cheek. So it was true. He bent to touch his lips to her forehead and whispered softly, 'We would have made a great team. I'll miss you.'

Sonoda lead him from the room. 'The police would like to ask you some questions, do you feel up to it?' He asked.

Alexander nodded.

'The Inspector speaks very little English, he asks if you would be willing to go with him to the Metropolitan Police Department near the palace, he has a colleague there who will be able to help.'

Again Alexander nodded as Akiko took his hand to comfort him.

They said good-bye to Sonoda-San at the hotel entrance, thanking him for the sympathetic manner in which he had handled everything, and stepped into the waiting police car.

The journey to the station was conducted in silence. Upon arrival they were shown to the office of the Chief Superintendent of Police. Several other policemen joined them, two in uniform and one in an ageing dark blue business suit.

The Chief Superintendent spoke first. 'Good evening Webb-San, Takino-San, please take a seat. My name is Hara.' He bowed slowly, handing Alexander his business card as he did so. 'I am saddened to hear of your loss, please accept my deepest sympathies. I hope you will bear with us, one of my staff would like to ask you a few questions. You are quite welcome to use my office, the interrogation rooms are so formal. Would you care for something to drink?'

'Black coffee for both of us please.' Requested Akiko.

The man in the blue suit took a seat opposite them and introduced himself as Captain Aono. A police Sergeant next to him opened his note pad and as if in preparation, licked the tip of his pencil. Aono began. 'Webb-San, will you please tell us how and when you first met Miss Sonya Martin?'

Alexander spent the next few minutes recounting the events of the past four days. From his arrival in Japan, to making the telephone call to the ANA hotel. Aono, visibly suspicious, had difficulty in coming to terms with how Alexander and Sonya had become so close in such a brief period of time.

'During your time together, Webb-San, did Miss Martin discuss with you any of her business affairs?' Aono asked.

'Not in any detail, no. She did say she was trying to convince your government to form a collection of precious stones, I believe she had an appointment at lunchtime today, to talk about the subject.'

'Lunch time today?' Probed Aono.

'Sorry.' Alexander looked at his watch, it showed two thirty am. "Yesterday." He corrected.

Aono turned to the Sergeant and asked him to fetch the box with Miss Martin's personal effects. Placing his pad and pencil on the table, the Sergeant left the room. Aono continued. 'Did she give you any details of who she would be meeting or where this meeting would take place?' He asked.

'I'm afraid she didn't. However, she may have written it in her diary. It's at my apartment.'

'We may need it to further our enquiries. Would you like me to arrange for it to be collected or would you like to bring it in yourself?'

'Leave it to me. I'll get it to you as soon as I can.'

The Sergeant returned carrying the box and a thermos flask of coffee. He placed the box at the side of the Captain's chair then returned to his seat and resumed his note taking duties.

'We found something very unusual in Miss Martins hotel room.' Aono said, reaching into the box. He drew out the gem case. 'Have you seen this before, Webb-San?' He asked, passing him the case.

'Yes. Sonya brought this with her from America,' said Alexander, 'It's her samples case. Why unusual?'

'Don't you think it strange, that a woman travelling alone, should be carrying such valuable merchandise?' He said, looking deep into Alexander's eyes, hoping for a reaction.

He got one. A rather sad fateful smile. Opening the box, he turned it to face the Captain. 'The most valuable thing here,' he said, 'is the box. These are glass samples. She said they were true to life replicas to show what her company had on offer.'

The Sergeant held up the flask, poised as a question. They all nodded. He started to pour.

'Oh, I see. That would explain it. They do look real though, don't they?' Said Aono-San, picking up the largest stone in the box.

'That's just what I said to Sonya. In fact, the stone you are holding even has a flaw in it.'

Curious the Sergeant's gaze drifted from a filling cup to the Captains hand. A pool of coffee began to form on the table. 'Careful, Sergeant!' Akiko said, reaching forward to help.

'I'm sorry, forgive me.' He said. 'It has been a long day.'

'For all of us.' Said Akiko, under her breath.

Captain Aono raised the stone to the light. 'A flaw? Interesting.' He said. After taking a few seconds to examine it, his brow furrowed. 'Where?' He passed the stone to Alexander.

He must be blind, thought Alexander. 'Close to the centre.' He said. Like the Captain, he held it up to the light. The Captain was right, no flaw. Confused, Alexander slowly placed the stone back into the box. *'That's not possible!'* He thought. *'It was there.'* He turned the box to see if there was a similar stone, it was the only ruby. He picked up the Emerald, Sonya's favourite, cut in a similar shape. He held that to the light, again no flaw. 'I don't understand.' He said, thinking aloud. 'Maybe I was mistaken. Were there any other sample boxes in her room?' He asked.

'No Webb-San, this was all that we found. You said yourself they were samples, perhaps she gave it to her lunch time appointment.'

'Perhaps?'

Captain Aono glanced at his watch. 'I think we have detained you long enough, you must be tired. Forgive me for having put you through this ordeal, I realise it must have been a stressing time for both of you. An unfortunate accident. I have no further questions. If you will follow me please, I will arrange for a car to take you home.'

CHAPTER 10

It was a little after eight thirty in the morning, Akiko would arrive soon to take him to the office. Alexander felt like he'd run a marathon and sat drained facing his uneaten breakfast. It had been a troubled sleepless night. Images of Sonya's bruised face disappearing beneath a closing black zipper had filled his consciousness; competing with the vision of a falling scimitar, each time he'd closed his eyes.

The doorbell rang. As he stood to answer it he spotted the camera next to Sonya's briefcase under the coffee table. His mind flashed back to the Friday evening and the hotel room. Sixteen compartments, sixteen samples. There were no spares!

'Come in Akiko.' He said excitedly, as he opened the door. She followed him in to the lounge. 'Last night, at the station, the stone, I said it had a flaw, remember?'

She nodded, bewildered at his change in mood.

'Well today I'm sure. She had no spares, I would have seen them in her briefcase. And that's not all, the ruby we were looking at was definitely not the one I had in my hand on Friday, and I have proof.' He lifted the camera. 'The one I saw is on the card in here.'

Takino read his thoughts well. 'We have a fast processing lab next to the office,' she said, 'we can drop it in on the way.'

'Do you think we should tell Higaki-san what happened?' Alexander asked, removing the compact flash card.

'Without doubt.' Takino replied. 'He is a very powerful man, and has many contacts, I think he would be sympathetic if you need his help.'

'Did you arrange for me to meet him this morning?'

'Yes, he said he would visit you sometime early today. He seems quite excited at the prospect of your new venture. He even told me that he admired your creativity, a great compliment, you must have made quite an impression on him when you met in England.'

Takino's news pleased him, it would be a pleasure working for someone who valued his talents, he mused. Picking up the computer printer and his briefcase he escorted her to the door.

Alexander's office was located on the top floor of the Tri-Star Motors building in Shinjuku, a matter of minutes from his Sendagaya apartment. The skyline of Shinjuku was reminiscent of La Defence in Paris, an area dominated by new, creatively designed sky scrapers, all now clearly visible from his full width office window.

Higaki entered, with a beaming smile. 'Webb-San, you are more than welcome.' He extended his hand in greeting. Alexander shook it. 'How are you settling in to our metropolis?' He enquired.

'It's certainly different, without Takino-San I'm sure I'd be lost in no time. She really is looking after me well.'

'Good, I chose her for you myself. Her English is excellent, I'm sure you will agree. How do you like your office?' He asked, knowing it would please him. It was a copy of his own. A large leather surfaced desk stood dominant at the end of the room, lined on one side by the window and on the other by a regency-style book case. Higaki sat in one of four comfortable chairs surrounding a similar styled meeting table. 'I took the liberty of shipping your personal belongings from Global design to make you feel more at home.' He said.

'You certainly are a man of your word Higaki-san, in England you said I would be well looked after, so far I could not ask for better. That reminds me...,' Alexander said, reaching into his briefcase, 'Glenmorange malt whisky. The nectar of the gods.'

'You really should not have bothered.' Said Higaki, pleased by the gift.

Alexander smiled, 'Should I take it back then?'

'Oh, no.' Higaki smiled, and held the bottle close to his chest.

With a brief knock at the door, Akiko entered. 'Forgive the Interruption, Higaki-san, Webb-San, but I thought you would like to see these as soon as possible.' She said, handing a brightly coloured packet over to Alexander.

'Photographs?' Enquired Higaki. 'Tokyo?'

'Not exactly. It's quite a long story, with rather a distressing ending, do you have time?' Alexander asked.

Higaki turned to Takino. 'Please inform my secretary that I am not to be disturbed.' He could see in Alexander's expression that it was something important.

Takino left as Alexander flicked through the pictures. He paused at the close up of the Chandra ruby. The fault was clearly visible in the centre.

'Good.' He sighed, relieved. 'Higaki-san. I met an American lady, last Friday, here in Tokyo. She had a box of samples showing gems like these.' Alexander passed the photographs across the table. 'She told me that they were all fakes, samples to convince your government to start a collection. Yesterday she was found dead in her hotel room, apparently as a result of an accident. I think she was killed,' Alexander pointed purposefully at a print of the ruby, 'for this!'

'Killed? Are you sure? Tokyo has the reputation for being one of the safest capitals in the world.' Higaki said.

'The proof is in your hands. I photographed the samples a couple of days ago out of pure curiosity. The large red stone has a flaw, as you can see.' He pointed to it on the photograph. 'Yesterday, Takino and I were questioned by the police, I mentioned this flaw to the police Captain, only when I tried to show him in the stone, it had gone. It was obviously a different stone. I'm beginning to believe the one Sonya showed me, unknown to her, may have been the real thing, and probably worth a considerable amount of money.'

'I think you should tell the police.' Higaki said firmly.

'Normally I would, only this time I'm a little hesitant. You see, the only people who could have substituted the gem were her murderer, a member of the hotel staff, a police officer or myself. If it was a police officer, he or she would have had ample opportunity to exchange it in the hotel or later at the station. The single undeniable fact is that the stone I saw in the station was different to the one in these photographs. That says to me that it was a premeditated murder.'

'I understand your predicament.' Said Higaki thoughtfully. 'However, we have to do something. The police Chief Superintendent, Hara-San, is a personal friend of mine. I've known him for some twenty years we grew up together. I can honestly say I have never met a man more trustworthy. I'm sure he would be discreet. Would you like me to call him?'

'Hara and I met last night, he seemed genuinely concerned, perhaps you're right.' Alexander conceded.

Higaki-san lifted the receiver and made the call, convincing Hara to join them for lunch at the office. At the same time Takino appeared with a tray of coffee and biscuits. 'You were right Akiko, Higaki-san does have friends in high places. Will you join us for a few moments?' Asked Alexander. She sat next to him.

'Higaki-san, over the weekend, Takino-San and I worked on a list of proposals and actions, that I believe need to be in place before my team arrive at the end of the month. Takino-San is quite capable and willing to carry out these requests, with your approval of course. I'm asking for your understanding. You know how I feel about what has happened. With your permission I would like to take a few days, until the team arrive, to gather my thoughts. I know I'll never be able to give the LX4 project my undivided attention with this still on my mind.'

Higaki leaned forward, resting his forearms on the table. Frankly he said, 'Webb-San. If you chose to do some investigating on your own I have my doubts whether you will be successful, if what you suspect is true, then you may be dealing with professionals. All the same, you have my blessing to try. If I can help in any way, you must not hesitate to call me. Tell me, where will you start?'

'I could see from the papers in her briefcase that Sonya had kept detail minutes of every meeting she'd attended since her arrival here. There must be some leads there. Also, in addition to the notes, she kept a diary.'

'I suggest that this information would be useful to Chief Hara, it will give him something on which to he can base his investigations.' Said Higaki.

Alexander nodded, collecting his jacket, he said 'I'll be back in time for lunch.'

Alexander returned to the office just before noon to find Chief Hara and Higaki chatting convivially in the executive conference room. 'Please forgive me for not being here, when you arrived.' Alexander said.

'Forgiveness, not necessary.' Hara replied. 'Higaki-san has explained to me your reasons for concern, I have arranged for one of my people to bring the collection from the station, they should be here at any moment.'

Taking a seat at the table Alexander drew the pictures from his inside pocket and offered them to the Chief. 'I took these in my apartment. There are a couple of close-ups of the ruby in there. I'm sure it's different to the one I saw in your office last night.'

Chief Hara looked thoughtful as he pondered over the photographs neatly arranged in rows in front of him. Looking up he smiled, 'You are a good photographer Webb-San. The detail is very clear. A Japanese camera I presume?'

'You presume correctly. One of many fine things your country produces.' Said Alexander flatteringly.

With a brief knock at the door, Akiko entered. 'Excuse me gentlemen. The police Sergeant is here.'

'Excellent.' Hara exclaimed, 'Please ask him to join us.'

The room was silent as Hara opened the lid to the case. All of the stones were present. Turning the box to Alexander he said, 'Webb-San, you will please examine the contents and remove the stone in question.'

The ruby felt cold in his hands as he raised it to the light. The reflected rays danced inside the faceted surface, causing it to glow. There was no mistake this time. Alexander's heart sank as with mixed feelings he passed it to Chief Hara. 'It would seem we have a paradox, Hara-San.'

Like Alexander, Hara also raised it to the light. The scimitar shaped flaw showed as a dark crack in the centre. 'Would you like to see this?' He said, passing it to Higaki.

'Very impressive. If I owned a stone like this I'd never have to work again.' He said, replacing it into the box.

With a nod from Chief Hara the sergeant stood, bowed, and with the case safely in his white-gloved hands, left quietly.

'What would you propose that we do now, Webb-San?' Hara enquired.

'As I have already said, the stone I saw last night was different, because of this I'm equally sure that Sonya, Miss Martin was murdered. You only have my word, I realise that. All I ask is that you investigate a little further.'

Hara's expression was pensive. 'Webb-San, your judgement is not in question here. If you say the gem sample you examined at the station was different, I am prepared to believe you. There is however a problem. My superiors will demand some form of proof before they will authorise me to instigate a murder inquiry. After all, this type of investigation involves significant manpower and financial resources. I'm sure you will understand when I say, officially, without proof, I am powerless to help you. Unofficially however, it is a different story. I will make some enquiries of my own. It worries me, if what you say is true, then the stone has now been substituted twice, and on the last occasion it must have been within the confines of the Tokyo police department, I plan to look into this immediately upon my return. If something turns up you will of course be informed.' Pausing for thought, he reached into his jacket pocket and produced a packet of filter-less Peace cigarettes. 'Smoke?' He offered.

'No thank you,' Alexander declined, 'maybe later after lunch.'

'Higaki-san tells me that you plan to do some research on your own.' Hara said, watching the smoke snake towards the extractor vent surrounding the centre spot light recessed into the ceiling. 'Normally I would advise against this, with the old line "leave it to the professionals". However, unfortunately in this case I cannot see any alternative. So if and when you need the resources of my department you are welcome to call on me in person, day or night. I can be reached at one of these numbers.' Taking the Government Issue biro from his pocket he added the telephone numbers to his business card.

'I appreciate your offer Chief Hara. Maybe these will help to give you some background.' Alexander placed Sonya's diary and meeting notes on to the table.

Chief Hara spent the next half-hour scanning the pages and drinking coffee, pausing occasionally to make notes.

'Considering the risks involved in taking these to the station,' he said, 'I propose you keep the documents here, locked somewhere safe. All I need for the moment is a photocopy of the pages detailing Miss Martin's movements over the last week, If I need more I will call you or Higaki-san. We can never be too careful can we?'

Once again, Akiko appeared at the door. This time she was carrying three black-lacquered wooden boxes. 'May I disturb you gentlemen?' She asked, 'Your lunch has arrived.'

'Yes, Takino-San, I think we are just about done.' Said Higaki. 'Webb-San, do you like Sushi?'

'I don't know, to tell you the truth, I've never had it.'

'Then prepare yourself for a culinary delight. Do you think a glass of Glenmorange would be a fitting complement to the delicate flavours of raw fish?' he asked playfully.

Alexander had to laugh. 'Undoubtedly.' He said.

CHAPTER 11

Despite the noise in the corridor he knew he would not be disturbed with the office door closed. It was a Met unwritten law, closed meant busy. All the same he could feel his heart thumping in his throat, the risk excited him in just the same way as being in on the kill. He could almost feel the adrenaline coursing through his veins and wiped the perspiration from the palms of his hands.

On the table in front of him stood a box with the legend "Personal effects, S. Martin, Miss. Case 1272'11." Next to the box laid the file with her American address. Unlocking the desk draw he removed a jar of coffee and proceeded to unscrew the lid. A few moments fishing with his fingers were rewarded by the cold touch of glass. "All change." He mumbled and grinned with satisfaction as the precious stone was once again back in his possession. He placed the Gem tray and its contents into the effects box and sealed it with two-inch wide scotch tape. Delicately he removed the official label and replaced it with Miss Martins company address.

It was now a race against time. Just fifteen minutes to catch the three o'clock post, then the two hour drive out to Gotemba and Matsumoto-San. No loose ends he had said, well he'd done his best, the rest was up to fate. Just one final thing before he could leave, his signature on the personal effects release form. Taking the pen from the side of his note pad he signed, T. Kumagai, Sergeant, Metropolitan Police.

CHAPTER 12

A bright silver reflection danced around the room. From the book lined library wall, to a framed picture of his father, then on to his collection of intricately hand carved Jade. Matsumoto grinned as he toyed with the paper knife. It was just like handling people. Control, that was what it was all about, even the smallest of movements could cause dramatic changes in direction, in the same way as a brief request to one of his staff would demand an instant response from the organisation.

The memory of a cold winters evening came to mind when the children would sit with him and he would do the same for them, telling them the reflections were enchanted fairies there to protect them while they slept. "Tinkerbell", he remembered. He owed a debt of gratitude to J.M.Barrie and Disney, it was the first word his daughter had spoken in English almost twenty years ago, a far cry from her language expertise today. She would be arriving soon to take her place at his side and act as translator and hostess at the gathering. The prospect of her arrival pleased him. It had been close to five years since her departure for Cambridge, he wondered how much she had changed. Matsumoto placed the knife carefully beneath the dragon headed desk lamp and rested back in the chair, closing his eyes.

The last of the fifty acceptance E-mails had arrived; it was going to be a full house. All day he had busied himself with the task of making their stay welcome and comfortable, arranging for their every need. Only the security still played heavily on his mind. Laser triggered surveillance cameras had been positioned at strategic locations in the grounds and a team of guards were at that very moment being trained down by the lake. It was a good start but would it be enough?

There was movement in the hall. He could hear the heavy oak entrance doors being opened and a muffled conversation. Although unable to discern the words exchanged, the visitor's recognisable voice promised good tidings. An idea began to germinate in his mind. Perhaps a potential solution to his problem had fortuitously presented itself.

With a brief knock at the study door Meena entered. 'Matsumoto-San. Kumagai-San is here, he would like to have a word with you.'

'Good! Have him come in. Bring us some cool refreshments and see to it that we are not disturbed.'

Moments later, Meena, acting as escort, placed a carafe and glasses in the centre of a low lacquered coffee table. She poured for them both, kowtowed and left. The room once again fell silent.

Standing before Matsumoto, Kumagai bowed deeply with respect, straightened and placed his hand into his jacket pocket to withdraw the Gem. He offered it smiling.

'You have done well, Kumagai-San.' Said Matsumoto, examining the prize. 'Very well. Tell me, how did it go?'

With a nod of permission, Kumagai made himself comfortable on the sofa. 'As you had anticipated, like clockwork. I made the switch in the girl's hotel room.'

'Yes, I was informed. Was it necessary to kill her?' Matsumoto enquired lightly, mesmerised by the internal fire of the ruby.

'She would have recognised me if she'd seen me again. I had no choice.'

'Understood.'

'There is however a minor complication, an Englishman, a friend of the girl's. To begin with he was unsure if her death was an accident.'

Slowly Matsumoto lowered the stone. 'How so?'

'His name is Webb. Our paths have crossed twice, last night at the Met. and this morning, I was summoned to his office by Chief Superintendent Hara. He appears to have photographs of the collection before the switch, and was under the impression, before my arrival, that the stone he'd seen at the station was a fake. I believe he is now convinced otherwise.

'A second examination of the stones struck me as unusual so I took the precaution of placing the original back in the box, just in case. It left him confused and embarrassed. I do not expect him to pursue it any further.' Kumagai paused to take a sip of the cool lemonade. 'And, to end the likelihood of any possible future investigation, the girl's possessions and sample box are now on their way back to her company in the United States.'

'Excellent!' Matsumoto, satisfied all was in hand, stood and walked to the door. 'Join me for a stroll in the garden.' He said.

When they had reached the lawns he spoke again. 'Your career in the police force, how important is it to you?'

'There are times that I wish I'd stayed in the army. I miss the action. Why?' Asked Kumagai.

'Would you consider working for me full time? I need someone who knows what they're doing to organise security. Considering your past record you are ideally qualified.'

'I would have to work my notice first.' Said Kumagai, pleased by the offer.

'How much holiday do you have left?'

'I never take holiday,' he said, 'it's been accumulating ever since I started on the force, there must be over a couple of months of it.'

'Good, then use that. Hand in your notice tomorrow, there's something I would like you to do for me.'

By now they had reached the shore of the lake which glowed red in the setting sun. A martial arts class was in progress with two instructors demonstrating weapon-disarming techniques to a circle of eager students. For some, this would be an unnecessary refresher course, for others it could mean the difference between life and death. Kumagai could see from the number of brief stolen glances that his uniform visibly made them nervous.

'What is it that you'd like me to do?' Asked Kumagai.

'Two weeks ago I received a letter from our Hong Kong brethren concerning the gathering, confirming the attendance of their representatives and the presence of a similar stone to the one you brought for me today. This morning I received a further, rather disturbing letter, airing their anxiety with respect to our security. That is where you come in. I would like you to go to Hong Kong to put their minds at rest. You know the risks we are likely to face while our guests are here so take the next few days developing contingency plans for any eventuality should we encounter a breach in security. If you feel comfortable with the system then I'm sure you will be able to convince them that their people and property will be protected. When you return, there will still be a few days left for briefing the staff and testing the efficiency of your security team, before they arrive. You may ask for anything you may need, cash, more manpower, equipment, it will be made available to you without questions.'

'Have you arranged a date for this meeting?' Asked Kumagai.

'Yes, the twenty seventh of May. I realise this will only give you seven days, however these two instructors will be staying on as part of your team, both good men, they can handle the implementation of whatever you decide. I should like you to concentrate on getting the systems in to place before you leave for Hong Kong, that should give them plenty of time to rehearse. Make a good job of this and your future will be secure. As you know, I control a large and diverse network, some of it is even legal.' He said smiling. 'It is my wish that you supervise all of the security aspects within this organisation. You will be reporting directly to me. Do you think you can handle it?'

'As you said, it's what I was trained for.'

'Good. Now to the other matter, the Englishman. As my father used to say, It's better to be safe than sorry. Have him followed, if he gets too close....kill him.'

CHAPTER 13

'You need some rest Webb-San, It's late.' Said Akiko reluctant to leave while Alexander was still at the office. 'Shall I arrange for the driver to bring the car round to reception?' She asked.

'In a while, please come and sit down. I've just been reading Sonya's diary, how anyone finds time for this kind of detail baffles me. Personal descriptions of everyone she met, where they went, what they ate, how she felt, It's all in here. Even me, and I can't for the life of me remember her having time enough to write a single word, let alone three pages. One thing's for sure, with this kind of background data we'll be starting on solid ground.'

'What do you plan to do first?' Asked Akiko picking up his enthusiasm.

'In principle there is no difference between this and any large project, they all need planning, implementation and resources and at the moment my most valuable resources are you and this company.' He said, closing the cover and looking up to face her. 'Akiko, I'm going to catch those bastards if it takes the rest of my life.'

Although outwardly calm, Akiko could feel his determination. Throughout the day she had watched his anger steadily develop, fuelled by frustration and Sonya's written word. Until now. All the signs of self-pity had gone, effectively replaced by the aura of action. 'I'll do everything I can to help.' She said.

'Sonya's last contact was a man called Koyanagi in Kyoto. I plan to go and see him, how do I get there?'

'The quickest way is the Shinkansen, you call it the Bullet Train. You can leave the booking arrangements to me, when would you like to leave, tomorrow morning?'

'No, the day after tomorrow, there are a few things we will need to do first. I will need business cards, in my name under the company heading of Gem International. You can copy this one.' Alexander handed her Sonya's calling card. 'They will serve as a useful introduction, without arousing suspicion. Secondly, when Sonya went to Kyoto she stayed with a friend called Tomoko, Tomoko Den. There's no address here, see if you can track her down.'

'That should not be difficult, the name Den is uncommon, an old Shogun name. When I locate her I will arrange an appointment for you to meet.' She said, now taking notes.

'A Mobile Phone. I will need to stay in contact with Hara-San and Higaki-san, preferably something small and light.'

'I ordered one for you this morning. I assumed you would need one for your duties here. The last time I ordered one it arrived the following day so you should have it tomorrow evening. Leave it with me'"

'Finally, I wish you would call me Alexander, Webb-San sounds much too formal, especially when we are on our own.'

Akiko nodded her agreement, then, almost cheekily said, 'Shall I order the car now, Alexander-San?' Reluctant to dismiss the formalities altogether.

Alexander smiled. 'Yes please, Akiko-San.' He said.

'Chief Hara wants to see you in his office.' Said the duty sergeant as Kumagai studied his holiday card.

'OK,' he said, counting the days, 'I won't be long.'

'He said, you were to go straight to him, the moment you came in, get a move on!'

Kumagai turned to face him. Hashimoto was one of the latest internal transfers from Osaka, he'd hated him on sight. 'You're new here Hashimoto, don't push your luck.' Walking over to him Kumagai stood within inches of his face, glaring into his eyes, 'If I were you I'd watch whom I pushed around.'

'Are you threatening me Kumagai?'

'You had better believe it.' He said, slapping the holiday request form onto the desk. 'It would give me the greatest of pleasure to post your epitaph in the Tokyo Times. Just stay off my back.' With that he headed off for the Chief's office. He felt good, stimulated, early morning confrontations were always good to get the blood flowing.

'Good morning Sergeant Kumagai, come in and sit down.' Said Hara, gesturing to the chair facing him on the opposite side of his desk. 'It's about our meeting yesterday with the Englishman, Webb. I would like you to arrange for a valuation of one of the stones amongst Martin-San's personal effects. The item we're most concerned with is the large ruby, although while you are about it you may as well get them to value all of the pieces. Probably worthless bits of cut glass, but its best to know for sure.'

'Forgive me, that will not be possible sir.' Kumagai cast his eyes downwards submissively for effect, reminiscent of his youth before the wrath of his once dominant headmaster.

'Why Sergeant?' Asked Hara, perplexed.

'After our meeting yesterday I thought the confusion had been cleared up and the case would be closed. So I sent all of her personal effects back to her company in America. Did I do wrong?'

'No, not really, although I would have preferred for you to ask me first. Well, what's done is done.' Hara sat back and thought for a moment. 'Send an E mail,' he continued, 'to Gem International. Inform them that they will be receiving the stones in the near future and request them to make the valuations for us.'

'I will do as you request sir.' Said Kumagai, inwardly thrilled that the ruse had worked. 'There is something else I would like to talk to you about, Sir.' He said, keeping his composure.

'Yes?'

'I've been offered another position, with Matsumoto Industries as Chief of Security. A position I really cannot refuse.'

'A large and powerful organisation Sergeant Kumagai, you are most fortunate.' Said Hara.

'The problem Sir is that Matsumoto-San would like me to start immediately, I would like to use my holiday entitlement as a bridge from now until the end of my notice period. In order to do this, I must first obtain your permission.'

'What is the status of your case load at the moment?' Asked Chief Hara.

'There is nothing I cannot pass on, mostly administration duties.'

'Good. I understand, it would be pointless for me to make you an offer of increased salary or promotion as an incentive to stay. With an offer like this one I would probably make the same decision as you. How long have you been with us?'

'Five years sir.' Answered Kumagai.

'In all of this time I have only ever heard good reports of you and your work. Because of this and in view of the fact that you will probably need every Yen you can lay your hands on during the first few weeks with your new employer, I will not insist that you work the required notice. Let me have your letter of resignation today, then you may leave when all of your affairs here are in order.'

'This is very generous of you Chief Superintendent Hara. I have the letter with me now.' Said Kumagai, handing it over.

'You may leave the formalities to me. We will be sorry to lose you Kumagai-San, I wish you well.' Said Hara honestly.

Kumagai stood and bowed. 'Good-bye sir and thank you.'

'Sergeant, leave a hard copy of the E mail with the duty officer.'

'Yes sir.' He said then closed the door to the office behind him.

As soon as Kumagai had left, Chief Hara lifted the telephone handset and called the personnel department to order the sergeants records. Within the hour the plastic bound folder lay open on the desk in front of him. What he read surprised him. In addition to the initial application letters and standard annual reports was an application for Special Forces. A detailed self-appraisal in Kumagai's hand was attached to a personal psychological profile, recommending refusal. Hara lifted his pen and started to make notes.

Toshiro Kumagai, now thirty-five, had been with the force for five years. This much he knew. His parents were both dead, killed during gangland violence in the nineties when he was only fifteen. This could explain his reasons for joining the police, he mused. All the same, he had managed to finish school and progressed to university where he'd graduated with honours in mathematics. Four years in the Japanese self defence force, where he'd specialised in small arms and martial arts had been rewarded with the distinction as a Marksman and Karate third Dan. The detail for the next three years was sketchy to say the least. A few names of military personnel in South Africa and Jordan as personal references and that was it.

Hara turned the page to see what the police psychologists had to say. An underlined hand-written note caught his eye at the top of the page, "Intelligence quotient = 185"

'He's a bloody genius.' Said Hara aloud.

He moved on to the typed text. Comments like 'Can be extremely violent' and 'Enjoys inflicting pain' were again underlined. That would explain the refusal, he thought. Hara scanned his notes again. He added a copy of Kumagai's resignation letter to the top of the papers and closed the file. Two key questions needed to be answered. What was he doing in South Africa and why had he not been told of the Special Forces application. He intended to find out. There's more to Kumagai than meets the eye, He reflected.

CHAPTER 14

There is a secret to travelling light; the richer you are the less you need, pondered Alexander, as he struggled with a large awkward sports bag slung over his shoulder through the morning crush hour.

Tokyo's central station was not as daunting as he'd expected; it had obviously been designed with Westerners in mind. Blue direction signs with the legend 'Shinkansen tracks' clearly indicated the route from the entrance to the turnstiles, where thoughtfully positioned overhead were digital display boards in both Japanese and English. The board was clear enough but his ticket was not. He'd better check he decided. At the gates stood a uniformed guard, with what looked to be a pair of pliers in his hand for clipping tickets.

'Kyoto?'

'Yes sir, track seventeen, nine o'clock,' he said, with a brief glance at the ticket, 'you have ten minutes.' His hand sprang into action, starting the pliers chattering and clipping the ticket with practised dexterity.

What a boring job, thought Alexander, mounting the escalator up to the platform. Directly ahead of him was a kiosk selling boxed meals. One sight of this made his stomach rumble, begging for breakfast. He handed over a thousand yen note in return for a packet of ham sandwiches and a small box of sushi. 'Do you have coffee?' He asked.

'Co-he, no, ven-in machin.' She said, pointing further up the platform.

All he could see was a machine with Coca-Cola emblazoned on the side, vending cans. On the front of the machine in two neat rows were samples of the drinks it contained and sure enough one of them was coffee, with milk and sugar at one hundred and fifty yen. The brown Georgia coffee can, too hot to handle found its temporary home in his jacket pocket as he set forth for carriage sixteen at the end of the graceful, projectile styled train.

The interior not too dissimilar to modern European trains was immaculate and Alexander soon located his pre-booked seat, number 6A, by the window.

Noiselessly the train glided out of the station and an English commentary followed the Japanese over the speakers. 'Ladies and Gentlemen, welcome to our Shinkansen, this is the Hikari Super-express bound for Hakata. We will be stopping at Nagoya, Kyoto, Shin-Osaka, Okayama, Hiroshima, Ogori, and Kokura stations before reaching Hakata terminal....'

The commentary continued, but Alexander was to preoccupied to listen, absorbed by the passing metropolis gradually blending with lush green countryside as the train gathered speed. Almost one hour later, a few miles after a high-speed pass through Mishima, Mount Fuji majestic in its snow capped splendour presented itself through the clearing clouds.

Alexander reached for his bag and took out his video and stills cameras to record the view. A view he'd seen so many times on film or frozen on a page, yet none of them could quite compare with the impressiveness of seeing this for the first time, with his own eyes. Every inch of the twelve thousand four hundred foot volcano was clearly visible, the sides were pure, almost straight lines, just as a child would have drawn it, before being scolded by an inexperienced teacher for his simplicity.

There was considerable movement in the carriage as other passengers, like Alexander were vying for positions to take their photographs. One of them sat next to him.

'I have lived in Japan all of my life,' he said, 'and I have never had so clear a view of Fuji-San. Fuchi the goddess of fire is smiling today, it is lucky. Make a wish Englishman.'

Alexander did as he was instructed; every ounce of luck would be welcome if he was to succeed.

With Fuji-San receding behind him, Alexander set to timing the kilometre markers in an attempt to see how fast the train was travelling. It was really flying; they were passing four markers every minute, equivalent to two hundred and forty kilometres per hour, about one hundred and fifty miles per hour. The strangest thing of all was the absence of any impression of speed from inside the train. *'I must try the TGV in France,'* he thought, *'it's supposed to be faster, I wonder if it's as comfortable.'*

A couple of hours after leaving Tokyo the train approached Japan's previous capital and Tokyo's anagram, Kyoto. The air was oppressive, hot and humid, forcing him to catch his breath as he stepped down onto the platform. He had a little more than an hour to kill before meeting Miss Tomoko Den at the Ryoanji Zen garden. Akiko's suggestion.

'It's a peaceful place,' she'd said, 'if she hasn't heard what's happened to Sonya, you may need somewhere like this to break the news to her.' Alexander had agreed and decided that the best course of action would be, to be there when she arrived.

A dozen or so Toyota Crown taxis were waiting at the entrance to the station as Alexander emerged into the bright sunlight. At the head of the line a nearside passenger door swung open as he approached. 'Ryoanji please.' He said, 'Take your time.'

'Hai.' Replied the driver, sedately manoeuvring the car out of the station and into the slowly moving traffic.

Kyoto was not what he'd expected. Instead of an ancient Japanese town, speckled with shrines and temples the taxi was driving past street after street of a modern city. Immediately in front of the station stood the Kyoto tower hotel, with what looked to be a two hundred foot radio mast reaching skyward, mounted to the hotel's roof. 'Progress.' He said, expecting the driver to have read his thoughts. There was no comment.

The car pressed onwards weaving through the traffic for a further fifteen minutes before pulling up in front of the temple's entrance gates at the side of a small deserted car park.

At a kiosk by the gate, Alexander handed the five hundred yen entrance fee to an old man in uniform. Both had seen better days. In return the old man offered him a pamphlet in English describing the temple and gardens and directed him to the path he was to follow.

The twelfth century gardens were a work of art, peaceful, yet full of colour. He paused for a moment to watch two mandarin ducks competing for a small piece of bread, close to the shore of the ornamental lake. Akiko had chosen well, he liked this place he decided. At a restful pace he walked on, following the signs to the rock garden, stopping frequently to take pictures.

Removing his shoes Alexander entered the main temple. The worn wooden floors felt comfortable underfoot, smoothed by the thousands of feet preceding his. He entered a long covered walkway with a panelled wall to his right and wooden steps leading down to the garden on his left. A courting couple seated on the steps at the far end looked up to see who had arrived to disturb their private moment. Alexander could almost feel them wishing he would leave. Setting his bag down on the floor at a discreet distance he sat to join in their contemplation. Like Kyoto the garden was not as he'd anticipated, he'd expected a typical ornamental Japanese garden. What lay in front of him was different. Low earthen walls surrounded a rectangular frame some hundred feet long and thirty feet wide, into which fifteen rocks had been placed on a bed of raked white gravel. The rocks were all different in size, some standing five feet or more high, while others were almost hidden by raked patterns. The simplicity of the design reminded him of a seminar he'd once had from a photography lecturer at college. He'd said, 'Keep it simple, the more information you have in a photograph the less time people will spend looking at it, the more you put in the less we see. Humans are basically simple creatures, we can only understand a little at a time.' Maybe he had something there, the old codger must have visited this place, he mused.

'May I sit with you?' The female voice came from behind him. Alexander turned and looked up.

'You must be Alexander Webb.' She said, moving to his side on the wooden steps and carefully arranging her dress as she sat down, so as not to crease it.

'And you must be Tomoko Den, I am pleased to meet you.' He said, gently shaking her hand. He held it for a moment, subconsciously unwilling to let it go. She had a face of the kind he couldn't help but stare at. Perfect in every detail, in essence the sum total of all his imaginations of oriental women in one person. A cascade of flowing black hair, minimal makeup, soulful brown eyes narrowing gracefully with a growing smile on her deep red painted lips.

'Sorry.' He said shyly, finally releasing her hand. 'How did you know it was me?'

'It was your camouflage, a dead give away. Your secretary said "Look for someone who's tall, well dressed and unmistakably British" and as you are the only Westerner here, I suppose the odds were probably in my favour.'

'Your powers of observation and deductive reasoning are truly amazing Miss Holmes.' Said Alexander.

'Elementary my dear Webb.' She countered, miming a pipe held between her thumb and forefinger.

'Tracking someone down is why I've come to see you.' He said, now looking back at the stones.

'Does this have something to do with the phone call?' Asked Tomoko, 'A man called Hara, a policeman from Tokyo phoned me yesterday.' Her voice had now turned serious with a hint of sadness. 'He said that a friend of mine, Sonya had met with an accident and would not be visiting me again, when I asked why..., he told me.' These last three words brought the moistness to her eyes. She produced a small lace lined handkerchief from her purse to pad it away.

'Sonya was a friend of mine too.' He said to comfort her.

'I know you are not from the police, so what do you want from me?'

'Would you like to walk in the park, its more private and we're less likely to be overheard.' Suggested Alexander, standing up and helping her to her feet.

'You're right, I'm not with the police,' he continued as they walked out of the temple, 'I met Sonya last weekend......' As they made their way down to the lake he told her everything, in as much detail as he could recall leaving nothing left unsaid.

CHAPTER 15

Tomoko sat in silence on a lakeside bench, gazing blankly out at the water. Alexander sat beside her, in a strange way comforted; Tomoko had believed everything he had told her.

'What are we going to do about it?' She asked.

'We?'

'Yes we. Sonya and I go back a long way. We started as pen pals when I was at high school. It was part of the system. At the end of every week as part of our language studies we all had to write letters to our twinned school in Utah. I used to write mine to Sonya. She was good for me, every time that she wrote back, she would send a copy of my letter with hers, with corrections in red, just like a teacher. We met up a few years later; she helped me get into college in America so we could study together, ever since we've been like sisters. So if you are going to do something about her murder, I'm going to be part of it.'

'It might be dangerous.' He said, secretly hoping this would not dissuade her, her help could be invaluable.

'Let me put it this way,' she said, 'If we can prove she was murdered and we can do something about it, it will be my way of saying thank you to her for everything she's done for me.'

'OK, it's a deal. Welcome aboard Partner.' Once again Alexander offered his hand, pleased by the prospect of not having to face the journey alone. 'The first thing I would like to do is find a hotel, take a bath and get rid of this bag.'

'Have you ever stayed in a Ryokan, a traditional Japanese Hotel?' She asked.

Alexander was intrigued. 'No, is it good?'

'It's different, I can promise you that and I know just the place. Come with me.' The smile was again on her lips as she led him back to the car park.

Like himself the prospect of action had stimulated her. He could sense it. She was obviously not the kind of person content with standing by whilst others got their hands dirty. In his experience it was a rare quality in men, let alone women.

Her car, a Nissan GTR was parked in the spot where he'd been dropped off by the taxi. 'Is this yours?' Said Alexander, seeing one close up for the first time. 'How does it handle?'

'You Brits drive on the same side of the road as we do, don't you?' She asked.

'That's right.'

'Then try it out. I'll give you directions.' She said, tossing him the keys.

To be behind the wheel of a powerful car again, pleased him. With a feather light touch on the red ignition button, the 3.8 litre twin turbocharged V6 engine burst into life. Selecting drive from the automatic gearbox and gently depressing the accelerator the black sports coupe purred out of the car park and quickly picked up speed, as Alexander retraced the route taken by the taxi only this time a little quicker.

As they approached the centre, Tomoko guided him through the back roads of the bustling town, avoiding all but a handful of the rush hour traffic jams. The scenery changed dramatically with every turn as they approached Gokomachi Street. *'It's just like driving back in time.'*

Thought Alexander, as she told him to pull up in front of one of the traditional wood fronted houses lining the street.

'There are very few roads like this one left in Kyoto.' She said. 'The architecture and gas lamps down here date back to the Meiji Era, thankfully it hasn't changed in the last hundred years, it's still the same now as it was then. A few years ago our local government passed new laws protecting this area from development. A little late in my view, but welcome all the same. It's nice to think that our future generations will still have the chance to see the way their ancestors lived, because of our actions today.'

'This seems to be a subject close to your heart Tomoko.'

'It is. This was my home for many years.' She said thoughtfully, gazing through the car's window at the illuminated hanging lantern, outside the Ryokan. 'I left a few years ago when I could afford a place of my own. It's strange; you only appreciate your family when you've left them. Collect your bag and I'll take you in.'

Sliding the latticework entrance door to the side they both entered the small stone paved reception. He could hear the clip clop of wooden shoes approaching from a hidden corridor to his right, stopping a few feet away. Part of the shoji screened wall in front of them slid to the side and a middle-aged European woman in a dark brown Kimono stood smiling before them.

'Tomoko my dear, your father and I were just talking about you.' She said in softly spoken Japanese. 'You should visit us more often, now come and give your mother a big hug.' Tomoko did as she was asked. 'Is this your boyfriend, Tomoko?'

'We've just met, a friend of a friend.' She said, answering in English and giving Alexander a wry smile,

'Mother, this is Alexander Webb, he's looking for a place to stay for a few days.'

Placing her hands together she bowed slowly to him. 'Mr Webb, you are very welcome. My name is Coco, I hope you will find our humble Inn to your liking. Tomoko my dear, will you be staying also?'

'I .....'

Before she could answer, Coco interrupted her flow. 'You so rarely visit us my dear, your father and I would be delighted if you'd spend a few nights with us. If you both stay, you can stay as our guests.' She stood before them with a sincere hopeful smile, knowing Tomoko would accept.

'How you make a living in this business mother, I will never know.' She said, turning to Alexander and shrugging her shoulders. 'It looks like we're both staying.'

Tomoko stooped to pick up a pair of wooden slippers from the floor and handed them to him. 'You'd better try these on for size, although I don't for one minute expect them to fit, they're made for a more delicate sized foot.'

Alexander resisted pointing out that if he had Japanese sized feet he would have considerable difficulty in balancing. Instead he settled for a sarcastic "Thank you" and hobbled uncomfortably behind them both as they lead him along the corridor and up a single flight of stairs, to his tatami floored room.

It was small by western standards and sparsely fitted. Dominant in the centre of the room, surrounded by cushions was a knee level dining table and beyond a small balcony overlooking the ornate enclosed garden. Despite it's size the obvious warmth of the family atmosphere glowed in the draped scroll paintings of Kyoto that decorated the manila coloured walls. 'Where do I sleep?' Whispered Alexander.

Tomoko lifted her hand to her mouth to hide a childish chuckle. 'You weren't lying when you said you'd never stayed in a Ryokan before, were you. I'll explain. In most Japanese homes space is very limited, this is also the case here. It helps with the feeling of nostalgia. After dinner my mother will run a bath for you. While you are soaking away your aches and pains, one of the staff will come to your room to remove the table and replace it with a Futon and some blankets.'

'A Futon?'

'It's a thin mattress. I hope you like a hard bed; you'll be sleeping on the floor. I would guess that there's not many hotels in Europe that would offer that as a sign of quality.' She said light-heartedly.

Shaking his head, Alexander smiled as she passed him a dark blue Yukata and brown quilted jacket. 'Change into these,' she continued, 'I think you'll find them very comfortable. It's a Japanese housecoat; all of the guests wear them. It's a kind of uniform.'

'Will you be joining me for dinner?' He asked.

'I wouldn't miss it for the world. But first, I must go and see my father, with a bit of luck he'll cook for us tonight, he prepares the best Kaiseki in Kyoto.' She said, following Coco out of the room. 'I'm off to get changed, I'll see you in half an hour.'

'Kaiseki, Futon, Yukata, it's all Greek to me.' Mumbled Alexander after they'd gone and set to changing his clothes before unpacking the sports bag.

The humid climate had taken its toll. Every piece of clothing packed into the bag was creased, as if pressed by a blind regimental sergeant major. The only respectable attire left for his appointment with Koyanagi was the light grey suit he'd been wearing all day. Even he had to admit it; a day's perspiration in this heat would hang like a cloud around him, if he wore the same suit for tomorrow's meeting. He vowed to ask Tomoko if anything could be done to help the situation.

The clothes were not the only things affected by the humidity. Sadly he lifted Sonya's diary from the bottom of the bag. The once slim volume had expanded with the now wrinkled pages. As he lifted it, the leather binding slipped away in his hand, leaving the bulk of the book still in the bottom of his bag.

'Are you decent? Can I come in?' Came a call from the hallway outside his room.

'Sure Tomoko, come in. I've got something to show you.' As she entered Alexander passed her the two separate parts of the diary. 'Have you got any glue? Sonya's diary's falling to pieces.'

'Yes, I'm sure my father has some wood glue in his workshop, will that do?'

Alexander nodded, 'That will do fine.'

A moment later they were both sitting at the table in his room with the leather binding open in front of them.

'What's this?' Said Tomoko, carefully easing a piece of paper from under the memo page, glued to the lining of the leather cover. 'It looks to me to be part of an official document.' She said, handing it over to Alexander.

Alexander read it quietly to himself, before asking 'Is there any more, another page?'

She looked and then shook her head. 'No, that's all there is, What is it?'

'It's the second page of a very recent valuation, dated May the sixth. That makes it only a couple of weeks old and after Sonya had left the States for the Pacific. The first page would have been the valuation, what we have here is a certificate of authenticity for a one hundred and fifty seven carat ruby.'

'Is it significant?' Asked Tomoko.

'Oh yes.' He said angrily. 'This means she lied to me. She
knew the Chandra Ruby was genuine.'

CHAPTER 16

The anger of the moment soon subsided. Alexander sat, thoughtful, on the tatami matted floor, facing Tomoko across the dining table. Sonya's predicament was now becoming clearer.

'We talked about the stones often.' He said quietly. 'She even acted surprised when I'd told her that I thought the ruby looked real. The hardest thing for me to come to terms with, is the fact that if she'd told me, I know I wouldn't have let her out of my sight. It doesn't take an Einstein to realise the level of danger she was letting herself in for. A couple of million dollars worth of gems would raise more than a passing interest in a monastery. If only she had told me, she would probably still be alive today.'

'You shouldn't blame yourself, Alexander. I'm sure there were reasons.' Tomoko said sympathetically, momentarily placing her hand on his.

'Oh yes, I'm sure there were.' He said sarcastically. Reaching for the sports bag he dragged it across the floor, drew back the zipper and searched for his crumpled packet of Marlboro. Then lighting up his first cigarette in weeks, Alexander soberly considered Sonya's motives for not telling him.

'The way I see it, there are a couple of possible scenarios. Firstly, there is the chance that she deliberately smuggled the ruby out of the states under false papers, for sale somewhere here in the pacific. I find this hard to believe and I'll tell you why. If this was the case, then she could have used the valuation papers accompanying the stones, in her briefcase. She wouldn't have needed to get another valuation done. That leads us to the second possibility, she must have discovered the true value of the sample sometime after she'd left for the pacific. Like me, she probably had a good look at the samples and found, just as I did, that one of them was flawed. In her job she would have been used to seeing small air bubbles or inclusions in cut glass stones and would have become suspicious by such a complex flaw. I would also be surprised if her company's quality control would have passed such a stone for sampling. No one in his or her right mind would have sent out a sample with such an obvious defect in it. It's one of the first rules of marketing; quality samples ensure quality results. After this discovery she would have had to be certain.' Alexander picked up the certificate. 'That would explain this and her independent valuation.'

'If this is true, then the stone was either placed in the box by mistake or it was a deliberate action. How does that help us find her killer.'

'I'm not sure, but it does explain why she couldn't tell me. She must have gone through the same thought processes as we have.' Alexander stood and walked to the balcony, deep in thought. 'Put yourself in her position. If you'd just discovered that you were carrying something that valuable, what would you do?'

'My first instinct would be to catch the next plane back home.' Said Tomoko.

'Probably mine too. Sonya obviously didn't. The question is, why not? My guess is that she thought she could sell it. She had the contacts, no doubt.'

'Then Sonya must have been killed by someone who knew the true value of the gem and also knew that she had it with her.' Said Tomoko, as a statement of fact.

'Make's sense!' Nodded Alexander. 'That narrows it down to someone who knew the stones had been switched in the states, or to one of Sonya's contacts in the pacific. Which ever way you look at it, it's a hell of a lot cheaper than shelling out the odd million when you've only got one individual to contend with.'

'How much have we got to go on. Have you any idea who Sonya's contacts were?' Asked Tomoko.

'According to her diary she came here via Bangkok and Hong Kong. Some names are there but no addresses. After Hong Kong she flew to Osaka and came straight to Kyoto to see you. I have an appointment with the man she met, tomorrow.'

'His name wouldn't be Koyanagi would it?'

'Yes it would.' Said Alexander intrigued. 'How did you know? What did she say?'

'Sonya was here for two days. The first day she spent with me. A little sightseeing, shopping and a lot of gossip, you know what its like when us women get together. She certainly seemed in good spirits, that was until she'd had her meeting with Koyanagi-San. She spent most of the second day with him. When she returned to my apartment she was in a foul mood. She used words like "arrogant swine" and "ungrateful bastard", to tell you the truth I'd never seen her so upset. It took her quite some time to regain her composure.'

'Did she say why she was so irritated?' Asked Alexander hopefully.

'Not in so many words. Although I do remember her saying that she'd made him an offer of a lifetime and he had turned her down.'

A brief knock at the entrance screen interrupted their conversation. As the screen slid to the side, Coco's smiling face appeared. From her kneeling position she bowed. 'I've brought you the first course of your dinner, may I come in?'

Over dinner they talked extensively about Sonya's visit and how they would approach Koyanagi the following morning. The game plan had been set. It all hinged on Alexander's ability to convince him that he was Gem International's new Pacific area manager. Although he didn't show it, Alexander had his doubts.

Satisfied by the delicate mixture of Sushi, Sashimi - raw fish, and Sake, Alexander and Tomoko sat relaxing in the two, low cushioned wicker chairs on the balcony, overlooking the floodlight enclosed garden.

'Forgive my curiosity, but I couldn't fail to notice, your mother's not Japanese.'

'This is what makes me pretty, No?' She smiled coquettishly. 'My father visited France thirty or so years ago, about the time when his father handed this Ryokan down to him. He could see the advantages of catering to the increasing number of western visitors, "Gaijin", which were visiting Kyoto. So he spent a little time, as you would say "checking out the competition". His stories of that time entertained me for many an evening during my childhood. He met my mother in a market selling bread. Both my mother and the variety of bread intrigued him. They probably had a few "rolls" together.'

Alexander's laughter could easily be heard on the other side of the courtyard. 'You're command of English is quite astonishing.'

'Thank you, so is yours.' She chuckled. 'Your bath will be ready soon, let me show you how we Japanese take a bath.'

Intrigued, Alexander followed her down the stairs to a small pine faced room. The floor space was evenly shared between the large cedar wood lined bath and a pre-washing area. Attached to the wall, a few feet above the ground were the shower heads and on the floor beneath them, two, six inch high wooden seats.

'When you undress you can place your clothes in the changing room just outside the door. Then, before you enter the bath, you must wash. You sit on these.' She said, pointing to the wooden stools. 'It's a bit like squatting in comfort.'

'Looks more like a form of Japanese water torture to me.' Said Alexander appalled at the prospect of having to do contortions before getting into a bath.

'When you've soaped yourself down and showered off you can get into the bath. The idea is to keep the bath water as clean as possible. It is meant purely for relaxation.'

'At what stage, do you get to scrub my back then?' He asked hopefully.

'In your dreams tonight, Webb-San.' She said musically, as she opened the door again. 'I must spend some time with my mother and father, you don't mind do you?'

'Oh no. Of course not. I would like to say one thing though; I am really pleased that we are working together. You make me feel lucky.'

'Likewise, I think we make a good partnership. Would you like me to go with you tomorrow when you meet with Koyanagi-San?'

'I'm counting on it!'

As Tomoko left, Alexander started to undress. 'I really must be loosing my touch.' He said aloud, walked naked into the bathroom, stared at the wall mounted shower unit, shuddered and lowered himself into the warm welcoming water. Sitting on a six inch stool was far too much to ask of his poor aching body.

The morning had arrived all too soon. Sleeping in a Ryokan was obviously a misnomer. With the paper-thin walls, it seemed that Kyoto had been holding a snoring and noisy, "let's try to be quiet", love making contest. Subsequently, Alexander felt like death warmed up as he stood at the downstairs washbasin, outside the occupied bathrooms.

'How was your first night in a Ryokan Alex?' Asked Tomoko, as she emerged from the door on his right, smelling of rose scented deodorant. 'Did you sleep well?'

'I can honestly say I've never had a more interesting night's sleep. It could have been warmer though with a little company.'

'Remind me to lend you my teddy bear, tonight.' She said, with a smile that made Alexander think the bear would be a very poor second choice.

'We should leave in about half an hour.' He said, picking up his travel wash case and following her back up the stairs, 'Does that give you enough time?'

'No problem, I'll come to your room when I'm ready.'

An hour later... they stepped out into the sunlight. The day like every other day so far had started cool with the inescapable prospect that it would turn into a scorcher by noon. Alexander settled himself into the passenger seat as Tomoko started the engine.

'Kinkaku ji is a beautiful place, I think you will like it.' She said as she pulled out of the parking place at speed. 'Who's idea was it to meet there?'

'Koyanagi's, apparently it's across the road from his offices. He told Akiko, my secretary, that he thought it would be good for my appreciation of Japanese culture.'

'In this case, he's probably right.' She said, forcing the engine into high pitch with the kick down and deftly negotiated her way around the slower morning traffic.

Alexander shrank back into the bucket seat. 'Do you always drive like this?'

Tomoko darted him a wide grin. 'No,' she said nonchalantly, 'sometimes I speed a little.' A piece of straight clear road loomed up in front of them and the needle flickered against the hundred mark. 'I think we might be a little early.'

CHAPTER 17

At the entrance to the temple grounds Tomoko handed him a pamphlet describing the buildings and their history. Emblazoned on the cover was the picture of a three-tiered golden temple, surrounded by still water. Alexander read with interest, picking out the salient details as they walked westwards along the gravel pathway leading to the lake.

Kinkaku-ji (Temple of the Golden Pavilion), situated at the foot of Mount Kinugasa was originally a country house belonging to Kintsune Saionji in the 1220's. *The great Shogun Ashikaga Yoshimitsu (1358-1408) relinquished power to his son Yoshimochi and chose this spot to retire to. He had the Golden Pavilion built in 1394 and the garden around it designed. All this was turned into a Rokuon Buddhist temple after his death. Most of the buildings disappeared at that time, and the pavilion was burnt down in 1950, when a young monk of the temple committed suicide. The temple that stands was reconstructed, identical to its predecessor in 1955. The Golden Pavilion, covered with gold-leaf, stands by a lovely pool. It is surmounted by two storeys, with a bronze phoenix on the very top. In the gardens is the 17th century 'Sekka tei' tea pavilion built by the Emperor Gomizuno o.*

A small group of school children blocked the pathway in front of him, causing him to look up from the text. The view that greeted him was spectacular. The inanimate words of the pamphlet seemed insignificant when compared with the actual scene. A perfectly symmetrical impression of the gleaming pagoda stood motionless in the crystal clear water. Dense green vegetation climbed the hills behind it, serving as the only possible compliment to the sparkling gold of the upper two tiers. Alexander knew a photograph could never do it justice, but reached into his bag for the Canon EOS all the same.

'I thought you'd like it,' said Tomoko, putting her arm around his waist, 'it's my favourite place. Most of the time the grounds are crowded with visitors. So it's only now, at this time of day that you can really appreciate it's beauty. I often come here if I need somewhere to think before I start a particularly hard day.'

The children were now moving away, giving Alexander a clear uninterrupted view over the lake. The motor drive of the camera whizzed quietly as several frames passed the shutter.

'I envy you Tomoko.' He said. Then with a faint secret smile, 'I also have a special place back home, a place where people gather to discus their pasts and futures. A place where the pressures of life are not permitted to enter. A place with an ambience and atmosphere, not too dissimilar from here.' Alexander spoke dreamily, as if describing a hallowed and sacred temple, inaccessible to mortal men, the quest of pilgrims. 'It's called the Kings Tavern and serves the best ale in Sussex.'

Tomoko sniggered.

The picture dissolved with a light tap on his shoulder. Alexander, annoyed at the interruption, turned. Before him stood an immaculately dressed Japanese gentleman, smiling. 'Please forgive the interruption sir, my name is Koyanagi. Would you by chance be Mister Webb of Gem International?'

Alexander returned the smile. 'I am indeed, it is so good of you to meet me, Mister Koyanagi, especially in such charming surroundings.'

Koyanagi, with hands clasped firmly to his sides bowed sharply in greeting. Alexander returned the compliment, only slower and lower, as Akiko had taught him. A brief ritual of exchanging business cards followed and when properly introduced they bowed again.

'Your name is new to me, Webb-San.' Said Koyanagi, as they started the gentle stroll around the periphery of the lake. 'I'd have thought by now that I would have met all of the representatives of your company.'

'It's a recent appointment, from our Antwerp office. I've spent most of my time in Europe on the diamond circuit, Mister Koyanagi, buying and selling for the jewellery trade. My company thought this would make a pleasant change for me, it is also supposed to be a promotion.'

'Then I must congratulate you, Webb-San. Tell me, what is your new assignment to be?'

'In brief, I have been entrusted with the responsibility of developing Gem International's penetration into the Pacific. What this means in reality is that I am in a position, to offer to you, the top one percent of the diamond and coloured gem stones currently on the international market. I am also empowered to act as an agent for you, and other pacific clients, should you require something special, or out of the ordinary. On a commission basis, of course. For myself, in the short term, I propose to learn as much as possible about your language and culture. I see this as essential preparation if I am ever going to be accepted into your world of business. As you can see, at the moment, I'm a little inexperienced in the finer details of Japanese protocol.'

'You will learn, Webb-San, You will learn.' Koyanagi stood thoughtful for a moment at the water's edge, watching a school of carp respond to the clapping hands of a group of children. 'In Russia, Pavlov trained his dogs to the sound of a bell. Here we train our fish and women to the sound of the clapped hand. The dogs get fed, the fish get fed, we get fed. Your first lesson Webb-San.' He said, looking directly at Tomoko. His reception was stone cold.

Returning to the path, he continued, 'Your call was not entirely unexpected. A colleague of yours visited me two weeks ago, Martin-San. I trust that you will prove to be more able, unfortunately our profession suffers greatly from enthusiastic amateurs.'

'I am eager to help you in any way that I can.' Said Alexander subserviently. 'Perhaps you will share with me your reasons for considering Miss Martin an amateur.'

'I will, in due course. But first, if you will permit me the indulgence, I would like to give you a little background, in order for your company's services to be fully in tune with my requirements. Over a century ago, my grandfather located a small deposit of Jade, on our southern-most island of Kyushu. The find, on land owned by my family for generations, was of considerable quality. In addition to this the Meiji Emperor declared war on China at roughly the same time, eighteen ninety four to be exact. Making the find potentially priceless. My grandfather was a very astute businessman and skilled in the art of trade. As a result the family prospered, supplying Jade to the royal family and wealthy landowners in and around Kyoto. Ever since I was a child I have been obsessed with collecting as many of these early pieces as possible. Only recently have I been expanding my collection to include other worthwhile gemstones, in particular, rubies. It is rumoured that he who wears rubies assures sexual appeal and guards against danger and ill health. All I can say in defence of this rumour, is that I have always experienced excellent health.'

The brief, faint smile looked uncomfortable on his lips, as if his attempts at the western practice of mixing business with a little light relief pained him. 'As you are undoubtedly aware, the demand, on a global scale, for coloured stones surged in the nineteen eighty's. Ruby prices soared faster than others did. Although they are among the most prized of all gems, their high price does not fully reflect their rarity. Large gem-quality rubies are thirty to fifty times more rare than diamonds and typically a ten carat top-quality ruby can sell for more than two hundred thousand dollars, a carat. A flawless white diamond might bring a fourth of that amount. Martin-San showed me, what she described as a feature-flawed ruby during her visit. It was undeniably one of the largest cut stones I have ever seen.'

Alexander reached into his inside jacket pocket for the photographs. 'Miss Martin was asked to market a selection of fine gems as part of her assignment. The ruby she offered, is it amongst these?'

Koyanagi quickly thumbed through the pictures, pausing at the close-up of the Chandra Ruby. 'Yes, this is the one! The fact that you have a photograph of this exact stone has answered a question that has troubled me, ever since her visit. As you know, in our business, reproduction and artificially grown gemstones are common. I am no expert, so when Martin-San offered me this stone for three million dollars my suspicions were aroused. As I have already mentioned an un-flawed ruby of this size would be worth somewhere in the region of thirty million dollars, this one, with the flaw, should be worth around twenty five. So I assumed the stone must have been either red Spinel, a similar gem of lower value, or a fake. I asked her if she would object to me having the gem analysed. She refused. Some nonsense about having limited time. It would seem that on this occasion, my natural caution has lost me the chance of owning one of the world's most valuable gems.'

Koyanagi handed the pictures back to Alexander and sighed, shaking his head in a gesture of disbelief. 'You British face failure with aplomb and phrases like "better luck next time" and "It's not winning that counts, it's how you play the game." Bullshit! You will soon learn, that in Japan, winning is everything. You must also realise, that this failure on my part, will be seen as your company's inability to make the sale.' He said testily. Then forcing his hands deep into his pockets he set off in front of them.

Alexander took Tomoko's arm in his as they followed Koyanagi up to the Tea Pavilion. Bending to her ear he whispered, 'He is not a happy man, Tomoko.'

She smiled.

Koyanagi had paused in front of the pavilion's wooden steps to light a large Havana cigar. He turned to face them. 'Tell me Webb-San, I am curious, is it normal for your representatives to be carrying original and highly valuable gems on their person?'

'Normal? No. Although sometimes, Mister Koyanagi, it is unavoidable. In this case I believe Miss Martin was left with no other choice.'

'I see. I don't suppose you have a Cullinan diamond or Long Star Ruby hidden in one of your pockets then?' He said, as if trying to make a point.

'If I was carrying something that valuable, we would not be having this discussion in a temple garden.' Said Alexander, acknowledging Koyanagi's logic, 'I would have insisted that we meet in the security vaults of Tokyo's Sumitomo bank.'

'My point exactly! A skilful salesman would not have chosen a second rate restaurant in the centre of Kyoto. Martin's blatant inability has cost me dearly. I will not accept incompetence in any facet of my organisation, you should not tolerate it in yours.' Koyanagi, now frustrated and angered, approached within inches of Alexander's face. 'A word of advice Webb-San, get your female staff out of Japan. They are far better suited to sales in cultures where the bedroom is preferred to the boardroom.'

'Arrogant bastard.' Thought Alexander, keeping his self-control. 'Your observation is well noted. Mister Koyanagi.'

'Good, Back to business. At the end of the month, I am invited to a function where a ruby such as this one would be very useful, at the moment I intend to decline; this stone of yours could change my decision. Is it still for sale?'

'Alas no,' said Alexander, apologetically, 'Miss Martin was instrumental in passing the gem into other hands last week, during her visit to Tokyo. However, If you would like me to locate another, similar example for you, I can put the wheels into motion immediately, today.'

'Not an easy task, Webb-San.' He said, pulling on the cigar. 'To my knowledge there are only four other comparable cut stones of this size in the world. The

Edward Ruby of course is the largest at one hundred and sixty seven carats, currently residing in the British Museum of Natural History in London. The next on the list would be The Rama's Hope at the Thai Royal treasury in Bangkok. Part of some statue I believe and interestingly of a similar cut to the one shown to me by Miss Martin. The Reeves Star Ruby in the Smithsonian Institution in Washington would be the third, a little smaller at one hundred and thirty nine carats, yet has quite beautiful and well defined asterism. The fourth I know little about, except for the fact that it is in private hands in Hong-Kong, owned by a Triad syndicate. So you see your search is unlikely to be successful, but you're welcome to try all the same. I would be prepared to pay up to twenty five million dollars for the right stone. And unlike my competitors, I am not concerned with where or from whom you obtain the gem, only the quality. I think we understand each other, Yes?'

'Basically you are unconcerned with the method of acquisition, as long as the price is right. Right?'

'Bluntly put, but you've got the point. Now if you will forgive me I have another meeting in fifteen minutes, I must return to my office. If you should ever uncover an item, which you believe fulfils my requirements, I will be more than pleased to have my secretary arrange for another appointment. I look forward to doing business with you Webb-San. I have enjoyed our brief conversation, I hope your Japanese studies go well, as you say, you're in need of them. Thank you for your time and interest.' Koyanagi bowed his farewell and left, retracing his steps back to the entrance gate.

'Well what do you make of that?' Asked Tomoko, feeling the morning's stroll had been little more than an exercise in accepting insults.

'Most enlightening. When I was a kid my dad often told me that easy money bred arrogance. Up until now I never believed him. You will learn, Webb-San, You will learn.' Said Alexander, mimicking Koyanagi and wagging his finger at Tomoko. 'I must confess to being a bit puzzled though. It's obvious that Koyanagi knows the stones on the market well, so, how come a stone as important as this one could come as a surprise to him? Put yourself in his position, if you hadn't heard of it, you probably wouldn't buy it either. You can understand his reaction when Sonya made him the offer.'

'Yes and did you see his face when it dawned on him that the stone that Sonya had shown him was the real thing?' Tomoko asked excitedly, 'Pure magic. And another thing, he answered one of our questions from last night! We now know that Sonya was trying to sell the Chandra Ruby for herself. Just Imagine, trying to make ends meet with three million in the bank?'

Tomoko linked her arm in his again as they walked back to the car. 'You were very convincing Alex, you should take up marketing, and you lie beautifully.'

'Thank you my dear, It's a god given gift.' Alexander bowed his head to salute the compliment. 'Next time it may not be this easy. If I'm to keep it up, I'm going to need some decent background, solid hard facts. I don't suppose there's an English library around here, is there?'

'An English library no. An English book shop yes! I'll drive you there.'

The flow of visitors was steadily increasing as Alexander and Tomoko passed through the entrance gate for the second time. A young man who'd been close all morning, now walked briskly in front of them heading for a green pay phone on the far side of the street.

At the car, Alexander stood hesitant by the door, watching him lift the handset, insert a card and punch the silver keys. It was not a local call.

The lingering remnants of euphoria, fuelled by the morning's success, quickly ebbed away, replaced by an overwhelming feeling of uneasiness. The prospect that they may have been followed was becoming all too clear. There was also something familiar about his face, He'd seen it before.

Alexander eased into the passenger seat next to Tomoko and closed his eyes to concentrate. At the Ryokan? No. Ryoan-ji? No. Tokyo? Maybe. On the train! Yes, that was it! He could picture the scene, behind the glass of the waiting room, on the Shinkansen platform in Tokyo.

Nothing would be gained by alarming Tomoko unnecessarily at the moment; after all, he could be wrong. There was a very real possibility it was just another tourist, travelling in their footsteps, and he was over reacting to the pressure of the last few days. He also knew from experience that his gut feelings were seldom wrong. He had to be sure. 'I think I can see a business acquaintance of mine over at the telephone booth,' he said with an air of indifference, 'would you mind driving over, I'd like to take a closer look.'

Tomoko started the engine and weaved her way through the maze of parked cars and coaches, pulling up at the side of the road.

The call was answered on the third ring and was immediately transferred to his waiting superior.

'Good morning sir, I have some interesting news for you. Your suspicions have just been confirmed. The Englishman, Webb, met with Koyanagi at nine this morning. He showed him a collection of photographs. From where I was standing they looked to be pictures of jewels, although I couldn't get close enough to be certain.'

'How did Koyanagi react?'

'After seeing the photographs, I'd say he was more than a little disturbed, angry would be a better description.'

'Fascinating! Keep up the surveillance. I want to know his every movement. If he leaves Kyoto, call me immediately.'

The sound of the Nissan GTR's throbbing exhaust caught his attention. He turned his head. The briefest of glances was enough to send a cold chill down his spine. 'If you will excuse me sir, I think we have a problem...'

Alexander studied him for a good fifteen seconds, he'd been right. 'I'm sorry Tomoko, it's not who I thought it was.' He said, satisfied, committing the face to memory. 'Let's go and buy some books.'

CHAPTER 18

Darkness had fallen through their hours of study. Alexander felt mentally drained and ached all over. How Tomoko and her fellow generation endured the discomfort of cramming for exams, on the floor, with crossed legs, eluded him. Between them, they had scoured the books for every morsel of relevant information, jotting each fact as an individual note and placing it onto the pre-determined piles.

Before them on the polished ebony table, lay five distinct researched areas. Mining, cutting, grading, marketing and counterfeiting.

A clear distinct picture was beginning to emerge. Pretty much the whole world trade in rubies focused in one place. Bangkok.

"That certificate of Sonya's came from Bangkok didn't it? Is there an address?" Asked Tomoko.

'I wish there was. All we have is the continuation sheet of the quotation. I guess the address must have been on the front page. All we have is the signature followed by two letters, R.L. It was obviously signed in roman characters for Sonya's benefit. It looks like we'll have to spend some time tracking down a chap called Khun Kraiwoot, tomorrow. We know he's in Bangkok from the diary, he must also have a pretty good reputation for Sonya to have used him. Where do you think we could start?'

'I would say the most logical places would be the Embassy of Thailand in Tokyo and your friend in the police. You can leave the Embassy up to me, I'll make a few calls. Are you thinking of going to see him?'

'Yes. We are!'

Tomoko shuffled over to his side and kissed his cheek. 'I do love travelling.' She said. 'And, I can get us cheep rates.'

'How so?' Asked Alexander.

'I'm surprised you haven't asked before. I run a travel agency in Kyoto centre. How would you like to pay sir? American Express?'

'British Airways Air Miles?'

Tomoko's smile glowed like an advertisement. 'That'll do nicely.' She said, reaching for the phone to make the booking.

The shoji screen entrance slid to the side revealing Coco's smiling face. The smiles were a matched pair. 'Your bath's are ready now, Webb-San, Tomoko. Shall I lead the way?'

The Ryokan buzzed with muffled movements as Alexander lay on the futon, listening to the sounds of the night. At last they were getting somewhere. He'd spoken to Chief Hara whilst soaking in the bath. With the hotel full to capacity it was the perfect place for an undisturbed conversation.

Hara had been as good as his word, the address for Khun Kraiwoot would be telephoned to him early in the morning, he'd even offered to arrange for their accommodation in Bangkok. "We'll find some way of hiding it in the department budget." He'd joked. More importantly he'd made progress on his own research. Hara now believed there was a clear connection between one of his force and Sonya's murder, although he wasn't prepared to divulge any names just yet without first obtaining what he'd called "concrete corroboration".

Outside in the hallway, a pair of shuffling feet caught his attention. The sound approached and ceased, outside his room. Involuntarily the face in the phone booth flashed instantly and consciously to his mind. Stock still, he could hear breathing, inhale, exhale, from behind the starched paper screen. Alexander's heart raced. Paranoid or not, he searched frantically for some form of weapon. Slowly, noiselessly, the screen slid to the side. Tense with apprehension, he drew his arm back, poised, ready to launch his camera at the intruder.

Cautiously a furry ear appeared at the opening, then a sparkling amber eye and a pert black buttoned nose. 'Shit! Tomoko, you scared the living daylights out of me.'

Her face appeared above that of her bear. 'Spooked you, eh?' She tiptoed over the tatami and slipped from her night-gown.

Tomoko's soft naked body moved towards him beneath the quilt. 'I promised you this morning that I would bring you my bear tonight....'

'And let me guess, you never sleep without it.' He placed his arms around her, he could feel her warmth and rising passion in every desirable curve. 'You're far more cuddly than your teddy bear.' He said, kissing her gently, tracing her full perfectly formed silken breasts with his fingertips.

'I have a confession to make Alex,' whispered Tomoko shyly, looking deep into his eyes with a hint of sorrow. 'You will not be the first man to make love to me.'

Alexander was unsure with what he should say. 'If you feel the same way in the morning, let me know.'

CHAPTER 19

Alexander Webb had been awake for hours, studying, absorbing and revising the text.

A fresh and fascinating world, totally alien to his own, had grown steadily, maturing page by page, before his eyes. Through the complex processes of formation to the intricacies of production and manufacturing, each facet in the realm of precious gems had irresistibly ingrained itself in to his memory.

Now he understood Sonya's passion. The subject was a pleasure to learn, both intriguing and captivating. With the uncertainty of ignorance behind him and aided by the Gem International manager's business cards and a gift of the gab, he felt confident he could acquit himself effectively, with assurance, should an occasion like his meeting with Koyanagi ever arise again.

At precisely eight o'clock in the morning, the cell telephone sprang into life. It was Hara with the address. Alexander reached for a pen to make the note. 'You work fast, Hara-San! I appreciate the help.' He said.

Hara's tone was cautious. 'It is given freely but advisedly. I have no jurisdiction in Thailand and few contacts, you'll be very much on your own. My advice Webb-San, would bc to talk to the man Kraiwoot then return to Japan as quickly as possible. In my experience, it is unlikely for you to be the only one to have made the connection, so keep your eyes open, anything out of the ordinary, go straight to the police.'

'I'll do that.' Said Alexander, assuming Hara was stating the obvious. 'One more thing, I think I've picked up a tail.'

'Baka na!' Hissed Hara with frustration, 'What makes you think that?'

'A young man, mid twenties, wearing a black tunic and trousers. I spotted him yesterday outside Kinkaku-ji.' Recalled Alexander calmly.

'The dress of a student? Clever.' Said Hara thoughtfully, 'Would you recognise him if you saw him again?'

'Certainly.'

'Good. If you do, return to Tokyo immediately. You can call me from the train. If he follows, we'll pick him up. Any more surprises?'

'No.'

'To Your travel arrangements. Are you flying from Narita or Osaka?' Hara asked.

'Narita, tonight at seven.'

'Fine, I'll meet you there. The executive waiting room at five thirty. And do us both a favour, stay out of trouble.' He hung up.

Tomoko stirred beneath the blankets at his side as Alexander placed his cell phone back into the travel bag. Gliding her hand across his chest, she slipped a leg over his hip and pulled him towards her. Her hot breath wisped teasingly against his cheek. 'Wake me up properly Alex.' She appealed, longingly, guiding his lips to meet her's. 'I'm sure we have time.'

'All the time in the world,' said Alexander, drawing her on top of him, 'quietly though, the walls are thin, your parents might hear us. I embarrass very easily in front of parents.'

Tomoko smiled knowingly. 'It's not them you have to please.'

The decoration of the Sun Wey Travel Agency was typical of travel agents the world over. They were all there, The houses of parliament, Sydney harbour bridge, there was even a poster of Kyoto showing a selection of temples above the legend, Cultural Japan. Alexander had studied each of them in turn and had drunk two cups of strong black coffee during his half hour wait.

'Well? How do you like my home from home?' Asked Tomoko, appearing in her office doorway, waving a pair of E tickets triumphantly in her hand.

'Not bad.' Said Alexander, positively. 'You managed to get the time off?'

'I did better than that.' She said. 'I called head office and told them that I thought it was about time one of the staff had some real, on the job, management training. They liked the idea. You know, they even commended me for my initiative. I've arranged for Suzuki-San to take over for a couple of weeks while you and I sample the bedrooms of Thailand. Pretty good for a morning's work, I think. We're having good luck aren't we?'

'Let's hope it holds up.' Said Alexander mischievously.

'You worry too much Alex, what could possibly go wrong? It'll be just like a holiday. We're booked on the two o'clock Hikari to Shinjuku connecting with the Narita express. That will get us there exactly two hours before the flight. On the train, I've reserved places for us in the Green Car, I thought a little bit of luxury was in order.'

'Why not! We may as well start as we mean to go on.' Alexander took her hand and led her out into the sunshine.

Back at the Ryokan, Coco ordered a taxi for them while Alexander collected his bag and Tomoko's suitcase. She bade them both farewell on the pavement outside. Taking Tomoko to one side, she whispered, 'Shouldn't you be getting married, before you go on your honeymoon?'

Tokyo's Narita airport was as chaotic as ever, check-in an interminable wait and the two thousand yen airport tax, complained Alexander, grossly overpriced. The only redeeming feature was a fully functioning air-conditioning system, a blessed relief from the baking afternoon sun.

With frequent apologies, Tomoko pushed her way through the crowds, down a flight of stairs and into the maze of corridors leading to the executive lounge.

'So, you made it in one piece.' Greeted Chief Hara at the entrance, shaking Alexander by the hand. 'Glad we had the chance to meet. I see you've brought a travelling companion. The spectre from Kinkaku-ji perhaps?' He asked, clearly charmed.

'In a manner of speaking, yes.' Grinned Alexander and introduced them.

Hara took her hand in his right and patted it gently with his left. 'I am delighted to meet you Tomoko-San. I shall arrange for a drink for you both, then perhaps we could talk.'

He led them to a table in the corner where Captain Aono stood to greet them. As they sat, a waitress in a dark blue pencil suit hovered, waiting for their orders.

The forty foot square room had a welcome air of relaxation. Illuminated by recessed ceiling spots and four standard lamps, the soft fawn colour scheme created the atmosphere well. Only the large functional square white clock looked out of place, dominant in the centre of the wall to the side of the bar.

Hara leaned forward, speaking in a soft voice so as not to be overheard, 'What I have to say must for the moment remain between the four of us. You will understand why as I explain. One of my officers sent Martin-San's personnel effects to Gem International in America on Monday. They received them at lunchtime today. I asked her supervisor if he would examine the ruby and describe it to me over the phone. He did.'

'And?' Prompted Alexander.

'There can no longer be any doubt. I am in total agreement with you Webb-San, your friend Sonya Martin was murdered. The stone he described was not the one both you and I examined in the Tri-Star offices. I have asked them to photograph the substitute and send it's picture along with that of the original from their files to me immediately. These two pictures will be enough to approach my seniors with a case for murder. I expect to receive them within forty-eight hours. Up until then our resources are limited.'

Hara paused to sip his glass of mineral water as a group of Korean businessmen passed in search of a place to rest. One of them, the youngest of the group approached, and after making his apologies for disturbing us, took the two remaining chairs from around our table. Hara waited until he'd rejoined the group before continuing, his voice a barely discernible whisper. 'Your suspicions that someone within the force tampered with the stones, I am sad to say, is now unequivocally confirmed. I have my suspicions and one or two leads regarding a possible suspect, yet without substantial evidence I can say no more for fear of incriminating the wrong man. As soon as I learn something, you will be the first to know.' Hara fished a packet of cigarettes from his pocket and offered one to Alexander. 'To more immediate problems. Have you seen the man who was following you since we last spoke?'

Alexander shook his head. 'My guess is that they've put a new man on the job. Some-what more professional by all accounts. The first chap was probably scared off when he saw that I'd recognised him.'

'It doesn't make it any easier does it?' Stated Hara, slowly shaking his head. 'How have your investigations been going?'

'Like you, we now know the Chandra Ruby was genuine. Tomoko and I met with one of Sonya's contacts in Kyoto, a Mister Koyanagi. He confirmed that he'd been offered the stone for a fraction of its true value. Sonya clearly realised the risks she was taking and must have wanted to sell it quickly. We also know that she'd had a valuation made in Bangkok, hence the address and the purpose of this trip. As far we can tell, outside Koyanagi and perhaps one of your officers, this expert was the only other person to know the true value and whereabouts of the gem. He seems like our most logical next step.'

'I agree. I wish I could join you.' Said Hara, his expression speaking volumes. Restricted by his departments procedures he felt powerless, professionally impotent and worst of all, envious of the carefree attitude in which the American dramas deceitfully portrayed the life of a police officer, committing himself and his department's resources on little more than a hunch. Such actions in Japan were inconceivable. 'Who knows, in two days, I might just do that.'

The hidden speakers of the address system crackled into life. 'Ladies and Gentlemen, Cathay Pacific flight, twenty seven, bound for Bangkok, is now ready for boarding. Please proceed to gate nine.'

'I'll walk with you to passport control,' offered Chief Hara, 'they will process your papers quickly with me at your side.'

Tomoko chuckled at the thought of their escort. 'With one look at Captain Aono's uniform, the other passengers will probably think we're being deported.' She said.

'No need to worry on that point, we will both bow regally to salute your departure.' Hara smiled.

CHAPTER 20

Two hours into the seven-hour flight, Tomoko watched as her country's emblem sank gracefully over the horizon and into the Pacific Ocean. She was angry, or was it disappointment, she couldn't decide which.

Alexander should have told her they were being followed. Did he think she would fall to pieces at the first sign of trouble? He didn't know her very well, did he? There would be time enough to prove herself, she was sure of that. What they were doing was right and just, they would surely be protected.

Ever since her childhood she had believed the teachings of Siddhartha Gautama, Buddha, her benevolent God, and his four noble truths. She closed her eyes to be closer to them. The First; a realisation that pain or ill existed. The second; that pain had a cause, third, to eliminate the pain, you must first eliminate the cause, and finally, the eight fold way of eliminating the cause: right understanding, right thought, right speech, right bodily conduct, right livelihood, right effort, right attentiveness and right concentration. Sonya had suffered pain at the hands of her attacker, and now, with the right effort and concentration, She and Alexander would see that he was removed from causing further suffering. Tomoko placed her hands together and repeated her pledge to Buddha.

'Are you praying?' Asked Alexander, assuming she'd been frightened by the meeting with Hara.

'For guidance.' She smiled, 'We will succeed Alex, I'm certain.'

'With your strength, how can we fail?' He could see his own confidence reflected in her eyes. 'Have you been to Bangkok before?' He asked.

'Two years ago, with the company on a fact finding tour.'

'What's it like?'

'It's a city struggling to embrace the future and its past in the palm of one hand. On one side you have an exquisite golden capital with jewel-encrusted temples, shrines and spires, delicate customs and a wonderful carefree nature. And on the other; a people barely surviving, in an economy as fragile as a piece of fine china. For those that live on the Chao Phraya River life must be particularly hard. There is undoubtedly great poverty. One time we were travelling up river on one of the ferries. I remember clearly, watching a family bathing together in the dirty water, as, at the same time, our guide told to us to keep our hands inside the boat, for fear of being bitten by one of the numerous poisonous river snakes. I was told that corruption was rife and drugs common, to be honest, as a tourist I never saw either. The one thing that faces you, almost the moment you arrive in the country and haunts you until you leave, is the fact that nothing will be done for you, without your first parting with a few Baht.'

Tomoko graphically demonstrated her words by running a thumb over her fingertips, 'Money, you can get anything if you have it, nothing if you haven't!'

'You paint a rather black picture, Tomoko.' As a tour operator, Alexander had expected her to emphasise the beauty of the country, with quaint anecdotes of Thai dancing and candlelight evening suppers. This reaction puzzled him. 'Has it always been this way?' He asked.

'Oh no. The influence of the west, and in particular, your ancestors are to blame. A couple of hundred years ago Bangkok was a thriving river city. Its streets were nothing more than a web of canals called klongs, highly decorated with flowers and trees. Progress changed all that. Although some still remain, most of the canals were filled to build roads and boulevards and the banks reinforced with concrete for the growing trade and commerce. The major modernisation started about a hundred and fifty years ago, around the time when the film, The King and I was set, did you ever see it?'

Alexander nodded, 'Getting to know you, getting to know all about you...' He sang cheerily, causing some of the passengers to turn their heads, some smiling, some were clearly not amused.

'Shhh. Not so loud.' She admonished with a whisper.

'What's the matter, don't you like my singing?' He said playfully.

'I do, he doesn't.' She said, pointing at an overweight passenger, reaching for his headphones.

'He's probably German, my guess is that he'd enjoy it more with a beer in his hand, should I order him one?' He jested.

'Should I continue?'

'Please.' Alexander patted her hand and smiled coyly.

'This some-what inaccurate film was actually based on a real event. The current King is Bhumibol Adulyadej, Rama the ninth. His great-great-grandfather, King Mongkut, Rama the fourth, had an English schoolteacher, Anna Leonowens brought to Siam in the 1860's to teach his children. In those days Tin, teak and rice were their major exports. Nowadays, rubber, sugar and of course from our research, rubies and sapphires have been added. This all adds up to an influx of "Farang", their name for Westerners, and the inevitable clash of cultures. That's basically what we can see today in the mirrored glass towers and the unashamedly blatant sex trade. Add to this unimaginable car pollution and you've got a pretty clear picture of modern Bangkok.'

'It all sounds pretty bleak to me. At this rate you'll have me hating the place before I've even seen it. What about the other side? The good side, there must be one?'

Tomoko didn't have to think for long. 'Of course there is. Outside commerce, tourism is their largest growing industry. There is an awful lot to see. Shrines, Temples, snake and crocodile farms, elephant theme parks, Thai dancing, music displays, the lists are almost endless. You could easily stay for a year and still be left wanting.' She reached into her handbag and retrieved a small guidebook. As she did so, a scarlet clad stewardess approached with two steaming trays. 'I'll show you after dinner, it's all in here!'

'Sounds interesting, we'll have to make time to see as much as possible. To start with, we will arrange our meeting with Khun Kraiwoot for the afternoon, tomorrow, that will at least give us the morning for ourselves and a bit of sightseeing.'

Alexander reset his Seiko Sports Chronograph back two hours to eleven thirty, in line with the time difference, as the 747 began it's decent. Through the half-shielded window he could see dancing lights in the distance. 'We're coming into land.' He said, rousing

Tomoko from her nap and reaching across her to draw back the curtain. 'Take a look.'

The land below was divided by a single silver tear, the temporary child of the Chao Phraya river and a full pacific moon. Small pockets of light were dotted over the smooth featureless plane, surrounded by recently flooded rice fields glowing like mirrors in the moonlight. It was indeed a peaceful scene.

Touchdown passed without event and the graceful leviathan of the air lumbered its way to the terminal. At the edge of the runway, to their amazement, was what looked to be the fourth tee of a meticulously maintained golf course. Alexander smiled. It would seem that seventy ton jumbo jets were only a minor inconvenience, to a dedicated Thai golfer settling down to that all-important difference between a birdie and par. He couldn't help pondering on the number of jet wind-screens needing replacement each year, falling foul of the demon slice, common to beginner golfers the world over and particularly prevalent in his game.

They disembarked on the stroke of midnight and passed through the customs of Suvarnabhumi airport with ease. At the arrival gate, a melee of taxi touts approached on mass, bidding for their custom.

Fatigued by the journey, Alexander was in no mood for bartering. 'You,' he pointed, 'how much to the Sheraton Royal Orchid Hotel.'

A short wiry Thai removed his cap and bowed. 'Three hundred Baht.' He said slowly, with a grin of crooked discoloured teeth. 'I good driver, safe driver.'

Alexander looked past him at the other drivers. One by one they each looked away, unwilling to compete with one of their own.

'Two hundred fifty Baht, best price.' He said. 'We go, yes?'

'Two fifty's fine. Let's go.' Said Alexander, handing over their luggage. 'Which is your car?'

'Plymouth, very good American car, this way, I show you. You American?'

'No, British.' Alexander opened the passenger door for Tomoko as he watched the driver put their bags in the boot. 'A similar culture, separated by a common language.'

The twenty-mile trip to town passed quickly. In spite of the dark, the driver appeared intent on giving them value for money, clearly believing it was his duty to point out places of interest on their way. They passed the impressive Chitladda Palace, the king's Bangkok residence. From the way that he spoke, the king was surely a benevolent and well-loved ruler. Further along the road, he launched into a blow by blow description of how, earlier in the day, he'd nearly won a thousand Baht, but in fact had lost five hundred by a short head, at the Royal Turf Club racetrack on their right. It was clear from the animated way that he spoke horse racing was his passion.

'Maybe he should have placed his bet on a horse with a longer neck.' Thought Alexander.

As they drove through the centre, competition for road space increased. Strange three wheeled two-seaters called tuk-tuks, a name aptly describing the sound emanating from their small engines, weaved in and out of the motorised pedicabs and other taxis.

'I take good route, yes? Direct route quicker, but this way better, you see more. You like?'

Alexander and Tomoko both agreed. The pavement markets were alive with people and an explosion of colour. The heady fragrance of new leather mixed with the sweet aroma of grilled foods, wafted through the taxi's open windows. Working girls in spray on jeans and tight fitting blouses sat in the open-air bars and stood in the night club doorways, smiling at all who passed. Several navy ships must have docked close by, as the familiar uniforms were everywhere, buying presents for folk back home and engaging in conversations with the ladies of the night.

'The author of the guide book must have spent a great deal of time here.' Whispered Alexander to Tomoko. His descriptions of Patpong, Bangkok's notorious nightclub district, were more than accurate, they were alive.

Ten minutes later they arrived at the hotel, and checked in. 'If you would be so kind as to follow me, I'll show you to your suite.' Said the one of the duty managers, leading them to the elevator. 'Your luggage and a complementary basket of fruit will be there when we arrive.'

The doors opened silently at the seventeenth floor and they followed him to the far end of the left corridor to seventeen o one. A porter waited with his head bowed as they approached. 'This is your suite, Mister Webb,' he said taking the key from the porter, 'I hope it meets with your approval.'

The light grey carpet and familiar classical western furniture, reminiscent of a large European hotel room, greeted them as they entered. The manager, wishing to fulfil his duty, walked passed them to show the features of the room. Alexander raised his hand, indicating that this was unnecessary. 'It's very pleasant. I'm sure we'll find everything. Thank you.' He said, Pressing a hundred Baht note into each of their eager open hands and motioning for them to leave. Without a word they bowed, turned and closed the door behind them.

Alexander walked to the window spanning the far end of the room as Tomoko stretched invitingly on the soft king size bed. 'This would be an ideal place to come to if we didn't have a care in the world.' He said, staring down at the inanimate snaking river two hundred feet below.

'Maybe we should stay on a while after meeting Kraiwoot. A bit of sightseeing, shopping, sunbathing, what do you say?'

'We'll see. It really depends on how much he can tell us, and if we get any new leads.'

Alexander's eyes were bloodshot, they should never have ordered that bottle of champagne before turning in. It was seven thirty and the hotel foyer was empty, save for a few staff. The plan for a late sleep in and a bit of sightseeing before meeting Kraiwoot had been shot to pieces. One mention that he worked for Gem International had been enough. Kraiwoot had insisted that they meet as soon as possible. He was undeniably anxious and had convinced Alexander that he should come straight over. So here they sat, waiting.

A short balding old man with thick glasses pushed through the glazed entrance doors wiping his forehead with a handkerchief. He scanned the foyer nervously, and then walked to the concierge. The concierge pointed across the marble floor towards the coffee lounge and Alexander.

'Tomoko, It looks like he's here.' They both stood to greet him.

'Sawat-dii Mr Webb, Miss Den, it is good of you to see me at so early an hour.' He said in a rasping voice, like nails on a blackboard, 'My name is Kraiwoot.' His hand quivered a little as Alexander shook it. *Was that fear?*

'We are very pleased you could spare us some of your valuable time Sir. Have you had breakfast?' Asked Alexander, hoping to put him at ease.

Kraiwoot shook his head. 'No, I would like that very much. It is not often I have the chance to eat in a hotel like this.'

Alexander handed over his business card as they walked to the Bho Tree Terrace.

'Sawat-dii,' the headwaiter said with a bow. 'Breakfast, please?'

Alexander nodded and raised three fingers. They followed the ornately dressed young man to a table by the flowered railing separating the hotel from the river.

The waiter smiled as they sat and waited for the order.

'Mr Kraiwoot, have you ever tried a full English breakfast?'
Asked Alexander reading the menu.

'Whatever you suggest Mr Webb.' He said, not really listening.

As Alexander ordered he could now see clearly Kraiwoot was on edge, searching the restaurant warily for a face he could recognise, his hands were clasped tightly in his lap.

'You sounded apprehensive on the telephone this morning Mr Kraiwoot, why?' Asked Alexander.

'You don't know?' He questioned, 'I'm not surprised. I only found out myself yesterday. A good friend of mine, one of your colleagues was murdered last week, and I think I know why.'

'Will you tell us?' Asked Tomoko.

'First, I must know why you are here.'

Alexander moved his chair closer to the table. 'Sonya was also a good friend of mine.' He said sincerely.

'Did she tell you about me?' Kraiwoot asked.

'No. We found your name in her diary.'

'Then you are in great danger Mister Webb. You must leave as soon as possible.' Said Kraiwoot, placing his fragile hand on Alexander's.

'We can't.' Alexander was determined. 'We need to know who killed her. Anything you can tell us, may help to track them down. Even the smallest detail could be important. So please tell us everything you know. Start at the beginning, how did you first meet Sonya?'

Kraiwoot breathed a sigh of relief at having the chance to share his story. 'I will tell you all I know.'

Alexander shook out his napkin and dropped it on his lap as the waiter brought their breakfasts. The table was silent as they were being served.

'I first met Sonya two years ago, when I still worked at the Royal Lapidary,' Kraiwoot began, 'I was the chief assessor in those days. It was my job to evaluate the rough stones and advise on which cut should be used, to bring out the best in each gem. I would also be called on to value the most important pieces. Everyone dreams that someday they will be given this job, it was offered to me on the day of my thirtieth year of service, fifteen years ago. Some say that I was the best in Bangkok, I'm too modest to comment. When I retired last year, Sonya travelled all the way from America to join me for my retirement party, at her own expense. This really meant a lot to me. After my retirement she still used to come for advice on how she should market or sell a particular stone. Sometimes she would bring small sapphires or rubies to me to check her company's valuations. They were always small stones of around one or two carats. I often told her, carrying anything larger than that would be foolish. Any way, a few weeks ago she came to see me on her way to Japan. She had a box of sample stones with her and asked my advice on how she should market them. One of them raised my curiosity, a big ruby She called the 'Chandra' Ruby. The rest were obviously cut glass, this one was not. I asked her if she would mind if I ran a few tests on it, she didn't object, so I did.'

Kraiwoot's hands were now steady. He raised his coffee cup, took a sip and scanned the terrace again.

'Where was I?'

'The tests.' Prompted Tomoko.

'Ah yes. The tests proved positive. So it turned out that Sonya had in her possession a ruby of considerable value. Around twenty six million dollars worth to be exact, or so I thought at the time.'

'You seem to be in some doubt Mr Kraiwoot?' Questioned Alexander.

'Yes, I'll come to that later. Anyway, someone had obviously made a very grave error in placing the wrong stone in the box. I told Sonya her best course of action would be to return home immediately or sell the stone for herself as fast as she could, let's face it, who would know? She told me that she knew of a man in Japan who would probably buy it, and made plans to go and see him. All went well until the following morning. Sonya caught her flight on time and I returned home. Around ten minutes later I had visitors. American I think. They introduced themselves as buyers looking to employ someone as a part time consultant for their company. Of course I was interested, so I invited them in. The conversation started innocently enough with a few questions about my past and the ruby trade in Thailand. It soon turned sour. They asked me about one ruby in particular, the Chandra Ruby. I do not lie very convincingly; they knew I'd seen it. So when I said that I hadn't, they got very angry.'

Kraiwoot showed them his forearms and the palm of his left hand. He was covered in small circular burns. So much so that Tomoko had to look away.

'Cigarettes! They strapped me to a chair and made me tell them about the stone in Sonya's box. You know? The strangest thing? They weren't at all surprised. It was as if they knew the stone was there all the time. They threatened to kill me if I breathed a word of their visit or the stone to anyone. So up until now I've kept it quiet. I don't mind telling you, they've got me scared out of my wits. I wouldn't be telling you this if it weren't for Sonya's murder. That changes everything. If they're prepared to kill her, they won't think twice about me.'

'What did they look like?' Asked Tomoko nervously.

Kraiwoot reached into his pocket and retrieved a couple of pieces of A4 paper. 'I drew these soon after they left. In my work sketching is an important part of recording flaws and creating designs, much more reliable than photographs. These faces will be ingrained in my memory for ever.'

Alexander couldn't help the look of surprise that appeared on his face as he studied the pencil sketches. Amazing as an adjective didn't seem to do them justice. Better than anything he had seen produced by portrait sketch artists around the streets of Montmartre in Paris. 'Would you mind if I faxed them to a friend of mine in the Tokyo police?' He asked.

'Would you? I'd be so pleased if you would.' Said Kraiwoot with growing confidence.

'Then I'll make a few notes on the back of them, telling the story you've just told me.'

When Alexander had finished writing he excused himself and walked to the hotel managers' office to make the call.

Hara answered on the first ring. 'Moshi-moshi, Hara des.'

'Alexander here, I haven't much time. I'm talking to Kraiwoot at the hotel. I've a couple of sketches, faces, I need to send them to you. Kraiwoot was attacked the same day that Sonya flew to Japan. He thinks they were both American, probably related and at a guess mid forty's. Can you see if you can track them down? What's your fax number?'

Alexander wrote as Hara dictated. 'Any movement on your police force suspect?' He asked.

'I'm waiting for military records, they should arrive late today. I'll call you around ten tonight, your time. If I'm right, we'll pick him up immediately.'

'Great. I have to dash now.' Said Alexander impatiently.

'I'll wait by the machine for your fax, it'll be safer. Talk to you tonight.' Hara replaced the receiver.

After sending the fax, Alexander photocopied the sketches, folded the copies and put them in his pocket, then returned to the terrace.

'Chief Hara's going to run a check on the faces, he'll call me tonight if anything turns up.' Said Alexander, taking his seat.

Kraiwoot smiled with relief. 'I'm so glad you came.' He said.

Alexander smiled in sympathy. 'You said earlier, you were in some doubt about the quality of your valuation?'

'Yes. I should explain. But, before I do, I would like you to see something in one of the temples next to the Royal Palace. Will you go with me? My explanation will be much clearer there.'

Intrigued, Alexander and Tomoko both nodded.

The waiter came over with the check as Alexander raised his hand. He signed his name and the room number and thanked him for his service.

CHAPTER 21

Alexander and Tomoko stood on the wharf at the rear of the hotel as Kraiwoot negotiated the charter. They all agreed that a private boat would be more prudent. He waved and beckoned them down to the Rua Hang Yao. A curiously designed craft. It was slender, thirty feet long and resembled a compromise between a long canoe and an alpine ski. The driver sat cross-legged on a crate at the rear, holding a control handle connected to a precariously pivoted four cylinder, tuned car engine. When the three of them were seated, he slowly raised the handle, lowering the long propeller shaft into the water. Cautiously they moved away from the jetty. Then, progressively, as the engine note changed with the opening throttle, the boat gathered speed and a white wake appeared at the stern.

Tomoko's face was a picture of his own, glowing with the delight of this new experience. Kraiwoot just sat, tight, behind them. At the first opportunity the boat steered off the Chao Phraya River and down one of the Klongs. Kraiwoot tapped his shoulder. 'A precaution,' he said, 'I have asked the driver to take the canal route, it is easier to see if we are being followed, I hope you don't mind.'

'Good idea.' Said Alexander. 'Very sensible.'

Thick banyan trees and flowering orchids lined the shore. Several yards ahead, a river snake skated quickly over the water's surface and under one of the many shacks built on stilts, half in the water and half on the bank. Further along he could see children fishing for their floating football with a broken branch, and their mother hanging a pair of light blue jeans, freshly washed in the clay brown water of the canal.

Tomoko opened the map in the last page of her guidebook, to trace their progress. She found her place with ease as they passed a small temple on their right. Through an elaborately decorated doorway facing the klong, four monks in saffron robes rushed out with their brass alms bowls, searching for their first meal of the day.

'At the next turn we should rejoin the river,' grinned Tomoko, demonstrating her map reading skills, 'the giant pagoda of Wat Arun will be on the left.' She was right.

The driver steered a course for the far bank and Tha Chang pier. Alexander watched him as he raised the propeller from the water at just the right time for the hang yao to glide effortlessly to the jetty with the briefest of kisses.

The driver waved farewell to Tomoko as she stepped to the shore. 'Thank you!' She called.

'Mai pen rai.' Came his reply.

'That means, Never mind or no problem.' Said Kraiwoot helpfully, 'I think he likes you.'

'Story of my life!' She said smiling, with a brief look back.

'It's this way, follow me.' Kraiwoot lead on.

The palace grounds were immaculate. Alexander walked to the kiosk and bought three entrance tickets at three hundred and fifty Baht each and rejoined the two of them admiring a postcard stand at its side. 'Shall we go?' He said with an air of expectation.

'If you wish to see the Grand Palace we can come to that later. But first I would like to take you to a rather special place. On the way I'll try to give you an impression of why this area was built and why there is so much splendour. Most of these buildings were built by Rama the first, in the late seventeen hundreds, immediately after his accession to the throne. His predecessor the King of Dhonburi lived on the other side of the river.'

As they walked onwards Alexander could see three magnificent pagodas on the far side of the red tile roofed wall. His heart quickened with anticipation. They passed through an ornate gateway defended by two, towering, and grotesque temple guardians with blue daemon faces.

'These are to ward off the evil spirits.' Informed Kraiwoot.

A little further and they stood beneath the pagodas. The first, resembling a conical bell was covered in pure gold leaf and glinted in the strong sunlight. The second was supported by slim blue and gold mosaic covered columns, capped by a complex structure of seven delicately carved concentric layers, surmounted by a blue and gold tapering spire. And the third, a white stone structure in the shape of a phallus surrounded by four red tile saddleback roofed arcades, facing north, south, east and west.

'The treasures of the Thai people are housed in the four main buildings of this courtyard.' Began Kraiwoot. 'The golden pagoda is called the Phra Sri Ratana Chedi, Chedi by the way means pagoda. Relics of the Buddha are stored inside.'

'I assume the gold is to signify enlightenment?' Questioned Tomoko.

'Quite so. Clever of you to make the connection.' He smiled. 'In the second, Phra Mondhob, we house the Holy Scriptures. I am one of the few people in Thailand ever to have seen them. Then, at the far end we have the Royal Pantheon. Inside there, we have enshrined statues of our past sovereigns of the ruling dynasty. You can see, scattered around these monuments on the terrace, many fanciful animals in our mythology, most of them are art treasures, evolved out of the imagination of our greatest artists. They are valued primarily for their aesthetic inspiration.'

Both Alexander and Tomoko raised their cameras for numerous pictures.

'We must move on,' said Kraiwoot, impatiently, 'the fourth building is what we have come to see.'

In the centre of the courtyard stood a building, stunning in its beauty. The outside walls were highly ornamented in gold leaf, cut glass and semi-precious stones arranged in complex decorative patterns. Through the gold plated entrance doors was a chamber adorned with a mural covering all four of the inside walls, telling the life story of Buddha. Tomoko was enthralled.

'Let's sit in the corner,' whispered Kraiwoot, 'we can talk there.'

The three of them settled on the rush matting at some distance from the other praying visitors, transfixed by the centrepiece of the room; A green statue of a seated Buddha on a throne of solid gold.

Kraiwoot moved to face Alexander and Tomoko with his back towards the shrine. He sat, cross-legged in front of them with his forearms resting lightly on his thighs. An unintentional imitation of the figure behind him.

'We are now sitting in the Chapel Royal.' He said, softly. 'The building was constructed around two hundred years ago, specifically to house this statue of the enlightened one. The Chapel was designed with all of the architectural features of a monastery, with the exception however of a residential quarter, monks are not permitted to live here. This assembly hall, or Uposatha, serves as the King's own private chapel. The statue, around thirty inches tall, is called the Emerald Buddha, and is in fact made from one solid piece of green Jade. Where and when it was carved is the subject of myth and legend, I'll get to that later, but all agree it was executed with incomparable skill. It is an object of national veneration; crowds come here from all over Thailand, not to mention the rest of the world, to pay their respect to the memory of the Buddha and his teachings. It sits high up on an altar of gold, designed to represent the traditional aerial chariot attributed to Hindu gods on the murals of this chapel and in many other holy temples across the country.'

He pointed to the embellished wall behind them, it showed a detail of the Ascension. The paint was beginning to flake and was in desperate need of repair.

'My father told me of this place when I was a child,' said Tomoko, 'I always thought it was a fairy tale. It fascinated me. Do you much of the history?' She asked.

'I know some of it, but not all. There are those that believe that the Emerald Buddha was created in Pataliputra, India in 43BC by a Brahmin sage called Nagasena. It remained there for three hundred years after which it was taken to Sri Lanka to save it from civil war. A thousand or so years pass where very little is known other than the passage of the statue through Burma and Cambodia and sometime during this period it was encased in stucco plaster, to hide its true value from avaricious rivals.

'In fourteen thirty two the Thais captured Angkor Wat and took it to Chiang Rai in the north of Thailand. Then, one stormy night in fourteen thirty four there was a lightning strike on the Chedi housing the statue. The temple Abbot noticed a green stone beneath the plaster. One can only imagine his expression when he removed the plaster to reveal once again this beautiful jade icon.

'It was then carried by elephant on an awkward and hazardous journey through jungle, a hundred and forty miles south to Lampang, where it remained until King Tilok took it to Chiang Mai, his capital. I believe this golden palladium was built for it there. Several generations passed and a new capital was built in Viangchan, a place we now call Vientiane. The ruler at the time was King Setthathirat the first. He ordered the Emerald Buddha moved to this new town in fifteen sixty.

'It remained in Vientiane for quite some time, until seventeen seventy eight in fact when the King of Dhonburi sent an expedition under the command of General Chao Phraya Chakkri to claim it for his own. General Chakkri subsequently assumed the throne and became King Rama the first. It was he who established the city of Bangkok with the Chapel Royal and the Grand Palace on the east bank of the river. The statue was moved once again and installed with much pomp and ceremony.'

'What has this to do with the ruby?' Asked Alexander, confused.

'Everything!' Said Kraiwoot, 'I'm coming to that. Tell me, what do you see when you look at this statue, Mister Webb?'

'A child sized carving in green Jade, wearing a golden bodice and an elaborate gold and jewelled head-dress.'

'Just so. The royal family changes the ornaments of gold and precious stones at the beginning of each season, in a great religious ritual. They are the only people permitted to look upon the Buddha at close range. At all other times the Buddha's breast is covered. There is a very good reason for this. At one time the Buddha had, in the centre of its chest a ruby, with four sides, to symbolise the four truths and in the centre of this stone, a flaw, symbolising the impure heart of mankind.'

'My God!' Gasped Alexander. 'Are you sure?'

'I believe I am. It never occurred to me at the time when Sonya was here, it was a few days later that I made the connection. It's not surprising, the last time I'd heard of the stone was forty-five years ago, during my training. Out of curiosity more than anything else, I visited our archives and searched through the ancient manuscripts for a description or a sketch, anything that would prove or disprove my theory. It was all there. Apparently the ruby was stolen by one of the King's guards on the journey from Vientiane to Bangkok. The guard was never found, neither was the jewel.'

Alexander unclasped the press-stud of the pouch on his belt and removed a small pair of Zeiss binoculars. Raising them to his eyes he examined the statue closely. Beneath the woven gold threads of the bodice he could see a shimmer of red.

'Can you see the stone?' Asked Kraiwoot.

'Yes?' Alexander was perplexed, 'Why...'

'The answer is simple. To lose the heart of Buddha would have been a catastrophe for the King. It would have caused mass revolts and widespread discontent. He had to locate a replacement. He scoured the country and those of our neighbours for a ruby of comparable size, unfortunately none could be found so he had to settle upon a compromise. What you can see there is a gemstone called a Spinel. A gem of lesser value and rarity. It has been there ever since. Few people outside the Royal Lapidary know the truth.'

Tomoko smiled in disbelief. 'How on earth did you manage to keep this to yourself? If I knew something like this I would be bursting to tell somebody.'

'You're quite right. I sat at home for days not knowing what to do. It finally came to me. In the whole world there is only one person I would trust with my life. I needed an audience with the King. Believe me, it was not easy. I had to ask a favour of my previous employer, I asked him for permission to present the anniversary designs, one last time before I died. He's a sympathetic man, he could see how much it meant to me, and so, he agreed. The next problem was to talk to King Bhumibol alone. I thought this would be impossible, as it turned out nothing could have been easier. I knelt before him with my head bowed and whispered five words. 'I've found the Rama's Hope.'

CHAPTER 22

The scorching Thai sun bore down, persistent and ruthless, relentlessly searching out every pore of his body. He hated the heat. The comforting early morning breeze had died an hour ago, now it was just plain hot. Kumagai waited impatiently in one of the scarce patches of shade across from the entrance to the Chapel Royal. *'Patience, the true test of a policeman.'* He mused. *'How right they were.'*

With only seven days to the gathering, and less than forty eight hours to the meeting in Hong Kong, he would have to act quickly. He wiped the perspiration from his brow into a sodden handkerchief and considered his options. The dilemma was a simple one. Who would be first?

He couldn't believe his good fortune at finding Webb in Bangkok, that had certainly been an unexpected bonus. Despite this, a voice at the back of his mind had nagged him all morning. *'Take extra care with this one.'* It said. *'Anyone with the initiative to have made it this far, is worthy of respect.'* Disposing of Webb and the girl would indeed need careful planning, they were rarely apart and Webb was sure to be alert.

His more immediate concern was with the elimination of Kraiwoot. Without doubt, the old man would have to be dealt with first. He was undeniably the most dangerous of the group. The American report had been explicit; Kraiwoot was an unnecessary risk. It was understandable; from their point of view he was the only person outside the circle to know the true value of the gem. More importantly, where Webb had encountered difficulty in convincing those in authority, Kraiwoot would be believed, instantly and without question. That made him a serious threat. Just one word, to the right people, and the whole operation would be in jeopardy.

Kumagai had started early that morning outside Kraiwoot's apartment in the prosperous expatriate quarter of Bangkok. By Thai standards he must have led a comfortable life. Living there would take an income normally reserved for the highflying business types of international corporations or government ministers on the take. He'd followed him from there to the Sheraton, and had even managed breakfast in the Benkay Japanese restaurant on the second floor, overlooking the terrace. The day had definitely started well. He'd also enjoyed the sedate passage through the canals following them at a discreet distance so as not to cause Webb alarm, the only one likely to recognise him. That had been over two hours ago and his patience was now wearing thin. What ever they were talking about in the chapel must surely be over soon.

He was right. The three of them appeared at the doorway, still deep in discussion. The girl, attentive, helped Kraiwoot down the steps to the courtyard. He was clearly frail; this would certainly work to his advantage, as he would need to rest frequently. An idea was beginning to form in his mind, the risks were high and he would need to get close, it hinged on Kraiwoot being alone and seated.

CHAPTER 23

The contrast in temperature and humidity to inside the chapel was astonishing. Alexander removed his lightweight, grey sports jacket and tossed it over his shoulder. 'We must have been in there for quite a while.' He said. 'I could do with a drink, You?'

Kraiwoot nodded. 'Yes please, something long and cool. You'd think that being a Thai and living here all of my life, I would have become accustomed to this heat. You never do you know. That's why we Thai's all carry umbrellas.' He opened his brightly coloured parasol to emphasise the point. 'It is rumoured that they were invented here in Thailand. There are still many villages up north whose sole income comes from manufacturing the wooden frames, turning the handles and decorating the canopies.'

'They are very attractive. Where can I buy one? I'd love one as a souvenir.' Said Tomoko.

'You may have mine, if you wish?' Said Kraiwoot bowing slowly, offering his as a gift, 'It is the very least I can do. Your presence here has me revitalized with new hope. I know now that something will be done.'

Tomoko accepted gracefully, kissing him lightly on the cheek. 'Thank you. I'll treasure it.' She said.

Alexander approached a small kiosk and bought three cans of soft drinks. They were refreshingly cold to the touch and glistened with condensation. 'There's still one open question. The Rama's Hope, how much is it actually worth?'

'Now that is rather a difficult question to answer Mr Webb.' Kraiwoot paused a moment searching for an analogy. 'I suppose you could liken it to the difference in price between two identical pianos. How much would you pay for a good piano in England?'

'Oh, somewhere in the region of one to two thousand pounds, I suppose.'

'Ok. Then how is it possible that a while back I read that a British musician, George Michael, paid two million dollars for a piano? The answer is the provenance. It was the one on which John Lennon wrote the song "Imagine".'

'I get your point.'

'History, provenance. It plays a huge part in the value of gems also. The Rama's Hope ruby is not just a valuable stone, it is unique. Potentially the first faceted stone in history. The Emerald Buddha has a recess in its chest where each facet on the rear of the stone is duplicated. No other stone in the world would fit. I have every confidence that the stone we have both seen will fit like a tailored glove.

'I would ask you also to consider the religious significance of this stone back in its rightful place to the sixty six million people of Thailand. I would conservatively estimate the value of the Rama's Hope at around One Hundred Million Dollars. For all intents and purposes, the Rama's Hope Ruby is priceless.'

The further they walked, the slower they walked. Kraiwoot was not in the best of health.

'Would you like to rest a while?' Asked Alexander seeing he was flushed with the exertion. They sat on a low wall facing the Grand Palace for him to catch his breath. He looked thoughtful.

'The name, Chandra, an interesting choice!' He said with laboured breathing, thinking aloud, 'I wonder if it was intentional? Whoever named it must have had some knowledge of its past. Our religious history is closely linked to that of India. A deliberate clue maybe?'

'I'm sorry, I don't follow you?' Said Alexander losing Kraiwoot's drift.

'Ramacandra. Pronounced Rama-Chandra, One of the most widely worshipped Hindu deities, the embodiment of chivalry and virtue. Legend has it that he was the seventh incarnation of the Lord Vishnu. His story is told at great length in the Ramayana, an Indian epic. King Rama the first sponsored the earliest full Thai version, we call it the Ramakien. When the gem was initially stolen he sent thousands of soldiers in search of it, the name Rama's Hope was inevitably coined at that time. I can just imagine the thief giving his new prize the name of Chandra as an affront to the king and his efforts to find him.'

'A fascinating possibility, I have a feeling that you are probably right. It would seem that some of the pieces are falling into place. I only wish we knew where the stone was right now. Any ideas?'

Kraiwoot shook his head. 'None. My best guess would be that it is in the hands of someone in Japan. After all it was stolen there.' Kraiwoot looked deeply onto Alexander's eyes. 'You know, I really don't think they have any idea just exactly what it is they've got!'

Alexander nodded and smiled. 'I do believe you're right.'

Kraiwoot stood offering his hand. 'If you will forgive me, I have to leave now, Doctor's orders!' He said, 'When you get to my age you'll know exactly what I mean. I must return home for some rest, you don't mind do you?

You both know where to find me if you would like to talk some more. You'd both be more than welcome.'

Alexander shook it warmly, 'We'll come with you.' He offered.

'Oh no, I wouldn't think of it.' He said turning to Tomoko. 'Enjoy the day! Look around the palace, it really is worth seeing. I'll be fine. Just do me one favour. If and when you find Sonya's killers, send me a letter, it will put my mind at rest.'

'It will be our pleasure.' Said Tomoko, With a farewell kiss to his cheek.

They both watched as he slowly made his way back to the entrance gate. Alexander took her hand. 'An honourable man Tomoko. We now know what we're searching for and why. If we succeed, we owe it to him to see that the Rama's Hope returns to its rightful place.'

CHAPTER 24

Squeals and shouts of delight filled the air as a party of Japanese school children in purple caps ran ashore at the Tha Chang pier. Their teacher paused in front of a fellow compatriot asking the way to the Palace entrance, he seemed pleased to oblige. Most of the passengers waiting to step aboard, watched the exchange. The Rua Duan river taxi was now empty but for the captain and a few crew selling tickets. Kraiwoot stepped down onto the wooden deck and took a seat at the back of the boat. The athletic looking Japanese man came to sit at his side.

'Where were they going?' Kraiwoot asked in English.

'To the Palace.' Replied Kumagai with a warm smile, 'I've just been there myself. Quite breathtaking.' The hidden insult amused him.

Kraiwoot nodded and returned the smile. The heat of the day had aggravated his chest, making breathing difficult. He closed his eyes and leaned his head against a circular stanchion, one of many supporting the canvas-covered roof.

Gradually the waves of tension and worry ebbed away. He fell into a light peaceful sleep. Tomoko and Alexander had lifted the burden from his shoulders and now a feeling of relief swept over him, an all-enveloping cloud, it was warm and comforting. There was something about those two, they inspired confidence, he would miss them. The adrenaline which had coursed through his veins for the past few weeks, causing many a sleepless night, retreated into its secret haven in his soul, it was no longer needed. He was at peace. His heart, barely murmuring, grew progressively weaker, its task completed. All that remained was the vision. A glowing pale green statue reunited with the Rama's Hope.

With his left hand, Kumagai reached into his right sleeve, he could feel the reassuring cold steel of the stiletto's pencil thin blade. Carefully he eased it into his palm, hidden from the view of the other passengers.

The boat slowed approaching the Oriental hotel, a perfect place to alight, he would be hidden in the waiting crowds. The time had come. He turned as if to gaze over the stern. The move was automatic, an instinctive flowing action. The Stiletto slid unimpaired through Kraiwoot's lightweight shirt, under the rib cage and into his heart as easily as a ski through powder snow. Barely a drop of blood showed, it was the perfect killing tool.

New passengers flooded on to the boat, the moment was one of disorganised chaos. As soon as he stood, another took his place on the wooden bench. He pushed his way through to the exit with his head bowed and when on the shore headed straight for Silom road to hail a taxi.

'Sheraton Hotel.' He ordered. Resting back into the rear seat, he wiped the remains of blood from the knife onto his damp handkerchief and pushed both of them into his boot for transfer later. He was elated. Totally unaware that he'd just killed a dead man.

CHAPTER 25

It was some hours later when Tomoko and Alexander returned to the hotel to find the note. It read 'I'm on holiday and just found out we are in the same hotel. If you would like to meet, I will be in the bar at seven. Best regards, Sergeant Kumagai.' There was a Ps in brackets. (I was the one taking notes during your interview at the Tokyo Metropolitan Police H.Q.)

'Read this Tomoko, What do you think?' Alexander passed her the piece of Sheraton notepaper.

'I think it is too much of a coincidence.' She said.

'So do I. Intriguing though, I think we should meet him. If he were the inside man I'd sooner have him where we can see him rather than the other way around. So, cocktails at seven. Formal dress?'

'Why not.'

They both had the same Idea. Arm in arm, they walked back to the tailor they had passed on their return to the hotel. The sign was still hanging in the window, boasting same day service for suits and dresses.

Nothing could have been simpler. They were measured at two, had their first fitting at four and final fitting at six. Both the cocktail dress and the Tuxedo were a perfect fit.

'You look radiant my dear.' Said Alexander affectatiously kissing her hand.

'You're quite handsome yourself.' She said, watching him preen his black bow tie.

'Only quite?'

Kumagai spotted them at the bar and boldly walked over. 'You are both very punctual.' He said, mockingly looking at his watch. 'I'm so pleased you could join me. I've been here for quite some time now, the days are full of adventure, the nights on the other hand are deathly boring. Can I get you a drink?'

Alexander ordered a glass of Singha beer, a local brew and Tomoko a tall cocktail crowned by a paper parasol and local exotic fruits.

'I think I will join you Webb-San, and sample the local offerings. Must mix with the natives eh?' Kumagai was clearly in a good mood. 'At eight, on the terrace, there is a buffet and a display of Thai dancing, interested?'

'Could be fun, what do say Alex?' Tomoko liked the idea.

Alexander smiled. 'It looks like you've both already made up my mind.'

'Excellent. Then I propose we move to one of the more comfortable chairs, we have about an hour, they'll bring the drinks to us.'

Kumagai lead them to a table midway between the bar and the band. 'To tell you the truth,' he said, 'I didn't think you would recognise me.'

'Oh I have a pretty good memory for faces.' Said Alexander, 'What's more intriguing is, how did you know we were here?'

'I saw you at breakfast. There's a Japanese restaurant here on the floor above us, I could see you on the terrace. I would have popped down to talk to you, but I didn't wish to intrude. I thought a couple of drinks later was a much better idea.'

'Very considerate of you. So what brings you to Bangkok? Holiday?' Asked Tomoko.

'Yes, some of my colleagues say it's about time. I've been in the force for more years than I care to remember. In all that time I never once took a holiday, couldn't afford it basically. Now that I can, I thought I'd treat myself. And you, what brings you here?'

Alexander took Tomoko's hand in his. 'Tomoko did. We decided a few days together in the sun would bring us closer together. I can't complain so far.'

Tomoko, with her eyes cast downwards, wearing the shyest of expressions, added, 'Neither can I.'

They all laughed.

'Tell me Sergeant, beside watching Thai dancing what else have you found to do in the evenings since your arrival.' Asked Alexander.

'The last few nights I've spent drinking in Patpong, as you English would say "getting pissed",' Kumagai playfully mimed his heavy drinking. 'That is of course with the exception of the first night. A most enjoyable evening. I found a magazine in my bedroom with addresses of local massage parlours. I chose the Chao-phraya, same name as the river, a most enjoyable experience. I'd recommend it to you both, nothing like a good massage to ease away the aches and pains of a days sightseeing.' Kumagai sat back with a sigh of satisfaction. 'The best four hundred Baht I've spent since I arrived. With luck, tonight will be even better.'

'In what way?' Asked Alexander.

'One of the local police officers has invited me to a Thai boxing match down in the Chinese part of town. It's an invitation bout, I'm told some of the best underground fighters in Thailand will be there. I'm sure he wouldn't mind if you came as my guests, you're both welcome to join me if you wish. It starts at around ten.'

Tomoko shook her head. 'I don't agree with blood sports. Watching two grown men beating each other up is not my idea of a good night out.'

Alexander sipped his beer, thinking of the proposition. Potentially this could be very hazardous. If Kumagai was what he claimed to be, no problem. If he was the one who switched the stones, big problem. Curiosity was beginning to get the better of him. He knew he would have to take risks if he was going to make headway, maybe this was the time.

'When I was a schoolboy, we had a school boxing team.' Said Alexander, 'I was quite good in my day. Nowhere near the standard of the chaps you see on TV, but I used to enjoy it. I think it would be fun to see how the Thai professionals fight. If my memory serves me correctly, I seem to recall that Thai boxers fight with their feet as well, is that right?' He asked, knowing it to be fact.

Kumagai nodded, delighted that Alexander had accepted his invitation.

'I always thought that was cheating.' Added Alexander.

'To a boxer constrained by the Queensbury rules it is. Here the rules are significantly different. The Thai's see it as a form of martial art. Unusual in so much that it is clearly an attack based form. In Japan, Korea and China they are purely defensive. I personally see it as the ultimate test of balance and skill. I watch it whenever and wherever I have the opportunity.'

'You sound very knowledgeable Kumagai-San.' Said Tomoko, searching. 'Are you an expert?'

'Heavens no,' said Kumagai on the verge of a smile, 'Like Webb here, I too gained a little experience in my youth, a long time ago now. Karate was my sport, should have kept it up I suppose, you never know when you might need it.'

Alexander barely picked at his food throughout the precision display. Beautiful girls dressed in gold lame and elaborate conical headdresses would normally have held his total and undivided attention. He had other things on his mind. While the others watched the dancing he wrote a brief note for Tomoko on the back of a hotel postcard.

It read: Tomoko, Hara calls at ten. Ask him about Kumagai. If Kumagai suspect, change rooms. Use name Maverick. Tell Hara story of Rama's Hope. Be careful, love, Alex.

'Kumagai-San and I will have to leave for the fight soon Tomoko, be a dear and post this to Higaki for me, will you? You'll find the address in my note book by the bed.' Alexander unclasped her handbag and placed it inside.

Alexander and Kumagai waited politely till the end of the dance, then stood to leave. Alexander bent to kiss Tomoko's cheek, 'Read the card,' he whispered, 'It's important.'

Outside the Hotel, Kumagai lead the way to a row of waiting tuk-tuks. 'A taxi will be too wide where we're going.' He said, 'Climb aboard.'

'Oh? And where exactly is that?' Enquired Alexander.

'One of the most fascinating areas in Bangkok, Chinese Town.' Leaning forward, he tapped the driver's arm. 'Take us to Chakkrawat.' He barked, barely audible over the sound of the clattering engine. The driver nodded.

The entrance to Chinese Town was like entering the wide end of a funnel. The deeper they drove, the narrower the lanes became. One tortuous, twisting street after another. The suffocating alleys, dimly lit by shop front neon lights reminiscent of Dickens's London, were deserted. It was an eerie place at night.

Kumagai leaned over the driver's shoulder guiding him through the last few streets then finally down an alley barely wide enough for the tuk-tuk to turn. It was a dead end.

Alexander could feel his heart thumping, a reaction to his growing anxiety.

'Webb-San, we're here.' Said Kumagai, jumping down from the seat, slapping a hundred Baht note into the drivers' hand. 'Come on, I'll show you the way.'

An Innocuous looking door opened as they approached. Inside, to the left of the passageway, an old man in black priest robes bowed to greet them. In his hands he held two thick white martial arts jackets. 'Change please.' He said, bowing again.

Before Alexander could object Kumagai had taken the jackets. 'It's the Thai way of ensuring anonymity,' he said, 'rich and poor alike, they all come here. What counts here is ability, not the depth of your pockets.'

Kumagai lead him into a changing room, the acrid smell of sweat hung heavily in the air. 'Remove your jacket and shirt and put this on.' He threw him one of the jackets.

'Your not expecting me to fight are you?' Asked Alexander, laughing nervously.

'Only if you want to.' He said stripping to the waist and removing his shoes. 'I did say it was an invitation bout.'

They passed through a final door into a large room with a sawdust-covered floor. Fifty to sixty people in similar dress were seated around the edges, the room was silent. In a corner to Alexander's right a group of musicians sat behind instruments similar to those supporting the dancers back at the hotel. A semicircle of tuned gongs formed the hub, surrounded at the rear by leather-skinned drums on red wooden frames. To the right three brightly coloured, hand-carved xylophones and to the left a blend of woodwind and guitar like strings. A mixture clearly designed for noise rather than musical appreciation.

Kumagai lead him to the front of three benches next to the left-hand wall, and motioned for him to sit. They were not the last to arrive.

Ten minutes passed without event, until finally a deep resounding gong rang, softly at first, rising to a deafening crescendo. Two thick wooden doors next to the changing room creaked open and the Sensei entered. Dressed in garish black and gold priest-like vestments, he walked slowly in front of them chanting and stepped up to an ornately carved podium at the head of the room. A shuffling of feet whispered throughout as the waiting crowd stood and bowed.

The gong sounded again, this time a single strike. The crowd sat. All with the exception of the Sensei and Kumagai.

Kumagai approached with respect and knelt before him to receive the old mans hands upon his head and what appeared to be a blessing. Gestures of friendship followed, making it evident they had unmistakably met many times before.

Alexander watched and listened as the gowned man bowed his head to hear Kumagai's request. As much as he strained to understand the exchange, it was of no use. Although perfectly clear to the rest of the spectators, he was still left guessing. Kumagai was speaking in fluent Thai.

The Sensei appeared to be proposing a place at his side for the contest, Kumagai had refused, with indications of a lack of time and pointing in Alexander's direction. The Sensei nodded with understanding, raised Kumagai to his feet and offered him his chance to address the assembly.

He turned to face the crowd with his arms raised like a preacher expecting attention. The room fizzed with anticipation, even Alexander could feel the excitement rise as he delivered the challenge at the top of his voice. A dozen or so hands shooting high into the air, eager to take up the task, answered it.

The Sensei pointed to a heavily built bald man close to where Kumagai was standing.

'This way if you please, there is someone I would like you to beat.' Said Kumagai, leading the volunteer over to Alexander's bench.

'What are you playing at Kumagai?' Demanded Alexander.

'Oh, the time for playing is long passed, my friend.' Joked Kumagai, 'I hope you can still remember some of your schoolboy boxing moves, you are about to fight for your life.' With a nonchalant wave he walked towards the dressing room. 'Don't worry, you won't be alone for long, with luck you're girlfriend will be joining you shortly.'

'You bastard.' Cried Alexander. 'Touch Tomoko and you're a dead man.'

Kumagai was gone. Alexander watched as the door closed behind him. His heart raced. The fighter moved to the end of the room between him and the door. There was no escape.

CHAPTER 26

Slowly Alexander removed the jacket from his shoulders and stood to face the Thai. He could feel there were still coins in his trouser pocket, he closed his hands around them, maybe they would help. He wasn't going to be eliminated without first putting up one hell of a fight.

The Sensei walked to his side. 'I look forward to a skilful contest. We have just one rule here, there can be only one survivor. Any style of fighting is acceptable. Your opponent is Lai Shin, he is an adept practitioner of Muay Thai, it will be interesting to see how he compares with your western techniques. Good luck young man.'

The music began slowly as Alexander and Shin circled each other. At first all he could think about was the exit, this soon changed.

Shin advanced with an air of invulnerability, jogging casually forward and lifting one leg in an attempt to land his first short stabbing kick.

Alexander easily avoided the move by dancing away from him, in return striking out with his first punch, a straight right to Shin's left cheek.

Unfazed, the bald man approached again throwing a hard kick at Alexander's waist, this time it connected, a shaft of pain shot through him causing him to back away. Shin pursued him, punching now with lefts and rights, some finding their mark, some raining down on his raised shielding arms.

Alexander had to do something, the battering was weakening him fast. He stepped inside Shin's attack, forcing his right arm upwards, in an upper cut to the jaw.

The large Thai took the blow with ease. Alexander pulled his head backwards then snapped it forward with all his strength smashing his forehead into Shin's nose, he could feel the crunch. Blood spurted like a river down his face and onto his chest.

Shin backed away, shaking his head, and fell into a protective pose.

The crowd incensed by the foul blow was on its feet screaming for a quick reaction from Shin.

Alexander could see his chance. He feinted with a jab and lashed out with a brutal kick to the groin. Shin roared with pain, and dropped to one knee.

Alexander moved in on the downed man with a combination of rights and lefts to his head aiming for the area of most damage, hoping to finish the fight. The punches had little effect, Shin took blow after blow with ease, standing as Alexander threw in his assault.

'My turn.' He said, grinning through the blood dripping over his lips. Shin jumped back and landed two quick kicks to Alexander's stomach, switched feet and caught him with two more to the kidneys.

Alexander staggered away, he couldn't take much more of this. He moved around Shin keeping his guard high. He tried a few jabs landing three of the gruelling punches on Shin's busted nose, the coins in his fist now having effect.

Suddenly, brutally, Shin slashed his foot out and landed a direct hit on Alexander's jaw. A buzz zipped through him and he span away, falling face down in to the saw dust. That was it, one more blow would finish him off.

Alexander felt rather than saw a man approaching from the bench nearest the exit. He came up to him and crouched. He was an athletic looking man of about Alexander's age, wearing a puzzled expression on his face.

'Having a spot of trouble Mister Webb?' He said. 'Make your way to the exit, you can leave this one to me.'

Under disapproving jeers from the assembly the man took up a wide stance between Shin and Alexander. His hands were held low, a classic attack pose of an experienced Karate master. A single combination of blows was all it took. Shin was smacked with two fast lefts and a final deadly ridge hand strike into the corner of his jaw just beneath his left ear. The daylight faded, he was down and out.

Alexander held the door open for his saviour's retreat. Once inside the changing room they threw the bolt to shield them from the inevitable onslaught and with his arm around the strangers' neck they made for the alley.

'I don't know who you are, but you came just in the nick of time. One more second, and I was a dead man.' Said Alexander staggering.

'Time to talk later.' He said. 'We've got to get out of here.'

A single tuk-tuk was waiting in the street outside, the driver was nowhere to be seen. Alexander climbed into the driving seat.

'Are you OK to drive?' The man asked.

'If we're going to get out of here alive I am. Don't worry, fighting is clearly your game, driving's mine.' The engine thrashed into life. Alexander gave it full throttle and the wheels squealed forward.

CHAPTER 27

Tomoko stepped from the shower and dabbed the water from her body, then wrapping the shaggy hotel towel around her hair walked naked into the bedroom. Her thick monogrammed bathrobe lay on the bed. She put it on to absorb the remaining trickles on her golden skin. Poised on the side of the mattress she removed the cap and sprayed liberally behind her ears and between her breasts. A sweet smelling cloud surrounded her. The whisky-coloured perfume had long been her mother's favourite, and was quickly becoming one of hers. She placed the bottle of Chanel No.5 Eau de Toilette next to the telephone and glanced at the travel alarm clock, it showed two minutes to ten. She knew in a minute or two the phone would ring.

Hara was clearly in a good mood. 'Tomoko, it is so good to hear your voice, how are you enjoying your stay.'

'We're having a great time, and we're doing better than we could ever have expected. We've got some news for you. We already knew that Sonya's ruby was authentic, what we didn't know was just how unique it really was. It now turns out that its part of a Jade icon of Buddha, the stone is not only irreplaceable, it's priceless.' The intonation in her voice reflected her excitement.

'I have some important news for you too,' interrupted Hara, 'I now know the name of the officer who switched the gems. My associates in the United States ran a finger print check on the large ruby, it turned up trumps. They ran the print through the Interpol computer and came up with the perfect match. Not only that, I ran a check of my own through the police forces in South Africa and Jordan, the same name cropped up on the mercenaries listing. It turns out that our man has quite a reputation. So far he's been indicted on eight counts of murder in seven countries. In all cases he escaped capture or was set free on the grounds of insufficient evidence. There's no doubt about it, he's a very clever and resourceful man. Is Webb-San there? I think he may have met him.'

'Alexander's out at the moment, he's gone to a boxing match with one of your officers.' A cold sweat broke out in Tomoko's palms, 'The name of your suspect, it's Kumagai isn't it?' She asked anxiously, dreading the answer and knowing it the moment she'd breathed his name. Over the thousands of miles that separated them she could feel Hara's reaction.

'You have to get out of that room immediately.' He said, confirming her suspicions, 'He's certain to know where you're staying. Call me back later, especially if you don't hear from Alexander.' The line went dead. Hara had realised, another word could cost her life.

Tomoko changed quickly into a pair of slacks and jumper, threw the rest of their unpacked belongings into her luggage and taking hold of her case and Alexander's bag ran swiftly to the lift.

At the desk the duty manager listened patiently. A family argument. There was nothing strange in this, particularly in Bangkok. It happened all the time with mixed marriages and couples cheating on their partners. In his judgement this was clearly a case of the latter. Sympathetic to her story he immediately arranged for another room. 'Shall I cancel your current accommodation Ms. Webb, er, Maverick?' He asked.

'That will not be necessary. Despite our disagreement my husband will still need somewhere to sleep. I have however a request, under no circumstances must you tell anyone which room I have been moved to. One exception, if I should receive a visitor asking for me by the name of Maverick and not Webb, show him straight up.'

'You can be assured of our discretion.' With a reassuring smile the manager struck the counter bell. 'The porter will show you to your suite.' He bowed and handed over the key.

Back in the lift and rising Tomoko released a sigh of relief. 'This had better be worth it.' She said aloud, unaware Kumagai had missed her by seconds and the ground floor call button had just been pressed.

CHAPTER 28

As the lift doors opened, Kumagai rechecked the note handed to him that morning by the concierge. He was right, seventeen-o-one. He walked the length of the corridor, rummaging casually through his pockets and keeping an eye on the chambermaid hovering at the entrance to the service stairs. A creek and the door hushed closed behind her. Save for a tray with the remains of a light supper the hallway was now deserted. With luck there would be time enough before she would return to collect it.

Retrieving his collection of passkeys from his pocket, standard issue to officers with hotels on their beat, he tried the first in the lock. The second one turned.

Softly the door eased open and he stepped into the darkened room. Taking a pencil torch from inside his jacket, he scanned the space. The bedroom was empty, the bathroom too. No clothes, no bags, no toiletries, nothing. The only sign that the room had been occupied was a ruffled bed and a single cigarette butt in the ashtray.

He left the room, leaving everything as he'd found it.

Down in the foyer Kumagai approached the desk, only to be told that Mrs Webb had checked out, leaving no forwarding address.

He sat for a moment to collect his thoughts. Could she have known? He doubted it, no-one was that good an actor. Had she decided to follow them to the fight? Impossible, he would have spotted her if she'd followed immediately, and she didn't know the address to follow later. He was baffled. Maybe they'd quarrelled earlier and she'd left for the airport? Without knowing her surname he would never find her there. He'd tried that once before on a previous case, it was pointless.

Frustrated, he decided to return to the fight and help dispose of the body. *'Webb's spirit would have to wait a little while longer'*, he mused.

He left the hotel and walked over to the driver of a waiting tuk-tuk.

CHAPTER 29

'Can't this bloody thing go any faster!' Screamed Alexander, pulling back hard on the throttle. A single objective fired his determination, all he could think of was getting back to the Sheraton, Tomoko was in grave danger.

The tuk-tuk howled it's resistance under braking, as again the back end broke away in a lateral slide with the feed in of more power on the apex of a ninety degree bend.

'Are you OK back there?' Alexander shouted, glancing briefly over his shoulder. 'You look a bit rough, you don't get car sick do you?'

'Yes...' The thought of it made him heave. He couldn't have been more accurate if he tried. The driver's window of a yellow Toyota taxi took the full force. Despite his condition, he couldn't help thinking it was an improvement.

Alexander looked back again, 'Good shooting partner, what's your name?'

'Call me Charlie.' He said.

'Well hold on tight Charlie, this bit's going to be a bit tricky.' It was a masterpiece of understatement. The road closed suddenly through the next corner, forcing the three-wheeler into a controlled skid, the rear end scraping inch deep gashes into an ancient brick wall.

'Are you sure you know how to drive this thing?' Said Charlie laughing nervously.

'We've all got to learn sometime I guess!' Alexander joined in the laughter.

Another tuk-tuk approached from directly in front of them. They passed with barely a hair's breadth between them.

'Step on it Webb.' Shouted Charlie. 'That was the Jap!'

'Who, Kumagai?'

'If that's the guy that took you to the fight, you got it in one.'

Through his wing mirror he could see the driver thrown bodily from the tuk-tuk, landing awkwardly in the gutter and Kumagai climbing into his seat.

'We have to loose him, which way?' Yelled Alexander.

'Take a right at the end, it goes down to the river. We'll loose him in the klongs.'

Alexander pulled out onto the main road, heading for Phra Pok Klao Bridge. Traffic was light and the road straight. He looked back again. Kumagai was closing.

'He's gaining on us, it must be a newer machine.' Said Charlie leaning close to his ear, 'Turn first right after the bridge, it'll take us down to the canals.'

Again the tuk-tuk resisted, sliding savagely in a three-wheel drift. A crack split the air as sparks scattered on the handlebars.

'The bastard's firing at us, move it Webb, move it!'

The tuk-tuk bounced brutally down the dirt track road, shaking violently as they hit one pothole after another. Alexander struggled to follow the path in front of them, the small headlamp on the fairing was next to useless in the blackness, dim lights from inside the shacks on the bank were his only true guides.

Another shot rang out, this time shattering their windscreen. 'That was close, Charlie. It's never like this in the movies.' Said Alexander concentrating hard, 'It's only supposed to be the good guys that can shoot straight.'

He could see movement in a darkened ramshackle cabin twenty yards in front of them, he slowed and killed his lights, turning tight around the bank and into the track on his left.

Kumagai strained to see them through the blackness, they'd disappeared. Pulling back the throttle for more power, he pushed onwards. By the time he'd reached the embankment it was too late. The tuk-tuk launched skywards, giving him fractions of a second to jump clear before it crashed thunderously into the rusting corrugated roof of the water front derelict. The water stank. He'd been lucky, landing within inches of a hang yao longboat.

'You can ease up now, your friend's got other things on his mind.' Said Charlie elated.

'Yes, about half a shack I imagine, I heard the crash.'

Alexander, still uneasy about Tomoko's safety pressed on at speed, crossing the Taksin Bridge and turning down New road bound for the Sheraton.

At the hotel Alexander and Charlie ran straight for the waiting lift.

'You!' Alexander was astonished. It was the first time he'd had the chance to see his face clearly.

'You recognise me?' Said Charlie with a smile.

'Kyoto, at the golden temple, you were following me. Why.'

'Plenty of time to explain later. You need rest. That was quite a beating you took.'

'You're telling me!' Said Alexander. 'But nowhere near the beating your stomach took on the streets of China Town! Were you aiming for that taxi, or was it pure luck?'

The lift doors opened and Alexander lead the way to his room.

The relief on his face said it all. She'd packed and moved. All that remained was the faint hint of her perfume in the air.

'She must have got out in time thank God. And, I've a pretty good idea where she went.' Said Alexander heading back to the lift. 'We'll call her from reception.'

CHAPTER 30

Still unsure of Charlie's motives for helping him, Alexander arranged for Tomoko to join them in the Garden Cafe of the Oriental Hotel, it was unlikely that Kumagai would look for them there.

'What happened to you?' She said, running to his side with genuine concern.

'My curiosity got the better of me. I went to the fight as a spectator and ended up as the main event, courtesy of your friend and mine Sergeant Kumagai. If it wasn't for Charlie here, well, I wouldn't be here.' Alexander pulled her to his side and hugged her tightly. 'I've been so worried about you.'

'Me too.' She said, reaching up to kiss him.

'Hey, steady on chaps, you're embarrassing me.' Joked Charlie, 'Let's go and sit down, there's a lot we have to talk about.'

The only table still unoccupied on the riverside terrace was located behind the partition close to the entrance doors. It would suit their purpose well. With twenty-four hour drink and snack service, it was popular with guests and visitors alike, especially after a heated night on the town. An ideal place to unwind before turning in.

Alexander gingerly took his seat and turned to Charlie. 'Charlie, a strange name for a Thai?' He said.

'I guess it is,' Taking a cigarette from his pocket, 'It's a nickname that's been with me since childhood. My given name is Chanarong Klahan Tan, I got the name Charlie when my parents moved to the States, that was when I was six. Dad was in the army, we travelled a lot in those days. If anything, it was good for my languages.'

'Yes, you surprise me, your English is perfect, you even speak with an English accent.' Said Alexander.

Charlie was pleased with the compliment. 'You can thank my mother for that, she did everything she could to remove any trace of an American accent, she's a bit of a snob to tell you the truth. Languages are a bit of a hobby of mine, you know the hardest thing in any language is understanding the humour. I don't mind telling you, you Brits are the hardest of all. I'll give you an example. Did you hear about the dyslexic, agnostic, insomniac? He sat up all night wondering if there was a dog.'

Tomoko looked puzzled and Alexander smiled.

'There you are, proof.' Said Charlie, rocking back in his chair, 'It took me ages to figure that one out.'

'Was it worth the effort?' Asked Alexander, still smiling.

'Ah, sarcasm. Now that really is a British speciality.' Parried Charlie.

'How many languages do you speak then?' Asked Tomoko.

Charlie raised his hands and counted them down on his fingers, 'Mandarin, Cantonese, Japanese, German, French, English and of course Thai.'

'Are you fluent in all of them?' Tomoko was impressed.

Charlie nodded.

Leaning forward, Alexander rested his elbows on the table, his face serious. 'Tell me Charlie, how is it that you were in the right place at the right time?'

'Before I answer that,' he said, 'I need to know something from you. I know you met with Khun Kraiwoot this morning. Did he say if he'd spoken to someone special, recently?'

'If you mean by that, did he speak to the highest authority in Thailand? Then the answer is yes.' Said Tomoko.

Charlie smiled again. 'You have told me all I need to know. The fact that Kraiwoot trusts you is good enough for me. I think we should work together.'

As a waiter passed the table Alexander ordered coffee all round. 'What exactly do you mean Charlie?' Asked Alexander.

'I'm looking for the Rama's Hope Ruby.' He said in earnest, 'I work for the government. An Interpol department that specialises in the location and recovery of stolen works of art. At present I'm on secondment to the Royal Lapidary. A couple of weeks ago I was called for an audience with the king. He told me Kraiwoot's story. I caught the next available plane out for Japan in search of the American lady, Miss Sonya Martin. I first saw you Mister Webb in the ANA hotel the night she was murdered. To tell you the truth I didn't know what to think. Some days before I'd called her head office in America to organise a meeting for the Sunday. We'd arranged to meet in the afternoon at the Okura. I waited in the hotel lobby for a couple of hours, and when she didn't show I tracked her to her hotel. It was crawling with police.'

Tomoko was still sceptical, 'Do you have any form of identification?' She asked.

Charlie reached into his back pocket and pulled out a wallet. The cover showed the globe, bisected by a sword, and flanked by the scales of justice. He flipped it open. The left side displayed the formal portrait in uniform and below this was his warrant in three languages, English, Japanese and Thai. Recognised approval stamps were on the facing page from numerous embassies. 'This card gives me almost unlimited resources anywhere in the world.'

'I could do with one of those myself.' Said Alexander thinking aloud.

Charlie smiled, tucking it back into his pocket. 'That will depend on whether we're successful or not.'

'What have you found out so far?' Asked Tomoko.

'Not a lot. I first thought Mr Webb had the stone, so I followed him to Kyoto. It became apparent that he hadn't after I'd seen the photographs you both showed, and my subsequent meeting with Koyanagi-San. I lost you soon after Alexander spotted me outside the temple.' Charlie lit another cigarette, this time offering one to Alexander.

'I'll never give up at this rate.' said Alexander, taking one. 'How did you find us again?'

'I didn't try,' Charlie continued, 'I decided to focus my attention on Kraiwoot. I followed him this morning to the Sheraton, and subsequently to you. That was also the first time I saw the Japanese "gentleman", Kumagai? The fact that he tried to eliminate you makes him my new flavour of the month.'

'I agree.' Said Alexander. 'I never thought I'd say this, but I hope he survived the crash. Without him we'll be back at square one. We'll have to check with the police tomorrow.'

'You can leave that to me.' Said Charlie.

Alexander's antipathy was building again, 'With luck he'll lead us straight to the gem and the murderous bastard that killed Sonya. If he's OK, then somehow we'll have to locate him before he leaves Bangkok, and if possible find out his plans. Any ideas?'

Tomoko lightly touched Alexander's arm. 'The airport would be our best bet. I'll call them in the morning. He's sure to be booked on a flight out.'

'Do that,' said Charlie, 'good idea, and I'll run a search through the hotel listings. But before we do anything else, we have one immediate matter to attend to. Kumagai will undoubtedly track you down if you continue to stay in your present hotel. I suggest you check out and allow me to find you alternative accommodation. OK?'

CHAPTER 31

Tomoko woke with a start. Disorientated. The unfamiliar discord of the traffic outside sounded surprisingly close, seemingly inches away from her pillow and offensive by comparison to the peace and quiet of their riverfront suite at the hotel. It was morning, the morning after her flight the night before. So much had happened and so fast that she could barely believe she had had the ability to rest let alone have the wherewithal to sleep.

The master bedroom of Charlie's apartment looked different in the daylight. Resting, with her hands behind her head, she explored the barren room. *'A typical male apartment,'* she thought, *'functional, clean and impersonal.'*

The white-emulsion faced walls surrounding her wicker-framed sofa bed were bare, devoid of any form of decoration, exactly as they would have been the day he had moved in. Only one feature of note saved it from the impression of a hospital recovery room, a hypnotic, softly spinning wooden fan, mounted in the centre of the ceiling. Tomoko smiled, the place was desperately in need of a women's delicate touch.

She peeled back the covers to permit her body to breathe. Despite the hour, the heat was already stifling in the south facing room. Alexander, still sound asleep, was lying with his back towards her.

'What did they do to you?' She whispered, wincing at the sight of his bruising. A patchwork of yellow, brown and violet spread from his neck to his waist. She didn't dare to touch it for fear of hurting him, instead, she smoothed her hand gently over his cheek to ease him from his slumbers.

'Good morning lover.' She said, as he regained consciousness, 'It's time to get up.'

Groaning, Alexander turned over to face her. 'Morning nurse.' He said, pushing himself to a seated position and drifting his gaze slowly from her face, down the smooth curves of her body. 'Uniform's in the wash, is it?'

Tomoko chuckled, 'On the contrary my dear. In Thailand our patients always get what they deserve. In your case it's shared bodily warmth. We believe in a personal service here Mister Webb.'

'And delightful it is too.' He closed his eyes again to block out the aches in his stiffening muscles, 'If you were truly an angel of mercy, you'd let me sleep.' He moaned, slumping back onto the pillow.

'Sorry, can't do. We have a delicate operation to perform today, we need to get an early start.' Tomoko slipped from the bed and tossed him his clothes.

Charlie was whistling one of the Thai top forty as she passed into the living room. 'Morning princess,' he said, toasting her with his coffee, 'breakfast?'

Tomoko nodded. 'Yes please. Can I use your telephone? I'd like to try the Airport before the rush.'

'Be my guest.' Said Charlie lightly. 'Did you sleep ok?'

'Fine. Better than Alex by all accounts,' she said, lifting the receiver, 'it took him hours to get comfortable.'

'Yer, poor old soldier.' Said Charlie, with a mocking smile.

Alexander walked into the room rubbing his side, 'Who are you calling old?' He croaked, taking a seat by the window. 'Have you got any tea? Oh, and painkillers!'

Charlie laughed. 'Coming right up!'

Tomoko was on the phone for almost an hour as Charlie and Alexander idly contemplated the passing traffic in the street below the balcony. 'How did you get involved in all of this?' Asked Charlie, sipping from his Snoopy printed mug.

'Why did I get involved in all of this would be a better question.' Remarked Alexander thoughtfully. 'I met Sonya ten days ago in a park in Tokyo, purely by chance. I wish you could have met her...'

Charlie listened attentively as Alexander revealed the poignant events of their time together and the days that followed. It quickly became apparent to him that the pictures were the key. If Alexander hadn't taken them, his girlfriend's murder would have ultimately remained an accident, his own personal pursuit stalled in its tracks and the Rama's Hope lost, perhaps forever. With them, it may well prove to be a different story.

'The photographs, are they any good?' He asked, disclosing his curiosity.

Alexander hobbled across the lounge to retrieve the packet. 'Judge for yourself.' He said, and tossed them to Charlie's seat.

Charlie skipped through them, from one print to another, selected those of the Rama's Hope and placed them separately on to the coffee table. 'Not bad at all! Sharp! Are the shots still on your camera card?'

Alexander nodded.

'Good, they may be useful.'

He thought quietly for a moment staring at the three photographs. When once again he lifted his gaze his face was alight with anticipation. 'I have a gem of an idea, Mister Webb.' The pun was clearly intended.

'It's Alex. You saved my life, remember? Tell me!'

'Ok. But first answer me this Alex. Why wasn't the stone stolen in America? They must have had the opportunity.'

'I would have thought ample opportunity, the first switch was made there. Then again, I suspect removing a valuable stone from any company like Gem International would be close to impossible. You'd expect security to be pretty tight in a place like that. No doubt that was the reason for using the sample box. My personal feeling is that it was destined for Japan from the outset, it stands to reason, why else would they use a Japanese market courier.'

'I agree. That takes care of the first switch. Now the second. Why should Kumagai go to the trouble of replacing the original with another copy?'

'For the same reason as the first, so as not to draw attention to the fact it was stolen.'

'Exactly. And it is just that fact that can work to our advantage. What I have in mind is this. We make another copy of the Rama's Hope ruby and perform the exercise for a third time. The closer we get, the higher the probability gets that we'll be in a position to make our own switch. Think about it. It's far less risky than trying to steal it. They'd be sure to send people after us to retrieve the gem the moment they discovered it was missing. This way, by the time it's reunited with the Emerald Buddha, it'll be too late. How's that for revenge?'

Alexander shook his head doubtfully. 'Sounds simple but we both know it's not going to be that easy. For a start, how on earth are we going to get a copy of sufficient quality made in a matter of hours.'

'You forget Alex,' said Charlie with a smile, 'this is Thailand! The home of the international ruby market, and the Royal Lapidary. Our success in this case is so important to the Thai people, that if I thought the King's crown would help secure the Rama's Hope, it would be given freely. All I would have to do is ask. That's the beauty of working on a king's commission. Basically, what Charlie wants, Charlie gets.'

Alexander picked up the photographs and examined them closely. 'Can they really make a copy from these?' He asked.

Charlie shook his head. 'From those alone, no. But thanks to Kraiwoot's research in the Lapidary files, we have sketches showing the exact measurements of the stone. A question, when you took these photographs did you correct for white balance?'

'I always do. It saves faffing about too much on photoshop.'

'That's brilliant! Then we have a good reference for the gem's colour also. With the photographs and the sketches together, it's more than possible.'

'How long is this likely to take?' Asked Alexander. Warming to the idea.

'It had better not take long.' Said Tomoko joining them, she'd been listening to the conversation whilst waiting for the flight information. 'We have until nine thirty tomorrow. Kumagai's confirmed his flight. He'll be leaving on Cathay Pacific flight CX 700 in the morning. He's going to Hong Kong.'

CHAPTER 32

'Take a drink, it's free. Customer relations, good eh?' Said Charlie, passing through the front doors of the Royal Lapidary and on to the tray of refreshments at the reception. A large group of mixed nationalities was also waiting. 'We've become quite a tourist attraction in recent years.' He said, taking a can of Coke for himself. 'I suggest that you join in with the tour while I go to see about the arrangements. I'll fetch you later, there is someone I would like you to meet.' Blowing a kiss to the pretty, shorthaired girl behind the desk, he strolled off down the corridor.

With an ice cool Singha beer in their hands an elegantly dressed stewardess lead them into a small cinema and requested them all to sit. The room darkened and the screen crackled into life.

A half-hour documentary followed, showing Thailand as one of the largest sources of gemstones in the world. From the open face mining of rubies and sapphires, two hundred and eighty kilometres south east of Bangkok in the Chanthaburi and Trat provinces, to the cutting and polishing of the stones by skilled craftsmen.

As the lights came up the same stewardess walked to the front of the auditorium. She bowed to them gracefully with her hands clasped together as if in prayer. 'Ladies and Gentlemen, if you will follow me please, I will lead you through our workshops, where you will see many of the processes shown in the film for yourselves.'

They followed her down a sterile looking arcade of glazed windows, the glass separating them from clinically equipped studios on both sides. As they passed, she explained that these were the rooms where the more precious gems were set. At the end of the corridor was a thirty foot square, air conditioned room buzzing with activity. It was filled with small individual workstations, laid out in two distinct zones. Sizing and rough cutting had been placed around the edges with a collection of green painted machines dedicated to polishing and finishing on a island in the middle.

The guide led them from one process to another. Alexander was fascinated. Watching with interest as a single rough stone, mounted in a pencil-like jig called a dop, was skilfully preformed into an oval with a diamond-impregnated grinding wheel. When that stage was completed it was passed to a scaife, with finer particles, for the grinding of dozens of facets into the surface. The stone quickly blackened with the dust, seeing the detail at this stage was largely a matter of touch. Each man in that room was undeniably a specialist in his chosen field. The stone was passed to one of the centre stations and yet another cutting wheel embedded with extraordinarily fine diamond grit for the final stages of polishing. The result, a stone with a mirror like surface in just over one hour.

Charlie came to his side, placing a hand on his shoulder. 'Most foreigners and Thai dealers find the local cutting prices in Bangkok and Chanthaburi highly attractive.' He said, 'As a rule we pay a little more to attract the best. But in general, throughout Thailand, workers who earn around Fifty dollars a day, collectively cut rubies and sapphires worth more than half a billion dollars each year.'

'How is it that Thailand has become so successful in this business?' Asked Alexander.

Charlie led them to the sales room as he talked. 'In addition to abundant natural resources, the Thai prospectors and dealers saw an opportunity and made the most of it. On a large scale, the local gem dealers persuaded the government to drop the import and export taxes to create a climate for growth. Then they systematically built a market to supply global buyers with a huge variety of polished stones and finished jewellery. Combine that with the luxury hotels and a non-stop entertainment district catering to every whim in Patpong, and you've got a marketing package that is almost irresistible.'

'Tantalising is what I'd call it.' Said Alexander, looking down into a glass topped cabinet. A whistle of amazement breathed through his lips, 'You'd need to be a millionaire to afford any of this stuff.'

One of the sales girls heard his remark and walked over. 'See anything you like, madam?' She said, addressing her remark to Tomoko.

'Everything, but I really cannot afford it.' She said.

'I think you will be pleasantly surprised. Please allow me to show you a few pieces.'

Tomoko pointed to a ring of seven rubies, glinting like fire in the halogen display lights. A total of point nine carats, arranged in a single bow, on a setting of pure yellow gold.

'Madam has excellent taste! Please, try it on.' Suggested the sales girl with the briefest of nods and a sparkling smile. 'Forgive me for testing you madam, but would you care to hazard a guess at the price?'

Tomoko flushed. 'Oh? I've no idea. Eight hundred dollars?' She said, hoping she hadn't quoted too low. The price would certainly be much higher in Kyoto.

The girl removed the folded price tag from the tray and opened it with the poise of a conjuror. It read two hundred and five U.S. dollars. Like magic, Tomoko reached for her American express card.

Charlie leaned over to the assistant and whispered into her ear. She nodded again and smiled at Tomoko. 'I'm sorry,' she said, 'I never realised. As a staff purchase, I am permitted to offer you a further fifteen percent discount.' She turned, and taking the card with her, walked to the cash register.

Tomoko beamed like a little child opening her first Christmas present. 'So, you really do work here!' She said, her doubts finally dispelled, 'Thank you Charlie.'

'I'm pleased to have been of help, my dear.' He said in an exaggerated English accent.

With the small lapis coloured box in her handbag, Tomoko followed Alexander and Charlie down a flight of steps to a pair of solid stainless steel vault doors. A video camera above them showed their presence on a monitor inside. The doors unlatched as Charlie approached.

Once inside, a middle-aged man in circular wire framed glasses walked up to greet them. With the air of a general, his mannerisms were that of a butler demanding the respect awarded him by the superiority of his position. Charlie shook his hand warmly.

'Alexander Webb and Tomoko Den, I would like you to meet Nukul Aksorn. Mr Aksorn is our Chief Assessor, Mister Kraiwoot's successor, and my personal friend for many years.' Charlie patted him lightly on the back.

'I'm pleased to meet you both.' He said calmly, 'Mister Webb, Chanarong Tan told me of your adventures last night, a most interesting way for you both to meet, I'm sure. Please, come to my office, it's at the back of the vault.'

Numerous dark green cabinets lined the passageway through the sealed chamber to a glass walled room at the end. Aksorn held the door open wide and beckoned them to enter. 'Please, make yourselves comfortable.' He said.

Charlie spoke to him in Thai, explaining their plans for making a duplicate of the Rama's hope, while Tomoko and Alexander examined the stones on his desk. The colours varied from a pure red with a hint of blue, which Alexander identified with the descriptions of a Pigeon's Blood ruby, to a pale pink more closely associated with Tourmaline Rubellite. None of the stones on the white baize was less than five carats.

'Well Mister Webb, Miss Den,' Aksorn had switched to English, 'you've set me quite a challenge. To put your minds at rest from the beginning, I believe I can help you. I will arrange for the facsimile to be delivered to Chanarong Tan's apartment at seven tomorrow morning.'

'Terrific, thank you! I imagine this request is something out of the ordinary. Do you make many fakes?' Alexander was curious.

'Oh boy! What a question!' Charlie raised his hands to his face and turned away in shame.

'The answer to your inquiry is, very rarely. We find the genuine articles a much more profitable enterprise. Of course, one of my duties for the Royal Lapidary is the identification of counterfeit gems, Mister Webb. So I know one when I see one. Recently the market has become, how should I say this, saturated with sub standard stones and deliberate forgeries. A sign of the times I expect.'

Aksorn walked to a cabinet of thin metal shelves to the right of his desk and pulled out a draw. He placed three, twenty-carat gems onto the baize in front of them. 'You like games Mister Webb?'

Alexander nodded and smiled uneasily.

'Good! Then let's see how you fare with this one. One of these is a true and valuable ruby, one has been artificially grown and the other is a piece of cut glass. Tell me Mister Webb, which would you pay a million dollars for?' Aksorn sat smugly in his chair waiting for the answer.

'If I had a million dollars Mister Aksorn, someone would probably want it back.' Said Alexander with a grin. Then picking up one of the stones, he raised it to the light and examined it carefully through a strong loupe. At twenty five times magnification the first appeared obvious. 'There are microscopic bubbles in this one, I would say this is the glass sample.'

'Good!'

The clarity of the remaining two was vastly different, both dark red, one was purer than the other. Alexander selected the cleanest one of the two. 'This is the other fake.' He said with confidence. 'You know I'm no expert, but from what I have read, I would expect some inclusions in a genuine ruby of this size, like those in the third stone, on your desk.'

Aksorn nodded slowly and looked towards Charlie. 'Your friend has studied well, Tan.'

'Mister Aksorn, how exactly will you make our ruby?' Asked Tomoko.

'Well you've already seen that glass is out of the question, in a stone of this size it would be far too easy to detect, even for an amateur.' He smiled at Alexander. 'No. What I propose is a process a little more sophisticated. It's called the flame fusion process, I believe it originated in France at the turn of the century. We start with colourless aluminium oxide powder as the base and mix other powdered elements to it to influence the colour. For example, with blue we add titanium and iron, for green we add cobalt, for yellow we use nickel instead of iron, and in this case, for the desirable red colour we will be adding chromium oxide powder. The sword shaped inclusion in the centre I'm afraid must remain my secret. The method for making the stone is surprisingly simple. The powder is dropped from a hopper through a hydrogen flame. As it passes through this flame the powder liquefies, landing on a seed crystal beneath, where it solidifies. At this stage the ruby crystal is called a boule. The largest one we've had cause to make so far measured seven centimetres in height and two in width, it took us around five and a half hours to grow it. I conservatively estimate that the boule for your stone will take in the region of eleven to twelve hours. After all, the Rama's Hope is quite a bit wider. No worries, we can easily manage it in the time.'

Alexander removed the photographs and camera flash card from his pocket. 'Charlie says that with these, and your sketches, you should be able to get pretty close to the original, is that so?'

Aksorn removed his glasses replacing them with a loupe to examine the photographs closely. 'Fine pictures young man, the detail in the inclusion is particularly good. ' He said, lifting his head.

'Thank you.' Alexander smiled, partly at the compliment and partly at the sight of Aksorn's comical stare, one normal eye twinned with the mechanically magnified iris on the other.

Aksorn returned to his study. 'Yes, a difficult task, but well within our capabilities I assure you, you have my word. With these and the original sketches, even I will be hard pushed to tell the duplicate from the original.'

Aksorn rose and walked to his wall mounted collection of butterflies. He stood there a moment thinking. 'It is just possible that this replica may cause some confusion at a later date. Although manufactured by hand, the very nature of it's quality, and the fact that it will have the same chemical composition as the real ruby, could make it desirable to an unskilled collector. After passing three centuries without one, It wouldn't do to have two Rama's Hope Rubies at the same time, now would it?'

Tomoko chuckled.

Aksorn was deadly serious. 'Because of this I will have to add a safety feature, a mark of some kind engraved onto the girdle of the finished gem. Nothing too obvious I assure you. It's a common practice with valuable stones nowadays and we have the latest state of the art laser equipment specifically for that purpose. It will be photographed and documented here and a copy will be supplied to you. If you don't mind, when you have finished with the duplicate, I would like you to return it. To save any future embarrassment, I will see to it, that it is destroyed. Is that satisfactory?'

Tomoko, Alexander and Charlie all nodded.

Aksorn walked to the doorway. 'Then I wish you the very best of luck in your venture my friends. If I am to get this completed before the morning, I will have to make a start immediately. I hope you will find time to come back and see me when you have the Rama's Hope safely back in your hands. Please, give me a call when you return.'

He shook each of their hands as they passed, acknowledging their thanks with a brief bow. Then, standing in his office doorway he watched as Charlie guided them back through the vault and up to the showroom.

'Can you imagine being sacked from a job like that?' Said Alexander emerging into the sunlight, 'You'd be set for life!' He mimed, playfully, sneaking a handful of gems and secreting them into his pocket.

Charlie laughed, 'You've got a criminal mind, Webb.'

'Yes! Maybe it takes one to catch one.' Said Alexander, climbing into Charlie's Volkswagen Beetle, 'With that thought in mind, I think we should return to your apartment. If I were Kumagai, I'd be searching high and low for us right now. So we may as well take it easy. For us, the pressure's off, we know where he'll be tomorrow morning and we'll have our own gem, I'd say that gives us an advantage.'

CHAPTER 33

Reclining his Japan Airlines first class seat, Charlie gave a sigh of relief, he was finally calming down. Breakfast had passed enjoyably in the relaxed atmosphere, and the tension of avoiding Kumagai at the airport was over. Undoubtedly, he would be preparing for his next appointment, somewhere near by in their shared sky on a parallel flight path.

The original plan of arriving in Hong Kong before him had been thwarted by their last minute bookings. The Thai International flights had all been full. Consequently the hour prior to take off had been filled with anxiety. Avoiding Kumagai's anxious stares around the departure hall, waiting nervously for him to board, then running like madmen for the flight, making their seats with barely a minute to spare. Both flights had departed on the dot of nine thirty.

'Alex. Tomoko.' Charlie handed them both a small walkie-talkie transceiver, 'If we're to find him, we will have to split up when we arrive. Our flight is scheduled to touch down five minutes after Kumagai's, so we'll need these to stay in touch. I suggest Tomoko, you take the arrival gate, Alex, the baggage claim, and as he is less likely to recognise me, I will take Immigration and the entrance. With luck they should let us through the customs formalities quickly with my pass. If you see him press this button and speak clearly.' Over the next few minutes Charlie explained the workings of the intercoms. 'If we loose him at the airport, heaven knows how long it will take to track him down again, so stay on your toes.'

'What's the range?' Asked Alexander.

'Around two miles.'

'Good. Then whichever one of us spots him, stays with him. If he takes a cab, we follow, alone if necessary. If we loose contact with each other, we'll meet at the ferry, Kowloon side at three, Agreed?'

'Agreed.' Said Tomoko and Charlie in unison.

A stewardess approached with a tray of sparkling champagne. 'Would you care for refreshment sir?' She said, addressing Alexander.

'Yes, thank you.' He said taking one of the JAL engraved glasses, 'I would also like to use the telephone, do you have one on board?'

The stewardess smiled. 'Of course sir. I will bring it to you directly.'

Chief Superintendent Hara was holding a staff meeting when the call came in.

'Forgive me gentlemen.' He said, glowering at his secretary. His request for her to hold his calls had clearly gone unheeded. 'Hara Des!' He barked.

'Hi Chief, its Alexander Webb.'

'Cha ta ma te - One moment please,' he said, changing his tone and covering the mouthpiece, 'Gentlemen, I'm sorry, but this is rather important, we will resume in thirty minutes.'

The staff stood and left.

Hara reached to the row of buttons on the telephone housing and pressed for Captain Aono to pick up the extension, to listen in. 'So you're still alive young man! I was beginning to worry about you. Tomoko-San, is she with you?'

'Yes sir. We're both well. I just thought you might like to know that one of your people, Sergeant Kumagai, tried to kill me a couple of nights ago.'

'Interesting. I'm pleased to hear he didn't succeed. Where is he now?'

'We're following him to Hong Kong, he's on flight CX700 from Bangkok. Have you managed to build a case yet?'

Hara was silent for a moment. 'Not exactly. Believe me I've tried. Every avenue we take meets with resistance. We're receiving all kinds of red tape from the Deputy Commissioner General's office and every order I give in connection with this case appears to be countermanded with feeble excuses. My resource request has been denied, and to top it all, I've been ordered to drop all further investigations. There is something very strange going on here. I fear it's much worse than we both first thought.'

Alexander could feel Hara's frustration. 'It sounds to me like Kumagai's not the only one involved.'

Hara sighed, 'I hate to say this, but that's becoming patently obvious, and there is very little we can do about it. All of our proof so far is circumstantial, even Kumagai's fingerprints on the stone can be easily explained away. You see, he was the officer who dispatched Miss Martin's personal effects to her company in America. We need something solid. As a contingency, and with the help of Captain Aono, I've formed a group of my most trusted men, they're prepared to take leave and are ready to act the moment either you or Kumagai return to Japan. One wrong move on his account and we'll pull him in.'

Alexander looked across the isle at Tomoko and Charlie, the smiles were back on their faces. Past them, through the window the South China Sea glinted in the sunlight. He'd known all along that they would have to face the task alone, Hara had just confirmed it. 'We'll do what we can to get you all the proof you need. I'll stay in touch.'

He handed the phone back to the passing stewardess and took a deep calming breath, 'So, it's just the three of us then.' He said, quietly airing his thoughts. He lifted his glass and silently toasted his travelling companions.

Waving for his attention, Tomoko pointed out of the window. 'We're coming into land.' She said.

Alexander moved to the seat behind them to take in the view. As the plane banked to the left, Hong Kong Island with its towering skyscrapers shone like a jewel. Ahead of them lay the runway of Chek Lap Kok International Airport and clearly visible was it's showpiece terminal, the biggest in the world. A truly breathtaking sight.

The 747 hit the tarmac hard and taxied noisily to the apron of the terminal building, all eyes were on the seat belt sign. The moment it went out they stood and moved towards the exit.

Charlie handed Alexander his jacket, 'The one advantage of travelling first class, is that you get to leave the plane first.' He said with a grin and lifting his walkie-talkie, 'Good luck, stay in touch.'

Tomoko led the way, walking quickly through to the gate, Alexander and Charlie followed. The corridors were surprisingly clear, a few dozen people, no more. Alexander checked the arrivals table on a high mounted television screen. Flight CX700 had landed on time. 'We'd better hurry.' He said breaking into a jog.

The walkie-talkie beeped and Tomoko spoke, 'Kumagai's plane's empty, I'll see you in the lobby.'

Alexander and Charlie ran hard for the immigration queues hoping to see him there. Just as they arrived they could see his familiar profile passing between the row of official's desks and through to the baggage claim on the far side. 'Dam!' Cursed Alexander, 'He's through, what now?' He called despondently, stalling to a walk. The remaining rows of passengers seemed endless.

'This way.' Shouted Charlie still running, 'At the far end! The Air Crew channel!'

Panting, he placed both of their immigration forms onto the counter beneath his official ID. 'Please, we're in a hurry.' He appealed breathlessly in Cantonese.

The official's face did not change. 'Passports.'

Alexander strained for a view past the cubicles, hoping to see the direction Kumagai had taken. He was gone. Precious seconds ticked by as the blue uniformed policeman checked the forms and Charlie's card. He nodded, slowly pressed the square immigration service black stamp into the visas page of their passports, raised his head and smiled. 'Enjoy your stay gentlemen.' He said.

Again they ran, this time in separate directions, Alexander headed for the baggage claim and Charlie for the customs and exit.

The spotless claim hall was packed. Walking quickly from one belt to another he checked the flight numbers. 700, this was it. Pushing his way through the crowds he searched for the face, scanning the area on tiptoe, the extra height didn't help, he couldn't see him. He lifted the walkie-talkie from his pocket, 'Tomoko, I need your help. Come to the baggage area I'll be at the customs counters, maybe I'll spot him there.'

'I'm on my way.' She responded, he could hear her running.

'Charlie, come in Charlie.' Called Alexander.

'Any luck Alex? I can't see him here...No...Wait...Got Him! He's leaving the building. You get the bags, I'll follow him.' With a squawk the walkie-talkie went silent.

Tomoko's touch on his arm startled him. 'You were quick,' he said leading her to the baggage carousel, 'Charlie spotted him.'

'Yes I heard, so did the guard at the passport desk come to that. Very embarrassing!' She smiled.

Picking up the bags they passed into the arrivals lounge. Charlie was standing by the exit with his fingers running through his hair. A clear sign he was desperate.

'I thought you'd be gone. What happened?' Asked Alexander anxiously.

'A car met him out front. I tried to call a cab, they were all taken. I'm sorry but I think we've lost him. I got the car number though, maybe we can trace it. DT 5877'

Tomoko moved to comfort him, 'What kind of car was it?'

'A Rolls. Green I think.'

'And the driver?'

'Chinese, in a white uniform.'

She smiled secretly and walked to a pay phone at the side of the glass doors to make her call.

'Sorry Alex, I really screwed up. Where's she going?'

Alexander shrugged his shoulders, 'Search me.' He said. 'Lets grab a coffee, maybe we can work something out.'

Tomoko joined them a few minutes later. They were both dejected, staring at themselves in the mirror behind the counter 'Cheer up you two, It's not exactly the end of the world, it could be worse. I've ordered us a taxi, it'll be here soon. I also took the liberty of booking us into a hotel. I felt sure you wouldn't mind.'

Without a word they both shook their heads. With the smile still on her face she sipped at Alexander's coffee. 'Ugh, too much sugar.'

Ten minutes passed and a white liveried chauffeur entered the lobby. Tomoko stepped from her chair and lifted her suitcase. 'Come on boys, the car's here. I've a sneaking suspicion we'll find Kumagai sooner than you think!' She said cheerily.

The chauffeur led the way and opened the boot to receive their luggage. The perfect deep green paintwork glowed with indulgence, matched only by the soft luxury of the Connolly leather interior and the classical sculpture of the "Spirit of Ecstasy" gracing the radiator at the front.

Alexander stared in amazement at Tomoko as her smile changed to a childish giggle. 'You knew all along didn't you!' He said.

Charlie stood at his side, open mouthed in disbelief. 'But how..?'

CHAPTER 33

With seemingly effortless progress the elegant Rolls Royce Phantom smoothed the ripples of the duel carriageway, on route to Kowloon. The roads, as expected, were far from clear. Alexander, gazing admiringly out of the window, he simply could not believe or even understand their good fortune. Resigned to delving the depths of despair, they had somehow elevated themselves to riding in the heights of luxury, with a Technicolor ray of hope on the horizon.

'You are an amazing woman Tomoko. How did you know?' He asked, easing the wire frame from the chilled Moet Chandon nestling in the silver cooler between them.

'I felt sure one of you would have recognised the car.' She said, steadying her glass as Alexander poured. 'We're heading for the Peninsular Hotel. One of the finest hotels in the Pacific. I was treated to an afternoon tea there once during a fact finding tour. The service was impeccable and the feeling of luxury almost unbelievable. I have a feeling you're going to like it, that is, until we get the bill.'

Charlie dismissed the comment with a wave of his hand, 'Don't worry about that, we're on an expense account!'

Considering his depleting reserves Alexander offered his champagne flute in salute. 'Thanks Charlie, it's appreciated.' He said.

'You're welcome Alex. Now, Tomoko, why are we destined to suffer this unavoidable decadence?'

'Well, the car was the key. The Peninsula happens to own one of the largest fleets of Rolls Royce cars in the world. As I've been down this path before, it wasn't difficult to make the connection. I called the Hotel to check if Kumagai-San had a reservation. When they confirmed that he had, I asked them to reserve us two rooms as close as possible to his and arrange for a chauffeur to pick us up from the airport. My final request to them was for them to keep our visit discreet, I told them he was a relative and it was meant to be a surprise.'

'And they agreed?' Queried Alexander.

'No problem.'

'That's my girl!' Said Alexander with a satisfied smile, placing his arm around her shoulders and closing it in a playful hug.

They chatted amicably for the remainder of the fifteen-minute journey to the crescent beneath the glazed entrance doors of the Peninsular. Two porters, as though by remote control, descended the steps as the car rolled to it's standstill, taking up positions one at the rear for the luggage and one at the passenger door. Both nodded politely in greeting.

'Hang on here for a minute.' Whispered Charlie, indicating they should wait in the car, 'I'll check the coast is clear first, there's still a chance he might be in the foyer.'

He turned from them and climbed the five steps between two stone Chinese lions and through the tended open door. He could imagine a president waiting in the car outside as he played the role, standing erect and scanning the large reception hall like royalty. No sign of Kumagai. He glanced over his shoulder and nodded slowly.

With a welcoming smile, the door porter guided them through the spacious gilt columned lobby and on to the reception desk. 'Good morning Miss Den.' Welcomed the duty manager, 'We are honoured to have you and your party as our guests. We have reserved two rooms both in your name. That is correct?'

Tomoko nodded.

'You are to be located on the fifth floor, the room of your cousin is between you. I assume this is satisfactory?' He asked, knowing it would be.

Charlie, standing close at her side nodded enthusiastically. 'That will be perfect.' He said.

With the check in formalities completed for them on their behalf, the duty manager leaned secretively forward to address Tomoko, as if sharing a little known confidence. 'As you requested Madam, your presence here has been concealed from your cousin, I sincerely hope your surprise will be all that you've planned it to be.'

'So do I!' Said Tomoko with a wry smile, 'So do I.'

A porter appeared at her side with the keys in his hands. 'Please to follow me?' He said, directing them towards the lifts. 'I show you to your rooms.'

The spacious florally decorated suite overlooked the courtyard and the bay beyond. Alexander stood at the window absorbing the spectacular skyline. Dwarfed in the distance, the high rise office buildings on the island of Hong Kong shimmered in sympathy with the sunlight dancing on the crests of the waves. A couple of ageing two tiered ferries jostled for position with sampans, container ships and sailing boats on the bustling waterway, and below on the far side of the road dividing the hotel from the promenade, courting couples walked arm in arm, oblivious to his observations.

A knock at the door disturbed his moment of reflection; he turned to answer it, leaving Tomoko to her unpacking.

Cautiously Alexander checked the spyglass before opening. Save for the two hotel staff the hallway appeared clear. Slowly he eased the door ajar and allowed them to enter. The first carried a silver tray bearing an assortment of imported soaps in ornate plastic boxes, he was followed by the second with a large bowl of exotic fruits to compliment the pot of Jasmine tea delivered to the room prior to their arrival.

As they filed past him he checked the hallway once again. Luckily his reactions were razor sharp. With the briefest of glimpses he stepped back into the room unseen. Extinguishing a cigar at the far end of the corridor stood Kumagai, alert, visually checking each of the occupants as they alighted from the deep pile carpeted lift. One second earlier and he would have been seen and their element of surprise lost.

With his back against the closed door Alexander breathed a sigh of relief. His heart raced, fuelled by the near miss and the conscious awareness that Kumagai's room was now unoccupied. He would have to act quickly.

He returned to the bedroom considering his options, passing a cursory glance over the tray offered by one of the waiters on his way to the telephone. He pointed to the embossed emblem of a horse and cart on the brown marble effect box, housing a bar of Hermes Equipage and asked the other waiter to poor the tea while he lifted the handset to call the desk manager.

The request was unorthodox to say the least, and he knew it. His appeal was for one of the waiters to accompany him into Kumagai's room in order to leave clues as to their presence in the Hotel, a continuation of their game of hide and seek. Thankfully the manager agreed, with one proviso, in the interest of security, he himself would assist them.

Alexander spent the next few minutes locating his automatic tape recorder; he replaced the batteries and wiped the digital memory to give the longest possible recording time. There was no telling how long this would take. Then selecting one of the Peninsula Hotel matchbooks from the stationary pile on the desk he wrote, *'Ferry pier, ten p.m.'* on the inside and handed it to Tomoko. 'This is for the benefit of the Manager,' he said, 'show it to him, then have him follow you into Kumagai's bathroom and place it next to the sink, that will get him out of the way while I place the recorder. Got it?'

She nodded, rapidly grasping the situation.

As the waiters left the manager appeared, all smiles. 'Your game has brightened my morning enormously Miss Den, how can I be of help?' He asked.

Skilfully Tomoko guided him to Kumagai's room chatting incessantly as he inserted the passkey into the lock. Alexander and Charlie followed close behind, watching Tomoko flip open the cover to the matchbook and lead the way into the bathroom. Within a matter of seconds Alexander had primed the recorder and placed it beneath the bed. Charlie headed straight for the desk, tearing the top few pages from the note pad beside the telephone before joining Alexander in his study of a watercolour of what looked to be an English country scene hanging in the hallway close to the entrance.

Alexander tapped his forehead as they were about to leave, an exaggerated gesture designed to give the impression of a momentary lapse of memory.

'We should have signed it Tomoko.' He said, deftly side stepping past the manager towards the bathroom door, 'He'll never guess it's from us if we don't. I won't be a minute.'

Once inside he switched the matchbook for one from the toiletry basket beside the sink and concealed the written one in his trouser pocket. The manager was just entering as he made his way back to the hallway.

'All done!' Said Alexander extending his hand towards him, 'Your help is very much appreciated sir, thank you. As Sherlock Holmes would have put it, the game is afoot.'

'My pleasure Mister Webb. Please let me know how it turns out.'

CHAPTER 34

Charlie sat thoughtful as Alexander and Tomoko sipped gingerly at the scalding Chinese tea. In front of him lay the top page from the note pad, locally blackened by the gentle rubbing of a soft leaded pencil over the white vellum.

The indentation was bold and legible. *"Chang,"* followed by a Hong Kong Island address and telephone number in Kana Japanese.

'Here's one for your address book Alex.' He said, passing him the sheet.

Alexander studied it. Upright, then playfully on it's side, it meant nothing to him. It did however resemble the trail of an ink footed spider, should such a thing exist and presumably after a few beers. He thought of mentioning it, but decided against it.

Taking the address back, Charlie copied it into his notebook. 'It may come to nothing, but we'll have to check it out. Assuming there hasn't been a Japanese visitor in the room before our friend, this could well be his local contact. I wish we'd heard the call.' His disappointment was curiously contagious. 'What we really need is a back up to the tape recorder. I should have thought of it earlier, we could have left one of the walkie-talkies in there.'

'You think that's wise?' Asked Tomoko.

'With the recorder on it's own we'll have to wait until morning when the maid cleans the room, that's about the earliest chance we'll have to retrieve it. With the walkie-talkie we'd be able to eves drop all night. Should something happen in there, we'd know instantly.'

'The walkie-talkie's too risky, they've already proved too useful to lose one. How about a baby intercom?' Suggested Tomoko, 'My neighbours have one to hear their daughter when she cries. They plug it straight into the mains and the signal comes through the house wiring system. It might work here.'

Charlie stood and slipped on his jacket. 'Just what we need! You two wait here, it'll be safer if you don't step outside until dark. I won't be long. Back in half an hour or so.'

Alexander followed him to the door to wish him good luck, and as Charlie left, placed the *"Do not disturb"* sign over the outside handle before closing it.

Tomoko was sat perched on the corner of the bed reading the hotel literature on his return to the bedroom. 'It's all here Alex, everything you wanted to know about Hong Kong, but were afraid to ask. Did you know that in Cantonese, Hong Kong means Fragrant Harbour?' She asked, reading from a small booklet entitled "The Official Hong Kong Guide". 'It says here that it gets its name from a pre-colonial fishing port near Aberdeen. Apparently, the area was known for producing and distributing incense. If my memory serves me correctly, Aberdeen is still a major fishing port today, on the far side of the island. It's where most of the boat people live. For a few Hong Kong dollars you can tour the area in a sampan, I'm told it's most enjoyable.'

Alexander sat at her side, peering over her shoulder at the pictures. Tomoko read on. 'Kowloon, Kow lung in Cantonese, is also a descriptive name meaning Nine Dragons, and derived from an ancient Chinese belief that the surrounding mountains were inhabited by them. Kowloon itself has eight peaks, the ninth being named after the boy emperor Ping, who because of his regal status, was also believed to be a dragon.'

Alexander drifted his gaze around the room as Tomoko read. A door between the bed and the outside wall focused his attention. It was a connecting door between their room and Kumagai's. He moved to try it. On his side it opened with ease, on Kumagai's, it was locked. *'Shame!'* He thought, and returned to the bed. Getting in there the first time had been easy, using the same method again would surely arouse suspicion. He would have to think of another way and what better place to think than up to his neck in bubbles, it worked during his studies, why shouldn't it work now? 'I'm going to take a bath.' He said. 'Join me?'

Tomoko nodded, smiled seductively and lead the way, reading as she walked, barely lifting her gaze from the page.

Using the key Alexander had given him, Charlie let himself back into the room and tossed the gift-wrapped box onto the bed.

'Oops, sorry,' he said, entering the bathroom, 'just checking you were still here.' He backed out and closed the door behind him. From the hallway he called, 'I've got the intercoms. Any suggestions how we get back in there?'

Alexander stepped from the bath and wrapped himself in one of the hotel's dressing gowns. 'There's a connecting door between the two rooms but it's locked.' He said, his voice echoing in the tiled room.

'I'll see what I can do.' Replied Charlie, settling down to unwrapping the box.

Alexander smiled as he watched Tomoko submerge in the bath water, rinsing the soap from her hair. 'I learned to swim like that.' He said, handing her a towel. 'Step out and I'll dry you off.'

As they emerged into the bedroom Charlie was lying on the bed watching the muted television. A distant thud of a closing door and a patter of footsteps emanated from a small white plastic box resting on the bedside table to his right. At his feet, cardboard and polystyrene packing lay strewn over the covers.

'You did it Charlie? How?' Alexander shook his head in disbelief.

Charlie raised a finger to his lips, 'Shh, I'm listening,' he said, then with the other hand he lifted a key ring with a selection of thin skeleton keys. 'Old hotel, old locks!' The statement was matter-of-fact, although his manner was clearly one of pride.

Alexander sat at his side and listened. He whispered, 'Can he hear us.'

'Only if you want him to Alex. You can press the button on the top to speak, I don't think it's a good idea to try it at the moment though.'

Kumagai was not alone, that was clear. The shuffling noises were too much for one person. Alexander guessed there were at least three.

CHAPTER 35

'Whisky?' Suggested Kumagai, approaching the recessed drinks cabinet to the right of the television.

Chang nodded his approval silently as Taylor walked to the window. 'On the rocks for me, Kumagai. Say, Matsumoto sure looks after you guys, nice place.' Taylor's drawl was pure Deep South.

Kumagai watched them both carefully in an attempt to assess which of them would pose the most resistance to his proposal. Taylor was obviously the more confident of the two. He guessed he would be Ling's security adviser. A powerfully built, flamboyantly dressed American, with undoubtedly a similar background to his own. Chang on the other hand was an unknown quantity. In his mid fifty's, short, wiry and quietly spoken. He presumably was Ling's eyes and ears. A shade too timid for this type of operation, he thought.

Kumagai placed the drinks on the coffee table between the florally decorated sofas and sat facing Chang. He smiled. 'At last we meet, Mister Chang. I find telephones so impersonal, don't you agree?'

Chang lifted his glass and raised it in a toast. 'Just so, Mister Kumagai. By your visit, may I assume Matsumoto has met with our security demands?'

'He has indeed. And, were he here now, he would almost certainly reprimand me for informing you it was with great personal dedication and expense. If you will permit me, I'll show you the detail.' Kumagai stood to collect a roll of drawings from his suitcase and laid them flat onto the table. Taylor turned to join them, sitting next to his colleague.

Removing a pen from his breast pocket Kumagai addressed the key to the top left. 'The castle is now equipped with the following systems. The crosses indicate monitored video cameras, squares armed guards, PIR mostly in the staterooms and the stars, laser sources for the electronic trip-wire net. All of the ground level windows are alarmed and the local external telephones, tapped with instant tracers.'

'That's quite a system you've got there, the security personnel, local men?' Taylor's tone made clear his mistrust of amateurs.

Kumagai could almost read his thoughts, 'Certainly some of them are, but most of them are from the circuit. It's quite possible you'll recognise a few faces, the instructors for example served in the Gulf. And before you ask, none of them will know the true reasons for the gathering. They will simply be serving under the impression that they are safeguarding the contents and dignitaries at a private auction, and we will keep that piece of information until the last possible moment. We thought it would be safer that way.'

Taylor nodded, sinking back into the sofa indicating that his work was completed. 'Looks good to me Chang, what do you think?'

Chang studied the plans with care. Kumagai had his answer, Chang took the decisions. Folding the drawings the lean Chinaman placed them inside a slim briefcase. 'I will keep these if you don't mind? Mister Ling, I'm sure would like to appraise them in person. You have still to tell us of the local police force. What have you arranged with them? Are they likely to be a problem?' His eyes were cold as his stare penetrated deeply into Kumagai's.

'A shrewd question Mister Chang, and I believe I have an astute answer. A particular item at the gathering will be withdrawn. Namely, the fifth century B.C. head of a bearded man in Greek terra cotta. I hope this was not one of the articles of interest for Mister Ling, as I would like you to remove it from your available item list. Matsumoto-San and I agree it would make a fitting reward for the Deputy Commissioner General of police in return for his co-operation. Apparently he's an ardent collector, and let's face it, everyone has their price.'

Chang bowed slowly with respect.

'An admirable compromise Mister Kumagai, you are to be commended.'

Kumagai returned the gesture. 'Thank you sir.' He said. 'Mister Taylor, In the interest of security, how may I ask do you propose to deliver your entry?'

Taking a pencil and paper from the desk, Taylor rested his forearms onto the coffee table and began to sketch. Kumagai looked on with surprise. For such a big man the developing drawing was delicate and full of detail. A simple walking cane crowned by a hemispherical globe fractionally larger than a half walnut to form the handle.

'Ling's no spring chicken, right?' Said Taylor, briefly looking up, 'so what better way than to have the old man bring the gem in himself, in his own hand. He loved the idea the instant I had it. We made him a walking cane with the ruby set as a bulb on the top. It's so obvious it wouldn't be spotted in a million years. A hundred and twelve carats in broad daylight and right under the customs officer's nose.' Taylor placed the pencil next to his sketch and lifted his glass of whisky. 'Brilliant, even though I say so myself!' He said, emptying the contents and presenting it for a refill.

'Then, am I to take it that you will be joining us?' Asked Kumagai hopefully.

Chang nodded. 'I will make my recommendations to Mister Ling. Suffice it to say that from what I have seen, I think we can assume he will be satisfied.'

CHAPTER 36

Tomoko scanned down her notes of the conversation, 'I'm worried Alex. Up until now I felt sure we were in control. Finding a murderer in one thing, but this is something else.'

'You're right to be worried. Remember our conversation with Koyanagi? The fourth ruby?' Alexander lifted his mobile phone from his breast pocket and dialled.

'He told us that it was in the hands of a Triad syndicate. Coincidence? Maybe, maybe not?'

Charlie reached for Alexander's packet of cigarettes, a nervous reaction. 'This is heavy Alex, Triad's are bad news. Have you any idea what we're getting into?'

Alexander shook his head. 'At the moment no. If we stay calm and stay out of sight, we'll be ok. Hara's the one I'm worried about, I'm calling him now.'

The distant end purred for some time before being answered by Captain Aono. Alexander asked to speak to the Chief.

'I'm glad you called Webb-San,' Aono was audibly nervous, 'we need to talk. Chief Superintendent Hara has been suspended. He's under house arrest. There's a team of officers turning over his office and apartment as we speak. I'll call you later when it's safe. Give me your number.'

Alexander relayed the number and ended the call.

The three of them sat in silence waiting, each of them hoping the other would speak first. Tomoko broke the ice. 'What do we do now Alex? We can't just sit here!'

'You're right. Let's take it a step at a time. What have we got to go on?' Alexander counted each item down on his fingers. 'One, Sonya was killed for the Rama's Hope, right? Two, the Triad's have another ruby they want to dispose of, or show for some reason. Three, there's a list of items for something called the gathering, and four, a castle with high security, probably somewhere in Japan.'

'Why Japan? Why not here in Hong Kong or China?' Asked Charlie.

'It must be Japan, or they wouldn't have bribed the Deputy Commissioner.' Added Tomoko.

'Exactly.' Agreed Alexander, 'The part I don't understand is the list and the Greek statue. Up to now I thought we were just dealing with some kind of trade in stolen gems.'

The telephone vibrated, Alexander stood to answer it. It was Aono.

'Sorry I couldn't talk earlier, too many ears.' He said, now relaxed.

'Where are you calling from?' Asked Alexander.

'My apartment, it's near the station. Hara-San's son is here with me. What can I do for you?'

'The first thing is Chief Hara. Whatever he is accused of is undoubtedly a fabrication. I've just learned that your Deputy Police Commissioner is on the take. If the order came from him to place Hara under house arrest, then he's in the clear. It's up to us now to prove it.'

Alexander could hear Aono passing on the news to Hara's son. Despite the language difference he could tell both of them were relieved. 'Thank you Webb-San. How can I help?'

'There isn't much to go on. See what you can find out about a fifth century B.C. Greek terra-cotta statue, it's a mans head with a beard. Apparently Kumagai has offered it to your Deputy Commissioner in return for his silence and assistance in an event called the gathering at a castle somewhere in Japan. There's a name, Matsumoto, he's somehow involved.'

'I've got that, anything else?' Captain Aono was obviously taking notes.

'Yes. I faxed a couple of sketches from Bangkok, faces, any news?' Alexander asked.

'I ran the check myself. No luck I'm afraid, both men are clean.'

'Shame. Another name for you to conjure with, Ling, could be connected with the Triad's here in Hong Kong. What can you tell me about him?'

There was a long sigh at the other end of the line. Then Aono replied, 'What are you into Webb-San?'

'Your guess is as good as mine Captain. Ling and one or two of his entourage will be on their way to Japan in the near future to take part in this gathering. At the moment, that's all I know.' Alexander was apologetic, knowing he was placing difficult questions in Aono's hands.

'Ling is what we call in Japan an Oyabun. In Europe you would refer to him as something akin to a Mafia boss or an Overlord. He is well known to us and well connected. He has visited our shores many times and on every occasion on legitimate business. If you're asking me to have him restrained at customs I'll need a very good reason and an order signed by Chief Superintendent Hara or the Deputy Commissioner.'

Alexander understood. 'Then the next step is clear. You have to find the statue and prove that it was given as a gift to your Deputy Commissioner. Agreed?'

'Agreed.' Aono took the instruction as if given by Hara himself. 'And Webb-San, call me the second you arrive back in Japan. For safety's sake we now have to work closely together. If anything develops, I'll call you again on this number.' Captain Aono rang off.

Charlie walked to the intercom and turned up the volume, they were still there. The sound was that of cutlery on fine china and the conversation changed to a discussion of an imminent Sumo contest to be held in Tokyo.

'The way I see it,' said Charlie, turning it down again, 'there's no alternative. We have to follow them. Somehow we must find out when they plan to leave, and where they plan to go.'

'How do you suggest we go about it? This is your territory.' Alexander was just as anxious to do something.

Picking up a quilted jacket Charlie slipped it on. 'You and I should wait downstairs. If all three of them come down Tomoko will join us. If Kumagai remains, Tomoko stays to monitor the intercom. We'll keep in touch by radio. Ok Tomoko?'

Tomoko was easy. 'Fine with me. As I said before, we have to start somewhere.'

CHAPTER 37

After a relaxing hour listening to a quintet playing on the cocktail lounge balcony, the walkie-talkie crackled into life. Tomoko's voice was calm. 'They're on their way down. Kumagai's still here, I can hear him shuffling papers in his room. Good luck, and, be careful.'

Charlie stood and sank the final dregs of his San Miguel beer, 'We're on. See if you can flag down a taxi, we may need it, I'll follow from behind.'

Taylor and Chang had taken the stairs and were easy to identify crossing the marble isle between the soaring square columns and gilded ceiling of the elegant lobby. He waited for them to pass through the entrance and followed at a suitable distance. Where ever they were going they'd decided to go on foot, passing the illuminated square of fountains in the centre of the crescent and turning right onto Salisbury road.

Alexander dismissed the taxi with sincere apologies and tracked them from the promenade, past the Planetarium and Space Museum towards the Tsim Sha Tsui Star ferry. He paid his two Hong Kong dollars at the turnstile and waited for Charlie.

'Just our luck,' said Charlie with a smile, dropping his coins into the slot, 'cattle class. You'd have thought high power business types like these two would have travelled upstairs, it's only another fifty cents.'

With barely a handful of passengers aboard, the gangplanks of the good ship Twinkling Star were noisily dragged ashore and the thumping diesel engines started for the twelve minute voyage over to the island of Hong Kong.

Charlie sat on the slatted wooden benches behind Taylor and Chang, while Alexander peered over the side at the setting sun. He recognised that even in Hong Kong the face of a Westerner would be easily remembered.

Chang fumbled with his briefcase and withdrew the map at Taylor's request. 'Looks like Matsumoto's gone out of his way to impress us, Ling should be pleased. I'll bet you it's a result of that letter I sent. A kind of power eh?' He boasted and began counting the squares. 'I think they're still undermanned for an operation of this size though, we should consider taking some of our own men. I'll talk it over with Ling when we get back.'

Charlie turned to signal what was happening.

Alexander was way ahead of him. The two hundred millimetre zoom lens of the Canon camera was already trained on the blue print and four frames at different exposures captured on film. He raised his thumb in the air with a grin and returned to the sunset.

Slowly the green and white ferry shuddered to a standstill at Central Wan Chai, ropes were tossed fore and aft and placed over stanchions by two of the green-overalled deck hands, the side barriers were raised and the passengers permitted to depart. Taylor and Chang were the first to leave.

Taylor rudely dismissed a straw hatted rickshaw driver with a push of his hand, shouting, 'Get a proper job, parasite!' on his way through the concourse to Connaught Road. Chang slowly shook his head, suffering his fellow countryman's derision in silence. Why Ling had hired this brash American bewildered him.

Again they were walking. It didn't take long to discover why, the roads and pavements had ground to a halt with homeward bound vehicles. Without doubt, it was easier on foot.

Alexander paused beneath the seventy-two storey Bank of China Tower. A stylish brushed steel and blue glass structure reaching skyward at the beginning of the gentle up hill climb towards Garden Road. Sky scrapers rarely impressed him, this one however was different. Slim, elegant and considering the effort it took to see the pinnacle, a real pain in the neck.

Their destination was becoming clear. Taylor pushed his way through the crowd and into the Peak Tram Terminus. Alexander and Charlie stayed close to Chang, within a few feet of his briefcase. The map would surely lead them to Ling, then with luck Matsumoto and the gathering and eventually the Rama's Hope.

The first tram with Taylor aboard began its ascent as they watched through the sliding glass doors. The platform was empty. With a hiss the doors opened again and the push began, starting the turnstile count from eighty to zero before locking. Both Alexander and Charlie headed for the far end and sat on the floor out of Chang's sight for the nervous eight minute wait.

Finally a replacement claret and white funicular appeared and opened its doors for boarding. Alexander watched as Chang stepped into the rear carriage before they entered the front. A bell sounded and they were underway on the one thousand three hundred foot climb to the Peak Tower.

Charlie was aware of two men, reeking of "security" waiting at the exit as they arrived on the summit. Both had Atlas's shoulders and wore dark grey pin stripe suits over their poorly concealed weapons. Chang walked straight to them. After a brief exchange indicating that there was something for Ling in his briefcase, all three of them walked down the pathway to the right.

For cover Alexander and Charlie followed with a group of camera laden Dutch tourists. The guide explained that the pathway ran the full periphery of the peak and it would take approximately an hour to circumnavigate it. She also pleaded for the group to stay together for fear of delaying the departure of their coach upon their return. Alexander nodded that he would do his best.

Ten minutes into the walk Chang and the suited escort turned from the path and down a flight of stairs to Old Peak Road then through a gateway recessed into an eight-foot brick wall.

Charlie paused to let them enter before jogging down the steps and through the passageway between the wall and the dense forest growth. 'We may only have a few seconds, switch off the motor drive and climb on my back. You'll probably have time for just one shot, so make it a good one.'

Alexander followed the instruction to the letter and carefully peered over the wall.

The ground fell away quickly on the far side and lead down to a floodlit lotus shaped swimming pool and a large modern flat topped house beyond. An attractive Chinese girl in an elaborately embroidered silk cheongsam now accompanied Chang, she was leading him to the red and white striped canopy at the edge of the water. An old man relaxing at the table beneath it stood to greet him.

'Hurry up Webb,' whispered Charlie, 'You're bloody heavy.'

Alexander glanced down, 'I thought you agents were supposed to have muscles in places, the rest of us haven't got places! Stop complaining.'

When he looked up again, Chang had laid out the plan onto the table and had been joined by Taylor. The old man was still there, it had to be Ling. Alexander raised the camera and covered it with his sweater to muffle the sound. The shutter release was almost silent and went unnoticed. He climbed down.

'What now?'

Charlie set off in the direction of the road, rubbing his back, 'We wait.'

The drapes of darkness drew in the hour that followed and with it the view from the lay-bye facing the house began it's spectacular transformation. Millions of iridescent lights danced below them in the twilight, defining every skyscraper and apartment of Hong Kong. Kowloon was also ablaze with a myriad of fireflies competing with its island sister.

'Another one for the album.' Thought Alexander setting up the camera to capture the scene. With the zoom pulled back as wide as it would go, he set the shutter speed to five seconds and released it. As he did so, a car with full beam headlights turned the corner behind them. 'Oh... Shit!' He exclaimed, he would have to do it again.

The car, an ageing Mercedes taxi slowed to a halt not twenty feet from them, and killed its engine.

CHAPTER 38

'Absolutely no doubt about it, Taylor's right.' Considered Kumagai, sipping luxuriantly from his chilled tumbler of twenty five year old Macallan single malt whisky, *'Matsumoto knows how to look after his own.'* He drew a light draught of air through pursed lips to savour the sherried lingering after-taste and sighed, without question, a masterpiece.

Muting the sound on the television he reached for the telephone, tapped the seven digit number and waited. There was a better than even chance that Chang would have spoken to him by now. A polite female voice answered and put him through.

'My dear young man.' Ling's voice was strong, unaccented English and as welcoming as a beloved grandfather. 'I have just this minute reviewed your security arrangements, you have indeed done well. I intend to make it a point to inform Matsumoto-San of your competence, myself.'

'Thank you sir,' Kumagai bristled with pride at the compliment, 'just doing my job.'

'Then come over and join us, I'd like to meet you. Perhaps you would care to travel with us? I have a private jet at my disposal. Where would you suggest we fly to? Narita?'

'Mishima. There's a small ex-military airfield close to the estate, I can make the arrangements if you'd like?'

Ling's manner was one of indifference, 'No, don't trouble yourself, I have people to do that for me. See you in an hour, yes?'

'I'll be there.' Kumagai cradled the phone and settled back. 'Quite a change from the old life. Private jets, expensive hotels and the minimum of work. Yes, this was infinitely better.' He said to himself as he downed the last mouthful.

A light traveller, Kumagai packed his shoulder bag in a matter of minutes and closed the room door behind him.

At the check out he handed over his credit card and waited.

'Such a shame you are leaving so soon Sir.' Crooned the duty Manager, 'I trust the room was to your satisfaction?'

'Perfectly, thank you. I'll tell my friends, I promise.' Said Kumagai turning on the charm.

'And your cousin, did you finally meet?'

'My cousin?' Kumagai was intrigued. If he had a cousin he would certainly know about it. 'Here?'

'Oh, forgive me,' apologised the Manager, 'I did promise not to tell. But as you are leaving, what harm can it do. At least I can ensure that you meet. She's in room five-two-five. Please don't tell her I told you.'

'I won't, you have my word.'

Leaving his bag by the desk under the Manager's watchful eye, he walked nonchalantly back to the stairs. Then taking two at a time, ran aggressively up the five flights back to his floor.

Outside five-two-five Kumagai checked the corridor before slipping his right hand beneath the rear of his jacket to pull the snub-nosed Smith & Weston Chief's special from his waistband. It was an old but truly tested design and the .38 Special ammunition could blow a sizeable hole in anyone who got in its way. He breathed in heavily to calm his pulse and tapped gently on the door.

'Who is it?' Came a voice from inside.

Kumagai feigned the highest voice he could manage, 'Maid service, Towels?'

The door unlatched.

Tomoko was taken aback by the speed of it's opening.

'Surprise! Greetings cousin.' Kumagai forced his way in and slammed the door behind him. 'Tomoko-San, I can honestly say this is a pleasure. A second-bite of the cherry, so to speak.' Kumagai's tone was as cool as ice.

'What do you want?' Whimpered Tomoko, backing into the bedroom.

'What I really want, is to kill you,' Confided Kumagai, checking the cupboards and wardrobes, 'but as I can see that wimp of an Englishman is probably with you, I think you should gather your things and come with me. It wouldn't do to have Webb calling the Police and airport in an attempt to stop me, now would it?'

Tomoko packed quickly, anything else would have been foolish.

'Good. Now sit.' Kumagai pointed towards the desk.

Tomoko obeyed.

'Write.' The order was firm and disturbingly amiable, 'Dearest Alex, or Mister Webb, it's up to you. Tell him exactly what has happened. I would, however, like you to add a footnote. Tell him, if he tries to follow you to Japan, before the second of June, I will kill you and send you to him as a welcome home present. After the second, you will be set free, unharmed. Got it?'

Tomoko nodded and wrote, passing him the letter upon completion.

'Very eloquent Tomoko-San. Although I think a final poetic touch is in order. Give me your hand.' Grasping her wrist Kumagai placed the pistol into his pocket and withdrew the stiletto. 'Hold still!' He commanded, then despite her struggling glided the blades edge over the tip of her index finger and placed it next to her signature. 'There!' He said triumphantly. 'Signed in blood.'

Tomoko pulled her hand away and sucked nursingly at the fingertip. 'Bastard.' She scolded.

'My parental background is no concern of yours. Get your things, we're going for a ride.'

With the .38 back in his hand, covered by Tomoko's coat, Kumagai rechecked the corridor. 'Just remember, one false move and Webb'll be buying you flowers for the last time.'

Tomoko understood.

Down in the lobby Kumagai collected his bag and smiled congenially at the Manager. 'One hell of a surprise eh?' He said, then turned on his heels towards the exit.

An old Mercedes taxi was waiting at the foot of the steps.

CHAPTER 39

Alexander took Charlie's arm and backed him into the shadows as the rear passenger door opened. Speechless they watched as Tomoko carried her suitcase and Kumagai's soft leather shoulder bag from the car to the gate. She glanced back twice to confirm her coat was over his arm before disappearing through the opening. It was clear to them both that she would not be returning to the hotel.

Stunned by the event Alexander slumped onto one of the park benches facing the metropolis and sighed with despair. 'Why isn't it ever easy?' He said.

'I don't know.' Replied Charlie equally despondent.

'Have you ever noticed? It always happens like that. Just when you think things are going smoothly, an angel piddles in your beer.'

Charlie sat next to him and drew his hands down over his face. 'Right. What now?' He asked. 'Do you think we should go in?'

'No, not yet. Kumagai wouldn't have brought her here if he meant to hurt her.'

'Then what do you suggest?'

Alexander dismantled the camera as he thought, placing the body and lens in separate pockets. 'I'll go back to the hotel and check out the recorder, there may be something there. Besides, the last thing we want is a maid picking it up now Kumagai's almost certainly checked out. It's probably best if you stay here and watch the place.'

Charlie reluctantly agreed and handed him the

skeleton keys. A brief description was all that was needed for Alexander to feel confident that he could open the door, if it became necessary. 'You may as well stop overnight at the hotel Alex and get some sleep.' Said Charlie, pulling his jacket collar up close to his ears, 'It makes sense for at least one of us to get a decent nights sleep. I'll call you on the radio if anything turns up. If the signal's too weak I'll find a phone. Don't worry about me, I'll be fine.'

Charlie's last comment, designed for sympathy, had the desired effect. Alexander removed his jacket and tossed it to him. 'Here. Take care of my camera, ok? There's some chocolate in the pocket if you get hungry. Bon appetit.' Then with a brief wave he set off on foot down the hill.

Alexander acknowledged the door boy with a nod and a smile before walking directly for the reception. He recognised the face as one of the Manager's assistants from earlier in the day. 'Good evening. Five-two-seven please.' He requested.

'Certainly sir.' The young man turned and drew the key from the pigeon hole, 'If you need anything the concierge will be pleased to assist you. I hope you sleep well.' He handed over the key with a brief bow. 'Goodnight sir.'

Alexander thanked him and walked to the lift. At the fifth floor the doors opened and he walked directly for Kumagai's room and rang the bell. No answer. Picking locks was really not his style. He inserted the key and entered.

Inside, the remnants of the dinner they'd heard over the intercom had still to be cleared. It was the only sign that the room had previously been occupied, as all traces of Kumagai's presence had gone.

Alexander located the recorder and intercom, picked an apple from the fruit bowl and left to return to the reception desk.

'I'm always doing things like this,' he apologised, handing over the key, 'Wrong number I'm afraid, I should have asked for five two five, my mistake.'

A trail of blood spots greeted him as he entered the hotel room. They were hard to miss. Perfectly formed small islands of russet red contrasting harshly against the pale green carpet. If he hadn't seen Tomoko with his own eyes the sight would have certainly triggered a thousand and one irrational thoughts. As it was, he knew she was safe, yet nevertheless they still had an unsettling effect on him. He followed the path they created from the door, to the bed and ultimately to the desk beneath the window where a final spot had etched its mark into a decade of polish. Calmly Alexander drew back the chair and sat.

On the desk lay a letter in Tomoko's hand and beside the signature a smudged fingerprint in her own blood. *'Kumagai's warped idea of finesse,'* he imagined, *'A sick joke from a sick mind.'* It angered him and reassured at the same time. At least now he knew the source of the diverting coloured trail. He read quickly.

The episode that had taken place earlier in the room was made crystal clear, he could even picture the scene. That, linked with other recent events begged for an inescapable and demanding question, could he trust

Kumagai to keep his word.

He decided not. He'd killed once, he'd kill again. Her survival would almost certainly depend on their ability to track him down and ultimately on timing, identifying the instant with the least risk to take her back.

Reaching for the recorder Alexander scanned through for the last moments he remembered hearing over the intercom and set it to play. At least a half hour passed before the telephone call. He listened intently. Mishima. The name was familiar, not only had he heard it before, he'd seen it on the train station at the foot of Mount Fuji. He read the letter again, without doubt they would be taking her there. What he needed to know was when?

The stress of the last few hours had been exhausting, it had been one hell of a day. He lay on the bed and briefly closed his eyes. The fight and drive that had been there on the flight from Bangkok was ebbing away fast. He knew he should call Charlie and give him the latest status but decided a little rest first would improve his judgement, the call could wait a minute or two.

Alexander's eyes snapped open. The blast of a car horn on the road outside startled him back to reality. It was almost daylight. He'd slept. Cursing, he grabbed the walkie-talkie and ran from the room, down the stairs and hailed a taxi.

Charlie was seated on the tarmac with his back against the wall as the taxi drew to a halt. 'I thought you'd forgotten me Alex. You didn't bring any more chocolate did you?'

Alexander shook his head. 'Sorry mate, I didn't think.'

'That's ok.' He said with a shrug. 'Nothing new here. You?'

'Mishima.' Alexander passed him the note and played the tape.

Whilst Charlie listened to the one-way conversation, Alexander's concentration drifted. There was something curious in the distance. At first the chatter was barely audible, like a playing card skipping over the spokes of a young boy's bicycle wheel. As each second passed the volume grew in intensity with its approach. Finally the craft appeared from above the trees, momentarily tossing the branches side to side before dropping gently from sight into the walled garden of Ling's estate.

They both stood and crossed to the gate. Through a gap in the warped lattice they could see Ling, Chang, Taylor, Kumagai and Tomoko pass from the house, stoop beneath the idling rotor and climb aboard the Helicopter. After a brief exchange between Ling and the pilot the throttles were opened and the graceful machine climbed skyward.

'That does it. I'm sick and tired of playing follow my leader with this clown. It's time we did something positive.' Alexander was visibly boiling with frustration. 'I don't mind telling you this guy's really pissing me off. Follow me.' He said and banged firmly on the gate.

The girl he'd seen the previous night opened it and bowed slowly. 'Can I help you gentlemen?'

Alexander handed her a Gem International business card. 'The name's Webb, and this is my colleague Mister Tan. We have an appointment with Mister Ling. I apologise for being a little late, but I'm sure he won't mind.'

As he spoke they walked passed her into the garden.

'I'm sorry sir, Mister Ling is not available, he's gone on a business trip.' She said, unbalanced by the intrusion.

Alexander smiled and dropped back to her side to guide her towards the house. 'No problem, I'll talk with his second in command then.'

'Very well sir. Please wait by the pool. I'll bring you some refreshments.'

Charlie sat in the lounger while they waited. 'I hope you know what you're doing Alex or we're both for it.' He stood to join him as a young Chinese, the picture of sartorial elegance, appeared from the patio doors.

'Good morning Gentlemen. My name is Wong, I'm Mister Ling's personal secretary. How may I help you?' He asked, motioning for them to sit.

Alexander offered him another card. Wong took it and nodded with interest. 'I'm sorry for our late arrival, I realise we should have been here half an hour ago. Believe me it's been one mad rush after another. A junior representative from my company called on me last night and asked for me to visit you this morning with regard to a delivery and ultimately a valuation service.'

Again Wong nodded passing his gaze towards Charlie, with the unspoken question, 'And your friend?'

'Mister Tan has kindly agreed to join me should you require clarification of any point in your own language. I was told that I should accompany Mister Ling on his visit to Japan to verify the value of one or two items he plans to purchase there. It's quite clear I've missed him.'

Wong looked thoughtful. 'I'm afraid Mister Webb, this is the first I've heard of your visit. Although I'm not too surprised. Your company is well known to us, I personally have had dealings with one of your representatives. Martin, I believe that was the name?'

'Sadly Miss Martin is no longer with the firm.' Alexander lowered his gaze, recognising the question was more of a test than an observation. 'An unfortunate accident, just over a week ago.'

'Yes I'd heard. Please pass on my sympathy. Am I to take it that you are to be her replacement?'

Alexander nodded. 'Exactly.'

Wong relaxed back into his chair. 'Well Mister Webb, as you know Mister Ling has already departed. So there isn't very much I can do to help you.'

Alexander drew the box containing the copy of the Rama's Hope from his pocket and passed it to Wong. 'I was asked to act as a courier for this stone to a meeting near Mishima in Japan, a meeting at which I believe Mister Ling is to be an honoured guest. I am also lead to believe that the meeting will be, how should we say this? Behind closed doors?'

Wong opened the box and spent a moment studying the gem. 'And the name of this meeting?'

'The Gathering.'

'Yes. Mister Webb, I believe I can help you. The address unfortunately is unknown to me. But, there is however a contact telephone number for guests encountering difficulty, I'm sure if you call it when you arrive in Japan you will be well looked after.'

Wong removed an address book from his inside jacket pocket and wrote the number neatly onto an adjoining note pad.

Alexander reached forward with his open palm to receive the returning box. He opened the lid once again to confirm the stone's presence before placing it back into his pocket. 'There is something else that perhaps you can help me with. The items which Mister Ling would like me to pay particular attention too. Do you have a description by any chance?'

Wong nodded. 'One moment.' He stood, and as he did so the servant girl approached with a tray of coffee. 'Please help yourselves, I'll fetch the list.' He said.

'You're in the wrong business, Webb.' Commented Charlie admiringly, watching Wong pass into the living room beyond the patio doors, 'If you ever need a job and a serious drop in salary, let me know.'

'Thanks for the offer, you never know someday I might just take you up on it. But first things first, we're not out of here yet, stay cool and maybe we'll come out on top for a change.'

Wong returned quickly with a leather bound folder under his arm. 'Gentlemen, as I'm sure you will understand, I cannot permit you to have a copy of this for security reasons. You are however welcome to study the lists. I expect Mister Ling will require your specialist skills on items fourteen and twenty one, a Trapiche Emerald and a Champagne Diamond.'

Alexander opened the cover and placed it onto the table between himself and Charlie. The list headed by the legend "The Gathering" and the date "Midnight 31st May" read like an exceptional museum catalogue. Mixed with the gems were names known the world over. Renoir, Vermeer, Rembrandt, Gainsborough, thirty two items in all, including one item, the Head of a bearded man, 5th century BC Greek terra-cotta eliminated by a single red line.

'There's not very much to go on here.' Commented Alexander pointing to the description of the diamond. 'I don't suppose there's a picture or a jeweller's description by any chance?'

Wong shook his head. 'That is all I have I'm afraid. Mister Ling has the master file amongst his personal papers.'

Alexander nodded. 'Well, you have my thanks for the opportunity to view this information. You understand, normally I would like to take a few notes for study reference in order to offer an accurate valuation. However considering the sensitivity of this document I will respect your confidence.'

Wong nodded and smiled. 'I will arrange for a car to take you back to your hotel.'

'That's very kind of you. But if you don't mind I would prefer to buy one or two souvenirs before moving on to Japan. If your driver could take us to one of the shopping areas in Kowloon I would very much appreciate it.'

'If that is your wish Mister Webb.' Wong stood and bowed.

Alexander did the same. 'It has been a pleasure talking with you Mister Wong. Please inform Mister Ling that my late arrival will not happen again.'

Wong walked with them to the car, a gleaming black Cadillac Limousine and gave instructions to the driver. One of the orders would undoubtedly be to keep them under surveillance.

CHAPTER 40

With the commercial sector in sight Charlie began his search in earnest. At least one hour of unmolested free movement would be essential if they were to have any chance of leaving Hong Kong alive. Once Ling had heard of their visit the warrant to apprehend them would hit the streets in a matter of seconds. Lead by instinct more than experience he scoured the doorways for a potential drop off point.

A brief tap on the driver's shoulder and a directive finger brought the car to rest in front of the Hyatt Regency, in the heart of the Nathan Road shopping district. An ideal place. The hotel would form half the decoy, the melee of international tourists the other. He and Alexander could blend and gradually disappear, just another pair of innocuous faces in the crowd.

Weaving his way through the maze of stacked suitcases Charlie guided the way, past the gilt edged stores frequented for the most part by the sheikh and foolish, through the congested hotel foyer, down an elegant corridor and on to the hotel's side entrance. Pausing on the pavement outside he cast a searching glance across the road. A bank of innumerable elaborate shop signs ran as far as the eye could see. He checked each one of them quickly, looked briefly over his shoulder back into the hotel and said, 'This way.'

Again he stepped out, this time at a quicker pace, Alexander followed close on his heels. 'Call me paranoid Alex, but these Triad gangs really put the wind up me. I've dealt with them in the past, they have eyes everywhere. If word gets out that we're not who we say we are, we'll be in serious trouble. Don't underestimate that.'

The sign on the door boasted of an incomparable one hour processing, with a sub-heading 'Satisfaction Guarantied.'

'You'll get an ulcer worrying like that Charlie. The way I see it, we've got at least four hours before they can check out our story.' Said Alexander, removing the memory card from the camera and handing it to the assistant. 'Ling will most likely be out of reach until he lands in Japan. And looking on the bright side, there's always the possibility that Wong won't even bother.'

Doubtful, Charlie shook his head. 'I wouldn't count on it. As far as Wong's concerned, we were unexpected visitors. If I was in his shoes, I'd call Ling at the earliest opportunity to verify our appointment. Just pray they don't contact the plane. I'll go and book our flights. Stay with the printer, make sure they only print one set.'

Alexander saluted. 'Aye, aye Captain. Two seats in first class, alright?' He shouted as Charlie passed through the door.

In front of him across the counter stood the assistant with an expectant smile. Alexander pointed to a new model Digital Nikon on the shelf behind him and drew up a stool. He grinned secretively to himself. *'If only you knew how long this is going to take.'* He thought.

Exactly one hour later the satisfied Englishman and the bewildered assistant parted company, Alexander with his pictures and the store without a camera sale.

On the pavement outside Charlie handed him his ticket. 'Just enough time to check out and travel to the Airport. Three-o-five this afternoon and we'll be airborne again.'

CHAPTER 41

Tomoko sat in silence as the Lear Jet reduced power on its approach to Mishima. She couldn't complain so far, despite the kidnap they had treated her with courtesy and respect. Even Kumagai had been almost civil. As far as he was concerned he'd made the right decision. The pictures taken by Aksorn had seen to that. Seated at her side, he thumbed through them once again for her benefit, and for the tenth time she regretted not having given them to Alexander for safe keeping.

'This is really a work of art.' He said, handing her one of the photographs showing the letters R.L. micro engraved onto the copy of the Rama's Hope ruby. 'Almost invisible to the naked eye. Truly the work of a master craftsman. Tell me Tomoko-San, where did you get them?'

Tomoko tore it in half without answering.

'Stupid bitch!' Kumagai snatched the two halves from her hands. 'No matter, there are others. You will tell us sooner or later, and believe me, sooner will be far more preferable for you.'

'You're deranged Kumagai. Theft, Murder, Kidnap and what next? Rape? You'll be quite the hero.'

Kumagai's smile sent a chill through her whole body. 'Rape? Now there's an idea to conjure with. You're a reasonable looking wench, the boys might enjoy it. Only twenty of them my dear, a mornings work for a woman like you I'd have thought.'

She turned from his leering stare and looked out of the window. Tears of desperation were welling up inside her. She fought them back with deep breaths. Kumagai wasn't worth them. What worried her most was that Alexander would have no idea where they were taking her. She would be on her own.

The heat hit Tomoko's face like a fist, her clothes drawn inexorably to her skin as she numbly crossed the fifty yards between the cool plane and the blessed relief of the air-conditioned stretched Toyota Century.

Light, easy conversation surrounded her, it was as bizarre as a dream. Like being the only unwelcome visitor on a school trip. She concentrated hard, casting her mind back to the halcyon days of school when her only worry was her language grades. The discourse was almost like code.

'Bauchel's ceiling'll be around twenty million for the storm. If he bids past it, stay with him,' Ling's tone was conspiratory and for the benefit of Chang. 'Past twenty, bid in units of ten thousand, it'll give him the feeling that we're coming to our limit, get it?'

Chang smiled. 'Got it.'

'Good. What ever it costs, I want it. Understand? The Rembrandt's mine.' Ling poured himself a shot of Suntory whisky from the cabinet between the two front seats and raised his eyebrows questioningly to Kumagai.

Kumagai smiled back. 'Just what I need. A small-one please. It's not far now, we'll be arriving at the castle in another five minutes or so.'

Ling passed him a short measure in one of the six plain tumblers and eased back into the comforting leather. 'Mister Kumagai, I am aware that your understanding of Cantonese is well above average, so I trust you will keep our bidding proposals in confidence. This painting means a lot to me. I should hate to return to Hong Kong empty handed.'

Kumagai assumed an air of professionalism. 'Your business affairs are no concern of mine Mister Ling. All that concerns me is your welfare and security during this visit.' He raised his glass and saluted the comment. 'To your success Sir.'

'Yes. To success!' Ling joined him in the toast drinking heartily. He leaned forward and touched Kumagai lightly on the knee, 'Tell me? If any one knows, you do. What's this special surprise Matsumoto-San's got for us?'

Kumagai gave a low chuckle. Clearly Matsumoto was teasing his guests with a bit of intrigue and drama to push up the price of the Chandra Ruby. 'Mr Ling, all I am permitted to say is, that it is well worth waiting for. I would however advise you to keep a little in reserve, not only will you find it irresistible, you may also find it expensive.'

'Very well.' Ling feigned disappointment. 'Matsumoto is indeed fortunate, loyalty is a rare quality. A quality I value most highly amongst my people. You're full of surprises young man. Maybe I should start recruiting from the Japanese police force? Now there's an idea!'

A pair of powered gates opened automatically as the car swept round the final bend of its hillside descent. The castle was directly in front of them, a picture of opulence at the end of the mile long, cherry tree lined drive. Fuji-San lay to the right across the calm waters of the sheltered lake, concealed behind a thin mist at its base and a band of cumulus surrounding the peak.

Tomoko grew edgy as they drew to a standstill at the foot of the rising steps. Her palms were wet with nervous anticipation, tense with the realisation that her fate would undoubtedly lie in the hands of Kumagai's boss,

Matsumoto. A thought ingrained in the forefront of her mind.

Great oak doors opened wide as they stepped from the car. At first a woman appeared in a gold embroidered kimono followed soon afterwards by a stockily built man appearing to be in his early fifties. 'Ling-San! Welcome to my humble abode.' Greeted the man, jogging athletically down the steps. 'I cannot tell you how pleased I am to have you as my guest.'

'Mister Matsumoto.' Ling extended his arms in friendship. 'I wouldn't have missed it for the world. Your invitation was impossible to refuse. Please, permit me to introduce you to my aides.'

Tomoko relaxed as the young kimono clad woman smiled at her and approached. 'Konnichiwa Den-San, my name is Jasmine Matsumoto, such a delight to know that I will not be the only woman here. Leave your bags, Meena will collect them later. I'll take you in.'

'You were expecting me?' Tomoko was taken aback by the informality and friendliness of her reception. At the very least she'd expected to be clasped in irons.

Jasmine put a reassuring arm around her shoulder. 'Of course, you were expected. Kumagai-San telephoned last night. Don't worry, you'll be safe enough here, I'll see to that. Come on, I'll show you to your room. One thing about living in a castle, we are never short of accommodation for last minute arrivals.' She said as they came up to the main door with its great-pillared porchway.

A Dutch marquetry long case clock announced its presence as they crossed the threshold, and as if on queue the telephone rang in the hallway. Out of reflex Tomoko checked her watch, it was three thirty.

As she climbed the stairs she peered down, Ling

was barking orders into the handset. Matsumoto and Kumagai were standing close by, faces solemn, listening intently to his side of the conversation.

'What?...Who?...You bloody fool! Find him!'

To Tomoko the exchange seemed animated in the extreme. One thing was clear, the name Webb was now known to all three of them and was a definite cause of concern. Her heart leapt, surging with hope. There was a slim chance Alexander knew where she was and judging by their expressions they were worried that he would attempt to find her.

CHAPTER 42

'You've got to be crazy to want to live here Alex.' Observed Charlie, stepping from the airport Limousine bus. 'Two hour's for a forty mile journey is outrageous.'

'That's one way of looking at it.' Alexander pointed towards the rising escalator inside Shinjuku station, threw the large awkward sports bag over his shoulder and marched for the J.R. line platform. 'On the other hand, what other city in the world can guarantee an extra couple of hours sleep, every time you travel.'

The video camera dug annoyingly into his ribs as he walked, he shifted the bag's position only to find the Dictaphone was intent on doing the same. He sighed with defeat. Not long, nearly home, just another two stops and he'd be brewing a pot of his favourite Brooke Bond PG tips back in the apartment.

Easing through the crowds to the ticket machines Alexander reflected on the last time he'd done the same thing. He remembered the occasion with fondness; Sonya had been at his side. The atmosphere was the same. It seemed that irrespective of the day or night the "son et lumiere" of Tokyo's stations was identical. The same suits, the same surging intensity and the same smell, perspiration, boiled noodles and soy sauce.

He passed one of the tickets to Charlie and together they walked for the platform.

'I honestly thought they'd never give up,' Said Charlie, boarding the train and feeding his hand through an empty grab handle, 'A persistent lot, weren't they?'

'Confucius he say, "Many ands make right wok".' Misquoted Alexander, squinting his eyes.

Charlie smiled, 'Careful Alex, remember where you are!'

As Charlie had expected the Triad surveillance procedure for undesirables had been implemented as a matter of routine. All tourist haunts, the airport and hotels had been covered and from the moment they had left the camera store in Hong Kong they had been shadowed. Even the hallowed halls of the Peninsular Hotel serviced its fair share of scouts. In total they had spotted five, although there were undoubtedly more. It wasn't until they had cleared the passport control of the airport terminal that the tails had been cut and the triads' curiosity appeased.

Two stops down the line the train gave a jerk and shuddered to a halt. Within minutes of the door's opening Alexander was inserting the key into his apartment's lock. 'I'll call Hara and set up a meeting.' He said in spite of the tiredness flooding over him. He checked his watch. It was fast approaching eleven.

He tried Hara's home number first. The voice that answered was unknown to him and decidedly official. He hung up and dialled again, this time to Aono's apartment.

'We were just talking about you!' Intoned Aono pleasantly.

'We?' Questioned Alexander.

'I have company. Hara-San is here with me. Would you like to speak with him?' Agreeing to Alexander's wish Aono past him over.

'Good evening Webb-San. Between us we've stirred up quite a hornet's nest, haven't we? Where are you calling from? Hong Kong?'

'Sendagaya, Tokyo. I'm back, and we have to meet.'

What seemed to be an enjoyable private party at the far end of the line turned stone cold sober at the mention of Tomoko's kidnap. Alexander had insisted that they meet immediately but was persuaded by Hara to delay a few hours until the morning rush hour when he was certain he could evade those controlling his house arrest. They finally agreed on eight the following morning at Alexander's apartment.

Alexander breakfasted on the balcony over looking Shinjuku Gyoen Garden. The suits were out in force. Early risers, walking their dogs and spouses along the white and pink blossom covered tracks surrounding the crystal clear water of Suiren Pond. The air was fresh and the coffee strong, dark and satisfying.

He picked up a gold-plated Cross pen and continued his list. A map of Honshu, Japan's central island lay as a tablecloth concealing all but a fraction of the table's surface beneath it. Thick red lines surrounded three possible alternatives. All of the houses bordered the lake identified on Kumagai's security plan and all were flanked by rising hills behind. He hoped Aono's research would help narrow down the options to a single choice. From the look of the terrain binoculars would be essential, the video camera, waterproofs, rope and a change of dark clothes would also be useful.

'Morning Alex.' Charlie leaned over his shoulder and placed a half-empty cup over Nagoya. 'Planning?'

Alexander nodded. 'It's not so difficult. Locate the house, rescue the girl, implicate the Deputy Commissioner

General, arrest Matsumoto and Kumagai for Sonya's murder, find the ruby, escape unseen and return the stone to Thailand in a blaze of glory. A piece of cake!' He handed the list to Charlie. 'We'll have to hire a car. Something small and inconspicuous.'

Charlie took the yellow pages in his hand and made the call while Alexander returned to the map and Kumagai's security plan. Frankly he had to admit it, he hadn't got a clue when it came to passing the more complex systems. Getting to the house was the easy part, from then on, as Charlie had put it, one eight foot brick wall after another. None of them insurmountable for an expert, except, he mused, there was never one around when you needed one.

The doorbell rang. Hara and Aono were a full half-hour early. He let them in and escorted them to the sitting room.

Alexander tried to read something in the Chief's weather-beaten face; it had aged considerably since the last time they had met. His dark brown eyes seemed strained and a small pulse beat high up on his right temple. He had the feeling that Hara's suspension was draining his will to live.

Charlie joined them with a fresh pot of coffee and poured. 'Hara-San? Two years ago, maybe three, you remember me Chief?'

Hara raised his gaze from the filling china cup to meet Charlie's eyes. 'My word! Tan! What are you doing here? Webb-San, why didn't you tell me?'

'You know each other?' Said Alexander in amazement.

'Of course! Tan-San and I joined forces a couple of years back. Bronze Buddha's, wasn't it?'

Charlie nodded. 'A good bust too, if you'll forgive the pun. As I recall you were a captain back then and a Superintendent a few days later!'

The sparkle was back. Enthusiastically Hara relayed the events of their first meeting for Alexander's benefit. 'As you may well know, taking religious artefacts out of Burma and Thailand is a serious offence, demanding severe penalties on those that get caught. Unfortunately, most of this trade goes undetected, however, on this occasion it was a different story to say the least. As I remember it, Tan-San was trailing a shipment from Burma that landed in Yokohama, twenty or so miles from here along the coast. He called me a couple of hours before the ship was due to dock with a rather belligerent appeal, demanding my co-operation and insisting on a search warrant. I don't mind telling you, it got my back up at the time, he's not the most tactful person in the world. Anyhow, I did as he requested and we met on the quay. The ship was impounded, searched and Tan-San got his Buddha statues back. The tale doesn't end there though. Unknown to Tan or myself at the time, the ship was also carrying a considerable consignment of opium concealed between the decks. It turned up during the search, discovered by one of the dogs, I remember. I shall never forget the look on the Ship Skipper's face, it was like a gift from the gods. I still laugh thinking about it. Without question the worst acting I have ever seen. Anyhow, a month of laborious paperwork later and the captain and four members of his crew were sent down. We both got a healthy pat on the back from narcotics and as a result both got promoted!'

Hara stood and shook Charlie warmly by the hand. 'It is good to see you again. I believe you and Webb-San should make a formidable team. The "rough and the smooth" so to speak. An ideal compliment of talents.'

Hara tapped the vacant space on the couch at his side, an unspoken request for Charlie to sit and join him. 'Right, too business.' He nodded towards the Captain.

Aono opened the discussion by laying a seven by five inch photograph and a hand drawn map onto the table. 'A portrait of the Deputy Commissioner General. I drew it from his personnel file.'

Alexander studied it. Vain was a good description. A perfect set of teeth, clear sincere eyes and head of hair Sassoon would have been proud of. A face, once seen, never forgotten. He could imagine him selling double-glazing to old age pensioners, on commission. 'How long ago was this taken?' Asked Alexander.

'Very recently.' Affirmed Aono with a hint of excitement in his voice. 'In fact I went to see him yesterday, it's a good likeness. As you suggested Webb-San, I visited his home on the pretext that should Chief Hara not return to his post, maybe he would consider me for the position.'

'The DCG is one of the new breed,' Interjected Hara, 'American style, he appreciates the direct approach. Don't worry, it was my idea.'

'I'm pleased to hear it. And?' Alexander prompted.

'You were right. It's like a museum. Antiques and statues everywhere you look. He could tell I was impressed and couldn't help showing me how proud he was of his collection. I never even had to ask to see them. Once he'd seen my interest he insisted on giving me the full tour. I paid most attention to the statues. There must have been over fifty of them, some in terra cotta but mostly in marble. The marble busts were the ones with beards, none of the terra-cotta statues had them. I looked everywhere, I'm certain there was nothing that fits the description you gave me.'

Alexander was heartened by the news. 'That means he hasn't got it yet. Excellent. If I were in Matsumoto's shoes, I'd have played it exactly the same way. My guess is that he'll get the statue at the gathering, that way they can ensure his loyalty until it's over, and more importantly secure his presence. I ask you, what would be your impression of Matsumoto, if you could see with your own eyes that he'd got Tokyo's Deputy Police Commissioner in his pocket.'

'Good point!' Commented Aono.

Alexander continued coldly, turning his attention to Hara. 'Am I to take it that your situation is still the same Chief?'

Hara nodded.

'Then the plan stays the same. Charlie and I will watch and wait at a suitable vantage point until the Deputy Commissioner General shows up. The moment he does, we'll call you.' Alexander turned Aono's map to face him. 'Matsumoto's house?'

'Yes.' Confirmed Aono. 'I filed for a warrant yesterday through Osaka. For such a high profile operation it needs a Commissioner or Superintendent General's signature before it can be presented to the judge. With luck we'll get it early on Friday, the last day of the month. You must understand, these things take time. Matsumoto is a powerful man, and with the Deputy Commissioner General involved everything must be by the book. How long do you think we have?'

Alexander lit a cigarette and inhaled deeply. 'From what I can gather, there's an art auction at midnight on the thirty first, so the timing is fine. My guess is that Tomoko will remain unharmed until it's over. We were warned to stay away so they'll probably look on her as additional insurance until Ling leaves.'

Hara's curiosity was aroused. 'What do you know about this auction?' He asked.

'We saw an inventory of the "Items" on offer yesterday at Ling's place in Hong Kong.' Offered Charlie, 'The Chandra Ruby wasn't listed, but that's not to say there weren't some big names there though Rembrandt, Vermeer and the like. Not my specialism I'm afraid, oriental art's my field, so I couldn't say if any of the pieces were suspect. But one thing is for sure, that with names like those, serious money will be changing hands. That says to me that Matsumoto's guests are not your ordinary run of the mill.'

Hara thought for a moment. 'Most of the guests won't appear until late that afternoon. So we shouldn't move at least until then. I have to confess, I'm curious, what kind of auction warrants the bribing of a Deputy Police Commissioner? Midnight you say?'

'Midnight.' Echoed Alexander.

Hara had decided. 'Then we'll let them have their fun and move in at two am on the first.'

CHAPTER 43

For Tomoko the minutes passed like hours. Frightened and vulnerable she sat perched on the edge of a blue velvet chaise longue in her French renaissance styled bedroom, gazing out at the clearing mist. It wasn't much of a view. A tree lined hillside fifty or so metres from the white stone castle wall.

There was no warning, just a sharp rap on the door and Kumagai entered.

Anxiously, she turned to face him. 'Thought you'd catch me with my pants down, did you?' Her nerves were close to breaking point. 'Well you're out of luck. Fuck off!' She screamed, returning to the view from the window, shaking.

After the remarks Kumagai had made on the flight from Hong Kong the previous day, she'd lived on a knife's edge. Sleeping in her T-shirt and Levis, forgoing her early morning shower and rising at the crack of dawn, to foil any advances he might have made on her whilst the castle slept.

'Come with me.' He ordered, ignoring her snide remarks. 'Matsumoto-San wants a word with you.'

Tomoko stood, and with as much dignity as she could muster strode past him and down her side of the flowing staircase to the marble floored entrance hall.

Kumagai passed her with a beckoning finger and showed her to the castle's southern terrace.

'Good morning sir.' Said Kumagai reverently.

Matsumoto remained seated, acknowledging them both with a brief nod. 'Kumagai-San, Den-San, please, join me.' He said calmly, offering them seats around his breakfast table. 'Tea?'

Without a word, Kumagai placed the pictures of the marked Ruby onto the table in front of him and bowed deeply before taking his place.

Matsumoto sifted through them slowly. At first with indifference, then as the full impact of their importance dawned on him his anger grew. 'Kumagai-San. Where did you get these?' The question, phrased slowly, hissed through his clenched teeth.

'With respect sir. Ask her.' Pointing directly at Tomoko Kumagai's reply held more than a hint of accusation.

Matsumoto leaned across the table within inches of her face, his whole body thunderous with fury. 'Well?' He barked.

Tomoko remained silent, staring arrogantly into Matsumoto's calculating eyes.

'Careful young lady, you're treading on very thin ice.' He said, throwing his napkin to the ground. 'Let's see if that ice is about to break.' He stormed from the table.

Matsumoto lead them through the house to a doorway beneath the stairs, Kumagai pushed her through and shut the door behind them.

They both sat on the sofa and watched as Matsumoto headed for one of the ornate golden-framed paintings. It slid to the side with the inaudible release of a single catch, revealing the concealed safe behind. Over the distance it was impossible to make out the numbers, although Tomoko was sure she counted six faint beeps before the latch was thrown. He reached inside and withdrew a black leather box, then turned and walked passed them to take his seat behind the large desk to their left.

Tomoko sat stunned, motionless. It was here. By now she'd convinced herself that Kumagai had stolen it, she had also guessed from his conversations in Hong Kong that Matsumoto was his new employer. Never the less, to see the jewel in Matsumoto's hand still came as a shock.

She stared at it transfixed by the glow as he examined the stone under the dragon headed desk lamp. His eyes, full of concern searched every facet in earnest. To the naked eye it was blemish free. He slid open the centre desk draw, retrieved a magnifying glass to assist with the scrutiny, and resumed his examination.

Sighing with relief, Matsumoto relaxed back into his chair and exhaled deeply, the stone was unmarked. 'You gave me quite a scare there Den-San.' He said, replacing the gem onto its bed of white silk and closing the box. 'So! There are now two identical Chandra Rubies. Why? What can you hope to accomplish by making a replica? Surely you can't be thinking of swapping yours for mine? No, I'm quite sure that would not be a good deal for me.' Matsumoto chuckled mockingly, 'Then, you plan to substitute it! Now that idea has merit! Believe me I know from first hand experience. Well then, how do you propose to go about that? Look about you my dear. Our security is second to none. Whilst we sleep, the estate is in the hands of well-trained sentries and sophisticated electronics, and you must have been blind not to see the patrols last night and this morning. You're living in a fantasy world young lady, who are you expecting, a knight in shining armour?' Again he laughed.

Tomoko sat passive and silent.

Matsumoto rose to return the box to the safe. 'R.L. Why R.L.?' He said, a private thought spoken aloud.

'I think I can answer that.' Said Kumagai knowingly. 'Kraiwoot! The ruby specialist in Bangkok,' he placed his right hand over his heart, 'God rest his soul.'

Tomoko glared at him, realising instantly the meaning behind his comment. Tears began to form in her eyes.

'I understand, that up until recently he was employed as the Chief Assessor by one of the oldest establishments in the pacific, namely the Royal Lapidary. Hence R.L.' Kumagai offered his hands wide and bowed slowly to salute his performance.

'Very astute of you! Kumagai-San,' said Matsumoto with admiration, "Very clever indeed.'

Kumagai stood and walked to his side. 'One question still remains to be answered though.' He said, glancing back at Tomoko, 'Where is the copy now?'

'Well Den-San, where is it?' Repeated Matsumoto.

Tomoko looked away, her only thoughts were for a kind old man who had given her a parasol. Unrestrained tears of sadness flowed freely down her cheeks. She searched her pockets for a tissue in vain and finally wiped them away with her sleeve.

Matsumoto patted Kumagai on the shoulder and accompanied him to the door. He glanced back, 'Very well my dear, I have guests to attend too.' His voice was calm and unfeeling; 'I will inform the guards that you are to be treated as one of my guests until the Gathering is concluded. If you attempt to leave the grounds you will be shot. Think about the question Den-San, you have until they leave to come up with your decision. I suggest you consider your answer carefully. Your life will depend on it.'

CHAPTER 44

Alexander smiled with satisfaction. It was gratifying to see Aono's sketch was leading them to one of the sites he'd identified with the sole use of a large-scale map and pure deductive reasoning.

He switched off the radio, reduced speed and glanced questioningly across to the passenger seat. Charlie nodded, yes this was the exit. *'How easy it would be to get lost on a motorway here.'* He thought. Without a command of the language, navigation was next to impossible. Piloting the Honda CRX off at the slip road, he turned down a country lane of heavily scented pines, completed the racing change from second to third and accelerated hard.

He recalled Kumagai's security plan to mind. A picture firmly ingrained into his memory. 'Charlie, what's P.I.R.?' He asked.

Charlie's thoughts were elsewhere, a nervous passenger in his own country and especially now. It was not a reflection on Alexander's driving; he'd been convinced of his ability during the episode in Bangkok. No, this was purely a feature of the dashboard layout. Normally there'd be a steering wheel on his side of the car. The question filtered through, 'P.I.R.? I don't know, Paid in Rupees? In what context?'

'Security systems.'

'Oh!' The penny dropped, 'The system at the castle, yes? Passive Infra-Red.' Charlie had found Alexander's wavelength. 'Why?'

Alexander pressed the car expertly through a series of S-bends and powered into the straight, enticing the engine to life with an enthusiastic roar. He watched as the rev counter climbed quickly past the six thousand mark and changed up into fourth.

'How do you get past it?'

'You pray that it's not switched on.' Offered Charlie seriously. 'In my experience I would say that it's almost impossible.'

'Almost? That's encouraging. Tell me what you know. I'm sure we'll think of a way.'

Charlie turned to study his profile. 'You're not going to wait for Hara are you?'

'Not on your life, it's too great a risk.' Alexander took the bend a little fast, swore, left-footed the brake, came out of the skid with power and had the car under control all in a matter of seconds.

'I wouldn't trust Kumagai as far as I could throw him. The longer we wait, the more dangerous it is for Tomoko. Besides, if the ruby's there when the police arrive, you'll be waiting for years for them to release it from evidence. Agreed?'

A minute passed in silence as Charlie considered Alexander's argument. With resignation he finally nodded his head. 'It's not going to be easy.'

'I know Charlie. That's why we have to put our heads together now. So, back to the sensors, what can you tell me about them?'

Charlie drew the plan from his pocket. The initials P.I.R. were in three locations. One inside what he presumed to be a large storage room in the basement, another in the study on the ground floor and the third set mounted to diagonally opposite corners of the banqueting hall, one level higher on the first.

'It really is a bitch of a system to pass.' He said thoughtfully, 'A couple of years ago, we installed a number of similar detectors in the Royal Lapidary, I guess that tells you something about their effectiveness. The principle is basically simple. Each unit has a pyroelectric sensor placed behind a plastic window which is transparent to infrared. The sensor detects changes in radiated heat. So when one infrared source such as a person passes in front of a different infrared source with another temperature like a wall the alarms go off. If I remember correctly, the units themselves were around four inches wide and three high, and operate on a twelve volt d.c. supply. Cut the supply and there's a battery back up. Most units cover an angle of a hundred and ten degrees and work over a range of up to thirty yards. That's why they've got two in the banqueting hall.'

'Then, more than likely that is where they'll hold the auction.' Concluded Alexander, dropping his speed to concentrate. 'Go on.'

'The system's stable within a temperature range from freezing to fifty degrees C and each unit is normally mounted six to eight feet above the ground for maximum effect. In most common installations the alarm signals are sent down the telephone line to the local police station, although in this case we know the signal will go directly to their security operations room on the third floor. Cut the line and the alarm trips automatically. Like I said a pretty difficult system to pass unless you have a thermal suit that matches the ambient in the room. Our only chance to disable it will be in daytime. There are ways. There's a better than even chance they'll switch it to stand-by while the house is in use, if we ever get that far, you can leave the details to me.'

'As you say, if we ever get that far.' Said Alexander with nervous laughter. A growing frown on Charlie's forehead caught his attention. 'What is it? Something wrong?'

'Aksorn's engraving.'

'What about it?'

'The photographs were in Tomoko's purse.'

'Oh Christ! I thought you had them.' Said Alexander shooting him a stare. 'If they know about it, the stone's next to useless. Can we file it off?'

'No way. Ruby's almost as hard as diamond.'

Alexander reduced his speed further down to thirty, they were entering the textile town of Fuji Yoshida. The traffic was light and the pavements sparsely populated with early morning shoppers. He passed his gaze from one shop front to another, searching for inspiration. 'Almost as hard as diamond, eh?'

'Uh-huh. You got an idea?' Asked Charlie rather dubiously.

'I think I have.' Said Alexander with confidence. 'The last one on the left, see it? Hardware and Car accessories! They'll have just what we need.' He drove the Honda to the side of the road, switched off and stepped out. 'A clue for you, "Non illegitimai Carborundum".'

'What's that, classical Latin?'

'Kind of, schoolboy Latin for Never let the bastards grind you down.'

'Eh? I'm sorry, you've lost me on that one Alex.' Charlie scratched his head. 'Stress, it's got to be stress.' He mumbled, following him to a wide glass fronted shop, displaying a set of cut-price aluminium racing wheels in front of a Toyota rally poster.

Under the watchful eye of the shop Assistant, Alexander drew the item. A model-makers electric screwdriver. He added further details to show battery or mains rechargeable power and a set of interchangeable polishing, cutting and grinding heads. On one of the heads he showed more detail and labelled it, "Carborundum / Silicon Carbide / SiC."

'Hai.' Replied the salesman, disappearing into the stores.

'Mohs hardness!' Alexander smiled. 'It's obvious, you need a harder material to scratch a softer one, right?'

Charlie shook his head slowly side to side. 'On a scale one to ten, with diamond at ten, ruby measures nine on the scale, you're aware of this?'

'I remembered ruby as nine from the research, that's what gave me the idea. Carborundum's nine point five.'

'You're not just a pretty face are you Alex?' Said Charlie impressed. 'We'll need something to lubricate the stone's surface. I'll see what I can find.'

The shop assistant returned with a selection of modelling drills, boxed sets, and all included to some degree accessories similar to those he had sketched.

'Have they got what we need?' Asked Charlie placing a rope, a couple of dark green car covers, penlight torches, a small pocket-knife and a can of lubricating oil on to the counter.

'I think so.' Said Alexander.

'Look's promising. We'll take the battery powered one and a couple of spare polishing heads as well, just in case.'

Back in the CRX, they were on the move again. Through the village of Kawaguchiko, past the Fuji National Park museum and heading northwards, with the edge of the lake far below on their left. Alexander turned from the main road and eased his way along the climbing track, parallel with the north shore. It was an enjoyable and challenging experience, swaying through the winding mountain roads that would lead them to Matsumoto's estate.

Charlie examined the torches and began to strip the cellophane wrapping from the batteries for installation.

'Somehow we'll have to disable the P.I.R. before we make our move Alex.' He said. 'And the way I see it, Tomoko's our best bet. We both know it's unlikely we'll be able to get her out in daylight, so we may as well make use of her while she's inside. With a good set of instructions from us, it'll be a breeze.' The moment he said it he could feel Alexander's reticence. He pushed on. 'She's a bright girl. If the ruby is there, I'd guess there's a high possibility that by now she'll know where it is.'

Alexander frowned, he could see Charlie's logic, and for him the ruby was his prime objective. Alexander's priority was somewhat different. Placing Tomoko in yet further danger went right against the grain.

'If I was in her position, all I'd want to do is get out.' He said seriously, 'We should see what the lye of the land is first, if using Tomoko is the only way, then so be it. But only as a last resort, ok?'

'Ok.' Charlie acceded and picked up the map to check their position for the final time. 'We're getting close. Go on for about a mile and pull over. We'll hide the car in the bushes.' He folded the map and placed it into the glove compartment. 'The element of surprise will be on our side so long as they don't see the car.'

Alexander slowed before a break in the undergrowth and eased the car gingerly through the scrub towards a dense green thicket. The screech of bracken scratching on the paintwork reminded him of nails on a blackboard and sent shivers up his spine. From Charlie's expression he was either feeling the same, or worrying about the hire car's insurance.

'This is far enough.' Said Charlie. 'We'll have to walk from here. The castle's through the trees on the far side of the headland, I estimate it will take us about half an hour at a slow pace.'

A sprawling rhododendron served as the basis for cover, completely obscuring the car from the road. They worked quickly. Alexander removed their bags and provisions from the inside the tailgate and repacked the new equipment, while Charlie cut further branches from the surrounding shrubs to conceal the remaining patches of red paint work still visible from the lake. 'Shouldn't we have put one of the car covers on, Charlie?' Asked Alexander, hoping it wasn't too late.

'Heavens no. Waste good camouflage on a car? Never. They're for us old-boy, keep us warm and dry. Come on, we'd better be going.'

The crisp undergrowth made progress in silence impossible. With the absence of rain since his arrival fourteen days ago each footfall sounded deafening, like they were telegraphing their presence to the whole valley. Only one sound seemed louder, the pounding of his heart. Alexander couldn't help reminding himself that this wasn't just a stroll in the park, this was for real. 'So this is how soldiers in battle discover the colour of adrenaline.' He whispered, hoping Charlie was feeling the same.

'If you're telling me, you're shit scared, then that makes two of us!' He confided, also in a whisper.

They paused often, listening, each time moving on with relief.

As they cleared the brow they could see it. A large white structure with a cascade of blue green roof tiles curling to raised gables on each corner of the three-tiered pagoda style mansion.

It was significantly larger than Alexander had expected from the floor plan. The grounds, laid mostly to lawn were immaculate, and were dissected by a file of cherry trees, leading from the shaded castle entrance to the main gates barely visible in the distance. He removed the Zeiss binoculars from his belt pouch and scanned the sun soaked terrace on the lakeside. There was no sign of Tomoko, but Kumagai was unmistakable. Stripped to the waist on the lawn, he was holding a martial arts demonstration with a group of ten similarly dressed guards for the benefit of a crescent of seated admirers.

Stealthily they continued down the slope until they were roughly level with the highest point of the castle, some seventy feet above the ground.

'This will do fine.' Said Charlie dropping his bag at the base of a large overhanging tree. 'We'll make camp here.'

Quietly they placed the car covers onto a cleared patch of undergrowth and buried all four edges of the lower sheet and three edges of the upper, to leave an opening on the side facing the castle. Charlie tied a rope around the centre of the upper, tossed it over a branch above them and pulled. The sheet rose to an apex in the middle as the rope went taut before being tied off. With a few selected branches carefully placed for extra disguise, the make shift shelter was complete and they moved inside.

Alexander unscrewed the white plastic cap off a thermos flask and pored. 'You've done this before haven't you?' He said, offering a cup of scalding coffee.

'Cheers. Once or twice. Its all part of the training, don't worry, you'll soon get used to it. You hungry?' Charlie asked, unravelling the aluminium foil from a packet of sandwiches.

Alexander shook his head, the tension had taken away his appetite. 'With these nerves, you've got to be joking.'

CHAPTER 45

A cold damp dusk gathered quickly around them, trading swiftly with patches of crystal moonlight as the ghost of Fuji submerged for it's nocturnal rest, engulfed beneath the rippling waves of the lake. So far, luck had been on their side and their cover was holding. Despite the efforts of two patrols earlier in the day, they'd remained undetected and now they could relax under the cloak of darkness, assured of their safety until morning.

Alexander had volunteered for the first two-hour watch and raised his compact Zeiss binoculars to his eyes to scan the white monolith for signs of activity. One by one the room lights flickered on, offering an insight into the castle's life.

For daytime observations their vantage point had been perfect, offering a clear view of the courtyard at the rear, a full view of the side and a perfect panorama of the terrace. Unfortunately the advantage fell with the failing light. In darkness the scope was limited to an occasional arrival at the entrance and the twenty or so rooms facing them on what he'd termed the poor side. It stood to reason, the more influential guests would more than likely be offered accommodation facing the garden and Mount Fuji.

So far he'd eliminated all but a half dozen of the visible rooms. Servants and guards occupied most, the rest remained dark. Alexander decided he'd give it another five minutes then make his way along the ridge to check out the windows above the entrance. He finished the dregs from the flask and packed the torch beneath his jacket into his shirt pocket and set off.

Barely two steps out of the shelter and a first floor room came to life. There was no mistake, the silhouette said it all. He'd found her.

Alexander raised the binoculars for a closer look. She was alone and approaching the window to close the curtains. He scanned the other windows in haste, praying the coast was clear, it was. Flash, Flash... Two brief signals from his torch. He checked again. Had she seen it? The curtains began to close. Again Flash, Flash... The movement stopped. Cautiously the drapes were drawn aside and the window creaked on its hinges. Tomoko leaned out.

'Alex?' A whispered plea, barely audible in the still night.

He flashed again.

An overwhelming sense of relief swept over her. 'Alex!' She cried, realising in the same instant her call had probably placed him in mortal danger.

'Dam!' He could see a patrol by the lakeshore doubling back to the castle, further signalling was out of the question. An attempt to reach her now would be suicidal. She'd have to wait until daybreak.

'Wave if you can hear me.' He whispered.

She did.

'Be at your window at five am. I'll be back!' He dropped from sight into the cover of the trees and retraced his footsteps as quietly as possible back to the shelter.

CHAPTER 46

'Stop! Don't move!'

Alexander froze at the command.

Cautiously, Charlie crept to his side at the foot of the tree-lined slope.

'Look.' He said, pointing into the early morning mist, an ethereal carpet separating them from the castle walls. 'We've got a problem.'

Alexander agreed. 'Where on earth did that come from. What is it?'

'A laser net.' Charlie crouched to examine one of the reflectors. 'We should count ourselves fortunate it shows up in the fog.' He stood again and scanned the fifty-yard expanse between them and the castle walls. 'There's no other way, we'll have to cross it.' Stepping to the manicured lawn, he glanced back over his shoulder. 'Be careful. Break one of the beams and they'll be down on us like a ton of bricks. Do as I do, and whatever happens, don't panic.' Charlie reached for change from his trouser pocket and let a single, silver, one hundred yen coin fall at his first footstep. 'Follow me. Where ever I drop a coin, step on it and if you want to stay alive, remember, step high.' He led on.

Each movement was painfully slow. Resembling the practised dawn ballet of an aged t'ai chi ch'uan master from one of Hong Kong's botanical gardens. Grace, balance and condition were undoubtedly the keys and Charlie had all three. Alexander envied him. He could only manage two of them; grace was never his strong suit.

Relieved, he watched as Charlie dissolved into the shadows beneath the first floor canopy, he'd made it. Just a few more steps over the knee-high shafts of red light and the muscle-tasking test would be over for him too.

He could hear the resistance of a window frame twenty feet above him, and a muffled male conversation on the far side of the building, it was getting closer. He glanced at his watch, not much time, just four more minutes and the half hourly patrol would be rounding the corner. Alexander looked up. 'Thank God,' she was there. He tiptoed on to the gravel path, unravelled the rope from his shoulder and tossed a coiled handful to meet her eagerly awaiting outstretched hands.

'Hurry Tomoko,' whispered Charlie forcibly. 'Hurry!'

Within seconds she'd reappeared, having wrapped the rope securely around the radiator and behind her back to take the strain. 'Ready when you are.'

Once again Charlie's experience showed, scaling the wall with the skill of a seasoned commando. He paused on the ledge.

'Come on up, hand over fist, just like I showed you.'

Alexander obeyed. Using Charlie's technique he climbed the rope with ease, pulled it over the guttering and lay face down, spread-eagled onto the tiles in silence. Their time had run out.

Three pairs of crunching footsteps approached and passed by beneath them. The procession stopped. *'Oh shit!'* His heart leapt into his mouth, they'd been spotted.

'Hey, look at this!' Said one of the voices, 'A hundred Yen, I'm rich!'

'Well don't tell Kumagai, he'll take it out of your bonus.' Replied another, laughing. 'You can stand me a coffee when we get back.'

The footsteps continued, taking an eternity to recede into the distance.

Alexander let out a sigh of relief and wiped the clamminess from his palms. 'I can't believe anyone getting their kicks out of this kind of thing.' He said under his breath, reaching for the window ledge. He hoisted himself into the room, turned and helped Charlie through the opening.

'At last!' Tomoko threw her arms around his neck excitedly as he closed the window. 'You came. I knew you would.' She said, searching for his lips to pass her gift of joy. 'You're one in a million Alex, I knew you wouldn't let me down, I just knew it!'

'I never could resist a woman in distress.' He teased, pulling her body close to his and moulding his arms gently around her. 'Or for that matter, in this dress.' He stroked his hand reassuringly down her back, willing his strength to pass between them. She was trembling.

Charlie crossed to the door and listened. All quiet. 'Oh, knock it off you two,' he said flippantly, 'I've warned you about embarrassing me before.' He moved to the bed and slumped onto the welcoming mattress. 'Nice place, staying long?'

Tomoko, chuckling nervously, sat at his side and took his hand in her's. 'Thank you Charlie.' She said, bending to kiss his cheek, 'Thanks for coming.'

'No problem lady,' said Charlie, hiding his bashfulness behind an attempted Humphrey Bogart accent, 'the pleasure's mine, the baby's yours.'

Alexander ignored the pun and joined them, perched on the edge of the bed. 'How have they been treating you?'

Tomoko shrugged nonchalantly, 'Not so bad. Three square meals a day and a space by the pool, I've stayed in worse places.' She grinned, 'If it wasn't for Matsumoto's threat this morning, I'd swear I was in a holiday camp.'

'Threat?' Echoed Alexander and Charlie in unison.

'Uh-huh. Kumagai found Aksorn's pictures in my handbag and showed them to Matsumoto, he got pretty angry when he saw them. Then, after he'd checked the stone against them...'

Charlie sat bolt upright, 'It's here? Where?' He asked, interrupting, his voice charged with excitement.

'That's just how I reacted when I saw it.' She said smiling, 'Yes! It's here,' her tone betraying the thrill of her discovery, 'in Matsumoto's safe, downstairs, in the study.'

'We'll get to that later.' Halted Alexander, raising his hand to Charlie. 'I want to hear more about this threat.'

'Well,' A faint tremor hovered as she spoke. 'They want to know where the copy is, and they've given me until Saturday morning to tell them. If I don't, then I'm certain Matsumoto will do everything in his power to make me talk, short of killing me. And I wouldn't rule that out either.'

Alexander stood and walked slowly to the window to close the curtains, a cascade of thoughts flashing through his mind. He turned to face her troubled eyes with a smile of reassurance. 'I wouldn't worry too much about that. If all goes to plan, he'll be securely behind bars by then. Hara will see to that.' Again he joined her, placing his arm comfortingly around her shoulders. 'At exactly two am on Saturday morning, Matsumoto won't know what's hit him.'

Tomoko bit her lip. 'I hope you're right Alex.'

'You bet your ass he's right.' Confirmed Charlie, reaching for his rucksack. 'I was there. And believe me, we're all going to get out of here alive and kicking, you can count on it.' He said, transferring a walkie-talkie and video camera to his combat jacket.

'Well one thing's for certain, we can't leave here until tonight.' Observed Alexander, 'The castle grounds are crawling with guards. I suggest we put the time to good use. What's the security like in here?'

'In the Castle? Non-existent. A few staff and guests, and that's it.'

'Are you sure?'

'Positive. It's all outside.'

'Extraordinary!' Said Alexander in disbelief. He flipped the lid of a packet of Marlboro, stared momentarily at the row of filters and decided against it. Tomoko didn't smoke and any guard on his toes was sure to check it out. 'Ok. For the first time since this thing started we've got the edge, and plenty of time, the rest of today and half of tomorrow. Let's make the most of it. They don't know we are here, right? So, I suggest we make a move on the stone. It would be a pretty poor show if we couldn't switch the Rama's Hope with those odds, now wouldn't it? Where exactly is it?'

Charlie offered Tomoko his enlargement of the castle's layout, unfolding it onto her lap.

'First of all, is this correct?' Asked Alexander hopefully.

She studied it for a moment before nodding. 'How on earth did you get this?'

'It's a long story, I'll tell you later.' He pointed to the study beneath the stairs on the ground floor. 'Is this the room with the safe?"'

Again she nodded. 'Yes, that's it, I spent most of yesterday there. No one seems to mind. They let me come and go as I please, providing that I don't leave the grounds.' She sat thoughtful for a moment studying the plan. 'I've got it! The briefing!' She said excitedly, 'They'll all be there. The place will be empty. I overheard one of the servants, late, last night. Matsumoto's called a meeting for all of the staff at eight thirty in the morning, in the banqueting hall. A final get together before the guests arrive.'

'Excellent. Then that's when we'll go walkabout.'

CHAPTER 47

A steady procession of wooden slippers, combat boots and soft shuffling high priced leather indicated their time was drawing near. Tomoko opened the door to witness the last of the attendants climb the stairs, pass in front of her and cross the marbled landing to the yawning double doors of the banqueting hall.

The carved portals closed solidly behind the final entrant and she could hear a muffled command for the hall's captives to sit in silence and await the address of their master.

With a large bathrobe folded carefully over her arm to conceal the intercom she descended the stairs alone, uncomfortable in the eerie silence.

She paused for a second on the last step, studying a solitary guard through the glass panel framing the entrance door. He was an untidy youth in green fatigues, manicuring his nails with a six-inch blade. Satisfied with a job well done, he sheathed his weapon and walked positively to one of the parked cars on the crescent.

Matsumoto's voice cracked the silence like a whip. 'Good morning, Den-San.'

'She-it! You startled me.' Said Tomoko anxiously, momentarily loosing her footing on the step. On an impulse he reached to help her, visibly taking offence as she shied from his touch. 'I can manage, thank you.' She said, regaining her balance.

'Very well. Going for a swim?' He asked with indifference.

'Uh-huh, and I thought I'd borrow one of your books to read by the lake. You don't mind do you?'

'You may do as you wish.' He said icily, permitting her to pass before climbing the stairs. He paused a third of the way up and looked down on her. 'Den-San. I will know where that copy is!'

Indignantly Tomoko turned her back on him and walked for the study. 'I'm sure you will. But not from me.'

'An amusing retort, my dear. Misguided, but amusing all the same.' He continued the climb with an admiring grin on his face. The girl had spirit.

Tomoko returned to the foot of the stairs listening intently. Like those before him, Matsumoto's heavy footsteps echoed on the veined marbled floor and reflected off the tapestry decorated stone walls. She could hear him wait momentarily at the doorway to collect his thoughts and then enter with authority, sealing it behind him.

A little shaken by the episode she turned her focus to the study and gingerly eased the door ajar on it's well oiled hinges. A light switch, recessed into the panelling fell readily to hand, she threw it and entered into the haunting "picture light" glow that illuminated the room.

'The hallway's clear,' she said, pressing the transmit button on the walkie-talkie, 'Come on down.'

Within seconds Alexander and Charlie had joined her, creating a sense of urgency in the room. 'We heard what happened, you did well Tomoko.' Said Charlie patting her back. 'Now, the safe, where is it?'

'Behind one of the paintings.' She said, scanning the wall. 'This one. It slides to the side.'

Charlie approached the dramatic canvas, taking a second to study it. 'I've seen this picture before, some years ago in Amsterdam. It's a good copy. The Original's in the state Van Gogh museum you know. Unless...'

'We don't have time for that.' Said Alexander edgily, sifting through the paper work on Matsumoto's desk, 'Get to the safe.'

Passing his attention to the frame Charlie traced two fingers down the left hand outer edge. 'What do we have here?' He said, feeling the cold touch of brass. 'Clever! It slides to the side you say?'

'That's right, I saw it.' Said Tomoko.

'If that's the case then the frame's booby-trapped.' His words were matter of fact; 'There's a hinge on this side, and a magnetic switch under the other.' He continued his visual search for a further minute. 'There are also Four other possible release catches on the frame itself, here I'll show you.'

Tomoko peered over his shoulder as Charlie pointed to the depressions, details in the gilded plaster of the lower right hand corner.

'Which one?' He asked.

'Matsumoto had his back to me when he opened it, I couldn't say for sure, is it important?' She could see from his face that it was.

Charlie stepped back a pace shaking his head. 'The frame's alarmed. If I open it on the hinge, it goes off, the same happens if I press the wrong release catch. A simple installation, but dammed effective. We have to be sure; it's too risky to guess. Matsumoto is going to have to show us.'

'You must be joking.' Said Tomoko seriously.

'Not at all.' Charlie took the video camera from his pocket. 'I'd anticipated something like this. Secondary or back-up systems are commonplace and thanks to Alexander's camera we have the means to see our way past them. We just have to make sure he opens it again before the auction.'

Tomoko was doubtful. 'And what if he doesn't?'

'Don't worry about it, we'll find a way. Take a couple of books from the case, focus the camera, and place it at a good vantage point,' He passed the machine to Tomoko, 'Alex and I will see to the sensor.'

Tomoko crossed the room to begin her task as Alexander rolled the leather button-backed chair from behind the desk, over the deep pile carpet, past a large screen LED television and came to rest beneath the dormant infra red unit.

The sensor was well located, a foot above the bookcase, high, in the far right hand corner of the study. It's field of view covering the entrance diagonally opposite, the bureau to it's left and a fine collection of oil paintings on the wall to the right.

He held the chair securely for Charlie to balance on the padded arms. 'Can you reach?' He asked.

'Just about.' Replied Charlie, unclipping the cover easily into his hand. 'Pass me your packet of cigarettes.'

Alexander did as he was asked without comment, intrigued by the request.

'It's truly amazing what you can do with a piece of aluminium foil.' Said Charlie, easing it from the packet and pressing the white paper side neatly against the inner surface of the sensor's lens. 'For our purposes it should work perfectly. The embossed face offers an impermeable barrier to the infrared and ideally reflects the signal internally. As for the outside, there's almost no visible change. Good eh?'

Buoyant, Charlie snapped the cover back into place and stepped down to further examine the room. 'The filling cabinets, they're worth a few minutes, see what you can find. I'll check the entrance for pressure pads and light sensors.'

Alexander returned to the desk and carefully drew the drawers to the cabinet at its side. There was nothing in the first or second, the reward came with the third, packed solid with files arranged under index letters. He called Tomoko to his side to translate.

They were mostly dossiers of business contacts, photographs coupled with descriptions of people with power and influence. Tomoko pointed to a romanji labelled tab 'G'. He pulled it out, opened it onto the desk and began to read. She'd guessed right.

Realising that time was short, Alexander selected a few of the pages in English, titled "The Gathering" and stuffed them into his jacket while Tomoko did the same with a selection of hand written Japanese notes before returning the file to the cabinet and closing the draw.

'There's no other systems and the camera's on stand-by,' said Charlie, wheeling the chair back into place, 'let's get out of here.' Quickly glancing around the room, he checked all was in order, just as they'd found it. 'Ok Tomoko, lead the way.'

For the remaining hours of the morning and afternoon Charlie and Alexander relaxed, playing cards behind the locked door of the bedroom. After the episode with Kumagai bursting in unannounced the previous day, Tomoko had successfully engaged the help of Jasmine in gleaning the key from the housekeeper. To all intents and purposes, they should be safe until nightfall.

Tomoko, reading in the drawing room across from the study, kept vigil. Watching and waiting for the safe to be reopened. Matsumoto had returned twice, on both occasions fleeting visits before returning to the terrace. The safe had remained untouched.

It had been a day of deliveries. Crates, parcels, packages, of diverse shapes and sizes, some demanding the sweat of numerous porters and some small enough to fit in to the smallest of pockets. All were destined for the security room in the basement.

With failing light, making further reading a strain on her eyes she crossed to the doorway to watch the latest arrival. A four-foot square, six-inch deep crate, man handled by two blue uniformed security guards.

All day Tomoko's curiosity had been gnawing away at the back of her mind; steadily nagging it's way into her consciousness. As the crate was carried down the narrow stone steps, the impulse to follow it became irresistible; converting her will into an uncontrollable need to know.

Grasping a note pad from beside the phone, she strode after them. Descended the steps with purpose, pushed the heavy oak door aside and walked confidently into the brightly lit basement.

Her confident steps grew shorter, as the full impact of the room's contents dawned. The cacophony and mayhem created by the unpacking of dozens of crates and boxes in no way affected the vision. The scene stunned her to a standstill.

She stood transfixed before a large extraordinarily fine canvas of a single-masted fishing boat, battling against the elements of a raging sea. A shaft of brilliant sunlight penetrated the storm clouds, illuminating the crashing waves and the vain attempts of a struggling crew to control the rigging. This was undoubtedly one of the finest paintings she had ever seen. The detail was almost photographic. The translucency of the waves and the strain on the faces of the panic-stricken crew were executed without doubt at the hands of a master craftsman. An elegant floral signature, barely discernible against the deep blacks of the sea caught her attention, she knew the name. Rembrandt. It was dated 1633.

She passed to another frame, housing a subject at contrast to the first. The technique was flatter, yet, no less appealing. A technically perfect composition, enticing her gaze from a cello laid in the foreground, across a black and white tiled floor, to a man seated with his back to her listening to the musical talents of what she assumed to be his daughters. There were two of them. One of them was singing, with a sheet of music in her hand and the other at the keys of a decorated piano. A tranquil European setting, frozen on an unsigned canvas.

Curiously, she searched for a description on an open packing case resting against the wall behind the easel. The customs documents had been removed, however one large purple sticker remained, "Do not open - U.S. Diplomatic delivery - First class" was printed in large white lettering against the contrasting background.

A young man in a dusty overall smiled at her as he placed a six-inch cardboard tube onto the table to her left. 'Who's the artist?' She asked, returning his smile and pointing to the musical scene.

'Vermeer's Concert, madam. Seventeenth century Dutch. Do you like it?'

'It's well executed, there's no doubt about that. I can't say as I could live with it though. If I had it at home it would serve as a constant reminder of how badly I play the piano.' She chuckled and moved to his side. 'I much prefer the Rembrandt. What have you got there?'

'Let's see.' He said examining the label. 'According to this, a selection of engineering drawings. Not very creative if you ask me.' He removed the plastic end cap and reached inside. 'Ah, I've been waiting for this one. There's a frame at your feet, would you mind?'

Tomoko placed the boxwood stretcher frame on to the table next to him. 'Who's that by?' She asked.

'Claude Monet.' He said admiringly. 'I have a passion for the French impressionists, you know. Renoir is really my favourite, although, at a push, I guess Monet would probably run a close second. It's unlikely that I'll ever get to own one, so, the next best thing is getting to frame somebody else's.'

'Can I help you?' The regimental voice came from behind her, a severe tone reserved for strangers and people interfering in the steady running of a tight schedule.

Tomoko ignored it, assuming the address was meant for one of the room's many labourers. The man moved to her side and tapped her arm impatiently. 'Can I help you?' He persisted.

'No thank you.' She said curtly, staring coldly into the ageing grey eyes of a tall, suited, distinguished gentleman sporting a handle bar moustache. Undeniably British. 'Just looking around.'

'Guest?'

'Guest.'

'Then, permit me to introduce myself, Claythorpe at your service. Auctioneer.' He extended his hand to receive hers. 'Forgive my abrupt approach, but I have orders to keep this area under wraps, so to speak, until midday tomorrow.'

'Indeed?' Claythorpe's stiff upper lip manner irritated her.

'So, if you would be so kind,' He gestured towards the doorway, 'you will have ample opportunity to view the exhibits then. I'm sure you understand. Matsumoto-San would prefer you to examine the paintings and other items with the correct lighting and atmosphere, without of course the confusion and disturbance we have around us at the moment.' With a gentle pressure on her lower back, he guided her towards the exit. 'Until tomorrow?'

She'd seen enough. 'As you say, until tomorrow.' She bowed briefly and climbed the steps away from the hall of treasures.

Outside her room, Tomoko fished for the key in her pocket, sneezed twice, a pre-arranged signal to inform 'the boys' that the rattling key was hers, and unlocked the door.

CHAPTER 48

'Do you think we should tell the police?' Queried Tomoko, passing the file-liberated auction catalogue to Alexander. 'It's all stolen, I'd swear it, every item on the list. I saw them with my own eyes, engineering drawings, machine parts and even a diplomatic delivery from America. Not exactly what you would call the actions of honest business men.'

'The police will find out soon enough Tomoko. Like I said, Hara plans to make a special house call, when the party's in full swing.' Alexander turned to Charlie with a knowing smile, 'You know I've just thought of something? When Hara bags this lot, he'll probably get promoted again! Without realising it, you've helped him a second time. I'd say that puts him two one up.'

'Two all if we get the ruby.' Laughed Charlie. 'I intend to retire on this one.'

'And so you will.' Said Alexander standing to pace again. 'Tomoko, any luck with the safe?'

She shook her head.

'I thought not. Then that brings me to an idea. I've been toying with it for most of the afternoon. I know at first you're going to hate it, but hear me out, given time I'll guarantee it'll grow on you.'

He sat on the chaise longue beneath the window, leaning forward in earnest. 'What do you know of the Aeneid of Virgil, the epic Latin poem? No? How about Trojan horses?'

Tomoko and Charlie stared at each other with shared confusion. 'What's that got to do with nicking a ruby?' Asked Charlie.

'A great deal, bear with me. The beginning of the Aeneid describes the fall of Troy. It's is all about deception, a beautiful woman held captive and a rather ingenious diversion...'

Midnight, and Alexander sat poised on the window ledge looking out into the blackness. So here it was. The "off". He stepped through the opening and glanced back.

'Be careful Alex.' Said Tomoko, wishing him well, 'Don't get hurt.'

'I'll be ok. Just keep Charlie Chan out of trouble for me while I'm gone.' He smiled at Charlie, doubt and concerns were written in every furrowed line of his face.

'You're a crazy dumb Englishman, you know that? You're going to get yourself killed. You're not trained for any of this.'

'Thanks for the encouragement Charlie. This is the easy part, just make sure you don't screw up when it comes to your turn or I'll have your guts for garters. If all goes well I'll see you in a couple of hours, keep your fingers crossed.' He shook Charlie's hand and nodded, they both knew the risk he was taking. 'There's an old Chinese proverb: "A journey of a thousand miles must begin with a single step." Lower away.'

Alexander crept backwards against the strain of the played out rope towards the edge of the roof and eased himself over the ledge.

In a third floor room, high up inside the thick castle walls, Taylor relaxed in the comfort of a recliner, with his feet crossed casually on the centre of the security console. He'd intended to doze but had drifted off into a deep sleep. The operations room was the perfect place. Away from the tactical laughing of his ambitious colleagues and hidden from the inevitable errands required of all security personnel when electronic surveillance was doing their job for them.

He'd volunteered for the duty to keep his sanity. Since the moment of his arrival he'd been bored out of his mind, hob-knobbing in rich company really wasn't his style. He'd read a little and studied the castle's systems in depth, there wasn't much else to do. Against an amateur the systems were adequate, but against a professional with inside knowledge? Only a test would tell. And that was exactly what he had planned for daybreak.

Under Charlie's careful control Alexander descended softly to the path, his trainers kissing the gravel with barely a sound. Quickly and silently he removed the rope from around his waist, tugged twice and waited for it to snake upwards over the brow before making his way back along the castle wall to the trail of coins. He checked his watch for the first time since the patrol had passed, twenty minutes remained, no need to rush.

Thankfully it was still a full moon and the coins were easily visible, the beams unfortunately had disappeared.

Listening carefully with each step he retraced the morning's crane dance to the safety of the trees and checked his chronograph again. Ten minutes. It was evidently easier the second time.

Under the cover of the tree canopy, he ran parallel with the castle a full thirty yards from his crossing point and waited. Five minutes lapsed before the sound of footsteps could be heard somewhere out of sight at the rear of the building. Crouching at the edge of the lawn he breathed deeply to lower his heart rate in preparation. The time had come. He thrust forward at speed, deliberately triggering the laser net and crossed the fifty-yard void in a matter of seconds.

Taylor's eyes snapped open at the insistence of the alarm bell, returning to full consciousness in an instant. A red patch flashed on the monitor's graphical display in sector six and the image intensifier's video display bloomed into life. He switched to the thermal imaging camera to check the surrounding woodland. No further traces.

'Action at last!' He thought, pressing a button on the desk microphone. 'Patrol platoon! Intruder alert, north west corner, sector six. I'm on my way. Move your arses, I want this one.'

Alexander had reached the castle walls without event and moving silently through the shadows crept around the corner towards the side entrance. 'Where the hell were they?'

He had his answer. As he reached for the handle of the door, he was caught in a sudden blaze of floodlights. A parade of warning shots rang out from behind them, splattering the wall above his head and causing a shower of stone splinters to be released by the ricocheting bullets, a sizeable section smacking painfully into his cheek.

'Freeze! Drop your gun and raise your hands.' The demand came in sharp staccato Japanese.

Alexander could guess the general idea. 'I'm unarmed.' He shouted, 'Don't shoot.'

The firing ceased. Two uniformed guards approached at the crouch, their weapons trained unerringly in his direction. A further two ran wide, one left, one right, dropping half way to assume the prone position. The sight made him nervous.

There was a light cough from behind him. Startled, Alexander shot a glance backwards. The side door was open, it's frame filled with the American's bulk. An electric fear ran through him as the stunted barrel of Taylor's machine gun pressed cold against his temple.

'In here.' Taylor lowered the well-used Uzi to his waist. 'Arms against the wall and spread your legs.'

Alexander reluctantly obliged.

The body search was thorough and physical; Taylor knew what he was doing. 'He's clean. Cuff him, Tomita.' He commanded, stepping aside for the patrol leader to carry out the order. 'Take him to Kumagai, I'll be along shortly.'

Tomita jabbed the barrel of his gun hard into Alexander's ribs. 'Move.'

'Hey, take it easy, that hurts.' Growled Alexander, paving the way along the dimly lit corridor, down several narrow passages and finally up a flight of steps to a metal fire door. 'You'll have to get it, my hands are tied.'

Tomita, alone with his first prisoner was cautious. 'Kick door, someone answer.' He said.

He was right. Kumagai stood within inches of his face.

'My dear Mister Webb, how kind of you to make an appearance. I've just been watching you on television. Not one of your better performances, I'm afraid. Thank you Tomita-San, I'll take him from here. This way Mister Webb, mind the steps.'

Kumagai held his arm in a tight grip and lead him across the hallway to the study. Matsumoto was seated behind the desk as they entered. 'Matsumoto-San, we have an unexpected guest. Permit me to introduce him to you.' He marched Alexander to the centre of the room. 'Miss Martin's lover, my adversary in Bangkok and Ling's gem expert from Hong Kong, I present to you Mister Alexander Webb.' He bowed theatrically.

'You're a persistent and resourceful man Webb-San. It is an honour to meet you at last. Tell me, what, may I ask, brings you to my home?'

'You have something that's rightfully mine, I came to take it back.'

Kumagai answered a knock at the door and returned with an extra chair, placed it at Alexander's side and pushed him onto it. Seated captives made fewer sudden movements.

'And did you succeed?'

'Partly.'

'Indeed?' Matsumoto rose abruptly from the desk, stood thoughtful for a second resting his knuckles on the surface, then walked slowly around it in the direction of the safe.

Alexander turned in an attempt to watch him only to have his view obscured by Kumagai standing between them. 'Eyes front Mister Webb, if you don't mind.'

'And, what was it exactly that you came for?' Continued Matsumoto, watching the painting slide quietly to the side.

'I think you know the answer to that.' Said Alexander, stalling. He could hear the safe-bolt release and the heavy circular door ease back. *'Part one accomplished.'* He thought. 'You do realise, kidnapping is a serious offence Matsumoto, even in Japan?'

'Only if you get caught Webb-San.' Said Matsumoto reflectively. The painting slid back into place and he returned to the desk. 'Kumagai-San, please, ask the young lady to join us.'

Kumagai was unnerved at the prospect of leaving his boss unguarded. 'With respect Sir, I'd rather stay and...'

'Oh, I'm sure Webb will behave himself. Won't you?' He asked condescendingly.

'All the same,' Kumagai unclipped the Chief's special from his shoulder holster and offered it. 'Insurance.' He said, bowing before leaving.

'Good personnel are so hard to find these days, don't you agree?' Matsumoto was pleased by Kumagai's gesture.

'I do, I have to admit it, I've seen worse,' replied Alexander blandly. 'not much worse I'll grant you. Still, you hired him...'

'You have a penchant for insolence Webb-San, I would choose your next witticism with care.' Advised Matsumoto, ruffled by the insult. He reached for a briefcase and opened it. 'What do you know of this?' He asked, slapping a photograph of the copied Rama's Hope on to the leather surfaced desk.

'Never seen it before.' Alexander answered flatly. Even with a cursory glance he could tell it was the stone given to them by Aksorn.

Matsumoto bore down on him. 'Oh, but I think you have! Look closely Webb-San, isn't this the stone you had made in Bangkok?'

'What ever gave you that idea? I wouldn't know were to start. If I was in your shoes, I'd be grilling Kumagai. He had ample opportunity. He was in Bangkok and he kills women for stones like this.'

'So! You have seen it before.'

'One like it, sure. But not that one.'

'How so?'

'Sonya Martin was a friend of mine, you know that. So I presume you also know that I photographed the collection she had with her. You can believe me, that stone was definitely not one of them. The gem I had in front of my camera was unmarked. That one has engraving on it.'

A light tap on the door drew Matsumoto's attention. 'Come in.' He said sharply.

'Tomoko!' Alexander stood to greet her as she ran to wrap her arms around his neck. It was a perfect replay of their rehearsal. With her head close to his, he whispered, 'Say nothing, leave all of the talking to me.'

'Sit, both of you.' Commanded Kumagai.

She took a place on the sofa beside Alexander's chair and reached behind his back in search of a cuffed hand for comfort.

'Mister Matsumoto, you're a reasonable man.' Pleading did not come easily to Alexander's lips, 'Please, Tomoko was the reason I came here. All I ask is that you let us leave safely. You have my word that you'll never hear from us again. No repercussions I promise. We'll forget about the kidnap, the stones and everything. Just let us go.'

The room was bathed in silence as Matsumoto thought. He considered Alexander's arguments carefully and weighed them against Kumagai's report. There was only one plausible conclusion. 'Webb-San, Den-San. Both of you deny knowledge of the copied ruby, yet, Den-San had the photographs on her person when she arrived and you were both seen in Bangkok in the company of a specialist from the Royal Lapidary. You must think I'm stupid. I have grown weary of your games and my patience is at an end. For the last time. Why was the stone made? And where is it now? Answer these questions for me and I will consider your future without prejudice.'

Tomoko cast her gaze downwards.

'Webb?'

'I came for Tomoko. Honestly, I've told you all I know.'

Matsumoto stood, walked to the door and called Taylor from the study. He crossed the hall to meet him half way. 'Armed?' He asked.

'Sure am.' Replied Taylor, snapping a full clip into the butt of his nine millimetre Browning. On safety, the Uzi remained hanging from his belt. With antiques about Matsumoto would probably disapprove of its inaccuracy.

'Good, then come with me. Cover the Englishman and take your lead from Kumagai-San.'

Allowing Taylor to enter first, Matsumoto remained in the doorway. He'd reached his decision. 'Kumagai.'

'Yes sir?'

'They're all yours. Take them away. I would advise you lose their bodies in the lake.'

Kumagai's grip of iron held fast against Tomoko's futile struggle. 'My pleasure sir.'

'You can't do this!' She screamed. 'Matsumoto-San, please, No!!!'

CHAPTER 49

Seated, with the Browning levelled squarely at the back of his head, Alexander Webb remained still, calm, analysing the events that had led to their immediate predicament.

In spite of their situation, the ruse had indeed been worth the attempt. He hadn't truly counted on Matsumoto allowing them to leave as a result of his plea, yet equally, hadn't expected quite so violent an outcome. A single regret, Tomoko, she had taken it hard, he would never forgive Matsumoto for that.

The results of the confrontation were more than satisfactory. The combination to the safe, a shrouded admission that Kumagai had killed Sonya and an order for their execution had all been recorded on the video. Assuming they would live to tell the tale, Matsumoto's days should now be numbered.

He looked thoughtfully towards Tomoko. The blind panic that had crossed her face with the command had subsided along with her resistance to Kumagai's grip. She sat defeated and stared listlessly back at him, her eyes pleading.

Shadowed by Taylor, Alexander crossed to the sofa to be at her side. 'There's a handkerchief in my pocket, it's yours if you need it.' He offered, concerned at her despair.

'You promised Alex,' she whimpered, 'You promised me.'

'I know.' His manner was that of a doctor caring for a sick child. 'Don't worry Tomoko, I always keep my promises. Pull yourself together and dry your eyes, I need you to be strong, especially now. The good guys always win, remember? Bear with me, we still have one or two cards to play.'

'They'd better be good.' She said, blowing gently into the soft white linen.

'All aces.' Alexander smiled with reassurance. He'd met Matsumoto's type before and on occasion guessed correctly at their Achilles heel. This time he was certain and knew without question Matsumoto's weakness could easily be beaten with a show of character. The overture had drawn to a close, it was time for the symphony to begin. As Kumagai raised the palm of his hand, indicating that they should both stand, he turned his head towards the doorway and drew a deep breath. 'Seventy million dollars Matsumoto!' He shouted. Four words, clear and concise, Matsumoto would have had to be deaf not to hear them.

Approaching the first floor landing the Japanese stopped dead in his tracks. The study, the hall, the whole building had fallen to a pregnant silence. He gave an irritated little sigh and leant over the banister. *'What would it take to get rid of this man?'* He thought. 'Are you addressing me Webb-San?'

'I am. Seventy million dollars. That's what we're worth to you alive, nothing if we're dead. I'd say that warrants a minute of your time, wouldn't you?'

Alexander waited uneasily for a reaction, knowing their fate hinged heavily on Matsumoto's greed. A wafer thin hand ticked by inside the cherry wood casing of a Masonic wall clock beside the door, agonisingly slowly at two heart beats to the second.

Finally, the response came. He could hear the soles of Matsumoto's shoes patter down the steps and return across the hall. 'Your bravado intrigues me young man, continue.' He said, re-entering the room.

'Then, take these off first.' Requested Alexander, shaking the handcuffs behind his back. 'I talk better with my hands free.'

'One step at a time Webb-San, you're in no position to make demands.'

'No? I think I am.' He said, now getting to his feet, 'In a word, you "need" me. I know, for a fact, that you have a ruby concealed somewhere in this building. A rather special ruby. Worth at face value, in the region of thirty million dollars. A lot of money I'll grant you, but a mere fraction of its true value. I can offer you a great deal. In return for our lives and a safe passage out of here, you'll receive my help in selling it. On the open market, I could promise you a sale in excess of a hundred million, without hesitation. At your auction, who knows? Maybe more, maybe less, it will all depend on the wealth of your guests.'

Matsumoto laughed mockingly. 'Again, you take me for a fool.'

'On the contrary Matsumoto-San. Misinformed maybe, but no fool.' Alexander's tone was deadly serious. 'The fact of the matter is, you have no idea of the importance placed on the stone in your possession. I, on the other hand, have information that will prove beyond doubt that you are holding one of the most significant gem stones in history."'

'I still say you are bluffing.' He was less convinced. 'Why should I trust you?'

'Because you have nothing to lose'

Matsumoto paced thoughtfully to his desk and sat down. 'What do you propose?'

Alexander had him. He knew it. 'A deal. In exchange for your word of honour, I will make a presentation to the auction assembly, the likes of which I'll guarantee will take their breath away. I will tell them a story, the fascinating and full history of the life of your ruby, heavily steeped in legend, yet all true and accurately documented. When I'm finished, I'll warrant that every man in the room would rather kill than lose the opportunity or indeed the privilege of owning it.'

Matsumoto's interest was evident. 'And, am I to assume that you intend to keep the provenance to yourself until the lot is called for auction?'

'That's the general idea. Call it insurance.'

Matsumoto toyed absently with the letter opener while he considered. It was truly an intriguing turn of events, and quite unexpected. He smiled secretly at the paradox, Webb's boast was so fantastic, he could conceivably be telling the truth and to pass this opportunity for the sake of a few hours would indeed be foolish. 'What of the copy?'

'Back in Bangkok I believe, in the hands of the Royal Lapidary's chief assessor.' Lied Alexander with confidence. 'He was with me during the interview with Ling's secretary, a Mister Wong. Helpful fellow.'

'And who told you of our auction?'

'Like I said, Wong was very helpful.'

An undeniable fact, he'd heard as much from Ling's own lips. 'You play an imaginative game Webb-San, a worthy opponent, you are to be congratulated.' He smiled. 'I may have misjudged you, I doubt it, but for the sake of argument, let us say that, for the moment, I am prepared to believe you. You say the Chandra ruby is valued at thirty million, double it and I will be satisfied.

Come up short and I will see to it personally that the next twenty four hours are your last. Those are my terms.'

Alexander bowed slightly. 'Agreed.'

Matsumoto swivelled his chair away from the desk, stood and walked to the door. He turned and gave a quizzical tilt of the head. 'Do you play chess Webb-San?' He asked, his manner changing to an air of familiarity.

Perplexed, Alexander nodded. 'Yes, why?'

'Good! Then I suggest you get some rest. We shall play in the morning, after breakfast, on the terrace. Kumagai, release the hand cuffs and take them both to the girl's room. Lock them in.'

CHAPTER 50

It was two o'clock in the morning and the castle was as quiet as the grave. By some miracle Tomoko had fallen asleep and lay loosely curled as a foetus at his side on the mattress, her head resting softly against his thigh. Too wound up to sleep, Alexander studied the subtle movements of Charlie's hands, well illuminated beneath the desk lamp next to the bed.

'Do you think it will be good enough?' Asked Alexander, absorbed in the too and fro rhythm of the counterfeit stone.

The Carborundum impregnated cutting head, greased with oil had proven to be effective in grinding the engraved girdle, now he'd moved to a fine textured polishing head and toothpaste for the final stage. It had taken a full thirty minutes to grind and polish and he was almost there.

'I wouldn't waste my time on it if I didn't.' Said Charlie, exercising the cramp from his fingers. 'It's been years since I last did this, I'd forgotten how hard these suckers are. After diamond, ruby is the next hardest natural mineral known to man. It's only a hundred and fortieth as hard, I'll grant you, but one thing's for sure, the tendons in my fingers will be wrecked by the time I'm finished.' He passed the stone to Alexander. 'Here, tell me if you can still see Aksorn's mark.'

Alexander examined the ruby carefully. 'Pretty good. You should try this for a living.'

'At the rates we pay, you must be kidding.' Charlie lit a cigarette and offered it. 'Besides, the stress would kill me. Can you imagine the owner's reaction if a stone like this should split while cutting? No thank you. I'll stick to snooping and leave that particular brand of nightmare to the professionals.'

'Split? You said rubies were almost as hard as diamonds?' Said Alexander, confused.

'They are. They're also very brittle. Like glass, hard to the touch, yet just as easy to break. The general rule with large rubies is to treat them like eggs, especially during cutting and setting.'

Charlie raised his gaze to meet Alexander's. Despite a nod of understanding, the eyes of his friend were anxious, undoubtedly a mirror of the apprehension in his own. Alex was right. The idle banter was comforting and distracting, unfortunately there was still a job to do, and it was indeed time.

He reached for the stone and dropped it into his breast pocket. 'I'd better make a move.' He said.

'Got everything you need?'

'I could use a good excuse for not going.'

'I know exactly what you mean. See to the lock and I'll check the corridor.' Alexander eased a pillow under Tomoko's head, stepped barefoot to the floor and crossed to his side.

Skilfully Charlie inserted the lock-picks into the barrel and turned. It took no longer than it would have done with the actual key. Amazed, Alexander rotated the handle and peeped out into the hallway. It was deserted. 'Enjoy your trip,' he said, patting him lightly on the back. 'Bring me back something nice.'

The short hairs on the nape of Charlie's neck tingled as the study door snapped shut behind him. He was inside. There was the normal desire to move fast, an overwhelming need to get it all over, but time served discipline made him cross the room at a slow, deliberate, tiptoe pace.

Cautiously, he reached for the video camera, pressed the stop button on the rear face and placed it onto the veined marble surface of the mantelpiece above the fire.

Now, moving with pace, he switched the television set to on, muted the sound and connected a yellow tipped video lead between the recorder and a component input on the television. He pressed play and carefully selected the camera input port. Grinning with satisfaction as the snowy image bloomed into an array of full colour. A crystal clear picture.

Applying a light pressure to engage the picture search, the hard drive advanced at five times its normal viewing speed causing the accelerated images to advance farcically on the screen. Soon, the familiar stockily built figure he'd studied through binoculars on the terrace, strode animatedly into view. *'This must be it.'* Play.

Matsumoto glanced to his left as though checking he was not being observed and positioned his body as a shield from prying eyes. Silently, Charlie thanked him. The view over his shoulder was now perfect. Pause, slow-motion.

He moved to the frame and waited patiently for his host's unwitting display, his hand hovering hesitantly over the four possible release catches. Lower right. He pressed it. *'Good.'* The frame slid to the side. Now for the numbers. 3,3, 2,2, 3,4. *'Jasmine?'* The notion intrigued him. Tomoko had said she was slim, she had also mentioned she was pretty. Perhaps one day he would have the opportunity to satisfy his curiosity.

Swiftly, he cleared his mind of the thought, re-applying himself to the task. He hesitated momentarily on the handle. The casing itself might be alarmed. Too late to worry now, he threw the bolt and eased open the door.

Save for a black leather box and an inch thick wad of ten thousand yen notes, the cavernous safe was empty. He reached inside, left the money untouched and closed his gloved hand over the case. With trepidation he drew it out, raised the lid and peered apprehensively inside.

A strange and unashamed feeling of achievement overwhelmed him. Generations of professional men-at-arms, detectives and mercenaries had tried and failed, yet, he, with the help of his inexperienced friends had succeeded. He cradled the jewel in the palm of his hand. The Buddha's heart. Cold and lifeless, oblivious to the life it would bring to his people, a nation desperately in need of hope. The stone was indeed well named.

Reaching into his breast pocket, he drew out Aksorn's copy, placed it snugly into the box and pushed the original into his sock to nestle in the arch of his left foot. Feeling it next to his skin, he would be less likely to lose it.

He closed the safe, and turned his attention to the television to return it to the state in which he had found it.

'Tomoko, Tomoko wake up!' Alexander shook her gently by the arm. 'Look! We've got it!'

She stirred with reluctance and stared lazily at the amorphous scarlet form separating Charlie's thumb and forefinger. She watched as an expression of contentment grew on his face and matched it with an engaging smile of her own. *'Why was he grinning?'* The thought perplexed her. She drifted her gaze back to his hand, blinking twice to remove the sleep from her eyes. Suddenly the realisation dawned and the stone snapped sharply into focus. 'You did it? When? How? Let me see.' She said, alive with excitement.

She took the stone and held it with reverence up to the light. Her face glowing like a child's at her first fireworks display. Holding it was an altogether different experience to just seeing it in Matsumoto's hands, rich and vibrant, with shafts of light dancing playfully through the scimitar formed flaw in it's centre. 'It's beautiful.'

'It certainly is.' Agreed Alexander with pride. 'I only wish it was ours to keep.'

'Hey, don't go putting ideas into her head, Alex.' Laughed Charlie, 'Haven't you heard, diamonds are a girl's best friend, not rubies. No, this one's going home with me, assuming of course we can get out of here.' He moved to the curtains and peered out.

Alexander could read the signs, escape was in the forefront of Charlie's mind. Impatience would soon replace his temporary elation. 'It's not a good idea Charlie.' He said warily. 'If you're thinking of crossing the laser net again, I'd advise against it. After my episode, the guards will be jumpier than a frog with haemorrhoids. Wait until morning.'

'Morning? You're losing your marbles Alex. If I wait until then, the place will be crawling with servants and porters lugging chairs and whatever up to the ballroom.'

Alexander grinned slyly. 'Exactly. Think about it. Dozens of unfamiliar faces?'

Charlie was quick to pick up the thread. 'You may have something there.' He said, allowing the curtain to fall back into its regiment of pleats. 'It's a better than even chance, I might get away with it. But what about you? You'll stick out like a sore thumb?'

'We'll leave later.' Alexander's voice had changed with the cold edge of determination. He cast a glance towards Tomoko for her reaction and was pleased with what he saw. Her thirst for vengeance was as strong as his own. 'We both have unfinished business to attend to here.'

'If you're going after Matsumoto and Kumagai, I should be with you, you'll need me.'

'I agree. Nevertheless, the safety of the stone has to be your first priority. Don't concern yourself with us, we'll be safe enough until you arrive with the police. There's an old saying, *"The only thing better than taking revenge, is watching someone else take it for you."* And that's exactly what we intend to do. Your skills are much more valuable to Chief Hara. Without you he'll be working blind. You know the layout of the grounds, the castle and the location of the auction. We just want to be around to see their faces when they're arrested. Maybe in some small way we can help you both from the inside.'

Charlie conceded defeat. 'Ok, have it your way. I'll wait in the car with one of the walkie-talkies, promise me you'll call if you need me.'

'We will.' Said Tomoko, heartened by the fact that he would not be far away. 'You can be sure of that!'

Removing his jacket, Charlie approached the wash basin in the bathroom and prepared to shave. 'When's the best time for me to leave then?'

Alexander stroked his own two day old growth and cursed. That was it. He always managed to forget something. 'Mid morning. Matsumoto, in his ultimate wisdom has invited me for a game of chess after breakfast.'

'You'll lose I hope.' Said Charlie anxiously.

'We'll see.' Chuckled Alexander. 'It all depends on how good he is. I'll take Tomoko down with me, that way the door will be left unlocked. Choose your moment any time after we leave.'

He walked to the bathroom as Charlie finished. Stripped, showered, dried himself and put on the towelling robe hanging readily behind the door. Then, taking a fresh blade from inside the handle he shaved with Charlie's razor and returned to the bedroom. It was the first time he'd felt truly clean for days.

Tomoko moved to the centre of the mattress and smiled cheekily. 'I've always wondered what it would be like to have two men in my bed.'

'Shameless hussy,' Alexander slapped her playfully on her behind. 'go to sleep.'

CHAPTER 51

The change of location had worked to Alexander and Tomoko's advantage. In spite of the continued spell of good weather, Matsumoto had insisted they conduct the contest indoors, in the drawing room adjacent to the hall. That way, he explained, purely by his physical presence he could ensure the diligence of his work-force during the preparations.

Tomoko, with feigned indifference to the game, sat alone on the window ledge overlooking the courtyard. An age had passed since it had began and she had become increasingly concerned for Charlie's welfare. *'What could be keeping him?'* The reoccurring thought troubled her, tormenting her piece of mind.

Through the glazing she could see the latest arrival. A white Nissan van with a display of elaborate cakes painted delicately on the side. It pulled to a rasping halt close to the entrance and a team of caterers stepped out.

She followed the driver's movements to the side of the van and watched dreamily as he rolled back the blind to distribute the boxes. Her stomach rumbled at the sight of the food and reminded her of the way she had picked at breakfast.

A motif on the driver's breast pocket caught her eye. A cream covered fancy with a cherry crown on top. "Not exactly an ideal choice of colours against white," she mused, "but what other colour could a caterer wear?" As the thought entered her mind she knew the reason for

Charlie's delay and knew exactly what she had to do to help.

'I won't be long,' she said, walking with poise for the door, 'back in a couple of minutes.'

Matsumoto nodded gracefully and returned to his move. 'I am pleased to see this is one game we play by the same rules.' He said, positioning his queen as a threat to Alexander's knight.

'Um.' Replied Alexander. He seldom spoke during a game and further comment was unnecessary.

The contest had begun with promise. Matsumoto had taken pains to present a convincing defence against Alexander's attack. It had even stood the test for the first half hour of play. But now, with an hour elapsed, Matsumoto's attention was drifting.

As a youth Matsumoto would have been a formidable opponent but the years had taken their toll. It showed in his concentration and in his ability to read the moves ahead. On occasion it had even been necessary to lose a piece with care to keep the even balance of the game. With Alexander's guidance the state of play had remained even. Both of them were left with an equal complement of knights, rooks, a half dozen pawns and a queen a piece.

Again Matsumoto had committed a basic error. The movement of his black queen close to Alexander's base line had left his king's rook vulnerable. It was only a matter of time before Alexander had him in mate. Win, lose or draw, he would have to decide soon.

'You play a fine game Matsumoto-San, we are equally matched. Perhaps we should agree on a fitting reward for the winner?' Said Alexander, lifting his gaze from the board.

Matsumoto smiled warmly at the suggestion. 'I have known since the beginning you have prowess at this game Webb-San, and frankly, I'm surprised you haven't cornered me already.'

Alexander had his permission. 'You do have the option to resign, you know.'

'Thank you for reminding me, your diplomacy does you credit. No, for the moment we shall continue, humour me and play to win. I should like to see your closing gambit. A brandy for the winner, yes?'

'French or Japanese?' A fine Cognac would indeed be worth the effort.

For the third time Charlie eased the door ajar and checked the landing. Blue uniforms and white monogrammed overalls were the order of the day. He had neither and the sight made him uneasy.

Already he had stripped to his jeans and T-shirt, packed the car keys, ruby, video recorder and walkie-talkie into his pockets and tidied the rest of his belongings into Tomoko's suitcase. It was now or never. With conviction, he opened the door wide and froze in mid-step, his heart missing a beat as the figure came from out of nowhere.

'I'm sorry, I didn't mean to startle you Charlie.' Said Tomoko, pushing past him into the bedroom. 'Come back inside.'

The scare had knocked the wind out of his sails. 'What's the matter?' He asked.

'You are. Your dress is all wrong. Put these on.' She pressed a white bundle into his hands.

'Overalls? You're a life saver! How did you get them?'

'From one of the caterers, I soaked him with a vase of flowers.' She raised her hand to conceal a childish snigger. 'Luckily, he had a spare set in his van. I promised him a personal fitting if he left them with me to dry until tomorrow. I dare say he will be disappointed.'

'I would be.'

'You are sweet Charlie.' She said, averting her eyes as he dressed. 'Ready?'

'I guess so. Let's get it over with.'

With his head bowed he followed her down the stairs, past the confusion of deliveries and out through the castle entrance.

Transfixed at the foot of the steps, Tomoko was amazed at the ease with which he crossed the gravel courtyard, passed between a pair of parked cars and disappeared from view into the bushes beyond. All of the clichés had been proved wrong. No-one gave him a second glance.

The true measure of a man's capabilities could always be judged by a game of chess. His father had taught him that, and as such, the morning's event had meant much more to Matsumoto than just a means of starting the day. It had given him the perfect instrument to look deeply into the Englishman's mind.

Webb was bright, no question, capable of clear logical planning and considerable lateral thought. Competent in defence and deadly in attack. The man's character, all be it in a game, was as clear to him now as crystal. He understood the drive that had brought the Englishman this far and was in no doubt how dangerous he was. Webb had to be eliminated. The question was, when?

It was a troubling dilemma. Run the risk of embarrassment at the Gathering, or cut his losses and remove his presence from the scene as soon as possible to save face.

The inability to make a decision frustrated him, as his actions were bound by a sense of duty and honour. His commitment to the other Oyabuns of obtaining an offering, so unique, that competitive lots would pale before it, had begun as a boast. Webb's proposed tale might well prove to be the fulfilling key. He needed to be sure. Besides, he was duty bound to undermine the assumed superiority of his western guests and prove to them, beyond doubt, his Japanese organisation could better all of their efforts with ease and as a matter of course.

'You play with amazing finesse Webb-San, I confess to having benefited greatly from the experience.' He said, studying Alexander's cool expression. 'You know, for one moment there, I thought you were going to let me win.'

'It had crossed my mind.' Said Alexander, casually rolling the amber liquid close to the rim of the glass.

'Well, I'm glad you decided against it. Two things I can't abide, losers and "yes" men. I'm pleased to see that you are neither of those. A toast. To success, in whatever form it may take.' He raised his Napoleon XO brandy in salute and drank heartily. 'It is good, yes?'

Alexander signalled his approval. 'Excellent.'

'Indeed.' Matsumoto raised the decanter for a refill. 'I have a strong feeling Webb-San that tonight you will perform beyond my expectations. Your mystery story surrounding the Chandra Ruby has me more than a little intrigued. Tell me honestly, this is not just another of your ploys to escape is it?'

Alexander shook his head and smiled. 'Not this time. The provenance is true enough. I see it purely as a means to an end. Wealth for you and immunity for me.'

'No clues?'

'Not yet. Have patience Matsumoto-San, it would be a shame to spoil the surprise.'

Matsumoto nodded slowly. 'Quite so. I see you enjoy the control Webb-San, on that count we are very much alike. So be it. A ten percent incentive for you should you succeed.'

A gong sounded discreetly, from somewhere in the far reaches of the castle.

'Lunch!' Announced Matsumoto, placing his empty goblet onto the chess board. 'I hope you don't mind, I would like you to return to your room. There is much for me to do and I must see to the arrival of my guests. I'm sure you understand.' He stood and walked regally towards the exit, pausing momentarily in the door frame. 'I will send Meena to you with food and liquid refreshment. Give her your clothing measurements and she will arrange suitable attire for this evening.' He bowed dismissively and called a guard for Alexander. 'A most interesting game Webb-San, thank you. I suggest you take the opportunity of this afternoon to prepare, after all, tonight you must be at your best. You will be sent for at eleven. Until then!'

Alexander downed the last drops of his brandy and reached for the decanter. 'You don't mind if I...?' He stalled, glancing towards the hallway Matsumoto had gone, instead, Tomita, in army fatigues, stood commandingly in his place.

'Forrow me, Webb-San.' He demanded. 'Woman alleady in room.'

'As you wish.' Tucking the decanter beneath his arm, Alexander followed in Tomita's footsteps, grinning privately to himself at his escort's failed attempt to pronounce his L's and R's. To be fair, at least he'd tried, it was more than he could manage in Japanese.

The sting of the bathroom's sachet after shave breathed new life into Alexander's cheeks. For a Japanese product it was surprisingly invigorating and it's lemon scented fragrance agreeably refreshing.

Again he checked his watch. They would be called soon. It was fast approaching eleven o'clock and the auction due to begin in just over an hour. Matsumoto had ordered him to prepare, so be it. He removed the glass stopper from the decanter, poured a short measure into a tumbler and swilled the brandy for a full thirty seconds around his mouth before discharging it into the sink. The decanter's contents followed. Preparation complete. He was ready.

The wolf-whistle was for Alexander's benefit.

Emerging from the bathroom, he bowed. 'At your service ma'am. You like?'

Tomoko nodded. 'It's a remarkable fit, not at all bad for an off the peg suit.'

'Modified of course. It would seem Matsumoto has influence over a local tailor.'

'No argument. Lets hope this one lasts longer than the one you bought in Bangkok.' Quipped Tomoko, applying the final touches to her mascara.

'Maybe they should sell tuxedo's with life insurance.' countered Alexander, 'Remind me to make a note.'

A sharp rap at the door was followed by a turning Key, Kumagai entered. 'Show time Mister Webb, are you ready?'

'As ready as I'll ever be.' Taking Tomoko's arm in his, Alexander escorted her from the room with a broad smile. 'Let's have some fun.'

CHAPTER 52

'Mister Alexander Webb and Miss Tomoko Den.' Announced the Master of Ceremonies, pausing them at the entrance.

Alexander had expected a larger crowd. Twenty perhaps twenty five had been announced before them and all were gathered eagerly around the exhibits. Jasmine caught Tomoko's eye and called her to view one of the show cases, leaving Alexander to enter alone. A uniformed commissionaire offered him a catalogue and at his request indicated the direction of the bar.

Resting casually against the rail he beckoned the steward, ordered a coffee, black with two sugars and looked around the room.

The lofty banqueting hall was resplendently appointed for the occasion. It had the look and smell of opulence and the two large chandeliers, to fit in with the period of most of the paintings, blazed warmly in contrast to the stark individual lighting afforded to each exhibit. Rows of glass display cases to the left and right formed an isle in the centre and each formed a gallery of its own with the sky blue velour dressed side walls, themselves adorned with tapestries and numerous framed canvases.

There were perhaps a hundred small gilt chairs arranged in arcs at the far end, vacantly waiting for the auctioneer to rise to his position at the wooden pulpit to begin the proceedings, no expense had been spared.

Matsumoto drew next to him at the bar. 'How are you feeling? nervous?'

'I was earlier, now I just feel queasy. A little too much medicinal brandy I'm afraid. It'll wear off, I'll be ok in an hour or so.'

Matsumoto's expression grew cold. 'You will still give your presentation I hope. I'd planned to start the proceedings with it.'

'Of course I will. We have an agreement. I only ask you to delay it for a while, that's all. Matsumoto-San, I don't wish to tell you your business, but to wait may in fact work to our advantage. Your guests will need time to settle, a pitch too early and they may err on the side of caution, saving their high bids for the middle and the end.'

Matsumoto nodded thoughtfully. 'An excellent observation Webb-San, you may be right. We'll do as you suggest, the middle it is. Now if you will forgive me, I must mingle with my guests. Enjoy the evening.'

With the reprieve he'd hoped for Alexander scanned the hall for Tomoko. The head count had swollen considerably since their arrival and she had proved difficult to spot. He estimated the group had grown closer to fifty and they were still arriving.

Through the sparkling gowns and the formal black and white his attention fell to an eighteen inch sculpture housed in a dome of glass. He knew it instantly and pressed through the crowds to examine it closer. Orange-pink in colour with traced lines of white, the bust was exactly as he'd imagined it to be. A head of tightly curled hair, a smooth blemish free face and a full majestic beard. The sign at its base read: 490 BC, Terra-cotta.

'A supreme work of Art. Reputed to be the likeness of Miltiades. The Athenian general and supreme tactician, whose strategy and planning routed the Persian attack on Athens in the battle of Marathon. Impressive, is it not?'

Alexander studied the expression of delight on the Deputy Police Commissioner's face. 'It is indeed. Marathon?'

'The very same. The celebrated battle in which a runner was dispatched to Athens to announce the Persian defeat before dying of exhaustion.'

'Fascinating. You talk with great scholarship, Mister...?'

'Tsugawa. I thank you for the compliment.'

'Deputy Commissioner General Tsugawa?'

'You have heard of me?'

'But of course. Your reputation recedes you. Shall we take our seats before the rush?'

CHAPTER 53

The short sharp staccato rap of gavel on wood drew an instant hush over the assembled throng, calling all eyes toward the regimental figure of Claythorpe at the podium. He coughed lightly and with a sweeping gesture indicated to the eight vacant rows of crescent seating before him. 'Take your places if you please, our auction will begin shortly.' He said.

Satisfied his message had been received he stepped down and passed behind the screens to supervise in the final preparations.

A gentle murmur of expectation stimulated the room as the remaining seconds ticked by on their approach to midnight. The gathering of guests, which had now swelled significantly beyond a hundred, jockeyed respectfully with each other for the best seats, positions with uninterrupted views of the exhibiting tables. To Alexander's mind the image was one of amusement. One of penguins leading peacocks. A silent power struggle, as the gentlemen of variegated races lead their finery adorned partners to sites previously secured by their respective bodyguards.

Past Tomoko to Alexander's left, Tsugawa sat oblivious to the commotion, absorbed in the contents of his catalogue. Periodically he turned the pages, read with typical Japanese intensity and with each new discovery made pencil notes in the margin. On his right a flamboyantly dressed Australian had secured the two remaining front row seats. He steadied his beer on the armrest at the second attempt, dusted the cushions pretentiously with a red satin handkerchief and offered the place at Alexander's side to his attractive teenage companion.

'Sit yourself down, darlin', take the load of yer feet.' He
drawled, flopping beside her. 'May as well get comfortable, we're
in for the duration.'

Amused, Alexander watched the man's expression develop as her cocktail dress climbed tantalisingly high up a bare thigh with her crossing legs. He found his eyes drifting in sympathy and agreed wholeheartedly it was a sight worthy of appraisal.

'Thank God it's in English.' Said the Australian with affected relief. 'I was dreading one of those translation thing-a-me's you stick in your ear, don't you just hate them?'

The girl shrugged her shoulders in ignorance and began to flick with disinterest from page to page, affording the same respect to the catalogue as she would have shown to an ageing magazine in a dentist's waiting room. 'Dunno what you're talkin about honey.' She said sheepishly.

'T'ain't important. See anythin you like? Name it, up to a mil and it's yours.'

A private smile grew on Alexander's lips. It was a different world. There was no doubt a girl with her looks would be used to generous gifts from admirers, who knows, she may well deserve them. But, a million dollars for a bit on the side, in his opinion, was a mite excessive.

Matsumoto stepped forward to take the stand, full of smiles and gestures of recognition for his guests. He nodded confidently, thankful of the polite applause rising before him, placed his notes onto the lectern and retrieved a pair of reading spectacles from his breast pocket.

'Ladies and Gentlemen. Friends.' He began. 'Greetings and welcome to this our first and hopefully inaugural gathering in Japan.' He paused momentarily to offer a bow of deference. 'I am supremely honoured to have been chosen as your host for this evening and thank each and every one of you for having accepted my invitation. I am in no doubt this promises to be our most rewarding auction assembly to date.'

He consulted his notes and continued. 'Many advances have been made in the arena of crime detection in the four short years since our last meeting. A period of major advancements in technology, with electronics and staged reconstruction's playing an increasingly important role. New teams of dedicated researchers with specialised investigators versed in the fields of antiquity, compete with your talents to safeguard the treasures of their respective nations. Yet! In spite of their efforts, you continue to succeed with ease. Truly a graphical demonstration of the superiority of your creative minds over the supposed expertise of the security services. My congratulations to you all.

'Much of our success can be attributed to the indefatigable assistance of one man. For twenty years, one amongst us has been perfectly placed to furnish strategic intelligence, advice on counter measures and key information to ensure the safety of our people out in the field. Our man on the inside so to speak. Tonight we honour him. He assures me that amongst the thirty two lots we have for you this evening, four of them are listed in Interpol's fabled top ten. A fine achievement and worthy of highlight. In order of merit, The Storm on the sea of Galilee by Rembrandt, The Concert by Vermeer, Manet's Chez Tortoni and a terra-cotta bust of a bearded man, dating five centuries before the birth of Jesus Christ. In effect, a collection par-excellence. I trust you will justify each of them with the bids they deserve. All that is, except the latter. Please join me, Ladies and Gentlemen in a warm hand, and welcome to the podium, Deputy Commissioner Tsugawa of the Metropolitan Police Force.'

Rapturous applause split the air as Tsugawa, visibly perplexed by the request, raised to his feet and crossed to join Matsumoto at the lectern. With a single tap of the gavel a white coated auction assistant appeared from the curtained wings to hand over the velvet draped gift.

Matsumoto held it aloft. 'In recognition for your unceasing guidance and support in our search for the finer things in life, we, the members of the gathering would like you to accept an offering of our appreciation.' Dramatically he removed the velvet veil to reveal the terra-cotta bust. 'We trust it is to your liking?'

Tsugawa, initially speechless, reached slowly forward to cradle the treasure in his arms. His delight at the encounter was evident. Carefully he traced the bust's features with his fingertips in a soft caress, assimilating as though by osmosis the perfection of the form. With the room silent, sharing the moment, he steadily lifted his gaze to the assembly. 'Kumagai-San insisted that I should be present this evening, cajoling me with the excuse he needed moral support at his first gathering. Now I understand the true reason, I shall probably never trust him again.'

A ripple of congenial laughter trickled through the audience.

'I really do not know what to say, I'm touched. To receive a gift for recognition from one's peers is invariably a pleasure, to receive such a generous gift from one's friends is...well...it's a joy beyond words. It's priceless!'

'No less priceless than the support you have given to all of us at some time or another.' Intoned Matsumoto. 'On behalf of the gathering, we thank you.'

The applause erupted into a standing ovation, enduring until well after Tsugawa had retaken his seat.

'Our thanks to Deputy Commissioner General Tsugawa.' Said Matsumoto, to quell the assembly. 'Ladies and Gentlemen, our proceedings will begin shortly, but first I would like to present to you two young men. The latest additions to our ranks.

'Our auction this evening may well include the finest collection of art ever to be offered under the hammer. Indeed some of the pieces have long been surrounded with the mystique of the Mary Celeste while others are recent acquisitions, the results of great daring. Cast your minds back to 1990, a significant date in the formative years of our Brotherhood. The art world was rocked by a spectacular robbery in Boston's Isabella Stewart Gardner Museum. Without doubt one of the most audacious and adventurous endeavours commissioned from within our organisation. Disguised as policemen, these two gentlemen, entered the premises, trussed up the guards and made off with a king's ransom. The Rembrandt and Vermeer gracing our auction room walls this evening, are testament to their success and to the security of our brotherhood. To quote the New York Times of the day, "Within three hours, about two hundred million dollars worth of irreplaceable creations had disappeared." Today, the estimate is no doubt closer to five hundred million.' Ladies and Gentlemen, I give you, the Borello brothers.'

Defying the applause Kraiwoot's sketches surfaced with lightening swiftness from Alexander's memory. Tomoko too had recognised them. The tightening grip of her fingers on his arm was undeniable proof. Reckless thoughts demanding an immediate reaction gripped him, as he recalled the callous torture they'd inflicted. The memory of the burns on Kraiwoot's frail arms pictured clearly in his mind and a flush of anger rose heatedly in his cheeks. Desperately he felt he should do something, shout out, tell someone, yet he knew his protest would fall on deaf ears and result in personal ridicule. He would have to wait, a rash move now would be foolhardy. Taking a calming deep breath he joined in, rather less enthusiastically, with the applause. A couple of hours were not too long to wait. Studying each of their faces, he vowed, these too would be marked for special attention when the time came.

To each in turn Matsumoto bestowed a silver award and his hand in congratulation.

'Danilo and Paolo, it is my privilege to present you with your spurs. As in days of old, proof of worth is valued as highly now as it was then. From this moment onwards you are welcome to call on any of us for financial aid, assistance in times of strife and guarantied support in all of your endeavours. In return, we ask for your loyalty and an offering of sufficient magnitude whenever we meet.'

In unison the Borello brothers bowed with acceptance.

Again the room filled with applause.

Amid the acclaim Matsumoto stepped down to leave way for Claythorpe to take up his rightful position of address. The gavel slapped twice and with a shuffling of chairs and catalogues the room settled back in to order.

'Ladies and Gentlemen.' He bellowed. 'For the sake of ease, all bids this evening will be accepted in American dollars. For those of you bidding with narcotics, our agreed conversion table may be found at the rear of the brochure, dollars per kilo and so on. You will also note that narcotic bids will only be accepted against those lots labelled with an initial, enclosed by a circle, to be found at the foot of each catalogue entry. The initials of course refer to the type of narcotic required. Is that clear to everyone?'

Flabbergasted at this new development Alexander turned to the back of his copy. As Claythorpe had said, Heroin, Cocaine and the rest with purity values, weights and cost were there, detailed in an innocuous kind of shopping list. He had heard speculation in television interviews of paintings being stolen to finance drug deals but had never imagined it could be true. Maybe he had been slow to make the connection, an organised crime syndicate, art theft and an international drug trafficking ring were probably a natural triumvirate. He shuddered to think of the extent to which this organisation had influence and tried as best as he could to distance it from his thoughts by returning his attention to Claythorpe.

'The electronic display board to my right will translate the latest bid into the nine currencies represented here this evening, and to my left, the item under offer will be revealed on either the easel or pivoting display unit.

'I draw your attention to lot number one. Entitled "Chez Tortoni", The work of the nineteenth century French artist, Edouard Manet. Recognised as a pivotal figure at the birth of the Impressionist movement and the first of those to attempt plein air painting. This particular painting was liberated as part of the Boston cache and we begin our auction with it to honour and celebrate the Borello brothers joining our ranks. I have a reserve price of seven hundred and fifty thousand dollars, what am I bid?'

A hand raised at the rear with fingers splayed.

'I have five hundred thousand to start it, at five hundred, six hundred, seven hundred...'

The bidding continued past the reserve.

A steadily increasing patter of rain drops drew Alexander's eyes to the window. Between the parted curtains he could see rivulets begin to form, channelled by the decay in the ageing wooden frames. The dry spell had evidently come to an end.

Solitary, Matsumoto stood before the tall decorated pane staring out into the darkness. Repeatedly he opened and closed the black leather box in his hand and occasionally glanced at its contents. He appeared troubled and stiffened visibly as Ling approached.

'Eight hundred and twenty five thousand I am bid. Eight fifty. Any more?' The hammer came down. 'Yours sir.' Said Claythorpe, his action provoking an instant response from the sales clerk to confirm the identity of the bidder.

'Lot two, an assortment of fifteen, hand painted and glazed plates from the hand of Pablo Picasso. A fine selection. Of especial interest, I draw your attention to a particular favourite of Francoise Gilot, his mistress from nineteen forty three to fifty three, a piece entitled 'Oseau sur fond bleu' and dated nineteen forty nine. A muster conservatively estimated in the region of one and a half million dollars and with a reserve, on this occasion, of five hundred thousand. What am I bid?'

The collection to Alexander's bewilderment attracted frenzied bidding from the audience. Warming to the atmosphere he twice raised his catalogue in fun to boost the ante before turning in search of the primary bidders. Following Claythorpe's eyes he quickly located them.

With feigned disinterest, a seated Latin, with a receding hairline, scratched the side of his nose, lowered his hand and inspected the dextrous nail for evidence, a prearranged signal for Claythorpe to transfer his attention to a Japanese displaying an apparent ear complaint. A tug at the troublesome lobe and the auctioneer returned his gaze for the Latin's counter bid.

Unaware of the event and ill at ease, Tomoko studied Matsumoto and Ling's exchange. 'They're talking about you.' She whispered.

CHAPTER 54

'And you believed him?' Said Ling in astonishment. 'With respect, Matsumoto-San, you have a reputation for shrewdness, a master with incomparable ability. Frankly, I am at a loss to conceive how you ever permitted yourself to be suckered by this Englishman. No ruby yet discovered can be worth that amount of money. He's up to no good, mark my words.'

'Your assumption is fundamentally correct my friend.' Said Matsumoto with a wry smile.

Ling's expression teetered between dismay and disbelief. 'Then why is he here? You realise he's simply playing for time.'

'You don't think I know that? If I were in his place I would be playing exactly the same game. Webb has much to lose and little to bargain with. He is here for one reason only, his ability to talk his way out of a difficult situation. His story, be it true or otherwise, is immaterial. Just so long as it raises the enthusiasm and loosens the purse strings of my guests. We understand each other?'

'We do indeed.' Said Ling with restored esteem.

Matsumoto released the stone from its box. 'A beautiful colour, don't you think?'

Comparing it with his own, Ling nodded his assent. 'Indeed, as you say, beautiful, one of a kind.'

'Should you wish to bid your stone as part payment against it at twenty five this will be perfectly acceptable.'

'And if it fetches less?'

'The Chandra ruby is valued at thirty million dollars, what ever the provenance Webb has to offer.'

'Very well, twenty five it is. On one condition, Taylor and Kumagai double check the grounds for my peace of mind. I'm sorry, but an outsider at our gathering makes me nervous.' Said Ling peering along the front row of seats. 'Webb looks far too comfortable for someone with no means of escape.'

The gavel fell at one million eight hundred thousand.

'I had no idea the Picasso's ceramics would be quite so popular.' Said Claythorpe with amazement. 'Should I remind you, Ladies and Gentlemen, these are "liberated" works of art?'

'Not necessary Claythorpe, old chap,' Quipped a facetious voice from the audience, 'split fifteen ways, these plates'll turn a tidy profit in the States.'

'My apologies sir. A clear example of why you are the purchaser and why I'm just a humble auctioneer.' Claythorpe offered his hands wide and bowed his head.

'You do ok.' Came the reply, amid a wave of chuckled laughter.

'Indeed I do. Astute of you to notice sir. We should move on. Lot three...'

The sight of Kumagai's summons to Matsumoto and his ensuing quick march from the Banqueting hall caused the hair on the back of Alexander's neck to prickle. Had something gone wrong?

He leaned towards Tomoko's ear. 'I'm off for a coffee.' He whispered. 'You? Milk, two sugars?'

Step for step Alexander followed Kumagai's passage past the bar and into the hallway. At the landing he paused. He could see them below, at the foot of the stairs, both Kumagai and Taylor. They checked their weapons, called on a night patrol for assistance and headed out into the blackness.

His thoughts turned to Charlie.

Alexander's voice echoed hollow in the stillness of Tomoko's bedroom. 'Charlie?' He appealed, pressing transmit on the walkie-talkie. 'Can you hear me?'

There was no reply. He tried again, raising the signal strength. Again, no reply save for a crackling emptiness.

Switching the transceiver to off he sat perched on the edge of the bed, pondering on his next move. It was out of character for Charlie to be out of reach without good reason. Distance was one possibility, yet having an insight into his reckless character, it was more than probable he'd still be close by, and at risk. He had to find out which.

Returning the set to the safe-keeping of Tomoko's suitcase Alexander stepped back out into the hallway, checked for observers and began to climb the stairs.

On the fourth step he paused, half expecting to be called back. A room adjoining the banqueting hall, he'd previously assumed to be a nothing more than a linen cupboard, had its door wedged open wide and a few paces inside a brace of propane cylinders. Further into the room and he could see a roaring wide mouthed furnace attended by a guard. Curious to the reason for it's presence Alexander felt drawn for a closer look. He checked his watch, five minutes had elapsed since leaving the hall. Kumagai's extracurricular activities had to be his prime concern. Given the opportunity he would investigate it later, for now it was prudent to press on upwards.

He slowed markedly on his approach to the top step. Facing the third floor landing the door to the security operations room stood ajar and a voice muffled by another's laughter came from inside.

Disbelieving the sight, he moved cautiously forward. Before him, astride the guard, sat a woman stripped to the waist, her eyes closed, her hands outstretched to his shoulders and her head thrown back. The surrounding monitors shimmered with the signals from the night vision cameras, bathing them both in a surreal green glow.

It was hard to see detail at this distance but the general location of the shelter was recognisable on two of the screens.

Alexander searched his mind for a word or two Tomoko had taught him. 'Anatawo! - You.' He commanded, with all the bearing he could muster, threw the door open wide and pointed down the stairs. 'Kumagai!'

It had the desired effect. The guard and his maiden fled without a word, each covering their modesty.

For however briefly, he was alone. The console, illegibly labelled in Japanese was as confusing as a flight simulator. Nothing was familiar. He sat in the guard's disagreeably warm chair in the vain hope of unravelling the puzzle. A functioning joy-stick zoomed and panned the image on the console's main screen, controlling a camera over the castles entrance. He tried the switches at its side in an attempt to change cameras to no effect. Without a close up of the shelter he couldn't be sure Charlie was safe. A set of buttons lay at his left hand. Colour coded in red, green and blue. Expecting green to be the current display, he pressed red. All of the screens changed. Blurred patterns of red and white replaced the clear images of the castle's guards. At an instant he knew the meaning. Thermal imaging cameras had been used to measure drive motor temperatures at the development lab of Global Design.

Glancing at the monitors covering the shelter, he'd guessed right.

'Bloody fool.' He said, under his breath. If he were in Charlie's position, that was exactly where he would be, close at hand.

Intensifying movement caught his eye on the main screen. The number of bodies had increased to double figures. For a full ten seconds they huddled together before breaking into an extended line for a walking assault on the surrounding hillside.

The knot of tension in his stomach grew agonisingly tighter with each advancing step, aggravated by a feeling of helplessness in his watch and wait for the inevitable. 'Get out of there Charlie.' He whispered through his tightening jaw, willing him to hear, "Move now."

There was movement, slow, barely perceptible, a deliberate rocking from side to side on the ground beside the shelter. The door creaking behind him, momentarily stunning Alexander's thoughts. He turned guiltily to face it.

'Having fun are we?' Asked Matsumoto, entering the room.

Stealing a final look, Alexander glanced for the last time at the monitor. Four bodies were now on the screen, one prone and three advancing. Then, quite unexpectedly and defying all comprehension, something strange began to happen. Gradually the image of Charlie began to diminish and fade.

'A night on the Peak in Hong Kong should have taught you the lesson.' Said Charlie mumbling to himself. 'God knows, you'll never learn.' Damp and miserable, he slapped his hands behind his back to keep warm. 'Talking to yourself? First sign of madness Tan. Second sign's getting involved in dam fool quests when it's raining.' He pulled the lightweight jacket up close to his face.

His watch read twelve forty five. He'd give them another half hour, to make sure all was quiet, then go in search of Hara.

'Action?' He lifted Alexander's field glasses for a closer examination of the entrance. Taylor and Kumagai, what did they want? He would have laid odds on them both being fair weather types.

In spite of the torrential rain the squawk from the walkie-talkie on his hip shocked without warning, threatening an early grave. By reflex he killed the sound. Message received and understood. Moving a fraction closer he lay prostrate on a soaking bed of leaves watching the scouting party form, first into a group and then into a line at the foot of the hill. His heart began to race at the sight of Taylor. Clearly no amateur, by the look of the apparatus emerging from his canvas hip pack he had come prepared.

Illuminated by the porch light Charlie could see the braided strap pass over his head and the equipment position carefully before his eyes. It was impossible to tell if the goggles were night-finders or Infra-red. Finding the shelter himself in daylight had proved hard enough so the image intensifying night finders would probably be no problem. The problem would come if Taylor could see his body heat. Which ever it was, the immediate risk, thankfully, was minimised by the rain. The effective range of portable infra-red would be reduced to little more than a hundred feet. With luck he would have time.

Back in the shelter he quickly unravelled the spent sandwich foil and began to feed it beneath his clothing. Most of his body could be covered this way and extra layers of clothes would also help. His hands and face still posed a problem. Crawling from beneath the covers to the nearest ditch he rolled himself in the mud, applying handfuls to his face and hands. Comfort, he reflected, would have to take the back seat. Distance would be his only other ally. At a crouch and as quietly as possible he began his run.

CHAPTER 55

Claythorpe by now was into his stride. It was Lot thirteen. The Monet described by Tomoko was on display and the bidding had already reached well into six figures.

'I was worried sick. Where have you been?' Asked Tomoko, feeding her hand into his.

'Misbehaving and getting my wrists slapped.' Whispered Alexander. 'Matsumoto felt sightseeing at a time like this was inappropriate.'

'Sightseeing?'

'Checking on Charlie. Kumagai's on the prowl outside.'

A look of concern clouded Tomoko's beauty. 'He's safe, isn't he?'

'Who, Kumagai? He'll catch his death if he's not careful, it's pouring out there.'

'Please Alex, be serious, I'm nervous enough as it is.'

Alexander smiled. 'He'll be ok. We're on next, before the Rembrandt.'

Over the bidding Alexander could hear the clock in the hallway strike the first quarter. The police would make their move in less than forty five minutes. If he screwed up they'd be dead in thirty. There was nothing for it but to make the best sales pitch of his life. Racking his brains, he began to make notes on the back cover of his catalogue. It was small consolation for Sonya's death, but the satisfaction of informing Matsumoto's Gathering of the truth about something none of them could ever own, in it's own way, justified a fitting revenge.

As the hammer fell Matsumoto strode confidently to the foot of the lectern, raised his hand to pause the proceedings and turned to the audience. 'Forgive the intrusion Mister Claythorpe, Ladies and Gentlemen, but I believe the time has come for me to put an end to the speculation. As in the past it has been the prerogative of the host to choose the moment at which he feels he can best benefit from the generosity of his guests, in essence the moment he feels most advantageous to reveal the unnumbered lot. Friends, you are right to have come to expect an offering of considerable magnitude, and I have no intention of disappointing you. On behalf of Matsumoto industries I have for you this evening an item I believe to be beyond your wildest expectations. Namely, one hundred and fifty seven carats of pure ruby. The Chandra Ruby. One of the largest of its type in the world and the result of a year's meticulous planning and endeavour.'

Easing the box open he passed it to his guests in the front row for scrutiny. 'Examine it carefully my friends, touch it, see it's clarity, this may be the only time in your lives you have a jewel of such beauty and quality, available and on offer.'

Slowly, with appreciation, the stone passed from hand to hand, each reluctant to progress it further.

Studying the expressions with care Alexander hoped to gain an insight into its acceptance. The interest was high and so he hoped would be the bidding.

Despite passing through nine hands the Australian was the first to lift it from the box and offer it to the light. 'Nice trinket Matsumoto, what's it worth?' He asked.

Matsumoto crossed to the Australian's left and looked hard at Alexander weighing the risk. 'Gem stone's of importance are not only valued for their material worth but also for their history. For this, I will invite my colleague, Mister Alexander Webb, to enlighten you further.' He said, placing a hand on his shoulder.

'On the face of it, twenty five to thirty million dollars.' Said Alexander, rising and making his way to the lectern.

'Jees..' Hissed the Australian amidst similar exclamations from the assembly.

'However,' Alexander continued, 'Mister Matsumoto is under the impression that I have come to offer you a provenance on the Chandra Ruby. If this is what he expects I fear he will be disappointed. The simple fact is that the stone you see before you is not the Chandra Ruby. In essence, the Chandra Ruby never existed.'

'What?' Exclaimed Matsumoto.

'Permit me to explain.' Said Alexander calmly. 'The stone we have with us this evening was cut over two thousand years ago in India, making it the first faceted gem stone in history. Essentially lost for fifteen hundred years it was rediscovered some five hundred years ago in the north of Thailand, set in a statue of Buddha and encased in clay. Moved several times from palace to palace the statue came to rest in Vientiane in fifteen sixty, where it became the private property of King Setthathirat and enshrined in a jewelled temple on an elaborate golden palladium. A Thai General from the south was dispatched by the King of Dhonburi to claim it for his own not long after. It was on this return journey that the Ruby was removed from the statue. Who stole it, nobody knows. A similar stone, a Spinel I am informed, was found to replace it and cut in a similar way to conceal the King's shame. That is, four sides signifying the four truths of Buddhism and a flaw in the centre to signify the impure heart of mankind. It is this stone which lives in the heart of the statue today.'

'The Emerald Buddha!' Said Ling, louder than he had intended.

'Exactly.' Said Alexander. 'As I have said before, this is not the Chandra Ruby. This, Ladies and Gentlemen, is probably the most valued gem stone in the east and possibly the world. Namely, the heart of the Emerald Buddha, the Rama's Hope. A symbol of a faith and in the true sense of the word, a ruby without price. Priceless.'

'Bloody hell!' Said the Australian breaking the silence.

'Bloody hell indeed!' Intoned Matsumoto, stunned by the revelation.

'You can prove this?' Stated Ling, hopefully.

'Every word, given time.' Answered Alexander, addressing Matsumoto. 'In principle the purchaser could receive a copy of all of the documents I've been privy to.'

'Claythorpe, your evaluation and expert opinion, if you please.' Requested Matsumoto.

Again the room fell silent. With loupe in hand Claythorpe began an examination. Following a cursory inspection he called for an attendant to have a table lamp brought for deeper analysis and resumed. Nothing could be gleaned from his expression, his manner and facial demeanour remained unchanged throughout.

Carefully replacing the loupe into his waistcoat pocket Claythorpe raised his head. 'Sir. As you, and many of those here can attest my curriculum vitae in the world of collectables is extensive. What may be less apparent is the considerable training I received in Lapidary and gem stone marketing during eight years experience in Antwerp. So rest assured you can trust my judgement and appraisal of this item.'

Having established his credentials Claythorpe paused to polish his glasses.

'I am familiar with the legend of the Rama's Hope and having heard Mister Webb's provenance, I am prepared to believe in its existence. Such a stone would indeed be priceless. Therefore, I would conservatively estimate the value of this stone to be somewhere within a region of ninety to one hundred..,' He paused to lock his eyes on those of Matsumoto, 'Dollars. Unfortunately, for your purposes this evening Mister Matsumoto, the stone is virtually worthless. This, I'm afraid sir, is a counterfeit, a flame fusion copy.'

CHAPTER 56

Shocked into silence the audience waited uneasily for some form of explanation. Unsettled by the tension, bemused Japanese, amused Chinese, disapproving Americans and suspicious Italians each focused with eager expectation on the reaction of their host. At the very least the situation called for a violent outburst.

With resignation Matsumoto approached the podium to receive the stone in his outstretched hand. Outwardly composed he offered a brief nod to acknowledge the auctioneer's prowess and turned with an open stance to face his guests.

'Ladies and Gentlemen, what can I say? Obviously there has been some degree of confusion. Taking the precaution of having a replica made for security, I had thought, until now, it had been an excellent idea. Please be assured, the Chandra, or should I say, the Rama's Hope ruby does exist and it is in my possession.'

Matsumoto paused to allow the relieving effects of his words sufficient air to defuse the anxiety in the room. 'A regrettable and unfortunate oversight, I can only assume our bank in Mishima must still hold the original. My sincere apologies. Bear with me my friends while I endeavour to have it collected. Mister Webb, a moment of your time if you please.' Determinedly he strode for the central isle, calling to the air as he went. 'You're doing an admirable job Mister Claythorpe, do continue, we will return as soon as possible.'

Quick on his heels Tomoko followed Alexander to the landing and down the sweeping gallery staircase, her heart thumping uncontrollably in her breast with the certain knowledge their life expectancy would be measured in seconds rather than hours from that moment on. They had almost made it. If Claythorpe had been a local auctioneer she was convinced they would have. She should have known. Or at least guessed. For an auction of this magnitude it was inconceivable for a man of Matsumoto's standing to have chosen anyone but a leading authority in the field of antiquities.

'Dam it Webb!' Matsumoto, boiling with rage, turned on them at the door to his study. 'You humiliated me! You cannot begin to imagine the damage you've done. And for what? This? This...Junk!' Aksorn's craft flew from his hand with the force of a baseball pitch, destined inevitably to cease existence the moment it struck the castle wall. With scarcely a sound the charlatan ruby shattered on impact. 'You have both put me to a great deal of trouble. If I do not receive a satisfactory answer I intend to put you both through a great deal of pain. Now talk fast Englishman, the original, where is it?'

'H..H..How should I know?' Stammered Alexander, feigning surprise. 'I thought that was it. I'm as stunned as you are. Do you think I could have delivered that presentation if I'd known otherwise?'

As Alexander spoke, Tomoko, in desperation, reached a second time for the vase that had proved its usefulness in acquiring Charlie's overalls. Taking a firm grasp about it's base she raised it precariously aloft. Its full weight was in her hands for barely a second.

Simultaneously with the deafening crash of porcelain innumerable shards burst into the air. Gossamer fragments dancing in slow motion before her, feather-like in their decent to the patchwork marble floor. A ceramic cascade pirouetting gracefully to a tinkling rest about Matsumoto's feet.

Time for the moment appeared to hang in suspension, the blow seeming to have no effect but to cause a trickle of blood to course down the nape of his neck. He looked incredulously towards her. Soundless mouthed words of disbelief faltering on his lips. Then with the clouding of his eyes the strength in his legs ebbed visibly away. He buckled at the knees and unceremoniously slumped to the unyielding tiles.

Reacting instinctively Alexander cupped his hands under Matsumoto's arms and dragged the leaden weight through the study doorway. There was only one would-be hiding place, the foot-well beneath the vast elaborate writing desk. With regard to security against detection it had it's limitations, but for a couple of hours he hoped it would suffice.

'I had to do something,' whimpered Tomoko, a base remnant of the Ming vase still in her hand, 'it was the only thing I could think of. Is he dead?'

'It'll take more than that to kill this parasite.' Said Alexander regrettably. 'See what you can do to clear up the mess in the hall. It could save us valuable minutes.'

While Tomoko worked furiously, office basket in hand to remove all traces of the event, Alexander checked through the glass panels flanking the castle's entrance. As a means of escape it was out of the question. One of a dozen or more chauffeurs was sure to raise the alarm. Undaunted he scanned for other possibilities. The side door passageway revealed on his capture flashed to mind. He tried the door, it was open.

Thankfully there was still no movement from the landing. 'I think we've outstayed our welcome Tomoko, it's time we left.'

Leading the way Alexander illuminated the passage with the flame from his petrol cigarette lighter. 'It's damp, mind your step.' He cautioned in a whisper, hoping he could remember the directions.

Twice the passageway split, on each occasion terminating in unexpected rooms. The first revealed a brightly lit and clinically clean kitchen, active with intent junior staff too preoccupied to notice them, and the second a guard's rest room, devoid of personnel.

A fleeting inspection paid dividends. Sheathed by a surgically stripped apple core on the dining table lay a bone handled knife with a Bowie style blade, and on the wall behind the door, a regiment of trench coats and caps hung dormant on wooden pegs. Why they were there and not in use against the foul weather outside left Alexander bewildered. Judging sizes he lifted a set apiece and returned to the passage, desperately hoping for third time lucky.

Within a few feet of the rest room door the stone floor felt slippery underfoot. He stooped to examine it, blessed the rain and carefully followed the footprints down to a junction with a familiar corridor.

'This is it Tomoko. Listen. Raise your coat collar, cap down tight, lower your voice and speak only in Japanese. Stay close. It's left out of here, along the path, around the car park and then up into the woods. Whatever happens, keep talking, keep your cool and hide your face. Got it?'

'Hai!...You're dead sexy when you're masterful, did you know that?' She said, her voice trembling.

'Really?' Teased Alexander.

With the first step outside the driving rain cold showered them both, instilling the feeling that each droplet would freeze on impact. Through Tomoko's incessant and incomprehensible chatter Alexander wondered which of Nara's three wise monkeys would suffer as a result, this was brass monkey weather, no question about it.

He glanced down at his patent shoes and across to Tomoko's black evening dress and again weighed the odds of crossing the laser net. The disguise of their coats and his recollection of Ninja's from television wearing full length black for battle would have to be good enough.

Placing himself between her and the line of sight of the cars for added security he dug his hands deep into his benevolent benefactor's warm coat pockets. Agreeably the right revealed an open packet of spearmint chewing gum. There were four left. Ideal for calming the nerves, he mused, and offered one to Tomoko. Another fifty yards and they would be in the moderate safety of the brush.

A perceived movement inside a brace of limousines beside the pathway triggered the adrenaline to course through his veins. A few paces closer and the movement was unmistakable. He lowered his head and quickened the pace. A gnawing ache of regret groaned at the back of his mind. The idea of crossing so close to a bank of parked cars had now begun to present itself as a manifestation of outright blatant stupidity. With each step his feet felt heavier, leaden with an overwhelming sense of foreboding.

'Sumimasen?' A chauffeur, the last in the line called through his open car door window.

Shaking with uncertainty Tomoko moved to the shroud of Alexander's shadow to answer. The discourse lasted barely a minute. A fast staccato exchange of words, a good-natured mixture of insults and pleasantries. He'd seen Alexander place a piece of chewing gum into his mouth and wanted some. Tomoko summarily obliged, tossing the remaining two strips across him onto the passenger seat at his side. Then grunting something to the effect of 'Next time bring your own', she slapped Alexander manly on the back and signalled to move on.

The car's interior courtesy light snapped on and was followed soon after by a call of 'Kansha!' and a rustling of paper from the inside.

Convinced the worst was over an audible involuntary waft of relief emanated from them both. So, Kansha means thanks considered Alexander, stepping upwards into the brush. He wouldn't forget that in a hurry. Stressful encounters always managed to teach something, not least Tomoko's resistance to pressure, she was full of surprises.

CHAPTER 57

'You ok back there?' He asked, ten minutes into the climb.

'Sure. Regular spy I am.'

He smiled. 'You've been around English sarcasm to long.'

'You think so? Maybe I should have picked a Frenchman.' She said wearily. 'Can we rest a while?'

With the castle still visible in the distance the risk would be high but acceptable. 'Certainly my dear.'

Alexander wasn't sure if it was the rain that was easing or the cover of the tree canopy that was stemming its fall, either way it mattered little. The ground underfoot was sodden and progress difficult, doubly so with vision barely a few feet before them in the blackness. Tomoko was right, all be it inadvisable, they should rest. Short sharp bursts were probably the best way to reach the car in these conditions.

A large fallen tree lay across their make-shift path, impeding the way ahead. Fortune at last was smiling on them, it was an ideal place. A towering pine at the log's end would also offer shelter and a welcome back rest.

Tomoko drifted to it without a word and slouched immodestly against the trunk.

For a time they sat in silence facing the way that they had come, breathing heavily, each knowing full well the other's discomfort. Bending at the waist Alexander stroked an open palm down his shins. They ached from bruising and his calves stung from constant scratching through the bramble. By comparison Tomoko's must be in one hell of a state, he thought. Any normal woman would have begun her complaining a long way back. With only stockings for protection, her's would be cut to shreds. He reached for her hand and patted it gently.

'This may not be the ideal moment for me to say this, but I think I'm...'

A crack, a hundred yards distant, stopped Alexander's declaration mid stream. Then another, this time closer.

'Absolutely still, don't move.' He whispered.

Stealthily Alexander slipped from the log and reached down into the mulch, dredging hopefully at his feet. Success. He closed his hand over a branch the thickness of a mans arm. It was hard, undecayed. It moved with ease and was at a guess three feet long. Charged and hardly daring to breathe he waited, his ear sensitive to each unseen sway of limbs through the distressed undergrowth. Who ever the person was moved quickly, he was muttering, cursing, English? No, there was an accent, American.

'...Seen better trained chimps in the god dam zoo. Nip's, waste of bleedin' time. Avn't got a fuckin' clue,...'

The voice was close. A yard, perhaps two. Too close not to react. Coiled to strike Alexander stole a glance in Tomoko's direction. From the approach of the footsteps she'd be invisible. Motionless, an amorphous shape fusing with the pine.

This was it. A combat boot crunched the bark above his head. It's twin landed an inch from his hand. With barely a rustle Alexander sprang. The branch drawing a perfect arc to it's objective, felling Taylor with a single blow. He was out cold, his face pitched down into the mud.

Resisting the temptation for a second blow, Alexander felt the side of his neck for a pulse. Thankfully the man was still alive. 'Keep your eyes and ears open, there's more of them out here.' He whispered.

Casting the branch aside he rolled Taylor's face to turn it from the sludge. Having failed to kill him by clubbing there was little point in succeeding by suffocation. Curiously an unusual texture filled his grasp. In place of the full head of hair he'd expected, his fingers closed over a stiff band of elastic webbing.

Intrigued, Alexander eased the apparatus free. Despite never having seen one before he instantly knew it's usefulness. Wiping the splashes of mud from the lenses, he stretched the straps over his own head and placed the viewfinder before his eyes.

The world around him immediately transformed into a sea of green images. A monochrome, electronically enhanced display of amplified light, converting night into day.

Initially the vision was strange, difficult to assimilate. His brain refusing the input from the stereoscopic video. It was only the appearance of Tomoko's features in softened detail that gave the image from the intensifiers a resemblance of reality.

'There's a small machine gun, two feet in front of his right hand. Check if it's loaded.' He said and set to searching Taylor's body for ammunition.

Stooped to all fours Tomoko patted the bed of leaves on the downward slope and offered the weapon with a glow of triumph.

'How on earth? You must have the eyes of an eagle.' She said.

Smiling secretly to himself Alexander glanced down at Taylor. He was breathing heavily with a laboured rasp. 'Would you believe, second sight?'

'For you? No chance.'

'Why not?' He asked, deciding to bind Taylor's wrists down his back to his bootlaces.

'If you had second sight, we wouldn't be in this mess!'

'Good point.'

Taking Tomoko by the hand Alexander chose his advancing steps with care, judiciously paving a way through the softer vegetation to save further personal discomfort. They were making good progress. A detour through the tea plantation flanking the edge of the wood, although longer in distance, had made the going easy. And now with a mile or more passed since their altercation with Taylor they were back in woodland and approaching recognisable terrain.

'Much further?' Wheezed Tomoko, throwing her head back, breathing hard.

'Not far. Ten minutes and we'll be at the car. It's just over the ridge.'

The all enveloping darkness had begun to break up. Shafts of brilliant moonlight appeared and disappeared with the race of cloud across the sky. From one moment to the next the scene ahead of them changed, switching rapidly from a land bathed in nocturnal daylight to a carpet of impenetrable blackness and then back again.

As a consequence, the image intensifiers, although a definite aid, were proving difficult to use. Slow to adjust and tiring on the eyes. With the sensitivity set for low illumination each breach in the cloud cover momentarily dissolved Alexander's image to a bright screen, making it necessary to pause for the stability to return. He quickly fell into the pattern of consciously removing the apparatus on each break to check the light and to set himself goals for the next large patch of cloud or extended period of open sky.

On one such break Tomoko gripped his arm. 'What was that?' She whispered, 'Did you hear it?'

Alexander had and was already surveying the woodland for movement. This time the full moon helped. A dozen moving silhouettes with shouldered weapons crested the brow of the hill and were descending in a V formation towards them.

'We've got company. In to the brush, this way!'

Unquestioning Tomoko followed, crouching beneath the enfolding umbrella of an established rhododendron, to hide in its shield of blackness.

The footsteps came. Heavy and tired. Lethargic flashlight beams apathetically scanning the bushes, singular in their objective, to search for a pathway back to the castle. There was no conversation, not even an attempt to examine the undergrowth as they passed.

Waiting silently, Alexander listened intently for the snap and crackle of footsteps to pass from ear-shot before retaking Tomoko's hand to press on up to the brow.

CHAPTER 58

'Charlie?' He called, in a loud whisper. His spirits surging at the sight of the car. 'Charlie! You sleeping? How can you possibly sleep at a time like this?'

With a metallic click the passenger door opened, a camouflaging branch slipped from the roof and a foot stepped out.

'You took your time.'

'Charlie?'

'He's here. Resting.'

'Who's that?' Demanded Alexander, cautiously raising Taylor's Uzi to the direction of the voice.

'You should know my voice by now Mister Webb.' Said Kumagai, moving into full view. A beam from his flashlight landing squarely on Alexander's face. 'Drop your weapon, there's a good fellow.'

Blinded by the light Alexander instinctively squeezed the trigger in his right hand. The report was deafening. Ten rounds spiting lead and fire from the climbing muzzle, two possibly accurate, the rest invariably missing their target with the rising recoil.

Had he hit him? No cry of pain, yet, he must have, the beam had gone. Expecting the worst his every sinew and muscle tightened, his eyes strained searching for detail in the developing image as agonisingly slowly the intensifier began its digital reconstruction.

The torch, still alight, lay discarded on the ground beside the car. Cautiously stepping closer he could see Charlie slumped inside, quiescent in the driving seat and to his left fractionally behind him, Tomoko taking cover in the brush. A body was nowhere to be seen.

'Good try Webb.' The voice was calm, at stark contrast to the explosive force that followed. Measured to perfection, Kumagai's foot slammed hard into Alexander's wrist. The Uzi spat again, this time uncontrolled in its flight from his hand. 'That makes us even. Prepare to die Webb.'

Alexander took a quick step back and to his right, out of range of the inevitable follow up. As he moved his heart raced faster, he could see a pencil thin blade in Kumagai's hand glinting in the moonlight. The hilt rolled gently between practised fingers, demonstrating the Japanese's dexterity and thorough familiarity with the weapon. He would need help. A swift glance skyward showed he had an ally. A bank of cloud was approaching rapidly. If he could keep Kumagai at reach until it arrived, god willing, the match could well go in his favour, he would have the advantage of sight.

Circling carefully he removed his large grey coat, slipped the bowie knife from its pocket and wrapped the bulky material tightly around his left arm.

Kumagai balked visibly at the sight, he hadn't expected his foe to be similarly armed with the Israeli firearm disposed of. He too circled, watching for weaknesses, airing on the side of caution.

Crabbing quickly to one side Alexander held the knife firmly in his right hand copying Kumagai, ready to thrust, blade upwards, thumb and forefinger to the front of the grip, weight evenly distributed over the balls of his feet, one foot forward for balance.

'The police are on their way Kumagai.' He warned, keeping a distance of eight feet between them.

'Sure they are.' There was a laugh in his voice. 'Very imaginative. You surprise me.'

'They're moving in now, Hara's men. Have no doubts Kumagai-San, you're going down for Sonya's murder.'

Kumagai, circling tighter, brushed the tall grass with his feet to check for debris, clearing it methodically with effortless flicks of his ankle. 'And not yours? That is disappointing.'

'No doubt you are better trained for this than I am. But then again, this is not about ability is it? This is revenge, and that makes it unpredictable.'

Kumagai began to toss his knife from hand to hand, the grip slapping the palm with a firm thump on each exchange.

'An unpredictable Englishman? Now there is a novelty.'

The blanket of darkness came. And as if on cue Hara's voice, at some distance, shattered the stillness of the night. Sharp orders in response to the gunfire.

'Over here!' Shouted Alexander, clearly defining his position to Kumagai before silently moving a yard to the left.

Kumagai's confident tone disappeared. 'Enough of this talk.' He stepped in abruptly, his right leg lunging out in a fencing thrust ten inches to the side of Alexander's waist, carving nothing but thin air. Seeing the blade Alexander countered, driving the Bowie hard down onto the stiletto's shaft hoping to separate it from Kumagai's hand. The clash of steel against steel rang as clean as a tenor bell but failed in its objective.

Back to circling Kumagai's stance was now wider, both hands high as though feeling for vibrations in the air. A classic attack posture, his karate grounding to the fore.

Controlling his breathing Alexander moved as stealthily as possible to position himself to Kumagai's right side. He thrust forward. Once more the clash of steel. The Japanese's response lightening fast.

How? A blind reaction or decades of experience? It was hard to tell. From the positive movement Alexander feared it was the latter.

'Stop it!' Screamed Tomoko, 'Stop it or I'll Shoot!'

For a split second Alexander lifted his gaze to that of Kumagai's and realised instantly his error. He tried to step back, stumbling in retreat to stem the inexorable onslaught. It was too late.

Sensing the hesitation Kumagai had made his strike decisive. A swift flight through the air to bury the slip proof tread of his leather boot squarely into Alexander's chest. It landed high, an inch below his neck.

Gasping for breath Alexander's head snapped hard forward, the whiplash ripping the intensifier brutally from his face. He could feel his body lifting out of control, staggering, unable to hold it's ground against the force. He was reeling backwards, a yard, two, powerless in his struggle to prevent himself from crashing against the confine of trees.

Landing with agility Kumagai pressed on, raising the stiletto to a dagger grip and thrusting it down with deadly accuracy towards Alexander's neck.

In a last ditch effort to protect himself Alexander raised his coat swathed arm as a token shield of defence. With more luck than judgement Kumagai's blow crushed into it.

A shaft of excruciating pain attacked mercilessly at his senses, nullifying his ability to assess the extent of damage. The sensation felt alien, like no other he had felt before. An unremitting rush of blood to countless tortured nerve endings swelling in the crushed and broken tissue. He knew without question the blade had found its mark in the flesh of his arm.

Weak and disorientated he tried to pull it free. It wouldn't come. It seemed to have a mind of it's own, thrashing unchecked.

Then, amidst repeated impassioned pleas to stop from Tomoko, a flash light beam landed squarely on them both. The reason for his inability to control the arm was now clear to see. An inch of the stiletto's blade was visible penetrating through the wrapped coat's folds. Kumagai's knife had lodged fast.

Mustering his last reserves of strength Alexander flailed the bowie knife wildly upwards. There was contact. Instantly, with the load on his arm releasing, the air filled with an agonising scream. His blade had caught Kumagai's face, opening a six inch fissure vertically from his neck into his hair line, severing a portion of his ear.

Wounded and distraught the Japanese staggered in retreat. Both hands locked fast to the left hand side of his face. 'You b......'

The detail in the curse was lost, drowned by a repetition of loud reverberating bangs. A cacophony of sound terminating with a slap of bolt against steel with the Uzi's last round.

Thrown physically from his feet Kumagai spun wildly in the air as a succession of soft lead bullets flattened on contact with his chest and shoulder, his fight for the day was over. A sprawling conifer at the edge of the clearing buckled under the strain of his weight and gave way. The thicket beneath crackling in protest offered little resistance. It swallowed his body whole and closed again to conceal it from sight.

Down to his knees, Alexander began to shake with nervous exhaustion. His stomach grew tight and with an involuntary spasm a taste of bile filled his mouth. He retched. He'd faced death, perhaps the closest he would ever come to it without meeting his maker, and he'd survived.

Tomoko knelt at his side. She spoke to him. Comforting words soothing the waves of attacking pain from his arm. He rested his head onto her lap, closed his eyes, allowed the clouds of blackness to form and lapsed submissively into unconsciousness.

CHAPTER 59

The noises from the undergrowth had grown louder. There was a snap of dead timber from behind the car, and to the right, a whisper in the bushes beyond the spent bullet casings, they were close. She could almost feel them. A beam of torch light bathed the ground about her, glistening like beads of opal in Alexander's perspiration. Two further beams panned the clearing, searchlights probing the stage for its principle players and then the movement came. A surge from all directions, barked orders to remain still and surrender weapons, countless men breaking cover racing decisively to secure the perimeter. And then a voice. Instantly recognisable as the voice of authority. It was purposely directing the attention of a brace of combat clad soldiers sporting red and white arm bands urgently in her direction. A wave of relief swept over her as she resolved the identity of the owner.

Hara's initial reaction, one of anger on hearing the foolhardy actions of his surrogate officers, had mellowed. As Tomoko's story unfolded a quiet admiration for their courage had replaced it. Not only had they successfully recovered the stone, revealed with much amusement from the aromatic depths of one of Charlie's socks, they had gleaned valuable intelligence; amply justifying the resources he had commandeered.

He had positively glowed at the established presence of Deputy Commissioner General Tsugawa. An officer beyond reproach, a recognised pillar of Japanese law enforcement, a man ultimately responsible for his suspension and now a man confirmed as having been seen receiving and assisting in the traffic of stolen goods. In recent days his faith had been tested to the limit, this single act had restored it.

'He's coming round sir.' Declared the police paramedic, wafting a phial of smelling salts under Alexander's nose. 'How's the other one?'

Leaving Charlie to a second medic Hara crossed to kneel at Alexander's side. 'A little groggy, but he'll live. He's a very resilient man. A fraction higher though and the blow would have killed him.'

'It looks to me Sir that they have both been very fortunate.'

'No argument. They lead a charmed life these two. Maybe some of their luck will rub off on the rest of us tonight, who knows?'

It had been fifteen minutes since the task force leader's digital wristwatch had announced it's deadline of 2 am and a sense of urgent impatience had begun to set in amongst the junior officers. Hara felt it too. Tomoko's de-brief had sown in him seeds of excitement. A tantalising account capable of securing a future few in his position could ever aspire to. Unfortunately it had fallen fractionally yet distressingly short of the mark. A significant key to the success of the whole operation was missing. Charlie's lucid report had added little more, Alexander's he hoped would do better. The decision between an airborne or land based attack would hinge upon it. All he could do was impotently watch and wait, mindful of the fact the auction would be drawing to a close at any moment.

'The Englishman, how badly is he hurt?' He asked.

'He's in shock, the cut on his arm needs dressing and there's some minor bruising. Other than that I can't say, I'll know more when he's fully conscious.'

'Well as soon as he is able, I have to talk to him. It's vitally important.'

Preparing an Entonox cylinder the paramedic began shaking his head. Vitally important, It always was. Maybe one day he would meet a police officer with a patient's best interests at heart, but he doubted it. 'Make it brief then, his body's been through a great deal of trauma. We should get him to a hospital as quickly as possible.'

'For Pete's sake, speak English!' Chided Alexander, clenching his teeth against the pain. His opening eyes fell on Hara's concerned face leaning over him. The sight forced an instant sigh of relief. 'If we ever get out of here alive remind me to buy you a beer. Glad you could make it chief. How's Charlie?'

'Charlie's fine. He tells me he's got a bad case of mood poisoning. As we Japanese would say, must be something he hate.'

'Breathe deeply.' Instructed the paramedic, placing a mask over Alexander's nose and mouth. 'It's gas and air, it'll take the pain away. Tell me when it begins to subside and I'll dress your arm. That's the way, deep breaths.'

Quietly insistent Hara lowered his head to Alexander's ear. 'Webb-San, please, listen carefully. The surveillance room, the room controlling the cameras, do you know where it is?'

Alexander nodded. Consciously he blotted out the pain, lifted the mask and drew greedily at the fresh air to fill his lungs.

'It's inside the castle on the third floor. Directly facing the stairs.' Assisted by the soothing gasses images from the encounter began to flow into his mind. He began to grin and then to chuckle painfully. 'They use it as a knocking shop, you can't miss it.'

'Is that so?' Said Hara with a wry smile. 'Thank you Webb-San, you've been a great help.'

Seeing his chief's satisfaction at the reply the paramedic pursued his questioning. 'Do you feel pain anywhere else?'

'Apart from the arm? No, I don't think so. Stomach's a bit queasy, a mixture of acid and shock I expect.'

'Considering the circumstances I would say that's quite normal, nothing to worry about. Could you move your fingers for me please. Good. Now raise your arm and rotate your wrist, does it hurt?'

Alexander shook his head.

'Ok.' Relieved there was no breakage, the paramedic set about dressing the wound. 'Breathe from the mask if you need it.'

As the paramedic folded the last of the micropore tape strips into place over the bandage Alexander's eyes locked hard onto Hara's, his face suddenly alert with realisation. 'You mustn't storm the castle.' He said.

Reading Alexander's expression as one of anxiety Hara convivially patted him on the back. 'Rest Webb-San. You don't have to worry yourself about us, we are well prepared.'

'It's not you that I'm worried about!' Responded Alexander, an edge of concern in his voice. 'The artwork's at risk.'

Hara's attention focused. 'Go on, I'm listening.'

'This may sound a mite far fetched, but they have a furnace in a room next to the auction. I saw it myself a couple of hours ago and it's just dawned on me what it is for. It's big, big enough for the largest of the paintings. If I'm right, at the first sign of your men, they'll destroy everything. It will be as if an auction never existed.'

'You're quite sure?' Pressed Hara, weighing its effect on the assault. Such a method was eminently capable, he knew it for a fact. In the case of a painting they would only need to inflict superficial damage to cast doubt on it's authenticity as being a work of a great master. He had seriously underestimated Matsumoto's ruthlessness. It hadn't occurred to him they'd consciously destroy something that was inherently valuable solely to protect their own liberty. The revelation troubled him greatly. 'You could not have mistaken it for the castle's boiler room?'

'Unlikely, they're using gas cylinders to fuel the furnace, it looks too portable to be permanent.'

Thoughtfully Hara stood, walked to the centre of the clearing and picked the discarded Bowie knife from the wet grass. He ran his thumb along its blade in contemplation, testing the keenness of its edge. If they were to succeed, penetration of the castle's defences would have to be swift. 'In my estimation we will have at most two minutes of confusion before they realise what is happening. You have a working knowledge of the castle's layout, long enough to reach it?'

Doubtful, Alexander shook his head.

'Then the room will have to be made secure before any action is taken. He unclipped a transceiver from his belt and spoke again in Japanese. 'Airborne primary confirmed, target, roof. Land forces, second wave. Await further orders.'

Knowing there was insufficient time to brief the assault force, Alexander, in spite of his injuries, could see only one logical course of action. 'You'd have a better chance of success with a man inside.' He offered.

'You? Go back in? Entirely out of the question.' Responded Hara firmly. Then, taking a moment to consider the proposal's advantages, he knelt once again at his side. Brave or foolish, Webb's idea had merit. 'You'd be in agony,' he stated, 'Wouldn't you?'

Cradling the protected arm in the palm of his right hand Alexander glanced sideways at the medic. 'That will depend on how good he is.'

CHAPTER 60

'Do you think Kumagai and Houdini could be related?' Puzzled Alexander whimsically, in the passenger seat of the Honda CRX.

'He's more likely related to Superman if what you say is true.' Scoffed Charlie. 'You're absolutely sure he was wounded that bad?'

'Stake my life on it. Mark my words, come daybreak they'll find him not a hundred yards from where he was shot. It stands to reason if the cut didn't finish him off the lead in his chest certainly did. Wind your window down, we're coming to the gates.'

An official hand raised in front of them to draw the car to a gentle rolling rest and another sentry in a crisp black dress uniform approached the window. 'State your business.'

'Sumitomo Bank security.' Informed Charlie with an air of command. 'Delivery for a mister Claythorpe. He's expecting us.'

'My apologies, you're too late Sir. From midnight we have orders to admit no-one. Sorry, no exceptions.'

'Too late! No exceptions! Rubbish!' Countered Charlie, showing signs of irritation. 'Matsumoto-San got me out of bed for this, he said it was urgent. I think you had better check.'

'As you wish Sir, but I assure you, it will be a waste of time. A moment please.'

In silent observation Alexander followed the sentry's actions. Through the condensation drenched pane of the guard house he could see the telephone receiver lifted, a number dialled and the start of conversation. A lens on the nearest surveillance camera rotated into focus and zoomed to pick the detail in their faces. It stayed at rest for a moment scrutinising them, then zoomed wide again and continued in its panning activity. They had evidently been examined by the operations room, a decision would follow shortly. The sentry uncomfortable with the delay shuffled his feet impatiently. Repeatedly he looked out towards them, apparently ill at ease at the possibility of action, or worse still of the potential consequences associated with keeping a VIP waiting. On a night such as this, when the majority of the world's criminal fraternity had passed through his gates Alexander could well understand why. The telephone handset cradled once more and the sentry turned back towards them. An element of surprise had appeared on his face. It would seem they had passed muster. He crossed to the desk-mounted panel and pressed one of the control buttons to trigger the low frequency whine of concealed motors. Steadily, with the semblance of apparent effortlessness the pair of towering gates before them yawned wide, audibly locking into place as the sentry reappeared in the doorway.

'You've been cleared to proceed. Straight on for half a mile, you will be met in the courtyard.' He said.

'Thank you.' Stated Charlie coldly. 'Just pray we're in time.'

Alexander started the stopwatch on his chronometer. 'So far, so good. Looks like Matsumoto's still out.'

'Perhaps.' Selecting first gear Charlie accelerated up the drive way. 'How's the arm? Is the morphine doing it's stuff?'

'Bloody marvellous. How's the neck?'

'Bloody painful!'

'Serves you right. You shouldn't have been sleeping on the job.' Gibed Alexander lightly. He passed the Uzi with Taylor's spare magazine across the centre console. 'Load this for me will you.'

Charlie did as he was bid, precisely and with care. 'Safety's off. Put it under your coat out of sight.'

With the castle looming towards them the car slowed a second time. Jasmine, enticing in a gown that praised her female form, descended the steps to meet them. To ward off the cold a mink wrap draped her shoulders and a catalogue folded close to it's final page flapped loosely from her right hand at her side.

'Matsumoto's daughter?' Enquired Charlie, mentally checking off the 33, 22, 34 statistics of the safe combination in his mind.

'Your type?'

Stepping out and jogging determinedly from the car he grinned admiringly back at Alexander. 'Could be.'

'Mine too.' Agreed Alexander. 'You've got taste.'

'Mr Webb, have you seen my father?' Jasmine asked anxiously as they passed her.

Alexander shook his head, momentarily pausing on the steps at the look of concern in her eyes. 'Not for an hour or more. Last time I saw him he was in the grounds looking for Kumagai-San. He's probably still out there.' He lied. It was strangely unsettling how easily lying came to him now, a month previously and anything other than the truth would have stumbled obviously on his lips. He centred back to the job at hand and pressed on.

Looking first to the perimeter of trees and then back to a disappearing Alexander she called after them,

'Are you sure? It's really not like him. What happened to your..?'

The oak portal thudded shut behind them.

'We've got sixty seconds.' Said Alexander urgently, racing the steps two at a time. 'It's at the top on the left.'

Through the open door, a carpet-less floor announced their entrance to a solitary guard. He was seated with crossed boots resting on the rim of a barrel. A newspaper rustled on his lap as he looked up, first to Charlie and then slowly, with curiosity, towards the ceiling. His face undoubtedly mirrored others in the building. The sound above was unmistakably recognisable as the chattering of rotor blades. His bewilderment morphed to anxiousness with it's increasing volume.

Lowering his gaze the guard's expression altered again to one of personal concern. Without inducement he unclipped the buckle securing his pistol, lifted it gingerly between his thumb and forefinger and lowered it to the ground. 'What do you want?' He asked nervously, as Charlie eased the door closed.

'Put it out!' Ordered Alexander, flicking the muzzle of his firearm in the direction of the furnace. 'Now!'

Fearful for his safety the guard, hands raised, slipped carefully from his seat, crossed to the propane cylinders and closed the gas delivery valves. Dutifully the flames lowered and with a barely audible pop, died. He stood there motionless, staring at the Uzi's barrel, awaiting his next order.

'Now cool the grid with water.' Demanded Alexander.

Whilst keeping a close eye on the guard's actions and preparing to move quickly should the contents of the fire bucket come in his direction, Charlie opened his pocket knife to a small blade and slid it through the hose between the cylinders and the furnace.

Alexander permitted himself a brief smile of satisfaction at the minor victory. If his supposition had been right the paintings would now be safe. Checking his watch. Their confusion time had run out. All hell would break loose any second. He returned his attention to the guard whose perspiration was now clearly visible on his forehead. 'Ok. Back to the chair.'

Once seated the guard sought again for Alexander's approval, resisting the temptation to check on Charlie's movements over his shoulder. Assuming Alexander's nod was for his benefit the guard relaxed. He never saw Charlie straighten his fingers or was even consciously aware of the blow when it came. He slumped forward, ungainly and without a sound.

'We still have unfinished business.' Said Alexander, turning to leave the room. He curled his hand over the doorknob and as he pulled so the action appeared to set off the first explosion.

It came like a double crump thirty feet above him. The castle walls shook on all sides and plaster powder billowed down in choking clouds, obscuring all vision beyond the first three steps of the raising stair well. Alexander counted the seconds, ...eight, nine, ten. They were in. The second explosion came, this time from inside, blinding the castle's electronic eyes to the direction of the land assault.

The doors to the auction room flew open. There was sudden chaos. People running in all directions. A disorganised rabble in a state of blind panic.

'Get out of the way, damn you!' Yelled a voice in Alexander's ear, 'Get out of the fucking Way!'

The corner of a heavy gilt frame rammed hard into his ribs, grazing his side as it pushed past. A second followed it in the hands of a coated auction assistant leading several others behind him.

Frame upon frame was thrown squarely in to the centre of the grate, each landing with a coupled look of confusion and disbelief at the inert hearth. The room began to fill with people exhibiting a need to do something, impotent in their ability to define exactly what. Within half a minute the noise of alarm and hysteria had grown to a deafening level.

'We've done what we came for.' Shouted Charlie, guiding Alexander out onto the landing. 'Let's get out of here.'

At the head of the stairs Alexander caught Charlie's arm. 'Not just yet. Find the commissioner and don't let him out of your sight. I've got a debt to settle for Kraiwoot.'

'Oh no you don't, not on your own. You're a car designer not a paratrooper, just remember that.'

Realising the morphine was clouding his judgement Alexander felt thankful for the reality check. 'You're right Charlie, Lets get out of here.'

A scream cut through the castle panic like the crack of a whip. 'Webb!'

As though through an instinctive reaction Alexander traced the source of the sound with the barrel of the Uzi. Within a fraction of a second it came to rest pointing at the centre of a mud and blood stained bullet-proof vest. A mixture of incredulity and fear began to overwhelm him. Facing him at the foot of the stairs stood an apparition of pure hate, in its hand was a pistol pointing in his direction. Simultaneously, as he registered the mussel flash he squeezed his trigger. The two opposing bodies fell in unison. The tortured face of Kumagai split vertically by a rising row of inch spaced holes leading from the top of his chest was the last thing Alexander saw.

CHAPTER 61

Monday had put an end to the unsettled weather of the weekend and an area of high pressure had once again firmly positioned itself over Tokyo. The Japan Times newspaper dated 3rd June rustled noisily as Hara searched for the article. Pages one and two had been dedicated to the events at the castle, he found what he was looking for at the top of the third page under the banner headline "British Hero Dies in Police Raid."

'Here it is. British detective, Alexander Webb, 35, unmarried, died in the early hours of Saturday morning. Following a Medi-Vac helicopter flight from the foot of Mount Fuji to Tokyo's Aoyama Hospital, the emergency medical team, in spite of a valiant effort, failed to save his life. Chief Hara, a spokesman from Tokyo's Metropolitan Police force gave the following statement: "Mr Webb died in hospital at 08:30 on Saturday morning as a result of a gun shot wound received whilst assisting a special forces operation in Mishima. He was instrumental in retrieving many stolen works of art and was unique in his contribution towards apprehending the perpetrators of these crimes. He will be sorely missed, his death is a great loss to law enforcement."'

He folded the paper carefully and placed it onto the bedside table. 'Well, there you have it. You're officially dead, Alexander-San.'

'I confess I've felt better.' Replied Alexander, raising his hand to the bandage surrounding his head.

'You have to understand, we're dealing with organised crime on a global scale, and the article was necessary to ensure your safety. A similar article to this one has been posted in all of the national and international papers, particularly in those countries where the Gathering members come from. Your embassy has been informed of the true situation of course. As to your occupation, well, I thought it would be prudent to misinform the press in order to protect you during your stay here.'

Alexander buried his head into his hands. The full impact of Hara's words was gradually dawning on him.

Seeing Alexander's distress Hara placed a reassuring hand onto his shoulder. 'Most of the people at the castle saw your body at the top of the stairway, I wouldn't expect any retribution.

'Thanks to you, we have every one of them in custody and recovered every item detailed in the auction catalogue. Matsumoto is facing a significant period of imprisonment for his part in Miss Martin's murder and due to your video evidence he has entered a plea of guilty. The recording may or may not be admissible as evidence, it may be considered as entrapment, we will have to see.' Hara glowed as he recollected an image from his interrogation. 'You should have been there when Matsumoto found out how you secured the combination to his safe, he was not pleased.

'Ling will be extradited to face charges of kidnapping, theft, illegal trade, and you can be certain, anything else the Chinese police can make stick. And as for Deputy Commissioner General Tsugawa, he has accepted indefinite suspension and is awaiting the result of two warrant searches, one at the castle and the other at his home. Although Tomoko's testimony may be sufficient to prosecute on the grounds of receiving stolen goods, we would prefer to build a case based upon supplying criminal intelligence and corruption. We believe corruption to be a rare occurrence in the Japanese police force so when it is suspected we must be seen to be dealing with it severely. We are currently holding him on a charge of conspiring to pervert the course of justice.'

'What will happen to the two men in Mr Kraiwoot's sketches?' Asked Tomoko.

'Rest assured, all of the people at the auction will come to some form of justice. My department is moving as quickly as is humanly possible. For example, we have enlisted the help of several international agencies to assist in closing the art theft related cases. Two officers will arrive later today from Interpol headquarters in Lyon. They may wish to question you both, nothing to worry about, they have been instructed to treat you like dignitaries. You have every reason to be proud of yourselves.'

Tomoko searched for Alexander's hand and squeezed it gently. 'I'm proud of you.' She said, 'How's your head?'

Alexander felt like a charlatan. The shot from Kumagai's .38 had only grazed the side of his temple. He was in hospital as a result of knocking himself out on the marble floor as he fell. By way of small consolation, his arm hurt like hell. 'Not too bad. Did the doctor say when I could leave?'

Before Tomoko could answer, the door to his private room swung open. 'Come on lay-about, the video conference is set up down the hall. Climb into this.' It was Greg Matthews with a wheel chair. 'I send you out here to work on a car and you end up getting yourself killed. Typical!'

Alexander smiled and eased himself from the bed. Greg had telephoned on Sunday evening, after his arrival with a team of three from Global Design, full of concern. 'It's good to see you're back to your belligerent old self Greg. How's Maverick?'

'He's keeping the wife company. I told you he'd be no trouble. We have to hurry, there's someone important who wishes to speak to you.' Said Greg, wheeling him down to the end of the corridor.

With Tomoko by his side Alexander watched as Charlie's face appeared on the screen. 'Good morning Alex, greetings from Thailand.'

'I hardly recognise you with a suit on Charlie, Have you returned the gem yet?'

'It was my first priority. There is someone here I would like to introduce you to, he wishes to offer his thanks personally. May I introduce His Royal Highness King Bhumibol Adulyadej, Rama the Ninth.'

Surprised, Alexander at first stood and then realised his face would be out of camera shot. Feeling a little foolish, he took his seat again. 'It is a pleasure to speak to you, your Majesty.' Said Alexander.

King Bhumibol briefly raised his right hand, 'The pleasure is all mine.' He Said, 'I felt that I had to offer to you a sincere and heart felt thank you personally, on behalf of the people of Thailand. Your efforts and those of Mr Tan are truly appreciated and I feel that we owe both of you a debt of gratitude.'

'That really is not necessary.' Stated Alexander overwhelmed.

'Your modesty does you credit Mister Webb. When your diary, and your personal recovery permit, perhaps you and Miss Den would like to visit my country as guests of the royal household?'

'That is very gracious of you Sir, we would consider it a great privilege.'

'Very Well. Arrange a suitable date with Mr Tan and you both will join me in the placing of the Rama's Hope back into its rightful home. In the meantime I have a request, please treat this as a private matter, not a word must be shared outside of our current circle. My subjects have believed the Rama's hope and the emerald Buddha to be as one for many years.'

'You have my word.' Said Alexander seriously.

'And I know that it will be kept. You strike me as a man of honour Mr Webb. Until we meet.'

The face of Charlie was once again on the screen. 'Mr Matthews tells me that you will return to work next Monday. I'll call you to set up a date, ok?'

'Before I can commit to a date I'll have to clear it with Higaki-San, the president of Tri-Star.'

Charlie dismissed the minor problem with a flick of his wrist.

'Bring him with you, I'm sure he will enjoy the experience. We'll arrange a few contacts for him. Thailand's a big market for a company with a royal warrant.'

Alexander would never cease to be amazed at Charlie's cheek. 'We'll talk on Monday Charlie. Take good care of yourself.'

With that the screen went blank.

'I wonder what scope there would be for a design consultancy based in Bangkok?' Wondered Greg out loud.

The sun had set outside the third floor hospital room and Alexander, after having his bandages changed and taking his penicillin tablets, was resting. Samuel

Barber's *Adagio for strings,* played through his MP3 headphones calming his every sinew. He particularly liked the way the music built, cadence upon cadence until two thirds of the way through when the music paused for a second or two, to begin again soft and romantic.

A knock at the door caused him to turn down the volume and bid his visitor to enter.

'A flying visit Alexander-San, please forgive the intrusion.' Begged Hara, walking to his side. 'I thought that I would call in on my way home.'

'It's after nine, your wife will have your guts for garters. All the same, it's good to see you. What's new?'

Alexander could see in Hara's expression that something special had occurred. 'We have found Deputy Commissioner Tsugawa's invitation to the gathering. There is nothing too damaging in that alone, the clincher is that Matsumoto has added a post-script. I made a note, listen to this; "Dear friend and colleague, please make every effort to ensure your attendance, I personally guarantee it will be worth your while. Years of faithful service to our organisation do not go unrewarded." With Tomoko's testimony, I do believe we have enough to convict him.'

'Does that mean that there will soon be a vacancy for a Deputy Commissioner of police' Said Alexander, playfully.

'Yes, it does, doesn't it?' Hara responded thoughtfully, turning to leave. 'Oh, I nearly forgot,' he said, pausing at the door, 'You said you had to return the copy to Thailand.' He tossed a small package on to the bed. 'We found it in Ling's pocket. There's no honour amongst thieves these days. Stay in touch.' With that he left.

Mystified and intrigued Alexander slowly raised the lid of the small box. He didn't know why but his heart started to beat a little faster. He had witnessed the Thai copy smashed with his own eyes, so what was this?

He pealed away the tissue paper inside.

'Oh my...!' he breathed. Hara knew what the Rama's Hope looked like from the photographs, he was sure of it. Perhaps this was his way of saying thank you?

He reached for his address book, found the number and dialled. Charlie would know what to do.

'Mr Koyanagi?' Enquired Charlie, into the telephone handset.

'Hai'

'I'm calling on behalf of a client in Hong Kong. Please forgive the intrusion at so late an hour, but I thought that you would like to be informed as soon as possible.'

'Your name please?' Enquired Koyanagi.

'My name is Wong. I am a associate of Mr Ling, perhaps you have heard of him?'

Koyanagi hummed as he thought. 'I'm sorry, the name means nothing to me. Tell me Mister Wong, the purpose of your call?'

'I am instructed to locate a buyer for a particularly fine gem stone. A one hundred and twelve carat cabochon cut ruby. We conservatively estimate the value to be in the region of twenty million US dollars. Would such a stone be of interest to you?' Charlie asked.

Koyanagi's voice changed to one of urgency. 'Indeed it would. Can we meet...?'

The End

ABOUT THE AUTHOR

Laurence Bradbury grew up in Coventry in the centre of England. He studied Electrical and Electronic engineering in the North East before deciding that a career in product and automotive design would be more varied and rewarding. Design projects enabled him to travel the globe with notable assignments in Japan, Korea, Holland, Sweden, Switzerland and the US.

Now a full time Author he continues to live and write in the stunning countryside of South Wales with his wife Honor, son Alexander and daughter Honor (As well as being a beautiful name it's a family tradition)

When he isn't hard at work on his next book, Laurence has a supporting career as a travel photographer. He says 'If you write about a place, you need to get it right. Also, it's amazing how well plot ideas coalesce when you're walking the streets of a foreign city.'

A keen musician he enjoys playing his Gibson 57 Black Beauty guitar, has a passion for films, likes to hone his skills at archery and tries to find time for an enthusiastic drive in his TVR Cerbera around the country lanes.

Made in the USA
Charleston, SC
27 April 2012